4/11 gate 320

AGAINST THE WIND

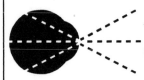 This Large Print Book carries the
Seal of Approval of N.A.V.H.

AGAINST THE WIND

KAT MARTIN

THORNDIKE PRESS
A part of Gale, Cengage Learning

GALE
CENGAGE Learning

Detroit • New York • San Francisco • New Haven, Conn • Waterville, Maine • London

Copyright © 2011 by Kat Martin.
The Raines of Wild Canyon Series #1.
Thorndike Press, a part of Gale, Cengage Learning.

Thorndike Press® Large Print Basic.
The text of this Large Print edition is unabridged.
Other aspects of the book may vary from the original edition.
Set in 16 pt. Plantin.

LIBRARY OF CONGRESS CATALOGING-IN-PUBLICATION DATA

Martin, Kat.
   Against the wind / by Kat Martin. — Large print ed.
    p. cm. — (The Raines of Wild Canyon series; #1)
  (Thorndike Press large print basic)
  ISBN-13: 978-1-4104-3638-2 (hardcover)
  ISBN-10: 1-4104-3638-1 (hardcover)
   1. Kidnapping—Fiction. 2. Wyoming—Fiction. 3. Large type books. I. Title.
  PS3563.A7246A43 2010
  813'.54—dc22   2010052848

Published in 2011 by arrangement with Harlequin Books. S.A.

Printed in the United States of America
1 2 3 4 5 6 7 15 14 13 12 11

For my husband, Larry,
the love of my life.

ONE

"Mommy, why do we have to leave?" Sarah Allen's six-year-old daughter, Holly, looked up at her with big blue, tear-filled eyes. "I like it here. I don't want to go."

Anxious to be on her way, Sarah reached down and lifted the little blonde girl into her arms. "Don't cry, sweetie. I promise you're going to love it. The mountains are beautiful and there are these rivers and big green forests, and you can have a puppy if you want." At least Sarah hoped so.

Surely the owners of the cottage she had rented wouldn't mind. The house was, after all, on a very large ranch, at least twelve thousand acres.

Holly sniffed back tears and looked up with interest. "A puppy? Can I really?"

"As soon as we get settled, we'll drive into town and you can adopt one from the pound." Sarah glanced nervously toward the door. The car was packed, the rest of their personal possessions boxed and shipped. She was leaving Los Angeles and she prayed she was leaving her troubles, as well.

The sooner they left town, the safer she would feel.

She set Holly back on her feet, took a last glance around the expensive Santa Monica apartment she had occupied with her late husband, surveyed the plush white carpet and chic black lacquer furniture that was Andrew's taste, not hers. There was nothing homey, nothing the least bit geared toward a family. The condo was just for show — no substance beyond the surface beauty. Just like Andrew.

Sarah started for the door, but the phone rang before she could reach it. She considered just letting it ring, a hollow echo now that her things were gone, but she was afraid it might be important.

She lifted the receiver and pressed it against her ear. "Hello."

"Sarah, this is Martin Kozak." His raspy smoker's voice grated over the line. "We need to talk."

A shiver went down her spine. Marty Kozak was one of Andrew's business associates. A few weeks ago, Marty had started calling, trying to set up a meeting. Sarah didn't want to talk to him or any of Andrew's other shady business acquaintances.

"What do you want, Marty? I told you I don't know anything about Andrew's affairs. He never talked to me about business. We never discussed it."

He didn't think I was smart enough, or savvy enough about finances, or he just plain didn't want to.

And Andrew never did anything he didn't want to do.

"Like I told you before," Marty said, "Andrew had something important I need. Did you find anything in his personal belongings? A list he might have been keeping? A computer disk, maybe, or a record book of some kind?"

"No. Before he died, we were barely speaking." That was an understatement. When they were together, Andrew did all the talking, mostly about himself. Sarah had been trying to leave him for years, but she had been afraid of what would happen if she did. "He didn't tell me anything, and he didn't give me anything."

"Maybe there was something in his personal effects."

"Not that I know of."

"I'd like to talk to you, Sarah."

"I'm sorry, Marty. I was just walking out the door. I've really got to go." By the time she hung up the phone, she was shaking. She had no idea what sort of trouble Andrew might have been in before he was killed, but she wasn't part of it and never had been.

Once you get out of town, she told herself, *everything is going to be all right.*

Things were bound to settle down. After her husband's murder, the police had questioned her extensively, but that had been months ago and they were certain his death was a result of his gambling debts or crooked business dealings. She figured Marty had waited for the police investigation to die down before he began to press her for whatever it was he wanted.

Sarah closed her eyes and dragged in a steadying breath. The past would fade, she told herself, and in time, even Andrew's associates would leave her alone.

Grabbing Holly's hand and the big leather purse that carried everything from bandages to emergency food — breakfast bars this morning — she took the private elevator down to the underground garage where her Mercedes, one of the few possessions Andrew had actually put in her name, was parked.

Everything else belonged solely to him and he managed to keep it that way with the prenuptial agreement she had signed. After he died, she was only mildly surprised to discover he owed more money than he had in his bank accounts and had mortgaged or sold all of the real estate he owned. He had even let his life insurance policy expire.

Sarah had been left with nothing. She had sold everything she could to raise enough money to move out of L.A., taken back her maiden name, changed Holly's name, and found a job over the internet in her home town of Wind Canyon, Wyoming. On a site for rental properties, she had happened upon a cottage on a ranch in the country not too far from town.

All she had to do was get there.

Still clutching Holly's hand, Sarah opened the rear car door, set her daughter in the booster seat and strapped her in, then rounded the vehicle and slid behind the wheel. It was a thousand-mile journey to Wyoming.

Sarah thought of Andrew, his extravagant lifestyle, his gambling and the crooked deals he made to keep the money rolling in. She thought of Marty Kozak and the rest of Andrew's so-called business associates.

She wouldn't feel safe until she got there.

Two

Jackson Raines tightened his hold on the steering wheel of his white Ford extended-cab pickup. The temperature outside was two below, the wind howling, the heavy snow blowing sideways. A Wyoming blizzard was nothing to sneeze at, even one this late in spring. Keeping his eyes carefully fixed on the road, he was surprised to see a pair of taillights up ahead, barely visible through the blowing snow, twin dots of red flashing in hazard mode, the car pulled off on the side of the road.

Jackson started slowing way before he reached the vehicle. He didn't want to slide into the damned thing, and on a road as icy as this one, it wouldn't be hard to do.

There was rarely any traffic on the narrow two lanes that led nowhere except to a couple of ranches in the area. He couldn't help wondering who would be driving out here in this kind of weather. Hell, he wouldn't be here himself if he hadn't been in town when the storm blew in, several hours earlier than expected. He should have known. In mountains like these, the weatherman was never right.

He slowed even more, downshifted until the pickup was moving at a crawl, then pulled in behind the stranded auto. California license plates. Through the blinding wall of white, he recognized the car as a newer Mercedes. *500S* gleamed in chrome on the left side of the trunk.

Jackson pulled on a pair of leather work gloves and climbed out of the pickup. He should have figured it would be some rich guy with more money than common sense.

Tugging his worn cowboy hat down over his forehead, he walked up to the car and rapped on the window. The driver flinched at the sound as if he'd been shot. He pressed the button and the window eased down, and Jackson frowned as he realized the driver was a woman. And in her lap, she was holding a little girl.

"Thank God you stopped," the woman said, her teeth chattering.

"What in blazes are you doing out here?"

"I thought we could get where we were going before the storm came in."

He could hardly argue with that since he

had done the same thing.

"What's the problem?"

"Flat tire. My cell phone's out of range. I thought about trying to make it on the rim, but I was afraid I wouldn't get there and just ruin the wheel, then no one would be able to put on the spare."

He nodded. "You did the right thing."

"Can you help us?"

There was something familiar about the woman's voice. He leaned down, trying to get a better look at her, but she was wearing a fancy fur coat and she had the collar pulled up over her ears, hiding most of her face. "Open the trunk."

She pressed a button somewhere inside the car and the trunk popped open.

"Should I get out and help?" she asked.

His eyebrows went up. He hadn't expected her to be the type to put herself out, especially not in the middle of a snowstorm.

"Nothing much you can do." He looked at the little girl, blond hair and big blue eyes, and he could see she was frightened. "I'll do what I can. Roll the window back up before you freeze."

Jackson pulled up the collar of his heavy down jacket and crunched through the snow toward the back of the Mercedes, silver, he saw, now mostly covered by at least an inch of fresh powder. He pulled the jack out of the trunk, walked around and stuck it under the frame. As he shoved the handle into the slot and started cranking, he thought about the woman.

He could only see enough of her to know she had thick, chestnut-brown hair about the color of her fancy mink coat and eyes as blue as her daughter's. Her skin was smooth and he thought she had a nice straight nose but he couldn't really be sure.

Still, there was something about her. . . .

Jackson pulled off the flat tire, got the spare out from under the luggage in the trunk, eventually got it on and replaced the lug nuts. It was ball-freezing cold and he wanted to get back to the ranch before the storm got any worse. When he finished putting the jack away, he reloaded the luggage, closed the trunk and walked back to the window, which slid open with a soft electric hum.

The woman stuck out a slim hand encased in a brown kid glove holding a twenty-dollar bill. "Thank you so much. I really appreciate your help."

"Keep your money," he said, only slightly annoyed. Out here people helped each other because it was the right thing to do. "It was only a flat tire."

"Are you sure? You must be freezing. I wish I could pay you more, but —"

"Consider it a favor. Where are you headed?"

"Just down the road." She checked the map that lay open on the console. "It's just a couple more miles."

It had to be one of the ranches up ahead. There wasn't much else out here. "I'll follow you to the turnoff."

She nodded and fired up the engine. The Mercedes didn't have four-wheel drive, but it was a good, heavy auto, and if she took her time, she could make it to where she was going. As if she were still on the freeway back in California, she put on her left turn signal and pulled cautiously onto the road.

Jackson felt the tug of a smile as she navigated the big car carefully down the lane. Again, he wondered who she was and what had brought her twenty miles from Wind Canyon, the nearest town.

Back in his pickup, he cranked the engine and followed them at a safe distance until her turn signal went on again and she made a very slow turn onto the private road leading to the Whittaker Ranch. He watched until he was sure she was close enough to the ranch to make it, then gave her a wave she probably couldn't see and drove on down the road toward home. It was only a couple miles farther. Olivia would have a pot of coffee on the stove and if he was lucky, stew and biscuits for supper.

Jackson pressed down on the gas pedal, eager to get in out of the weather.

Sarah rounded a corner and saw the sign for the Whittaker Ranch. Biting back a swear word she couldn't say in front of Holly, she cautiously stepped on the brake.

"What's the matter, Mommy?"

"I turned too soon. This is the Whittaker Ranch. We're looking for the Raintree Ranch."

"Do we have to turn around?" Holly gazed worriedly out the window into the storm.

"We'll turn around as soon as I can find a wide enough spot in the road." She wasn't taking any chances. The next time she ran into trouble, her old classmate, Jackson Raines, wouldn't be there to help her.

Sarah released a shaky breath that turned white inside the car, even with the heater running full blast. Though he looked older, more rugged than he had when he was a senior at Wind Canyon High, she had known him instantly. She had kept her head down, hoping Jackson wouldn't recognize her, and she didn't think he had.

She knew he'd left town after high school. According to her friend, Nancy Marcus, he had gone to the University of Wyoming on a boxing scholarship. Everyone in Wind Canyon had watched the Barcelona Olympics the year Jackson had competed in the light heavyweight division, and though he hadn't won, everyone in Wyoming had been proud of the effort he had made.

Sarah had never heard any more about him.

She certainly didn't know he had returned to Wind Canyon. Maybe he was working as a hand on one of the local ranches. She remembered he had done that during the summers when he'd been in high school.

Driving carefully, she continued along the road and finally found a turnaround spot, her thoughts still on Jackson, the gangly teenager he had been and the lean, broad-shouldered, rugged-looking man he had become. With his high cheekbones, dark eyes and nearly black hair, he had been a good-looking boy. Now, at thirty-five — three years older than she — he was a man, with an air of confidence that made him even more attractive.

Focusing her attention on getting back to the main road, Sarah used the circular turnaround made for just that purpose. It

18

was nice and wide and she was able to change direction without a problem, even with the building layer of snow.

She had taken Holly out of the backseat when the tire went flat so they could huddle together and stay warm. For the few miles left to their destination, the six-year-old was strapped into the passenger seat with the air bag turned off.

Sarah kept the car going slowly all the way to the entrance gate, then turned right, back onto the two-lane road. The next two miles felt like ten, with the car slipping on the ice beneath the snow and the wind making an eerie moaning sound.

Then she spotted the big sign, Raintree Ranch, hanging from a gate framed by huge pine logs. The name was different now, but the ranch had been there for as long as Sarah could remember. She had driven by a dozen times over the years but never actually been on the property — which was, after all, privately owned, and the no-trespassing policy had always been strictly enforced.

Sarah had left Wind Canyon two days after graduation. Having taken out a student loan, combined with the money she earned from a part-time job at a small café, she was able to attend UCLA. She had a cousin in Westwood named Betsy, who had offered her a bedroom, which Sarah gratefully accepted. She majored in literature with the goal of becoming a journalist, a goal that had never been reached.

Until now.

"Are we there yet, Mama?"

Sarah smiled. "Almost. It's only a little ways farther. Keep your eyes open for the ranch house."

Holly sat up straighter in the seat, trying to see through the heavy snowfall. In the distance, the main house came slowly into focus until it took the shape of a shadowy fortress, a big, rambling, two-story wooden structure with a balcony off the second floor. It was built sometime in the twenties, Sarah recalled, by the descendants of the ranch's original owners. There were a couple of lights on downstairs, but Sarah didn't stop.

It was after eight o'clock. When she sent in her rent deposit on the cottage, she had told the housekeeper, Olivia Jones, that she wasn't sure of the date or time of her arrival. The letter she received in return said it didn't matter, that she should just go directly to the cottage, which was another hundred yards down the road. There was a map, as well as the location of the key —

beneath a flowerpot on the front porch next to the door.

The snow was getting worse. The main house sat some distance off the lane she was traveling, and as the Mercedes drove slowly past, no one seemed to notice. Though Sarah looked forward to meeting the woman who had been so kind to her when she had called about the rental, she was grateful for a quiet night to settle into her new home.

Sometime in the next few days, the rest of her meager possessions would arrive, not much since most of her things had been sold to raise money for the move from California. Thankfully, the cottage was furnished, so she didn't have to worry about that. Tonight she and Holly would eat the sandwiches she had picked up in Wind Canyon and go straight to bed.

Sarah smiled. She was back where she had been born, a town she had once wanted desperately to escape. But she was a grown woman now, not a schoolgirl. Wind Canyon was the perfect place to raise a child and she was incredibly glad to be home.

Still smiling, Sarah pulled the car up next to the little batten-board cottage and turned off the engine. But as she sat there working up the courage to climb out into the storm, the sweet feeling of homecoming began to

21

fade. She had a lot of regrets about her life. One of the biggest was the way she had treated Jackson Raines.

THREE

A brilliant Wyoming sun shone down on eight inches of fresh snow that blanketed the landscape. In the distance, the branches on the pine trees climbing the sides of the mountains drooped with their heavy burden of white. Already it was melting. It was mid-May, a little late in the year for a storm this size, though it wasn't that uncommon, either.

In the mountains, the weather was always unpredictable. It was one of the things Jackson liked best about living here, the fierce storms and wild winds, the sun so bright it hurt your eyes. As he walked toward the barn, pulling on his work gloves, he smiled. When he'd left Wind Canyon sixteen years ago, he wasn't sure he would ever return.

Now he was home and he was damned glad to be back.

He glanced ahead, his steps slowing as he spotted the Mercedes with the flat tire he had worked on last night. What in blazes was the car doing parked at the cottage?

Jackson turned in that direction, each step leaving a deep boot print in the snow. He had almost reached the house when he heard his housekeeper, Olivia Jones, calling from behind him.

"Jackson, wait! Jackson!" She was breathing hard as she hurried toward him, a woman of sixty, broad-hipped, thick-waisted and gray-haired. She'd been a real beauty in her day, still had the dimples in her cheeks to prove it, and the same sweet smile she'd had when she worked at the ice-cream shop in town when he was a boy.

She wasn't smiling now. "Jackson!"

"Take it easy, Livvy. You'll give yourself a heart attack."

She cast him a look, then drew in a panting breath and slowly released it. "I forgot to tell you — I rented the cottage."

"You what?"

"We talked about it, remember? You said we ought to do something with the place instead of just letting it sit there and rot into the ground."

"I didn't say we should rent it. My brothers stay there whenever they come back to town."

"Which is almost never. They're too busy

making money."

"Yes, but —"

"You said do something, so I did."

He lifted his cowboy hat, then settled it back down on his forehead. "All right, I guess that's fair." He looked over at the cottage. The gabled roof had just been replaced and the slight sag in the porch had been repaired, making it nice to sit outside where you could watch the small, rushing stream that passed by the house. "So what's that car doing parked there?"

"That's the new tenant."

"Tell me you didn't rent the place to some rich society woman from the city out here for the summer."

"Of course not."

"I changed the lady's tire last night and that's what she looked like to me."

"She's not *some society woman.* She used to live in Wind Canyon when she was a girl. She recently lost her husband. She wanted to come home and I thought this would be the perfect place for her to recover from her loss."

Jackson frowned. "What's her name?"

"Sarah Hollister."

"Doesn't sound familiar."

"She was Sarah Allen when she was a girl."

Jackson took the news like a sucker punch

25

to the stomach. *Sarah Allen.* Damn, he had known her voice sounded familiar. Sarah had been two grades behind him in school, though he was three years older. He thought she was the prettiest, sweetest girl he had ever seen.

Man, had he been wrong.

Oh, she was pretty. From what little he could see last night, she still was. But even back then, Sarah was a social climber, a middle-class girl who wanted to be part of the in crowd, to socialize with the kids whose parents had money.

It had taken him weeks to work up the courage to talk to her. That first time, she had seemed almost shy. A few weeks passed while he madly saved his money. Like a lovesick fool, he had asked her to his senior prom.

Sarah hadn't just said no. When she realized some of her friends were watching, she had pointed at him as if he were something stuck on the bottom of her shoe, and started laughing.

"Jackson wants to take me to the prom!" She ignored his red face and the hands at his sides balled into fists. "How would we get there, Jackson? In that old, beat-up car of yours? Or maybe your brother could loan us his bicycle."

He had turned and walked away when he wanted to punch something, maybe hit the guy laughing even harder than she was, the school's pretty-boy quarterback, Jeffrey Freedman. Jeff was the guy who gave him and his younger brothers, Gabe and Devlin, more grief than any of the other kids in school.

He and Freedman had gone at it once before and Freedman had come out the loser. Jackson might have hit him again except that by then he'd started team-boxing and his coach, Steve Whitelaw, had taught him that the street fighting he was so good at would only get him into more trouble. He was learning to channel the talent he had with his fists into a sport that eventually won him a scholarship.

Jackson glanced back at the cottage. He was no longer that same insecure boy who had left Wind Canyon sixteen years ago. But he would never forget the girl who had made him feel less than a man.

"You remember her, don't you?" Livvy asked, breaking into his thoughts. "She was real pretty, thick dark brown hair and big blue eyes. She was kind of shy back then."

"Shy? I'm afraid that isn't the Sarah I remember. And I don't want her here." He started toward the cottage, but Livvy caught his arm.

"What are you doing? I've already taken her money."

"Then give it back."

"She doesn't want it back. She wants a place to raise her little girl. I thought it would be nice to have a child around — and maybe some female company once in a while."

"Fine, but not here."

"Why not?"

"Because I said so. Go back to the house, Livvy. I'll take care of this."

"But . . . but . . ."

Jackson just ignored her and kept on walking. He tried to tell himself he wouldn't get the least satisfaction from throwing Sarah Allen off his land.

But he knew it wasn't the truth.

Sarah hummed as she worked in the quaint little cottage, unpacking her and Holly's things. She had tied a bandanna around her head to hold back her heavy dark hair and though the place was immaculately clean, busied herself lining drawers with the shelf paper she had found in one of the closets and generally taking inventory of what was in the house.

She glanced around the larger of two cozy

bedrooms, one with twin beds, the other with a queen-size four-poster, each covered with what looked like handmade quilts. Surprisingly, considering the age of the cottage, there were also two bathrooms, which Sarah viewed as a major bonus.

She was on her way back into the living room — wide-planked wooden floors, a stone fireplace, a comfortable sofa and chairs — when she heard a brisk knock at the door. For a instant, fear gripped her. Living with Andrew had instilled a defense mechanism that set her adrenaline rushing in an instant.

She forced herself to relax. Assuming it must be Olivia Jones, the lady who had rented her the property, she hurried over, lifted the wrought-iron latch and pulled the door open.

Her eyes widened. It wasn't Olivia; it was Jackson Raines.

And he didn't look happy to see her.

"Hello, Sarah."

She wet her lips, which suddenly felt stiff as paper. "Hello, Jackson."

"You don't seem surprised to see me. I guess you recognized me last night."

"I . . . umm . . . figured it out."

"And you must have been headed here and not the Whittaker Ranch."

"I made the wrong turn." She tipped her head back a little farther to look at him. He was even taller than she remembered, somewhere around six foot three. He had certainly changed in sixteen years. Each of his features seemed more distinct, his dark brown eyes more intense, his cheekbones more sharply defined. She remembered the slight cleft in his chin, but now there was a faint scar along his temple and another bisected one of his nicely shaped eyebrows.

A little tremor of awareness went through her that she was surprised to feel. It had been years since she had felt any sort of attraction to a man. After Andrew, she thought maybe she never would again.

"Do you . . . umm . . . work here on the ranch?" she asked.

The corner of his mouth edged up. "You might say that." He looked over her shoulder into the living room, surveyed the boxes on the sofa and the suitcases on the bed he could see through the open bedroom door. "I'm afraid we have a problem."

"We do? What is it?"

"Mrs. Jones made a mistake. The cottage is not for rent."

Her stomach tightened. "That . . . that can't be right. It was listed on the internet. The details have all been worked out."

"I'll see your money is returned. And I'll pay for any extra trouble this might have caused. Just tell me how much and I'll write you a check."

Her voice rose. "I don't want a check! This is going to be our home. Holly and I . . . we need this place. We love it here already." Tears welled in her eyes. She couldn't stand to think of being uprooted again, of searching for somewhere else to live, of disappointing Holly. Just then the little girl raced into the living room.

"Mommy — there's a nest of baby robins under the roof right outside my window! The mother bird is feeding them!" She slid to a stop just a few feet away from Jackson. "You're the man from last night."

"That's right."

"Holly, this is Mr. Raines. Jackson, this is my daughter, Holly."

"You saved us. Mommy said she didn't know what we would have done if you hadn't come along. Maybe we would have frozen right out there on the road."

His lips twitched. "I don't think you would have frozen but I'm glad I could help."

"Please," Sarah pleaded, "isn't there any way you could speak to the owner, tell him

31

how important it is for Holly and me to stay?"

His eyes drifted over her turtleneck sweater and jeans, the white sneakers she wore that would be worthless out in the snow. "Just how important is it?"

A lump began to swell in her throat. Being here meant everything. Since the moment she had walked through the door of the cottage, for the first time in years, she had felt as if she were home.

"I have a job in town, working for the *Wind Canyon News.* It's freelance, so it's only part-time and I'll be able to take care of Holly. I had to pull her out of school two weeks early but I figured it would be worth it. She's never lived anywhere but the city. I want her to know what it's like to live somewhere free and open — a place where there are trees and animals and birds, where the sky is blue and clear." She glanced away, afraid he would notice the glitter of tears in her eyes. "She just lost her father. She needs this, Jackson. Please . . . I need it."

He was frowning. He looked down at Holly, who was staring at him as if he were a real-life hero — which, to her, being a cowboy and their savior last night, he was.

He took a deep breath and slowly released it. "I suppose it wouldn't hurt if you stayed for a while. Just don't get too comfortable. If things don't work out, you'll have to find another place to live."

Relief hit her so hard her knees went weak. A bright smile broke over her face. "Things will work out. We won't be a problem, I promise."

He nodded.

"So you'll talk to the owner? You'll make sure it's okay for us to stay?"

He made a scoffing sound. "I'll take care of it." Then he turned and started walking away, out the door and across the porch, out into the snow.

Sarah ran after him. "I meant to ask . . ." she called out. "What's the name of the man who owns the ranch?"

He kept on walking, his boots crunching in the snow. Over his shoulder he called back to her. "Jackson Raines."

Sarah just stood there staring. Jackson Raines owned the ranch where she and Holly were going to live. Of course, after the way she had treated him all those years ago, no wonder he wanted her to leave! She dragged in a breath and slowly released it. Sooner or later, she would have to talk to him, apologize and try to explain why she had behaved so badly — not that there was any real excuse.

"He's a really nice man, Mama. I like him."

She managed a smile. "It was kind of him to let us stay." But clearly, it was only a temporary reprieve. He would be looking for a reason to get rid of them. He didn't want her here, and she couldn't really blame him.

Still, she wouldn't make it easy.

She intended to keep to herself, do her job in town and not cause any trouble.

Surely that wouldn't be a difficult thing to do.

Two days later, Jackson stood at the kitchen window, watching as a car hauler drove down the lane past the ranch house and rolled to a stop in front of the cottage. There was an old Toyota pickup on the flatbed, rusted and at least ten years old. The driver unloaded the little truck that looked like a miniature version of a real pickup, then pulled Sarah's fancy Mercedes up on the carrier and began to strap it down.

Jackson frowned. What the hell was going on?

Taking a last swig of coffee, he tossed the rest down the drain, grabbed his jacket off the coatrack beside the door and headed toward the cottage. Most of the snow had already melted, leaving the ground a muddy, soggy mess. His old work boots squished with every step. As he strode toward the cottage, he spotted Sarah standing on the porch, dressed in jeans and the same white sneakers she'd had on the last time he saw her. He wondered why she didn't have the good sense to buy herself a decent pair of boots.

"All set, Ms. Allen."

"Thank you, Mr. Roderick."

The driver waved, got back into his truck, turned the carrier around in the open space between the cottage and the barn, and headed back down the lane toward the road.

"Car trouble?" Jackson asked, wondering if she would explain or tell him it was none of his business.

"I sold my car. It wasn't any good for country living, anyway."

He walked over to the little Toyota pickup. The first thing he noticed was that all four tires were bare.

"I know I probably shouldn't say this, but you realize those tires have got to be replaced."

She frowned. "What do you mean?"

"I mean they aren't safe for you to drive on, let alone haul your little girl back and forth to town."

She started toward him down the steps, the white sneakers instantly sucking down in the icy, slushy mud. "Are you sure?"

"I'm sure." He walked around the pickup, saw that the leather seats were cracked and the carpets worn. "Did you have anyone look at this truck before you bought it?"

"I didn't know who to ask. I don't know anyone around here anymore. It looked like it would get good gas mileage and it has four-wheel drive."

"The damned thing's ten years old."

She stiffened. "It was all I could afford. Now if you will excuse me —"

"Whoa — wait a minute." She turned back to him. He tried not to notice how pretty she looked in the morning sun with her dark hair pulled into a long gleaming braid and her skin glowing as if it were lit from within.

"What do you mean, 'all you can afford'? Word around here was you married some wealthy guy in L.A. If he just passed away, you ought to be pretty well fixed for money."

"Well, I'm not. By the time the estate paid Andrew's debts, there wasn't much of anything left."

"Couldn't tell by that fancy fur coat you were wearing when I saw you on the road."

Her chin inched up. "That's sold, too, if

36

it's any of your business." She turned and started walking and when he looked at her mud-covered sneakers, it occurred to him that she really might not have any money. He should have been elated by this little crumb of payback but he wasn't.

Christ.

No wonder she wanted to stay in the cottage. It was all she could afford. Which could be the reason she didn't seem particularly grief-stricken by her husband's death. She had probably married the guy for his money and then found out he didn't have any.

Sarah disappeared inside the little house. Against all his better instincts, he followed. He rapped on the door, and an instant later, she pulled it open.

"Was there something else you wanted?"

"I just thought I'd check, see if you're getting settled in all right."

"The rest of our things are supposed to arrive tomorrow."

"The rest?"

"There isn't all that much. I sold everything I could to get enough money to come out here." She sighed, looped a wisp of dark hair behind her ear. "I don't know why I'm telling you this. It's hardly your concern."

"Maybe not." But somehow it almost

seemed as if it was. "How's Holly doing?"

"She loves it here."

"Mr. Raines!" She spotted him on the porch just then, bolted through the door and slid to a halt at his feet. "Mama said the next time I saw you I should ask you if it's all right if I get a puppy?"

He couldn't help a smile. His foreman, Jimmy Threebears, and his two boys had a couple of mutts. One more could hardly hurt. Still, it would just make things harder if he decided to send them packing.

Holly was looking up at him with big blue eyes so full of hope Jackson groaned inside. He loved kids. There was no way he was going to say no to this sweet little girl.

"It's all right. Matter of fact, my foreman's dog just had a litter. They're border collies. You want to take a look? You might like to have one of the pups."

Holly whirled toward her mother, her long blond ponytail swinging out behind her. "Mommy, can I, please?"

Sarah smiled. She had pretty white teeth and full pink lips. Jackson remembered that smile and his jaw tightened. That same warm smile had been deceptive in the past.

Likely, it still was.

The UPS truck delivered the boxes with the

rest of Sarah's clothes and personal items the following day. Olivia Jones, the house-keeper she had met the day after her arrival, came over with a hamburger-mac-and-cheese casserole that smelled so good her stomach growled.

"Looks like you got plenty of work ahead of you. I figured with this you wouldn't have to stop and cook dinner."

"Thank you, Mrs. Jones. It looks wonder-ful."

"It's just Livvy, same as when you used to come into the ice-cream shop."

Sarah remembered her from back in those days. Livvy had always been friendly and smiling, just as she was now.

Livvy set the casserole down on the kitchen table. "I figured macaroni might be something your little girl would like."

"Holly likes just about everything. Except avocados." Sarah laughed. "She calls them squishy green things."

Livvy chuckled. "I'll remember that."

For the rest of the day, Sarah unpacked and put things away while Holly played with the puppy Jackson had given her, a black-and-white border collie Holly named Rags.

Sarah had gone with them out to the barn so that Holly could choose which pup she wanted. They met Jackson's foreman, a big

Sioux Indian named Jimmy Threebears. Jimmy had two boys, one ten and one twelve, but no wife.

According to Livvy, Annie Baylor Threebears, a waitress at the Wind Canyon Café, had left her husband and sons five years ago and never been heard from since. From what Sarah could tell, Jimmy had done a good job raising his boys.

Eventually, the long day came to an end and Sarah surveyed her work in the cottage, pleased with all she had done. Tomorrow would be her first day working at the newspaper. She had found a day-care facility not far from the office and Holly was excited at the prospect of making new friends. Sarah was excited to be starting her first real job as a reporter.

Oh, it wasn't anything big. Not much happened in a town the size of Wind Canyon, which was one of the reasons the job appealed to her.

She smiled as she broke down and stacked the last of the empty cardboard boxes. Writing stories about everyday occurrences, working to make them interesting and entertaining, was going to be fun. She had done something similar when she had written for the *Daily Bruin* at UCLA — before she had dropped out in her senior year to marry Andrew.

An image of her husband in one of his rages popped into her mind and a shudder ran down her spine. God, what a fool she had been.

She shook her head, dislodging the memory. A few years after the marriage, she had started taking correspondence courses and eventually gotten her Bachelor's degree, which had helped in getting her the job in Wind Canyon. Andrew wouldn't let her take night classes or she would have finished sooner.

Sarah thought of the husband she had once believed she loved, the cruel, hateful man he had become, and resisted an urge to shiver. She walked over to the window and stood in the sunshine pouring through the glass, hoping to erase the chill.

FOUR

Sarah pulled her blue pickup over to the curb in front of the Busy Bee Day-Care Center. Holly waited on the porch, along with a couple of other kids. The little girl ran around to the passenger side and climbed into the truck, settled herself in her booster seat, and Sarah helped her fasten the seat belt. The pickup was sporting a new set of tires, thanks to the small amount of room she had left on her credit card, so she wasn't worried about getting safely home.

She turned the vehicle onto the street leading out of town and settled in for the drive back to the ranch. She looked over at her daughter, who peered at the thick growth of forest passing by outside the window.

"How was your first day, honey?" Sarah asked.

"I met a girl named Alice. Everyone calls her Allie. She showed me how to play a really cool card game called Go Fish."

Sarah smiled. "That's great, baby."

She thought of her own first day. She had been introduced to the owner of the paper, Smiley Reed, an older, pudgy, balding man with a penchant for cigars. And just like in the movies, everyone called him "chief."

The paper's only other reporter, Mike Stevens, was a couple of years younger than Sarah but had more experience. He was tall, sandy-haired and not bad-looking. Mike covered the headline news, weather and sports, while Sarah was assigned to personal interest stories, and pretty much anything newsworthy that she could come up with.

"To start with, just get out there and get acquainted with the town," Smiley had said, handing her a box of business cards he'd had printed especially for her. "Stop in the stores and meet the owners, see who's doing what. You'll be surprised what you might find out."

Sarah proudly held on to the cards, the first she'd ever had. She was fine with the idea. She'd had to come up with news for the college paper. This shouldn't be any more difficult.

She spent the afternoon milling around town, getting reacquainted. Wind Canyon looked just like a Wyoming town should, with a long main street that still had old covered boardwalks running along both sides. Bars, restaurants and boutiques lined the street, a lot more of them now that the quaint little Western town had been discovered by tourists.

Wind Canyon had grown quite a bit in the years Sarah had been gone and now there were shops and restaurants on the side streets, as well. She was surprised to discover some of the people in town still remembered her.

"I sure was sorry about what happened to your folks," Fred Wilkins said, owner of Wilkins' Mercantile. "They were real nice people."

"Thank you." Sarah fought a wave of sadness she hadn't let surface in years, not since the awful news of her parents' death had reached her when she was in college. Her overwhelming grief and loneliness were part of the reason she had married Andrew that year.

Sarah left the mercantile, leaving a card with Mr. Wilkins, as well as Mrs. Potter at the antiques shop and a number of other business owners, asking them to call her if they had something of interest for the paper. She smiled to think how well she had been received.

Sarah was still smiling when she arrived back at Raintree Ranch and she and Holly drove up in front of the cottage. Then she saw the front door standing wide-open and her smile disappeared.

"Who's in our house, Mommy?"

"I don't know." She cracked open the car door and climbed out. "You wait here, okay?"

She walked toward the house, wondering if the wind or an animal might have pushed open the door. The lock was old. Maybe it had just given way. As she climbed up to the porch to inspect the lock, she caught a glimpse of the living room through the front window.

"Oh, my God!"

She forced herself to walk inside, her legs beginning to tremble. The entire cottage was a shambles, the sofa cushions ripped open, the curtains torn down from the windows, pots and pans tossed out of the cupboards, broken dishes all over the floor. "Oh, my God," she repeated a second time.

Holly raced through the front door. "Mama! Someone tore up our house!" The little girl started crying and it was all Sarah could do not to join her. She lifted Holly into her arms and turned at the sound of a man's deep voice.

"What the hell . . . ?"

"Jackson . . ." Of all the people she didn't want to see in that moment, Jackson Raines topped the list. She had promised there wouldn't be any trouble. This looked like very big trouble to her.

She set Holly back on her feet and the little girl clung to her waist. Sarah swallowed. "Someone . . . someone broke in."

"I can see that."

She covered her mouth with her hand to hold back a sob.

"You stay here," Jackson commanded. "I'll make sure they're not still around." He left her there and went through each room in the house, then returned to the living room.

"Whoever did it is long gone. You have any idea who it might be?"

Sarah shook her head. She looked at him and her eyes filled with tears. "Why would someone do this?"

Jackson's gaze held a trace of pity. It was overshadowed by anger. "I don't know, but I'm sure as hell going to find out." He surveyed the overturned sofa and chairs, then the destruction in the bedroom, which looked as bad as the rest of the house.

"What are we gonna do, Mama?" Holly stared up at her with tears in her big blue eyes.

Jackson strode toward the little girl, crouched down in front of her, and she went into his arms as if she had done it a thousand times. "Don't you worry, honey. We'll put this place back just the way it was." He looked over at Sarah, must have noticed the pallor of her face and the way she stood there trembling.

He came to his feet, but kept hold of Holly's hand. "That goes for you, too, Sarah. I'll get Livvy over here to help and between the three of us we'll have this place back in shape in no time."

She just nodded. Her throat was too tight to speak.

Jackson let go of Holly's hand and she ran back to Sarah.

"Nothing like this has ever happened on the ranch before," Jackson said. "We'll find out who did it and make sure it doesn't happen again."

Sarah made no reply. *Nothing like this has ever happened before.* The words sent a chill down her spine. Surely this had nothing to do with her, nothing to do with Andrew and the past she had run from in L.A.

Surely her problems hadn't followed her.

But as she looked at the destruction in the cottage, Sarah felt sure they had.

■ ■ ■ ■

Jackson met Sheriff Weber in front of the cottage and they walked inside together. Livvy had taken Sarah and little Holly up to the main house and was distracting them with milk and cookies.

Weber, a tall, heavyset man with iron-gray hair, lifted his brown felt cowboy hat and scratched his head. "Worst case of vandalism I've seen round these parts in years. Any idea who might have done it?"

"No, but a woman and her little girl just moved into the place. I imagine they aren't feeling real safe right now."

"Who's that?"

"Sarah Allen. Her family used to live here. Livvy tells me her folks died about ten years ago in a car accident. Husband died not long ago."

"I remember the accident that killed her folks. Some drunk crossed the center line out on the highway coming into town. I'll talk to Sarah, tell her we're looking into this. Odds are it was a bunch of teenagers, maybe someone whose family is camped around here. I'll take a drive through the campgrounds, see what I can come up with."

"Thanks, Ben."

The sheriff went out and got his camera, took a string of photos documenting the damage. "Insurance gonna take care of this?"

"Only the building's covered."

"Figures." The sheriff walked back outside and the two of them went up to the main house so Ben could speak to Sarah.

As soon as Weber left, Jackson led the small group back to the cottage to begin cleaning up.

"Looks like you'll need a new sofa and chairs," he said to Sarah. "Some new curtains, too. Soon as you get time, we'll go into town and get whatever you need."

She gazed up at him in surprise. "You're going to replace everything?"

"You didn't think I would? What happened wasn't your fault."

Sarah glanced away. "Thank you."

When she looked back at him, there was something in her face . . . It had never occurred to him that Sarah's presence might have anything to do with the vandalism. Watching her now, he wondered.

Jackson made a mental note to call his brother, Devlin, have him do some digging. Dev owned a chain of security companies in the Southwest, including one in L.A. Mostly he managed them from his house in

49

Scottsdale, close to the Phoenix branch. These days, his employees did most of the legwork, but Dev was still one of the best investigators in the business.

Jackson would ask Dev to sniff around, find out what he could about the young widow and her daughter.

Dev wasn't home. His brother was off somewhere with one of his lady friends, or so Devlin's Phoenix office manager said. Jackson wasn't surprised. A few years back, his youngest brother had suffered a bad breakup with the girl he planned to marry and since then, had become a dedicated bachelor.

"Can I take a message?" the manager asked.

"Tell him Jackson called. Tell him I need to talk to him." Jackson hung up the phone. He'd get a return call sooner or later, but he wasn't holding his breath. Dev liked to live big and he usually did just that.

Instead of waiting anxiously to hear from him, Jackson spent the morning in the basement, working out on the weights, punching the heavy bag, then spending some time on the speed bag. He liked the physical exercise that had come to be a habit, liked to keep in shape. When he finished, he showered and pulled on his jeans and headed down to his foreman Jimmy Three-bears's house, part of the original ranch compound, three bedrooms with a wrap-around, screened-in front porch.

The residence, which sat on a knoll across from the barn, had been remodeled a number of times, and Jackson had done a bit more modernizing of the old wooden structure when he bought the ranch four years ago. As he approached, he saw Jimmy's boys playing ball out in front.

"Where's your dad?" Jackson asked.

"He's up on the ridgeline, sir." Sam, the twelve-year-old, shoved a hand through his gleaming black shoulder-length hair. He was a good-looking kid — both of them were. They got good grades and were very good athletes. Jimmy had a right to be proud of them.

"Dad says those loggers are filling the stream up with mud again. He went up to take another look."

Jackson's jaw tightened. He had actually thought he'd had problems when he'd worked in Houston. After high school, he had used his boxing scholarship to earn a degree in geology then landed a job with the small, newly formed Wildcat Oil. He had taken part of his salary in stock — the smartest move he ever made.

When the company expanded, then went public, he made enough money to retire from the oil business and live in comfort, buy the old Simmons ranch and become a cattleman — which had been his lifelong dream.

One thing he'd learned — a rancher faced just as many problems as an oil company and made a whole lot less money.

And now the damned logging companies were making things worse. They were cutting down trees in the national forest that bordered the ranch and causing him all kinds of trouble.

He shook his head. He still couldn't believe the taxpayers paid to build roads so the bastards could cut down trees. They were taking out those big seven-hundred-year-old ponderosas as if they had a right. Only God had a right to those trees as far as Jackson was concerned. Somewhere along the way, the politicians had sure as hell gotten things screwed up.

He looked over at the older boy, who was nearly as tall as his dad but lean and lanky instead of muscular like Jimmy. Sam tossed the baseball into the air and caught it.

"I could use a little help," Jackson said. "You boys game?"

"Sure." Gibby grinned, a ten-year-old version of his older brother with slightly shorter black hair. "Just tell us what you need us to do."

Always ready for a little diversion, both boys followed him off toward the barn. Half an hour later, they had loaded the old sofa he remembered storing in the loft into the back of his truck, dusted it off real good, then the boys jumped up in the bed and he drove the load down to Sarah's cottage.

Sarah's. Jackson blew out a breath, amazed he already thought of the place that way and none too pleased about it.

"Found a couch you can use," he said when she opened the door. "Hope this'll do till we can buy you a new one."

"Anything we can sit on will do." She gave him one of her pretty white smiles and he felt the same kick in the stomach he used to feel in high school. He wished he could believe that smile was real.

With the boys' help, they situated the sofa in front of the fireplace. With the rest of the house cleaned up, the place was again in fairly livable condition. He made a mental note to have Livvy bring down a few of the extra dishes, enough to make do until he could buy some to replace the ones that were broken.

The boys took off, leaving him with Sarah.

"So when can you get away?" he found himself asking, wishing like hell he wasn't so eager to hear her answer.

"I'm working in town tomorrow, but I'll be done by three. Holly can stay at the day-care center while we go shopping if you want."

He nodded. "Great. I'll pick you up in front of the newspaper office."

She flashed him another warm smile and his groin tightened. He tried to tell himself he shouldn't be the least attracted to a money-hungry woman like Sarah but in the his mind's eye he was untying that long, thick chestnut braid and running his fingers through it, unbuttoning her blouse and —

Jackson clamped down on the image. He needed to go a couple more rounds with the heavy bag, maybe let the speed bag hit him a few times in the head.

He had been fooled by Sarah Allen once. It wasn't going to happen again.

Sarah's cell phone rang. Sitting behind the desk Smiley had assigned her, she jumped, startled by the unexpected jangle. Ever since the break-in, her nerves had been on edge. Thank God nothing else had happened, which made her think she might be wrong, and it was, as the sheriff believed, just teenagers bent on making trouble.

The phone rang a second time before she could dig it out of her oversize leather purse. Hoping someone might be calling with a news story, she flipped open the phone without checking the caller ID and heard Martin Kozak's rusty smoker's voice on the line.

"I've been trying to reach you, Sarah. Don't you check your messages?"

Her hand shook. Vaguely she heard the bell ring above the door, but didn't look up to see who it was. "I've been busy, Marty. And my phone's been out of service." That was the truth. There were only certain places around the cottage where she could get cell reception. She reminded herself to get a landline, though she had few people to call.

"I need to talk to you, Sarah."

"I don't have anything to tell you, Marty. I don't have what you're looking for. I don't know anything about Andrew's business. We never discussed it."

"You moved out of the condo. Where are you, Sarah? Tell me where you are, and I'll meet you."

She swallowed. Her hand kept shaking. She tightened her fingers around the phone to make it stop. "Leave me alone, Marty." Sarah hung up the phone. She was breathing hard, her pulse racing. She closed her eyes, trying to bring herself under control, and when she looked up, Jackson Raines stood next to her desk.

"Who's Marty?" he asked. The look in his eyes said he had overheard her conversation. He expected an answer, and he wasn't going to settle for less.

"H-he was a business acquaintance of my husband's."

"What did he want?"

She moistened her lips, worked to make them form the words. "I don't know."

Jackson slid a hand beneath her elbow and urged her up out of her chair. "You're trembling. Come on, let's get out of here."

She didn't argue. Marty's call had shaken her. She had been so sure he would leave her alone once she left L.A. Now she wondered if Marty had been lying about not knowing where she lived and had followed her to Wyoming.

If he had sent his thugs to search the cottage for whatever it was he was looking for.

She waved to Mike as they walked out, letting him know she was leaving, and stepping outside, into the crisp mountain air. Sarah took a deep breath, felt a little steadier. Jackson just kept walking, hauling her around to the passenger side of his truck, opening the door and boosting her up into the seat. His hand accidentally brushed her thigh as he helped her get settled and a little tingle of awareness went through her.

She was wearing a lightweight apricot sweater and a pair of tan slacks — and it was a darned good thing. She imagined what that light touch might have felt like on bare skin and a rush of heat slid into her stomach.

Embarrassment sparked a little burst of hysterical laughter.

"What's so funny?"

She shook her head, then sobered at the sudden memory of Martin Kozak's call. "Not a damned thing."

One of his dark eyebrows arched up. He pinned her with the same look he had used in her office. "Why don't you tell me what's going on." It was an order, not a question.

Sarah sighed and leaned back against the black leather seat. "I suppose, since I'm living in your house, you have a right to know." And there was something about him that made her want to tell him. Maybe it was just that she had known him from before, or maybe it was that he seemed so strong and capable, a solid shoulder to lean on. Whatever it was, she just hoped that once he knew, he wouldn't toss her out in the street.

He drove the truck to a shady area off the road at the edge of town and turned off the engine, then shifted on the seat to face her.

"I overheard some of your conversation. Does the guy you were talking to have something to do with what happened at the cottage?"

She looked over to where he sat. His dark eyes were mostly hidden by his battered cowboy hat, but the hard line of his jaw and the indentation in his chin were clear. "I don't know. I don't think he even knows where I live."

"Then why were you so upset?"

She bit her lip, wondering how much she should tell him. "To put it bluntly, my husband — that is to say, my *late* husband — was a crook. I didn't know it when I married him and I was never involved in any of his shady business dealings, but I knew whatever he was up to wasn't good."

"Why didn't you leave him?"

"I tried more than once. He was . . . determined I would never get a divorce. He said he would do whatever it took to keep me from taking his daughter." An ugly memory surfaced of Andrew's fist connecting with her cheek and Sarah fought not to flinch. "I believed him."

She looked out the window, into the dense grove of dark, shadowy pines trees that climbed the sides of the hills. "I came here to start a new life. I just want to be left alone."

For several moments, Jackson said nothing. Maybe he was the one person she knew who understood what it was to want to start over. In high school, Jackson Raines had a wild reputation. He was in trouble off and on all through his early teenage years. Until he'd been recruited by the boxing team. After that, he had settled down, come up with a solid set of goals, and become the sort of boy she found attractive.

She hadn't dared let on. He had made an enemy of the varsity quarterback, Jeff Freedman, the most popular boy in school. Jeff had taunted him into a fistfight then taken a beating for his foolishness. Jackson had been completely ostracized, and unless Sarah wanted that same treatment, she was forced to ignore the attraction she felt for him.

But Sarah was a woman now and Jackson no longer a boy. It was far more difficult to ignore that attraction today than it had been back then.

"What's this guy's name?" Jackson's deep voice jolted her back to the present.

"Martin Kozak."

"You said you didn't have what he was looking for. So what is it he's looking for?"

She sighed. "Marty called me a number of times before we moved. He said Andrew had something he needed. A list of some kind, maybe a computer disk or a notebook. I told him I didn't know anything about it and I don't."

"So what makes you think Kozak's not responsible for ransacking the cottage?"

"On the phone Marty asked me where I lived. He said if I would tell him, he would come and meet me. It seemed like he really didn't know. I said to just leave me alone."

Jackson watched her closely. "Why do you suppose he's come after this now? You said your husband passed away some months back."

"I don't understand that, either."

Jackson cast her another penetrating glance. "Do you think Kozak is a danger to you and Holly?"

She looked away. There was something about Marty Kozak that frightened her. She wasn't sure what it was. "He lives in L.A. I can't imagine he would come all the way up here, even if he knew where to find me. I'm just hoping the sheriff is right and it was just a bunch of kids."

Jackson studied her face, searching for the truth, she supposed. "All right. For now, that's the assumption we'll go on. In the meantime, let's forget about Kozak and go buy that sofa. We'll worry about the rest of it as it comes."

She looked at him and something squeezed inside her. "You're . . . you're going to help me?"

"If we're lucky, you won't need my help. This guy will stop looking for you and that will be the end of it."

"And if he doesn't?"

He shrugged a powerful set of shoulders that must have been a nightmare for his boxing opponents. "If he doesn't, we'll figure out where to go from there."

Her throat closed up. It had been so long since anyone had done anything at all to help her. One by one, Andrew had managed to destroy her personal friendships. Oh, she had tennis partners, mostly the women at the country club, and there were the wives of his business acquaintances. But none of them were real friends.

Her grandmother was still alive, but she was in her seventies and she had a heart condition. Sarah had been afraid that if she called her, she would inadvertently spill out her pain and it might aggravate her heart condition. With no friends or family she could talk to, she had no one to depend on but herself.

"I know what you must think of me," she said. "I know you haven't forgotten what I did to you in high school."

He flicked her a glance. "Maybe not. But we're not in high school anymore. And we're both too old to play games." He cranked up the engine, started to put the truck into gear, but she caught his arm.

"I'm sorry about what happened that day. I know it doesn't change anything, but it's true. I've regretted the way I behaved, the way I treated you, a thousand times."

Jackson said nothing, just shifted the truck into Drive and stepped on the gas. She didn't think he believed her. He probably thought that she was just being nice to him because he was successful now, obviously a man of some means, instead of a boy from the wrong side of the tracks.

Maybe he was right and what she'd done no longer mattered.

Oddly enough, it still mattered a great deal to Sarah.

FIVE

Jackson called himself ten kinds of fool. It was sheer insanity. Total stupidity. But every time he saw her, watched her doing some simple task, desire for Sarah Allen hit him like a fist to the solar plexus.

Something had shifted, changed the day she had told him about her husband's shady dealings and the man she was afraid of, Martin Kozak. Maybe it was the vulnerability he had seen in her face, maybe it was the way she had looked at him when he had offered to help her. Whatever it was, since that day, the attraction he had felt had grown into full-blown lust.

Jackson lifted his cowboy hat and settled it low on his forehead. He told himself it was just that he hadn't had a woman in a while. He wasn't like his brother, Dev. He wasn't into one-night stands. He dated, got to know a lady before he took her to bed. His relationships usually lasted until the heat was gone and the affair turned into friendship. The women knew from the start he didn't make promises and didn't want a woman who expected them.

Which didn't mean he was *completely* opposed to marriage. Hell, he always figured someday in the distant future he'd get married and have a couple of kids. Just not right away.

Still, he liked sex and he didn't have much trouble finding a willing bed partner, even in a town as small as Wind Canyon. It was just that lately, he'd been busy.

Or maybe he just hadn't met a woman who appealed to him.

As he strode toward where Jimmy Threebears worked with a couple of new saddle horses, he passed Sarah's cottage and caught a glimpse of her sweeping the porch. She bent over to use the dustpan, pulling her jeans tight over a very round, very nice ass, and pressure began to build in his groin.

It was insanity. Total stupidity.

He told himself he ought to give Maddie Gallagher a call. They had dated off and on. Maddie was a few years older, divorced, always up for a round of steamy sex. Maybe he should call her . . . but he didn't really want to.

He forced himself not to look back at the

porch, carefully kept his attention on the big man working one of the geldings on a lead line in the pen. From the corner of his eye, he saw Jimmy's two boys tossing a ball to little Holly, whose black-and-white puppy sniffed and yapped at her feet. The boys had already grown protective of her.

Just as Jackson had grown protective of Sarah.

It was insanity. Total stupidity.

Sarah was probably playing him, just like she had in high school.

"Hey, boss!" Jimmy waved, dark-skinned and dark-eyed, his long black hair pulled into a ponytail fastened low on his neck. He handed the lead to one of the hands and walked out of the pen.

"You been up to the ridge today?" Jackson asked as Jimmy approached.

"Not today. But it sure didn't look good the last time I was there. There's slash clogging the water upriver, making it overflow the banks, and with the trees clear-cut on the north side of the hill that last storm washed a shitload of dirt into the stream. Those cows in the upper pasture are having a helluva time getting anything decent to drink."

"Let's move 'em down into Pine Meadow. The grass isn't quite as good, but at least the water will be clean."

"I'll get a couple of the hands and trailer some horses. Won't take long to move 'em."

"Keep an eye open while you're up there. I don't trust those loggers. The Barrett brothers are in for the quick buck and they don't care what they do to get it. If we aren't careful, they'll do something else we'll have to pay for."

Jimmy nodded, turned and started organizing the men. He was hardworking and efficient. Jackson couldn't run the place without him. On top of that, not counting Gabe and Dev, Jimmy was his closest friend.

Jackson left the men and returned to the house. As he walked into his study, he saw the message light blinking on the phone.

He pushed the button, heard his youngest brother's deep voice. "Hey, bro, what's up? Give me a call."

Jackson dialed Dev's home number and his brother picked up on the second ring.

"Thanks for calling me back," Jackson said. "Sorry to bother you, little brother, but I got what could turn into a problem and I was hoping you might be able to help."

"What's going on?"

"You remember a girl in your high school class named Sarah Allen?"

"Sarah Allen . . . Sarah Allen . . . dark

hair, big blue, heartbreaker eyes and a luscious little body? The girl who had you tied in knots half your senior year? Nah, I don't recall."

"Very funny. The thing is, Sarah is back in Wind Canyon and I think she might be in some kind of trouble. I want you to find out everything you can about her and get back to me."

"What can you give me to work with?"

He dug out the application Livvy had taken from Sarah over the internet and read what little was on the printed page: her social security number; her residence address in Santa Monica, a former address on Sunset Drive, the make and model of her Mercedes, which had now been sold. Jackson told Dev about the break-in, and about the call from a guy named Martin Kozak, who wanted some kind of list that Sarah's husband supposedly had.

"I'm trying to tell myself the break-in had nothing to do with Sarah's past, but I don't believe in coincidence."

"Neither do I. What else can you tell me?"

"Sarah has a six-year-old daughter named Holly. Her husband's name was Andrew Hollister."

"*Late* husband, is it?"

He could almost see Dev's knowing grin.

"Just do what you can, will you?"

"You got it, bro." Dev signed off and Jackson hung up the phone.

His brother was an ex-Ranger. Both his brothers had gone into the service after high school. Gabe had enlisted in the Marines, then a year later, Dev, the youngest and determined to prove himself, had joined the army and become a Ranger. Once he got out, he had used the specialized skills he had learned to start a security company, and eventually became one of the best investigators around.

Officially, he didn't take cases anymore, just ran his business. Unofficially, he still got involved whenever a case intrigued him — and he was always there if one of his brothers needed his help.

Jackson thought of the destruction in Sarah's cottage, of the ominous phone call she had received, and hoped his brother called back soon.

Three days later, Sarah stood at the window in the living room, watching Jackson at the barn. She liked the way he moved — his long, confident strides, the purpose that was clear in every step. She liked the narrow, masculine span of his hips in contrast to the width of his shoulders.

Something had changed between them the day she had told him about Marty. She still wasn't sure why she had done it — not that he had left her much choice. Maybe it just felt good to talk to someone instead of being afraid to open her mouth.

She hadn't told him everything, of course. The years she had spent with Andrew were too ugly, too frightening — the end too terrible to recall. And she had no idea how much she could really trust him.

Still, she didn't leave the window, just stood there watching, smiling at the way he angled his hat over his eyes, how natural he looked in his worn jeans and boots, as if he'd been born to ranching — which she knew he hadn't.

In truth, he had lived in a ramshackle house at the edge of town. His mother had been a drunk and his father had left when Jackson was a boy. Thanks to boxing, he had been able to stop the downhill spiral that had been leading him into trouble and turn his life around.

He paused to talk to some of his ranch hands, saw them nod and head out to do whatever it was he asked. He was truly a man's man, but then he always had been. Maybe that was what she had liked about him even way back then.

"Are we going to work today, Mama?"

Sarah looked down to see Holly standing in front of her. "Yes, honey. I got a call from Mr. Wilkins at the mercantile. He reminded me about the big Memorial Day celebration coming up the end of the month. The paper needs an article written about it." She loved the fact she was a freelance reporter. It gave her a wonderful control of her time — as long as she got her work done.

"So you're gonna write it?"

"That's my job, honey. There's a picnic and a parade every year and the whole town turns out. Doesn't that sound like fun?"

Holly jumped up and down. "I love parades!"

Sarah smiled. "I know you do." And the community spirit in Wind Canyon was one of the things that had brought her back home to raise her daughter. "After I get finished in town, we'll drive over and see your great-grandma, just like I promised." Sarah had been anxious to visit her grandmother, a woman she hadn't seen in years.

Holly fell silent. She ran the toe of a small bare foot over the planked wooden floor. "Do you think she'll like me?"

Sarah reached out and caught her daughter's small hands. "Grandma Thompson is going to love you. I brought you to see her

70

once when you were a baby, but you were too small to remember. She thought you were the prettiest baby girl she'd ever seen."

But Sarah had paid for that defiant visit dearly. When she'd gotten back to L.A., Andrew had been furious. During the terrible fight they'd had, he had blackened her eye and broken her arm.

Sarah took a deep breath and shoved the painful memory away. She smiled down at her daughter. "Go get your socks and sneakers, grab your jacket, and we'll get going."

Holly dashed off, and Sarah went to collect her sweater and purse. She glanced around the cottage. The new sofa and chair and the rest of the furnishings she and Jackson had purchased wouldn't be in for a few more weeks. She told herself the vandalism was never going to happen again. It was just out-of-control kids, nothing more.

But even if it weren't, she was home and she was going to stay. She had paid long enough for the foolish mistakes she had made.

And nothing — not even one of Andrew's crooked friends — was going to drive her away.

Jackson spotted Livvy's stout figure hurrying toward where he unloaded sacks of grain

71

from the back of a flatbed truck.

"Jackson! Jackson, your brother's on the phone! He says it's important!"

Jackson waved, thought again that he should add a line out in the barn so he could take his calls. Then again, he didn't like talking on the phone. He'd talked from dawn to midnight when he had been in the oil business, which was the reason he hadn't put a phone out in the barn in the first place.

He started jogging toward the house, passed Livvy on the way and took the call in his study.

"Hey, Dev."

His brother's deep voice reached him over the line. "Are you sitting down?"

He sank down in the chair behind his desk. "That bad, is it?"

"Afraid so. You said Sarah's husband was Andrew Hollister?"

"That's right."

"Ever heard of Louis Hollister?"

"Seems to ring a bell, but I'm not sure why."

"Louis Hollister was a blue-collar guy from the San Fernando Valley who made it big in the heavy equipment business. He owned Blacktop Tires, owned some big manufacturing plants, a couple of mining

72

operations, a demolition company — the list goes on and on. The guy dabbled in just about everything that dealt with machinery and usually made money. By the time he died, he was worth a nice round forty mil."

"Not exactly chump change."

"Not exactly. His estate went entirely to his son Andrew — money, business interests, even his Spanish-style house on Sunset Drive."

"I guess Sarah found what she was looking for."

"No quite. For a while, Andrew lived high on Daddy's money. So high, in fact, he began to run out. He was a big-time gambler and he liked life in the fast lane. He married Sarah and they had a kid, but it didn't slow him down. Andrew kept right on spending."

"Sounds like a great guy."

"Yeah, well, according to my sources, he made enemies wherever he went. Four months ago, he was murdered, apparently by someone he pissed off. Probably one of his business cronies or someone he owed money."

"So the police never found the killer."

"I don't think they were highly motivated. No one thought much of Andrew. The Feds were looking at him for tax evasion, probably the only thing they could hang him on, but everyone knew he was into a lot of bad shit. I think the cops wanted to pin a medal on the guy who offed him."

Jackson mulled over the information, trying to imagine Sarah with a no-good like that. "I really appreciate it, Dev."

"There's one more thing."

He braced himself. "What is it?"

"Hollister was a wife-beater, Jackson. Sarah went to the hospital on more than one occasion. It was fairly common knowledge that he used his wife as a punching bag whenever he felt the urge. Rumor mill says his wife was scared to death of him."

He said he would do whatever it took to keep me from taking his daughter. I believed him.

Jackson took a steadying breath. He couldn't believe how angry he was. His chest was squeezing as if he'd fought ten rounds, and one of his hands had unconsciously fisted.

He forced himself to relax. "What about the little girl?"

"Hollister worshipped her. No record of any hospital visits. I don't think he ever laid a hand on the kid, just took out his frustrations on Sarah."

"Thanks, Dev."

"Listen, I'm supposed to head down to Mexico with a lady friend for the next ten days. If you need me here, I'll cancel."

"So far I'm just trying to stay ahead of the game. Have fun in ole Meh-he-co."

Dev chuckled. "You've got my cell number . . . though I'm not sure there'll be any service."

"Not to worry. Watch out for bandits," he said.

"You, too," said Dev, and hung up the phone.

For long moments he just sat there, trying to wrap his mind around the fact that pretty little Sarah Allen had married some bastard who had hurt her so badly she'd wound up in the hospital. A gangster involved in gambling and shady business deals. If he'd had any doubts about the man or men who had tossed the cottage, he didn't anymore.

He needed to talk to Sarah. Unfortunately, he'd seen her drive out this morning in her beat-up truck. He'd have to wait until she got home.

He told himself not to worry.

But he couldn't seem to make himself stop.

"She's a lovely child, Sarah." Her grandmother, Abigail Benton Thompson, watched fondly as Holly chased a butterfly across the covered porch in front of her small wood-frame house. "You've done a good job raising her."

"Thanks, Gran."

"Sometimes I wondered if I'd ever see the two of you again." She was silver-haired and broad-hipped, robust on the outside, though her heart was frail.

"I know. My calls were far too rare. The truth is, I had problems at home and I was afraid you'd be able to hear it in my voice. I didn't want to worry you."

"I worried anyway, darlin'. I'm your gran. You should have called. I might have been able to help."

Sarah managed a wobbly smile. There was nothing her grandmother could have done — nothing anyone could do. "It doesn't matter — not anymore. Andrew is gone. He's out of my life and I'm finally able to do what I want." Sarah kept other thoughts of him at bay, as she had learned to do, though sometimes they crept in anyway.

She leaned over and hugged the older woman. "I've missed you, Gran. It's going to be wonderful to be living so close again."

The town of Sheep River sat just the other side of the Wind Canyon County line. It was a good long drive, but manageable. And it was worth the time it took to get there to be with the only family, aside from a few distant cousins, Sarah had left.

"It's getting late," she said. "We'd better be getting home. I promise I'll be back next week."

"You'd better. Else I might have to pull that old Ford of your granddad's off the blocks in the garage and drive myself on over to your place."

Sarah laughed. Her grandfather had been dead since Sarah was seven years old, but Gran had insisted on keeping his car, the only new vehicle he could ever afford to buy. The tires were rotted off now, but Gran still went out to the barn just to look at it. She said it made her remember the good times.

Gran was still a romantic, even after all these years.

Sarah wasn't. Not anymore.

It was dark by the time she and Holly reached the cottage. Yesterday, she'd had a landline installed and the phone was ringing when she walked through the front door. She lifted the receiver.

"Sarah Allen?"

Her stomach knotted. Almost no one knew her brand-new number. "Yes . . . ?"

"This is Deputy Carson of the Sheep River Sheriff's Department. I'm sorry to have to tell you, but your grandmother's had a heart attack. She's been taken to community hospital."

"Oh, my God!" Her knees turned to water and she sank down in the chair next to the phone. "I — I was just there. She seemed fine when I left."

"I'm afraid there was an incident. Two men broke into her house. They threatened her, told her they wanted whatever it was you gave her to keep for you."

"But I didn't give her anything! All I brought was a bouquet of flowers." *She always loved flowers.*

"I guess she told them that, but they didn't believe her. They tore up her house pretty bad, looking for whatever it was they were after. I gather your grandmother tried to stop them, but her heart began acting up. She called 911. She gave the medics your phone number when they got there."

Sarah swallowed, her lips trembling. "Is she . . . is she all right? Is she going be okay?"

"I'm afraid I can't tell you. At the moment, she's in intensive care."

She beat down her fear and swallowed past the knot in her throat. "I'm on my way. I'll be there as fast as I can." Sarah hung up the phone, her hands shaking so badly she could barely get the receiver back into its cradle.

She whispered a silent prayer. *Please, God, don't let her die. We only just found each other again.*

When she turned, Holly stood there, holding on to Jackson's hand.

"I could tell it was something bad, so I went to get help," Holly said.

Sarah glanced up at Jackson, saw that his jaw was hard, his face lined with worry. She swallowed, tried to pull herself together when what she wanted to do was walk into his arms and just let him hold her.

She fixed her attention on Holly. "Grandma's had a heart attack, honey. Mama has to go to the hospital to make sure she's all right."

Holly started crying. "I don't want her to die like Daddy did. Please, Mama, I don't want Gran to die."

Sarah lifted the little girl into her arms. "She isn't going to die. But she needs us right now. Can you be brave for her?"

Holly nodded, sniffed back tears.

Jackson's gaze locked with hers. "I'll drive you. I'll get my truck and be right back."

"You don't have to —" But he was already gone and she didn't think he would let her go without him even if she wanted to.

He had only been gone a moment when Livvy knocked on the door. "Your little one says you got a problem. Anything I can do to help?"

Sarah released a shaky breath. "My grandmother's had a heart attack. Jackson is driving us to the hospital over in Sheep River."

"If that's the case, you're liable to be there a while, all night maybe. Why don't you leave Holly with me?"

Sarah bit her lip. She hated the idea of her daughter sleeping in a corridor all night. She trusted Livvy. She remembered how good she had been to the kids who came into the ice-cream shop. The salt of the earth was Livvy.

"Are you sure?"

"Of course I'm sure. Don't be silly. There's a spare room off the kitchen. I stay there whenever it storms. I'll stay tonight and Holly can sleep in the other twin bed."

Relief swept through her, so strong it made her dizzy. She knelt in front of her daughter. "I want you to stay here with Livvy. Will you do that for me?"

"We'll bake some of those chocolate-chip cookies you like," Livvy promised. "What do you say?"

"What about Gran?"

"Gran's going to be all right," Sarah said,

praying it was true. The heart attack was all her fault. Her past had followed her, just as she had feared. If she caused her grandmother's death, she would never be able to live with herself.

She squeezed Holly's hand. "I'll call you as soon as I know for sure she's okay. Be a good girl and do what Livvy says."

"I could sure use the company," Livvy added. "You and me can worry together."

Sarah's heart squeezed. Somehow in returning to Wind Canyon, she had begun to make friends. She couldn't believe how good it felt.

Holly said nothing, just walked over and caught Livvy's thick-fingered hand.

"Thank you, Livvy," Sarah said. "You don't know how much I appreciate this."

"You just go on and take care of your family."

Sarah nodded, heard Jackson's big Ford pull up in front of the house.

"Holly's staying with Livvy," she told him as she walked to the truck.

Settling a hand at her waist, he walked her around and helped her climb into the passenger seat. In minutes they were rolling down the highway, headed back to Sheep River.

Neither of them talked until they passed

through Wind Canyon and started farther east along the road.

Jackson tossed her a glance. "We need to talk, Sarah."

At his tone of voice, anxiety trembled through her. She wasn't sure if she was more worried about her grandmother — or what Jackson had to tell her.

SIX

"It's a ways to Sheep River," Jackson said. "You're gonna sit there and worry until we get there. You might as well tell me what I need to know."

He could read the uncertainty in her face. Sarah sliced him a glance and nibbled her lip. "What exactly are you asking me?"

"You just got back from visiting her, right?"

"Yes."

"I want to know if what brought on your grandmother's heart attack has anything to do with what happened at the cottage?"

She kept her eyes straight ahead, staring at the yellow line in the middle of the darkened highway. "I went to see her today. After I left, two men broke into her house. They thought I had brought whatever it is they're looking for to my grandmother for safekeeping. She told them I hadn't brought anything, but they didn't believe her. They tore up her house, just the way they did the cottage."

Her lips trembled. "She tried to stop them. She has a heart condition. If something happens to her, it's my fault. Everything that's happened is my fault."

She started crying and pressed her fingers against her lips to hold back a sob. Jackson pulled the truck to the side of the road. Leaning over, he caught her face between his hands.

"This isn't your fault. You married some bastard who gave you nothing but trouble. That trouble followed you here. This is where it's going to end."

He let go of her and she straightened, seemed a little steadier. "Y-you know about Andrew?"

"Some of it." Jackson fought an urge to pull her into his arms, tell her everything would be okay. Instead, he put the pickup in gear and pulled back onto the road.

"When Kozak called," he continued, "I figured your past was somehow connected to the destruction in the cottage. My brother's in the security business. I called him, asked him to do some digging. He called me back this afternoon."

Sarah pulled a tissue out of her big leather purse and blew her nose. "How . . . how much did he tell you?"

"Enough to know that Andrew Hollister was a no-good SOB who treated you badly. I know he inherited a fortune from his father and spent it like there was no tomorrow — which for him, apparently, there wasn't."

"Then I guess . . . I guess you know he was murdered."

"Sounds to me like he got exactly what he deserved. Are you the one who found him?"

Sarah's hand went to her chest. He could tell she didn't want to remember.

She took a deep breath and slowly released it. "We . . . we were still living in the house on Sunset, but Andrew had put it up for sale. He'd bought a condo in Santa Monica and I had already moved in. I went back to the Sunset house to pick up some more of my things, but Andrew was there so I didn't stay long. After I left, I picked Holly up from her ballet class and drove on to the condo. The cleaning lady found him in the morning."

"You weren't worried when he didn't show up that night?"

"After the first few years we were married, Andrew rarely spent time at home. I didn't expect to see him that night."

"So the two of you were estranged?"

"If by *estranged* you mean we barely spoke to each other, had separate bedrooms and hadn't slept together in years — yes, we were estranged."

"Must have been a rough ten years."

Sarah gazed out the window as if she looked into the past. "He wasn't always that way. In the beginning, he treated me very well. He had a lot of money and he showered me with presents. He was handsome. To a twenty-two-year-old girl, he seemed like Prince Charming. I actually thought I was in love with him."

"Coming from a small town like Wind Canyon, I can understand how you might be impressed."

She sighed, raked a hand through her hair. "He started having money problems and as those problems grew, he turned violent. The slightest thing could set him off. I wanted to leave him but I was afraid. I'm only grateful he never hurt Holly. But I always worried that sooner or later he would."

Jackson made no reply. Every time he thought of what Sarah had suffered, he wanted to kill Andrew Hollister himself.

They finally reached the hospital, a three-story brick building big enough to service the rural community surrounding Sheep River. Jackson dropped Sarah off in front then drove into the lot to park the truck.

He found her outside the intensive care unit, talking to one of the doctors, a woman in her forties with salt-and-pepper hair.

"Do you think she's going to be okay, Dr. Ellis?" he heard Sarah ask.

"No heart attack is good, but we don't think she suffered any major damage. We'll be moving her into a private room in the morning."

Sarah's shoulders sagged in relief. "Thank God."

"You won't be able to see her tonight. Why don't you get some rest and come back in the morning?"

"I don't want to leave her."

Jackson introduced himself to Dr. Ellis. "I'll take care of Sarah," he added. "See she doesn't overdo. For now we'd like to stay."

"Suit yourself. I'll let you know if there's any change."

"Thank you, Dr. Ellis," Sarah said. The doctor walked away and Sarah looked up at Jackson. "You don't have to stay."

"Neither do you, but we will."

Her eyes misted, a soft clear blue, like the sky on a cloudless day. "Thank you." He felt sucker punched by the look in those eyes, the need and the trust. She was getting to him again.

Jackson told himself it would be different this time, but he was afraid it wouldn't.

Sarah called Holly at the ranch house and told her Gran was going to be all right. She urged Jackson to go home and said she would call him in the morning. Jackson solidly refused. He wasn't the kind of man to abandon a friend in her time of need.

Or at least that was the way he seemed.

But in the beginning, Andrew had seemed a different man than he actually was. Sarah wrapped her arms around herself against the chill in the empty corridor. Just the smells and the sounds dredged memories of her time in the emergency room, once with a broken arm, twice with broken ribs and lacerations, not to mention the concussion.

After a while, Andrew got better at hurting her without leaving traces. And over the years, she learned to stay out of the path of his anger.

It was his threats that kept her from leaving.

He had said he would kill her.

Sarah was certain he would.

She and Jackson sat in the hallway all night. In the morning, a tall blond nurse walked over to where they sat on a padded vinyl bench that didn't feel the least bit padded.

"We're moving Mrs. Thompson into a private room on the second floor. As soon as she's settled, you can go up and see her. Just don't stay too long."

"Thank you." Sarah waited with Jackson for another half hour before the nurse was ready for them to go upstairs.

"She's in Room 204. Like I said, don't stay long."

Sarah stretched to loosen her stiff, aching muscles. Sometime during the night, she had fallen asleep against Jackson's shoulder. She wondered if he'd gotten any sleep at all.

She flicked him a glance as they made their way along the second-floor corridor to her grandmother's room. His dark hair was mussed and a shadow of beard lined his jaw. He only looked more attractive.

"I'll wait for you out here," he said when they reached the room.

Sarah nodded. The door was open and Gran was awake when Sarah walked in. Her gray hair stood out all over her head and she looked tired, but some of the color had returned to her face. They talked for several minutes, Gran reassuring her, as the doctor had that morning, that she was going to be all right.

"I brought it on myself," the old woman said. "I knew those men were dangerous. I should have stayed out of their way, but they just made me so darned mad."

Under different conditions, Sarah might have smiled. "This wasn't your fault, Gran."

Watery blue eyes fixed on Sarah's face. "This has something to do with your husband, doesn't it?"

Gran had always been perceptive.

"I don't have a husband anymore, but yes, it has something to do with Andrew. Unfortunately, I don't know exactly what." Sarah squeezed her grandmother's hand. "Can you tell me what the men who broke in looked like?"

A sound of disgust came from Gran's throat. "One was skinny and blond. He had a tattoo on his hand that said Mother. The other was Mexican . . . what do they call it now . . . Hispanic?"

"That's right, Gran."

"He was short, lots of muscles, wearing one of those tight black T-shirts with a skull on the front. Neither one of them seemed to care —" she dragged in a shaky breath "— that I'd seen their faces."

"Probably because they don't have a record." Jackson walked up beside the bed

90

and Sarah introduced him as the friend who had brought her to the hospital. "They probably weren't concerned because they have no prints on file, no criminal record, that kind of thing."

"He brought you here?" The old woman's shrewd gaze surveyed the man at her bedside head to foot.

"Jackson owns the Raintree Ranch, Gran, where Holly and I are living."

She nodded with obvious approval. "A Western man. 'Bout time, girl."

Sarah flushed. She didn't dare look at Jackson. "Those men didn't find anything in your house. I don't think they'll bother you again. And while you're in here, I'm going to make sure your house is put back in order."

Gran patted her hand. "You're a good girl, Sarah. You didn't deserve a husband like that." The old woman's eyes began to droop and Sarah gently eased her hand away, letting her grandmother drift back to sleep.

She leaned over and kissed the old woman's forehead. "I'll be back tomorrow," she whispered and caught a last faint smile on her grandmother's wrinkled face.

Jackson walked her out into the hall. She shouldn't be thinking how sexy he looked in his low-slung jeans and scuffed boots, shouldn't be feeling this sweep of desire as he walked beside her — not with her grandmother lying in a hospital bed — but it was happening just the same.

How long had it been since a man had appealed to her the way this one did? In truth, not even Andrew in the days when she so foolishly thought she was in love with him.

"She sounded good," Sarah said, determined to distract herself. "I think she's going to be fine. I told her I'd come back tomorrow."

"So I guess that means we can go home."

She nodded. "I imagine we're both ready for a few hours in bed." Her cheeks flushed at her poor choice of words.

She flicked a glance at Jackson, hoping he hadn't noticed, and sucked in a breath at the flash of heat that burned in those dark brown eyes. For the first time she realized she wasn't the only one feeling the attraction.

After her nightmare marriage to Andrew, she wasn't ready for a serious relationship. She wasn't sure she ever would be. But she hadn't had sex in years. Maybe it was time she gave in to the growing need she felt for the man beside her.

His hand settled at her waist, guiding her

out of the hospital, and that slight touch made her stomach contract. She could only imagine what it would feel like to kiss him, touch him, have him touch her.

She was a grown woman. For the first time in years, she was free to live her life as she pleased. And it was becoming increasingly clear, it would please her a very great deal to make love with Jackson Raines.

Jackson cast a glance at Sarah, who rode in the passenger seat as they drove out of the hospital parking lot. "There's something I need to do before we go home."

"What's that?"

"Take a look at your grandmother's house. We need to see if there's something there that might give us a clue who's behind this."

"I know where the spare key is — if the door's even locked. Gran figured living in a place like Sheep River, she didn't have to worry about locking her doors."

"Used to be that way. Unfortunately, times have changed." As he drove toward the old woman's house at the edge of town, Jackson glanced over at Sarah. He tried to concentrate on his driving and not think of the desire he felt for her that was growing all out of proportion. During the night just listening to her breathing as she slept against his shoulder made him hard. Her soft breasts had nestled against his arm, and desire clawed into his belly. He'd been hard off and on all night.

Damn.

He couldn't remember when a woman had gotten to him the way Sarah Allen did.

He amended that. As his brother had reminded him, the same woman had tied him in knots through most of his senior year. Though she had never known how strongly he wanted her, she had never been far from his thoughts.

She wasn't now.

Christ.

Boxing had taught him self-control and he prided himself on being a master. Unfortunately, when Sarah was around, that control grew thin and strained. He flicked her another quick glance. He wanted to kiss her more than anything he could think of. He wanted to feel those soft breasts in his hands. He just flat out wanted her — to a degree that had rarely occurred in his orderly world.

Jackson didn't like it.

Not one damned bit.

They pulled up in front of Abigail Thompson's little wood-frame house and he turned off the engine. He rounded the truck and

94

helped Sarah down, tried to ignore the brush of fine strands of chestnut hair that floated across his cheek.

His groin throbbed. When he looked at her again, she hadn't moved, just stood there staring up at him as if she felt the heat pulsing between them. He couldn't stop himself. He bent his head and kissed her.

Soft, full lips. Cinnamon from the breakfast roll he'd bought her in the hospital cafeteria that morning. She softened against him and his body went achingly hard. He started to pull away, end the kiss while a thread of sanity remained, but her sweet mouth opened in invitation and his tongue slid inside.

His arm went around her waist and he hauled her flush against him, deepened the kiss, lost himself in the taste of her, the feel of her slender body pressed the length of his. Her breasts were even fuller than he had imagined, softer, the tips like firm little berries. It was all he could do not to rip open her blouse and fill his palms, to bend his head and taste them.

It took a moment before he realized she was pressing her hands against his chest, trying to break free of his hold.

Instantly, he let her go.

"God, Sarah, I'm sorry. I didn't mean for

that to happen. I can't believe it did." He ran a hand along his jaw, felt the roughness of his morning beard. "I know the kind of man you were married to, the things he did to you. I didn't mean to scare you. I don't exactly know what happened."

The tension left her shoulders and a faint smile rose on her lips. "You're a man. I've learned to distrust them. You scared me a little, but I think I mostly scared myself." She reached up and lightly touched the roughness along his jaw. "It's been a long time, Jackson."

His erection pulsed. He ached to kiss her again. Instead he stayed where he was. "You don't have to be afraid of me, Sarah. Not ever."

She studied him a moment, then turned away and started for the house. Jackson followed, not the least bit happy with his loss of control.

And aching for it to happen again.

The front door was locked when they got there, a small piece of yellow crime scene tape still attached to the porch. The tape was mostly gone now, but the sheriff had obviously been there. When Jackson got back to the ranch, he would call Ben Weber, tell him about the second break-in. Maybe the two law officers could piece something together.

They went into the house, saw that it looked pretty much the same as the cottage, the sofa cushions torn open, the chair upended, the lace curtains pulled down.

Sarah went over and examined them. "The curtains aren't torn. If I had a ladder, I could put them back up."

Jackson walked over, reached up and did it for her.

She gave him one of those soft smiles that turned him upside down. "Thank you."

The kitchen drawers had been pulled out, the contents strewn on the kitchen floor. Sarah bent and picked up the silverware, put it in the sink, and Jackson helped her. They worked for a while, Jackson searching while he helped Sarah straighten. As he walked out on the back porch, something dark and shiny caught his eye near the base of a flowerpot, the object partly covered by the blooms of a pink petunia. He picked up an empty matchbook, examined it in his palm.

"Look at this." He showed the blue-and-gold matchbook to Sarah. "It came from a place called The Blue Parrot." He turned it over, read the address. "It's in California, on Ventura Boulevard in Studio City. Ever heard of it?"

"No, but Marty Kozak is a smoker. Unfortunately he doesn't fit Gran's description of either of the men who were here."

"Maybe he hired them." He stuffed the matchbook into his pocket and finished inspecting the house, which wasn't torn up quite as badly as the cottage.

"I'm coming back to visit Gran tomorrow. I'll buy some throw covers for the sofa and chair. I don't think she'll mind. In fact, she'll probably be happy for the change. She's always been kind of adventurous."

"I'd be happy to buy —"

"This isn't your problem, Jackson. It's mine. It isn't your responsibility to replace Gran's furniture, and I can't afford to do it myself right now. But I'm pretty good with decorating. And the men didn't do that much damage. As I said, Gran will probably like the change."

He nodded. He was beginning to think he'd been wrong about Sarah. Or maybe she had just learned that money wasn't everything. Sometimes the price you paid for having it was just too high. It occurred to him that he could like this Sarah Allen.

And as he thought of the men who had put an old lady in the hospital, he was even more worried about her.

SEVEN

Sarah drove to Sheep River for the next two days to visit her grandmother in the hospital and put the little wood-frame house back in order. She took Gran home the morning of the third day and smiled at the surprised, pleased expression she received for the work she had done.

"Looks real nice, honey," Gran said, assessing the dark blue flowered throws over the sofa and chair, the light and dark blue accent pillows. "Place has been needin' some sprucing up. I guess there's always something good comes from everything."

Sarah wasn't convinced about that, but she didn't say so. "Are you sure you'll be all right?"

"Dr. Ellis says I'm good as new. I've got a couple of check-ups along the way, but Doc says, long as I take it easy, I'll be fine."

Sarah hated to leave her there alone, but as Gran reminded her, she had been living by herself for the past twenty-five years. And the men had already been there, searched and found nothing.

Satisfied Gran would be all right, Sarah returned to the office to finish the articles she was writing about the Memorial Day celebration coming up the end of the week.

Using memories from her childhood in the first article, combined with old photos from the 1980s she found in the newspaper's archives, she hammered out a piece she felt pleased with. She printed the pages at the end of her shift and set them aside, and headed for her pickup, parked in the lot down the street.

She had just reached the corner when a man stepped up beside her, tall, mid-forties, with a long, pointed nose and very smooth dark skin. He was wearing an expensive dark brown sport coat and tan slacks and looked as out of place in Wind Canyon as he actually was.

She stiffened as she felt hard steel shoved into her ribs. "Keep walking," he said. "Make a sound and I won't hesitate to pull the trigger."

Her pulse kicked into high gear. The man looked foreign but his accent was purely American. She had no idea who he was, but she knew he must be somehow connected to Andrew. She had known Andrew's business dealings bordered on illegal, but she hadn't believed they would haunt her from the grave.

He urged her around the corner, into the parking lot. "What . . . what do you want?"

"I want the disk your husband kept — the one he was using to blackmail his customers."

"Andrew was . . . blackmailing people?"

He prodded her with the gun. "I want the disk. I think you know where it is."

"I — I don't know anything. Do you work for Martin Kozak?"

He frowned, ignored the question. "Just tell me where to find the disk and you'll never see me again." She gasped as he shoved her hard against the rough brick wall.

"If . . . if I had it, I'd give it to you." She dragged in a shaky breath. "Andrew never trusted me with anything. He certainly didn't give me any blackmail list."

His hard look sharpened. "Then how did you know it was a list?" he said smugly, not really expecting an answer.

Sarah wet her lips, tried to push him away, but his body was as hard as the wall behind her and the forearm he pressed beneath her chin felt like an iron bar.

"I want that disk. If you don't have it, you'd better figure out where it is." He shoved her again, slamming her head against the wall.

For years she had let Andrew bully her, let him hurt her. "Get off me!" She shoved the man with all her strength but he moved barely an inch.

A slow smile curved his narrow lips. "I'll be back. You say anything to the cops, you won't like what happens when I get here."

Turning away, he started walking and Sarah sagged against the wall. At least she'd fought back. She remembered the day she had been watching TV when an item came on about an online battered women's group. There were other women just like her, she had discovered, and the chat room they shared became her refuge.

And her strength.

She bit back a sob. She had no idea where Andrew might have kept a disk that apparently held information he used for blackmail, but she knew she had to find it.

The man had threatened her. He hadn't mentioned Holly, but there was no doubt Sarah wasn't the only one in danger.

She pushed away from the bricks and moved on shaking legs toward the pickup. From the corner of her eye, she spotted

Jackson striding across the parking lot in her direction. Without thinking, she turned and ran toward him. When he saw her face, he hauled her straight into his arms.

"You're shaking all over. For God's sake, what's happened?"

Sarah clung to him. For a moment, she couldn't speak.

"Take your time," he said. "I've got you. I won't let anyone hurt you."

She lifted her head from his shoulder, saw by the hard set of his jaw he meant every word. "A man came . . ." She swallowed. "He . . . he had a gun. He said he wanted the disk Andrew was using to blackmail his customers."

"Blackmail? That's what he said?"

"Yes."

"Was he one of the men your grandmother described?"

She shook her head. "He seemed more . . . sophisticated than the men who ransacked Gran's house." She glanced around the parking lot, but saw no sign of him. "I've got to find that disk, Jackson." She felt the sting of tears and blinked to keep from crying. "Somehow, I've got to find it."

Keeping an arm around her, he started walking her back toward her truck. "We'll talk to the sheriff, tell him what's going on, see what he can do."

She jolted to a halt in the middle of the parking lot. "No sheriff — not unless we absolutely have to. These men . . . Jackson, they're dangerous. And if they were associated with Andrew, they're powerful. I'm afraid of what they might do."

Jackson made no reply, but a muscle flexed along his jaw.

"Can you drive?" he asked when they reached her blue truck.

She nodded. "I'm just a little shaken. I'll be fine."

"We'll pick up Holly then I'll follow you back to the house."

She opened the door of the pickup. "What were you doing in town?"

"I had some grocery shopping to do. You usually finish around three. I thought I'd buy you a cup of coffee or a soda or something." His gaze shifted toward the brick building where the man had dragged her. "Too bad I didn't get here a little sooner."

Her stomach churned. If Jackson had tried to rescue her, the man might have shot him. A sweep of nausea rolled through her. She didn't want him getting hurt because of her.

What on earth was she going to do?

Sarah pretended everything was normal.

She picked up Holly at the day-care center, then turned onto the highway leading back to the ranch. Jackson followed to make sure she got there safely.

"Everyone is going to the parade tomorrow," Holly said as they rolled toward home. For the past fifteen minutes, she had been chattering away, mostly about the upcoming weekend. "Allie says her brother's going to be on the Boy Scout float. She says her dad's going to take her while her mom helps with the picnic."

Holly prattled on, excited at the prospect of the big celebration. The thought of going made Sarah sick to her stomach.

What if the dark-skinned man were there? What if he threatened Holly?

"Mama, what time does the parade start?" Holly shifted in her seat. "Mama, did you hear me?"

Sarah forced herself to smile. "I'm sorry, honey, what did you say?"

"I asked what time does the parade start?"

She had to think. It seemed impossible to concentrate. "It starts at eleven."

"Is Jackson going with us?"

Jackson. Just the sound of his name sent her pulse up a notch. "I don't know." But secretly she hoped he would. She didn't think the man would bother her if Jackson were with them.

She pulled up in front of the cottage and as soon as she turned off the engine, Holly unfastened her seat belt and jumped down from the truck.

She ran straight back to the big Ford pickup pulling up behind them. "Jackson!" It seemed her daughter and her landlord were now on a first-name basis, as Holly also was with Livvy. "Are you going with us tomorrow?"

"Tomorrow?" Bending down, he scooped her up in his arms and settled her against his shoulder. "What's going on tomorrow?"

Watching them, Sarah felt a pang in her chest. Andrew had adored Holly, but he rarely had time for her. Jackson was just the opposite. No matter how busy he was, he always made time for Holly, or Jimmy's boys, Gibby and Sam.

"Tomorrow's the parade, silly. Everyone's going to be there — Mama said so."

He set Holly back on her feet, cocked an eyebrow at Sarah.

"I'm covering the celebration for the paper," she explained. "I have to go."

He looked more resigned than excited. "Looks like we're going then," he said to Holly.

"Yippee!" She jumped up and down, her

ponytail bobbing. Jackson looked over at Sarah and smiled. He had the nicest smile, the straightest, whitest teeth. She tried not to think of the searing kiss they'd shared, but the image was crystal clear, and soft heat curled in her stomach.

She clamped down on the dangerous memory. "You don't mind going with us?"

"You think I'd let you go alone?"

She didn't answer but relief trickled through her. Though deep down, she had known he would insist on coming along.

"Why don't I see if Jimmy and the boys want to come with us? We'll go to the picnic, too, make a day of it."

Sarah smiled and nodded, figuring he probably wanted Jimmy there in case there was trouble. The first time she'd met Jackson's big brawny foreman, Sarah had sensed the bond between the two men.

From the corner of her eye, she caught a flash of color and turned to see Olivia bustling up to them in a pale pink sweater and jeans.

Livvy set her hands on her plump hips. "I heard what you said. Tomorrow's the big celebration. Everyone in town will be there and don't think for a minute you're leaving me home." She grinned. "I'll make us all some nice fried chicken and potato salad.

We'll have a real old-fashioned family outing."

Something sqeezed in Sarah's chest. If it weren't for the trouble that had followed her to Wind Canyon, she would be delighted at the prospect of a family outing — even if the family wasn't truly her own.

If it weren't for the trouble that had followed her . . .

Sarah's stomach churned.

Jackson left Sarah and Holly and headed for the house. Before he reached the back door he spotted his top hand, Wheeler Dillon, hurrying toward him.

Blond and gangly, Wheel was a cowboy in the truest sense of the word, a man who, at forty, had the suntanned, weathered features that came from spending most of his life out of doors.

"What's up, Wheel?"

"It's those damned loggers, Jackson. They had an accident up there along that new area they started working. Log pile broke loose, knocked down a big section of fence. The crew boss called, said some of our cattle got loose and were wandering around their equipment. I was just heading out with Shorty and Mac to round them up and move them down with the rest of the herd

108

in Pine Meadow."

"Where's Jimmy?"

"He's out on the south range. Ought to be back any minute."

He spotted Jimmy's pickup just then, pulling up in front of the barn. Jimmy jumped down from the driver's seat and started walking toward them.

"What's going on?" he asked, and Wheel filled him in. "I'll go with you," Jimmy said.

"We can go up together," Jackson told him. "I've got a couple of phone calls I need to make, then we'll take the ATVs and ride on up. I want to take a look, see for myself what's going on up there."

Jimmy nodded, his long black ponytail blowing in the wind. "Sounds good."

Wheel took off with the men, a trailer and three horses, and Jackson went into the house to use the phone. If they were going to find that disk, they would have to go to L.A. He picked up the receiver to make arrangements with Mountain Air for a trip to California.

As soon as his calls were finished, he and Jimmy headed out on the four-wheelers, taking the road to the top of the mountain to assess the damage that had been done.

"They'll have to pay for that fence," Jimmy said as they pulled the four-wheelers to a stop in a spot that overlooked the upper pasture.

Jackson grunted. "You can be sure I'll send them a bill — but I won't hold my breath waiting for the check."

Bannock Logging was notorious for the destruction it caused. It was the kind of company that took its profits, then filed bankruptcy to avoid any claims for financial restitution or having to replant any trees.

Jackson figured the two brothers who owned the company were just the sort Andrew Hollister would have had dealings with, the sort he had been trying to blackmail. No wonder the guy had been murdered.

Wheel sauntered up beside them. "We'll need more fence line and posts than I thought."

"You and the boys get started with what you've got. Jimmy and I will go back down and get the rest of what you need."

"You got it, boss."

"The bastards," Jimmy muttered, surveying the ugly sea of stumps that dotted what had once been dense, old-growth forest.

They called it fire protection.

Well, they were right about that. You didn't have to worry about a forest fire if you cut down all the trees.

Jackson and Jimmy drove the dirt road back down the mountain, loaded a flatbed trailer with posts and barbless wire fence line. As they worked next to the barn, Jackson explained to Jimmy what was going on with Sarah, about her murdered late husband, and the danger she and her daughter might be facing.

"We're going to have to go to L.A., try to figure out what the hell is going on."

"If you have to go — then go. Things are pretty well under control around here, and Livvy and I can look after Holly. You just take care of Sarah."

Jackson clapped Jimmy on the back. "Thanks, Jim."

"Just call if you need anything."

"I will." But there was only one thing Jackson needed. His gaze strayed to the cottage and the dark-haired woman he could see through the living-room window.

Heat pooled low in Jackson's groin. Softly, he cursed.

EIGHT

The parade was flashy, with lots of red, white and blue. The Cougars high school marching band in their red-and-gold uniforms played rousing John Philip Sousa tunes. There were a string of floats: Chamber of Commerce; the district recreation baseball team, the Wolverines; a war veterans VFW float sponsored by Fred Wilkins at the mercantile.

"There's Allie's brother, Rex!" Holly waved at the group of boys atop the Boy Scout float, jumping up and down as if she knew the boy, though she had never met him. Next came the sheriff's posse, riding palomino horses wearing silver-mounted saddles. Clowns on bicycles tossed out candy near the end.

Sarah scribbled notes. She had thought about bringing her small portable tape recorder, but it was noisy along the parade route and a regular old notepad worked just as well. Unfortunately it reminded her of the notes Andrew must have kept to black-mail the people with whom he did business.

She wondered what they had done that Andrew could hold over them, knew it must be illegal if someone wanted the informa-tion back so badly.

She had to find that disk.

Sarah closed her notepad and sighed. The last thing she wanted to do was go back to L.A. Too many bad memories, too much fear. Still, she needed to talk to Stan Green-berg, Andrew's attorney. Maybe he could tell her where to look for the disk.

Then again, Andrew had died owing Stan money. There wasn't enough in the estate to pay him for all the hours he had billed. She wasn't sure how much help he would be willing to provide. Or if he knew anything at all about the blackmail list.

Or if he did, if he would admit it.

She tried to think what else she might do. The house on Sunset had finally sold — way below market value because of the death that had occurred there. The escrow had closed and what was left of the furniture that hadn't been sold had been moved into storage. Eventually that would go, too — more money into the probate coffers to pay the attorneys and a little more of Andrew's staggering debts.

The Santa Monica condo was up for sale but hadn't sold yet. She wondered if the apartment had suffered the same fate as the cottage and thought that it must have been the first place the men had searched.

It just indicated how bad the market was that the Realtor hadn't shown the place, discovered the vandalism and called her with the news.

"Look, Mommy, a fire engine!" It followed the last float, signaling the end of the parade.

"We'll drive over to the park," Jackson said, "and find a nice place to eat that chicken Livvy fried." He made another sweeping glance of the area. She noticed he had been doing that ever since they arrived in town.

"Let's head back to the cars," Jimmy said. "You boys look out for Holly."

Rags yapped and danced on the end of the leash Holly held. Sam and Gibby's little dog, Feather, one of two they owned, was also there for the festivities.

All kinds of activities were scheduled at Wind Canyon Park: a pie-eating contest, a three-legged sack race, a kayak race in the small lake in the middle of the park. The Memorial Day weekend weather was perfect

— crisp, clear and sunny — just a few puffy clouds floating across the sky.

Still, Sarah was nervous. She hadn't seen any sign of the man who had accosted her, but there were a lot of people milling about. She told herself to relax, that she was with Jackson and Jimmy. She was safe and she should enjoy herself.

They were busily climbing into the pickups when she heard someone calling her name.

"Sarah? Sarah Allen, is that you?"

Turning, she spotted a freckle-faced redhead with a big wide grin. Sarah let out a shout of excitement. "Nancy! Nan Marcus! I can't believe it's really you!"

The two women hugged. "It's Nan Hargrove now," said her old friend. "You look fantastic!"

"So do you!" Nan was a few pounds heavier, but still curvy in all the right places.

"Actually, I'm divorced," Nan said, casting a sideways glance at Jimmy.

Sarah took the hint. "Do you know everyone? You probably know Livvy. This is Jackson Raines and his foreman, Jimmy Threebears. These are Jimmy's sons, Gibby and Sam."

"I know Livvy and Jackson. I've seen the boys and Jimmy around but we've never actually met."

"Nice to meet you," Jimmy said, and there was a tightness in his features Sarah didn't understand.

She smiled at Nan. "And this is my daughter, Holly."

Nan lowered herself to the little girl's level. "It's very nice to meet you, Holly. You're just as pretty as your mother."

Holly grinned. "Thank you."

Nan returned her attention to Sarah. "I never had any kids. I wanted them but Ron said we should wait, and then things . . . well, things just didn't work out."

"I'm sorry, Nan."

She shrugged. "It's all right. We never were very well suited. I just felt like it was time to get married and so I did. Not a good idea."

"Are you here by yourself?"

"I'm here with my mother. She's waiting for me in the car."

Sarah glanced at Jackson, caught his faint nod. "Why don't the two of you join us for lunch? Livvy made fried chicken and she always makes more than enough."

"I'm afraid my mother gets tired pretty easily. I was about to drive her home."

"Then come back and join us. Please, Nan. I'd love a chance to catch up. It's been so long and it's so good to see you."

Nan's gaze strayed to Jimmy then back. "All right. I won't be long."

"We'll watch for you."

For the next few hours, Sarah was actually able to think of something besides the problems she was facing. Nan joined them and they ate fried chicken, potato salad and peach cobbler on a picnic table covered by a white cotton cloth in the shade of an old sycamore tree.

She and Nan shared old memories of their youth and lots of laughter. It was heaven.

Until a big-bosomed woman with long blond hair and even longer legs in tight jeans walked up to the table.

"Hi, y'all." She flashed a smile that was clearly meant for Jackson.

"Hi, Maddie," he replied and there was something in the look that passed between them that told Sarah he knew the woman well — very well. He introduced Maddie Gallagher to Sarah.

"It's nice to meet you," Sarah said.

"Same here."

Nan knew Maddie through her ex-husband's restaurant, The Cedar Inn, where Maddie worked as a part-time waitress.

"I guess you been busy," the woman said to Jackson, glancing from him to Sarah as if she were sizing up her competition.

"A little."

"Give me a call sometime. I'll fix you supper — just like I used to."

"I'll do that," Jackson said, but he didn't seem enthused.

As the woman walked away, Sarah couldn't help wondering if Jackson would make the call. It was clear Maddie Gallagher could give a man what he needed.

Sarah felt a stirring inside her, a combination of jealousy and heat as the thought occurred that if Jackson needed a woman, why not her?

The afternoon passed and all too soon it was time to head home. Sarah's nervousness returned as Jackson took her hand and led her away from the group.

"I wish I didn't have to bring this up, but we can't put it off much longer. Whoever these guys are, they aren't going to give up — not as long as they think you've got whatever it is they want . . . or know where to find it."

"I know." She looked up into that ruggedly handsome face, felt the same hot stirring she had felt before. She forced herself to concentrate. "I've got to go back to L.A. Since I don't have the disk, it must be there."

"We need to know who these people are. If we can't find the disk, we're going to have to deal with them some other way."

A chill slipped through her even though she stood in the sun. "Marty owns Kozak Construction," she said. "It's a pretty big company. He rented heavy equipment from one of Andrew's companies. Maybe he was using the stuff for something illegal."

"If so, we need to know what it was."

She nodded. "I'll talk to Andrew's attorney, see what I can get him to tell me."

Jackson dug the blue-and-gold matchbook out of his pocket. Sarah had forgotten all about it.

"This might be a lead. The Blue Parrot. We'll need to find out."

She plucked the matchbook out of his hand. "I'll make a point to go there, see what I —"

"*We,* Sarah. You're not going to L.A. alone — I'm going with you."

"But —"

"There's no point in arguing."

"But —"

He cocked a dark eyebrow and she closed her mouth a second time.

"Livvy can take care of Holly while we're away. Monday's a holiday. Can you be ready to leave first thing Tuesday morning?"

"I — I guess so."

He smiled. "Too bad my brother, Gabe, isn't up here. He flies a big twin Aerostar. But he's living in Texas these days. Be kind of out of the way for him."

She remembered Gabriel Raines, who had been a year ahead of her in high school. Like Jackson, Gabe had been a bad boy, always in trouble. When Jackson had begun to change, so had his two younger brothers. He had that kind of influence on people. From what she could tell, he still did.

"I've already called Mountain Air. Their planes are comfortable and well maintained. I use them whenever I have to fly."

"I can't afford —"

"I can."

Sarah glanced away. It was funny. Jackson was the sort of man who took charge, took care of things. At first she'd believed Andrew was that way. But Andrew mostly took care of himself, and he got what he wanted by force, not the lift of an eyebrow.

She shouldn't have liked being looked after. She should have craved the independence Andrew had stolen from her. But Jackson didn't make her feel cheated. He just did what he thought a man ought to do.

Sarah almost smiled.

Then she thought of the trip to L.A., of what they might find, of the demons she would have to confront, and any thought of smiling slipped away.

NINE

They flew out at eight-thirty Tuesday morning in a twin-engine Cessna Jackson had chartered a number of times before. He hated the crowds and the security hassles at the airports and he could afford to fly private.

After a four-hour flight, plus a refueling stop, they arrived at the Santa Monica Airport, their destination, and a smaller, easier place to land than LAX. They grabbed their bags and made their way over to retrieve the rental car Jackson had reserved.

As Sarah watched him wheeling his carry-on bag across the asphalt, she found herself smiling. He looked almost as good in tan slacks and a short-sleeved shirt as he did in faded jeans and boots. He loaded their luggage into the trunk of a snappy red, four-door Infiniti and they climbed into the plush interior. Jackson checked the map he had printed off the internet and pulled the car out onto the road.

"Where are we going?" Sarah asked.

"I think we should check into the hotel first, get settled and get our bearings, then we can head out again."

She was only a little surprised when he drove the rental car up in front of Loews Santa Monica Beach, an expensive hotel that fronted the ocean.

"Can't beat Expedia," he said as he pushed through the doors leading into an impressive lobby lined with potted palms. "Living so far out of town, the internet is invaluable for travel."

Sarah had been to the hotel bar for drinks with Andrew and his friends. She caught hold of Jackson's arm, felt his very solid bicep harden at her touch, forced herself to ignore the little flutter in her stomach.

"Are you sure, Jackson? This place is expensive."

He smiled. "You know how much a gallon of gas costs in L.A.?"

"Depending on the economy, as much as four dollars."

"Until a couple of years ago, I owned a pile of oil stocks. They made me more money than I can spend. If my conscience hadn't started nagging me, I'd still own them. As it is, I'm now investing in Green."

"Green?"

"You know, wind machines and solar products developed to benefit the environment. So far, my stocks are doing great. I'm not Bill Gates, but I'm more than comfortable. I can do pretty much what I want."

He had reserved a two-bedroom suite with ocean views, a lovely room, she saw as they walked in. The bedroom doors were open. The minute he noticed the king-size bed, his gaze turned dark and smoky.

"Take your pick," he said, his eyes never leaving her face.

Sarah swallowed. She wanted to tell him that whatever room he chose was the one she wanted to sleep in. That she wanted him to make love to her and this was the perfect place.

She didn't. Just turned and walked into the nearest bedroom, leaving him the one with the ocean view. She picked up the phone and dialed the ranch house, spent a few minutes talking to Holly, telling her they had made it safely to L.A.

"Me and Livvy baked a cake, Mama. We're gonna invite Sam and Gibby and their dad over for supper."

"That sounds great, honey. I'm glad you're having fun."

"Sam says if it's okay with you, he could teach me to ride Midnight. She's a pony, Mom, and she's just my size. Can I?"

Uncertainty rolled through her. Sarah glanced over at Jackson, who had just walked into the doorway. "There's a pony named Midnight. Do you think it's safe for Holly —"

"Midnight's twenty years old. Both Jimmy's boys learned to ride on her. Holly couldn't be safer."

Sarah turned back to the phone. "You can ride her — as long as Livvy or Sam's dad is out there with you."

"Yippee!" The sound of clanging pots and pans came over the line. "I gotta go, Mom. Livvy's taking the cake out of the oven."

"Have a good time, sweetheart." The line went dead and Sarah hung up the phone, wishing she were there instead of in L.A.

"Everything okay?"

"Everything's fine. She's having a great time. I don't think she's missing me — especially not when she's got a pony to ride."

He chuckled. "She's living on a ranch. She needs to learn to ride."

"I suppose. I just . . . I worry about her."

"That's what mothers are supposed to do. Don't worry, she'll be fine." His expression changed and so did the subject. "Do you still have a key to your condo?"

She nodded. "I meant to leave it there when I left that last day, but I was so anxious to get on the road I forgot."

"We'll go there first."

"All right. I'd like to call Gran before we go, make sure she's doing okay."

Gran was fine. She told Sarah to enjoy the trip with her handsome cowboy.

"We're just friends," Sarah tried to convince her, but Gran just chuckled into the phone.

The rental car still sat in front of the hotel. Jackson waited until Sarah got in, closed her door, then went around to the driver's side and slid behind the wheel.

It didn't take long to reach the impressive Whispering Sands condominium development where Sarah had been living before her move to Wyoming. They parked in guest parking, then Sarah used her key to the private elevator, which they took to the seventh floor.

She steeled herself, expecting the worst, and handed Jackson the key to the door. When the door swung open, she saw that the apartment had been trashed as she had feared.

"Look familiar?" Jackson asked.

"Unfortunately, yes."

"I was pretty sure they'd hit here first."

"So was I." She surveyed the overturned cream-colored sofa and chairs in the living room, the cushions sliced open and the stuffing torn out. They had done a thorough job, she saw, even pulling up the carpet in the bottom of the closets. Still, the impact wasn't nearly as painful as it had been in the little cottage she thought of as home.

"When we get back to Wyoming, I'll call the real estate office," she said. "Tell them what's happened. They'll need to get the place cleaned up."

"You'd better call the police."

She stiffened, turned away from surveying the wreckage to face him. "I'm not calling the police, Jackson. I had more than my share of dealings with them after Andrew died. If I call, it'll start all over. I can't go through that again."

He said nothing for several long moments, just stood there studying her face. "All right, we'll play it your way. For now."

She knew he was worried about the danger she might be facing. But there was a danger in all of this that Jackson didn't understand. She turned away from him, walked into the master bedroom, surveyed the destruction in there.

Jackson walked up beside her. "Looks like they did a pretty thorough job."

"Very thorough."

"Any place they might have missed?"

"That's what I was trying to figure out." She gazed past the cream-colored bedspread to the black lacquer nightstands and matching armoire. The furniture had been thoroughly searched, the drawers and doors left standing open.

"There was a safe at the back of the closet," she said, heading in that direction, "but once my clothes were gone, it would be easy to spot." She walked inside, saw the door to the safe standing open.

"From the looks of things," Jackson said, "Andrew didn't leave the disk in the condo or your friends would have found it and they wouldn't be bothering you."

"As I said, Andrew didn't spend much time here."

"Where *did* he spend his time?"

She glanced away, barely able to look at him. "He traveled a lot. He spent a lot of time in Vegas. And then there was his mistress."

One of his dark eyebrows went up. "Sounds like Andrew was a very busy man."

"Thank God for that."

"Do you know her name?"

It was embarrassing to have a husband who openly flaunted his women, even if their marriage had been over for years. "The latest one you mean? I heard him call her Mitzy. I don't know her last name or where she lives. I didn't really care."

"We need to talk to her, Sarah. Maybe she has the disk — or at least some kind of information about it."

"If she had the disk and they threatened her, she probably would have given it to them." Sarah looked up at him, read the tension in his face, ignored the pity. "We need to talk to Stanley Greenberg. Stan was Andrew's attorney — his right-hand man. He would know where to find Mitzy."

Ditzy — Sarah had secretly called her. Though she had never seen the woman, she could describe her: perfect body, perfect face, pea-size brain. That was the kind of female Andrew always chose.

Too bad he'd made an exception in Sarah's case.

Too bad she hadn't figured it out before she'd married him.

"Let's go," Jackson said, catching her hand and pulling her out of the bedroom toward the front door. "Like I said, if the disk was here, they would have found it."

They left the apartment and Sarah gave

Jackson directions to Stan Greenberg's office in Santa Monica. They drove into the underground parking lot, then took the elevator up to Stan's office.

Recognizing the attractive older woman seated behind the reception desk, Sarah summoned a smile. "Hello, Rosemary. Is Stan in? I need to talk to him."

The woman wheeled back her chair and stood up, smoothed the skirt of her apricot linen suit. "Mrs. Hollister — I thought you'd moved out of town."

"I have. I'm just here a few days on business. As I said, I need to speak to Stan." She continued to smile. "It shouldn't take very long."

"I'll see if he's in." Which meant, *I'll see if he'll talk to you.*

They waited only a moment before Rosemary returned. "He says you can go right in."

"Thank you."

Jackson followed her into Stan's office, elegantly decorated in dark wood and forest green.

"Sarah!" Stan rose and rounded his desk to greet her, kissing her on each cheek in the Hollywood style that always seemed so phony. "It's good to see you, Sarah." He was a balding man in his forties with the hint of a paunch beginning to show above the waistline of his navy-blue suit pants.

"You, too, Stan."

He turned a smile on Jackson, extended his hand. "I'm Stan Greenberg."

"Jackson Raines." The men completed the handshake.

"So how can I help you two?"

"A couple of things, Stan." Sarah went on to explain about the men who had pursued her to Wyoming, about the book or disk or whatever it was that they wanted.

"Andrew was blackmailing someone, Stan. We think it was Martin Kozak. Do you know anything about that?"

"Of course not. You know I would never do anything illegal."

Sarah refrained from rolling her eyes. "I'll need a copy of the probate documents. I need to find out what was going on."

"Are you sure you should be involving yourself in this, Sarah?"

"Involving myself is the last thing I want. I don't have any other choice."

"I see."

"I need a copy of the probate, Stan."

"That shouldn't be a problem. I'll ask Rosemary to mail you one. Just give her your address before you leave."

"I'll just wait here while she gets it."

It was clear he wasn't pleased. Still, he leaned over and pressed the intercom button, instructed Rosemary to get the information Sarah had requested. Though she had signed a lengthy prenuptial agreement before she and Andrew were married, giving him sole rights to the companies he owned, she was his widow and a party to the probate proceedings.

She just hoped the information would help.

"The copies will be ready for you when you leave," Stan said.

"Thank you."

He walked behind his desk, sat down and opened the file in front of him.

"There's just one more thing," Sarah said.

He looked up. "Which is . . . ?"

"I need to talk to Mitzy. Maybe she knows something that will help us."

His face colored slightly. "I didn't realize you knew."

"I've known for years, Stan. Before Mitzy, it was Gloria, and let's not forget Susie. The list goes on and on."

Stan flipped open the card file sitting on top of his desk and dug out the information. "Her name is Mitzy Bender. Unfortunately, she left town just after you did. I tried to call and check on her — as Andrew would have wanted — but I never reached her. She seems to have disappeared completely."

"I think I know why," Jackson said softly.

"Are you sure there's nothing you can tell us that might help us find the disk?"

Stan shook his head. "I wish I could. If anyone comes to me asking questions, I'll tell them you have no idea where to find whatever it is they're looking for."

"Thanks, Stan."

They left his private office. Sarah collected the probate paperwork from Rosemary and they carried it down to the garage. Sitting in the front seat of the Infiniti, she began to skim the documents, paying particular attention to the page listing the companies requesting payment of debt from the estate.

"God, there are dozens," she said, a sick feeling in her stomach.

Jackson leaned over to examine the list. "Looks like your late husband owed money to half the people in California."

"And most of the people in Nevada — though his gambling debts don't appear on the list."

She turned to the page showing his current assets. "Andrew's been selling off his father's businesses for years. Here's a list of the businesses he still owned when he died.

Doesn't look like there's that many left."

"Read off the names, tell me what you know about each one."

"Not much, I'm afraid. Andrew wasn't very forthcoming when it came to his business dealings." But she looked down and began to read. "Blacktop Tires. That's a chain of retail tire stores located throughout the West."

"I've seen them."

"Speedway Manufacturing — a small company that makes specialty racing tires. It's kind of an offshoot of Blacktop."

"What else?"

"Axis Mining. As I recall, they closed down operations a couple of years ago. Andrew used to own a company that made ore crushing machines, but he sold that sometime back." She looked at another name on the list. "Hollister Equipment is a company that leases heavy machinery for big construction projects. I'm pretty sure that was Andrew's connection to Kozak. Kozak Construction builds roads, mostly. I'm not sure what else."

"That it?"

"There's one more listed — Southgate Demolition. They tear down buildings. That's all I know."

"It's a start."

"I guess. But what exactly are we looking for?"

"I'm not sure. If Kozak was doing something illegal, we need to figure out what it was."

"So how do we do that?"

He shook his head. "I wish my brother was back in the country. He's got lots of friends in low places, people who can dig up dirt when no one else can."

"When will he be home?"

"Not soon enough. We'll have to do the best we can while we're here."

"There's something that's been bothering me," she said. "I've been thinking about the man who accosted me in the parking lot . . . I'm not convinced he works for Kozak."

"Why is that?"

"I don't know exactly . . . just a couple of things he said."

"If he isn't Kozak's man, there may be more than one company Andrew was blackmailing."

"That's what I'm afraid of." Sarah sighed and leaned back in the deep red leather seat as Jackson stuck the key in the ignition.

"It's late and both of us are tired," he said. "We'll get something to eat, get a good night's sleep, and start again in the morning."

Sarah glanced over at Jackson. His gaze locked with hers and her heartbeat quickened. It wasn't food he wanted, those hot brown eyes said. And it wasn't sleep.

As the engine roared to life, Sarah ignored the flood of heat that roared into her bloodstream.

TEN

They decided on room service. As much as Jackson liked the idea of taking Sarah to one of the fine restaurants along the beach, he also liked the notion of sharing a meal with her alone.

He tried to tell himself not to think what might happen after they had finished eating and enjoyed a bottle of wine. He told himself not to imagine running his hands through all that glorious chestnut hair, capturing her face between his hands and kissing her until he'd had his fill. He tried not to think of undressing her, carrying her into the bedroom, easing her down on the king-size bed and making love to her.

She was exhausted, worried, and on top of that was the not-so-small matter that the last man she'd been with had abused her so badly she had wound up in the hospital.

Letting him make love to her was probably the last thing she wanted.

They ordered two filets, medium rare, and Jackson added a bottle of Stags' Leap, Napa Valley cabernet. The plates came piping hot with fully loaded baked potatoes, two big green salads, and there was strawberry shortcake for dessert.

The server had placed the food on the linen-draped table in front of the sliding glass doors to the balcony overlooking the ocean. Mostly Jackson just picked at the food on his plate, his mind on Sarah and how pretty she looked in the moonlight streaming in off the white sand beach and how much he wanted her.

He had no idea what Sarah was thinking. She made pleasant conversation and smiled often enough, but she didn't eat even as much as he did.

When the meal was finished, Jackson rounded the table and pulled out her chair.

"We've got a big day tomorrow." They planned to start with Hollister Equipment, investigate the connection to Marty Kozak, and make some calls, see what they might learn. "Why don't you go on to bed, try to get some sleep?"

Exactly what he knew he wouldn't be able to do — not with Sarah in a bed on the other side of the wall.

"I suppose we should." But she didn't

move away from him, and the longer he stayed close to her, the harder it was going to be. He was so damned hard now he ached with every heartbeat.

"Good night," he said gruffly. Turning, he walked into his bedroom.

It took every ounce of his will.

Jackson closed the door and leaned against it. *Dammit to hell.* But it wasn't fair to Sarah to press her. Not after what she'd been through.

With a sigh, he stripped off his shirt and tossed it over the end of the bed, took off his loafers and socks, then padded over to his suitcase and pulled out a paperback book. He tried not to listen for sounds in the room next door. It was going to be torture just knowing she was in there. Knowing he couldn't kiss her, touch her, couldn't pull off her nightgown and run his tongue over those soft, full breasts.

Jackson groaned.

Sarah paced the bedroom. She knew he wanted her. Or at least she thought he did. All through dinner, whenever he looked at her, the heat in his eyes made her giddy. Desire was there in every gesture, every glance. She'd been sure when they were finished with the meal, he would kiss her, do something that would lead to making love.

Instead, he had practically run from the room.

Sarah paced the bedroom. She remembered the kiss they had shared in front of Gran's house. True, she had been a little frightened. She had never been with a man whose passions ran so hot — and clearly his did. She had known it the moment he had touched her.

But mostly she had been afraid of herself — of her own fierce need, stronger than she ever could have guessed.

It was that kiss, she believed, that kept Jackson in his room, instead of in her bed. He was afraid he would frighten her, that he might lose control and hurt her in some way. He knew how cruel Andrew had been and he was going out of his way to protect her.

From himself.

Sarah glanced at the clock. Half an hour had passed and still desire pulsed through her. Her skin felt so sensitive the slight breeze coming in through the bedroom window seemed to scorch her flesh. Her nipples were as hard as diamonds and the place between her legs throbbed and burned.

All day she had thought of what it would be like to make love with Jackson. She had been so sure, so certain it would happen tonight.

She paused in front of the mirror, opened the silk robe she had put on in the hope he would come. At thirty-two, her body was still firm, her waist small and her hips nicely rounded. Her breasts were a little heavier since she'd had a child, but they were high and nicely shaped and as she looked at them in the mirror they seemed to swell with anticipation.

A noise sounded in the room next door.

Jackson was still awake. What would he do if she simply walked into his room? Would he send her away? Or would he take charge, as was his nature? Would he make love to her as she had dreamed he would do?

Her shoulders straightened. There was only one way to find out.

Refusing to allow the terrifying thought of how she would feel if he rejected her, she walked into the living room, crossed the carpet, and knocked on his bedroom door. She didn't wait for permission to enter, just turned the knob and walked in.

Jackson lay propped on a pillow, his rugged, handsome features immersed in the pages of a book. He spotted her, came up off the bed in the same tan slacks he'd had on earlier — and nothing else. Sarah sucked in a breath. He was tall and lean and all solid muscle — wide, muscled shoulders; slabs of muscle across his chest; an abdomen laddered with sinew. A light furring of dark hair spanned his chest and arrowed down into the waistband of his slacks. She had never seen a man with a more beautiful body.

"You must . . . must have kept up your boxing."

He stood there unmoving, his chest heaving in and out. "There's a gym in the basement at the house. I like to stay in shape."

She wet her lips. "Yes . . . I — I can see that."

He reached for the shirt lying across the foot of his bed, but Sarah held up a hand.

"Don't. You look perfect the way you are."

Dark brown eyes burned into her. "Sarah . . ."

"Do you know how badly I want to touch you? It's all I can do not to —"

"God, Sarah . . ." He didn't let her finish, just moved the short distance between them and hauled her into his arms.

His kiss was hot and fierce, a wild, burning, taking kiss that turned her inside out. He opened the front of her robe and one of his suntanned hands cupped a breast, began to mold and caress her.

"I've dreamed of this," he whispered, sliding the robe off her shoulders, lowering his head to take the fullness into his mouth. He tugged softly. His tongue curled around the hardened tip and it felt so good she swayed against him. She slid her fingers into his thick dark hair and arched her back to give him better access.

"Jackson . . ."

A shudder passed through him. His white teeth fastened on a nipple, raked gently, and hot sensation poured through her. Her legs gave out and Jackson caught her, lifted her into his arms and strode back to the bed.

"I've never wanted a woman as much as I want you," he said, settling her on the mattress and capturing her lips in another scorching kiss.

The words thrilled her, burned away any second thoughts she might have had. Held in thrall by his magnificent body, she watched him strip off his slacks and white cotton briefs. He was big and hard and her insides tightened at the thought of him entering her. Her mouth watered as if she wanted to eat him up.

"I want you, too," she said, and then he was kissing her again, joining her naked on the bed, taking her deeply with his tongue. Her own tongue swept in, tangled with his, and she heard him groan.

Jackson kissed the side of her neck, trailed hot kisses down over her breasts, and he suckled her there. Sarah began to writhe, to arch upward in a silent plea for more.

"I need you," she whispered, moving restlessly, urging him to take her.

"Soon, darlin'. First I want to taste you." She wasn't sure what he meant until she felt his tongue circling her navel, moving lower, felt the wetness of his kisses on the inside of her thighs.

"Jackson!" she cried out at the feel of his mouth on her sex, the slick heat of his tongue. Hot sensation flooded into her core, gripped her like a fist. The first climax hit like a tidal wave, shattering the last of her reserve, immersing her in a wave of pleasure that threatened to pull her under and never let go. She came a second time before he left her, moved above her, settled himself between her legs.

She tasted herself on the kiss that followed, and renewed desire swamped her, so powerful she barely noticed when he paused to slip on a condom. She was drenched and ready but, as big as he was, it took an effort to ease his way inside.

"It's all right, darlin'." He kissed the side of her neck. "We don't have to rush."

When he filled her completely at last, he paused and she realized he was fighting for control.

"Don't move," he whispered, bending to press a soft kiss on her lips. "Stay exactly where you are."

Sarah just smiled. She loved that she could do this, keep him on the very edge. She shifted, took him deeper still.

Jackson cursed softly, and then he began to move. She could feel the hot need burning through him as he pounded into her, took her with long deep, furious strokes that had her moaning and arching beneath him.

"Jackson!" she cried out as a fresh climax shook her, splintered her into a thousand pieces. An instant later, he followed her to release, his muscles tightening, a low growl coming from his throat.

Long seconds passed. He was still hard inside her when he rolled over, taking her with him, letting her lie across his chest.

He looped a strand of dark hair behind her ear. "You were amazing," he said, pressing a last soft kiss on her lips.

"So were you," she said. From somewhere deep inside her, Andrew's image flashed through her head — Andrew demanding she yield to him, Sarah giving in though whatever they had shared was long gone, enduring his touch but gaining no pleasure. Until he no longer came to her at all.

She shook her head, refusing to let him intrude — not now, not in a moment that belonged to her and Jackson.

"Are you all right?" he asked, his voice changing, roughening with concern. "I didn't scare you?"

A sweet warmth filled her that he should care. "You didn't scare me." In fact, she had never enjoyed lovemaking so much, never really known how good it could be.

She leaned down and kissed him, her hair falling forward, cocooning them in a world of their own. Jackson's erection stirred inside her, grew thicker, turned rock hard.

"I want you again," he said, "but I don't want to hurt you."

But the only one who had hurt her was Andrew and he would never hurt her again.

Sarah shifted, sat up astride him. She smiled as she lifted herself a little, then slid back down his hardened length. She moved that way again, felt the tension return to his body, felt his building desire. She had no idea what tomorrow might bring, whether the past would put an end to her future. Soon tomorrow would come, but tonight belonged to her.

Sarah meant to take this moment and hold it close to her heart.

As was his habit, Jackson awakened in the gray light of dawn. Beneath the covers he was hard. A beautiful woman lay beside him and he wanted her again.

He would not wake her. She needed her sleep, needed her strength to face the day ahead.

He sighed into the dim light slipping into the bedroom. The morning traffic was still sparse enough he could hear the waves rolling up on the beach. He looked over at Sarah, admired the way her glossy dark hair spread over the pillow, noticed the swell of a breast, barely covered by the white cotton sheet, and hardened even more.

Jackson softly cursed. Sliding out of the bed, he padded over to the closet, pulled out one of the terry cloth robes the hotel provided, and went into the living room to order coffee and breakfast rolls. He closed the door softly behind him, thinking of Sarah and the fantastic night they'd shared.

He couldn't stop wondering about her, how she had survived a man like Andrew, what made her the strong woman she seemed to be when she should have been defeated and weak.

He would find out, he vowed. There was something about Sarah Allen that made him want to know all of her secrets.

Then again, the more he knew, the more he might be drawn to her, the more easily he might fall prey to the charms that had captured him sixteen years ago.

He wasn't ready for that.

He would have to be careful.

But then *careful* was Jackson's middle name.

Sarah awoke with a start. For an instant, she didn't know where she was. Then she remembered — she had seduced Jackson Raines.

Embarrassment burned through her. There was no denying it. She had gone brazenly into his room and practically demanded he have sex with her.

Not that he had minded.

Her embarrassment slowly faded. Jackson was an extremely virile man and an amazingly satisfying lover. It had been no hardship for him to make love to her.

And certainly no hardship for her.

They had made love three times last night, and it was one of the best nights of her life.

No, *the* best night, she corrected. Everything that had happened between them had been wonderful.

But wonderful had a way of disappearing, leaving heartbreak in its wake.

Sarah shivered. What she had shared with Jackson was special, but it couldn't last. There was too much pain in her past — and too many problems ahead.

She rose from the bed, grabbed her silk robe off the floor and slipped it on. She refused to lie to herself. She was free of Andrew but her life was still a mess. Danger lurked behind every corner. Beginning any sort of relationship wouldn't be fair to Jackson.

And it wouldn't be fair to her and Holly.

Sarah wasn't ready for any kind of commitment. Her one-night stand with Jackson — the first ever for Sarah — had perfectly filled her needs. Of course she wanted him again already — which could only be expected. Jackson was exactly the sort of lover every woman wanted: passionate, considerate and tireless. Sarah was thirty-two, at the height of her sexuality. It was only normal that she was attracted to such a virile male.

Still, she knew the terrible consequences of falling under a man's spell — even one who, on the surface, appeared to be exactly the sort a woman would want. Sarah had learned the hard way how deceiving appearances could be.

One thing she knew for certain, the closer she allowed herself to get to Jackson, the more difficult it would be to end the affair.

No more hot, unbridled sex, she told herself. *No more fierce kisses and heated embraces, no more touching, aching, wanting.*

She had to stop now — before it was too late.

Jackson didn't notice Sarah standing in the bedroom doorway until she walked barefoot into the living room, wearing the same sexy, flowered silk robe she'd had on the night before. As she made her way toward the coffee pot, he went hard beneath his white terry robe.

She poured herself a cup of coffee but never once did she look at him, and right then, he knew he was in trouble. "You might as well say it. I kind of thought you would."

She added cream to her coffee, carefully stirred it in, then turned toward where he sat on the sofa. "All right, I'll say it. Last night was great — fantastic, in fact — but . . ."

"But it was a mistake."

She sighed, unnecessarily stirred her coffee a few more times, set the spoon back down on the tray. "It was my idea, so if it was a mistake, I'm the one who made it."

"That so? Maybe it wasn't a mistake. Maybe it was just great sex and we both enjoyed it."

She smiled at that, seemed a little relieved. "Yeah, maybe it was. It's been years for me. I suppose I'm entitled."

That was exactly what he wanted to hear. Great sex, no strings. So why did hearing it make his insides draw into a knot?

"Actually, I've been wondering about last night . . ." he said.

"Wondering?"

"Yeah. Wondering why you weren't cowering in fear. I'm a man, after all, and a fairly demanding lover. After what your husband did —"

"Fairly demanding?"

"All right, I like sex. I like a partner who enjoys it, too."

"So you thought that after Andrew, I'd be afraid of you, afraid of your passion?"

He nodded. "I'm surprised you didn't run screaming from the room."

Sarah sighed, shoved back a lock of her heavy dark hair. "The truth is, for a long time, I was the coward you expected me to be. I was terrified of Andrew. I did whatever he told me to."

"Considering he beat you so badly he put you in the hospital, I can understand that."

"You know about that?"

"My brother's fairly thorough."

She walked toward him but sat down in the chair instead of taking a seat beside him on the sofa. "I was afraid to leave him. I was sure he'd wind up with custody of Holly — one way or another. And I was terrified that if he did and I wasn't there to take the brunt of his wrath, he would take it out on her."

"You thought he would kill you and then hurt your daughter."

"Yes." She glanced away, staring out the wide glass sliding doors as if she could see into the past. "Three years ago, I found a site on the internet, a support group for abused women — SBW. It stands for Support for Battered Women. I had my own laptop — something Andrew gave me so he could email me from wherever he happened to be, make sure I stayed close by."

"Kind of like Big Brother."

"Exactly. But it worked against him. Once I was in the chat group, little by little the women made me understand that I didn't have to let him break me, that I could find ways around him, ways to be my own person, even if I stayed."

"Do you still interact with the group?"

She nodded. "As soon as I get home, I'm hooking up to a server. Some of the women have become close friends. I've missed talking to them."

"I see." And he did. She had endured and become stronger, found ways to protect her daughter and herself. He couldn't help admiring her for it.

"So what about the disk?" she asked. "Where should we begin?"

He moved the paper lying open on the coffee table and she spotted the probate documents he had been reviewing. "I read through the paperwork this morning. I didn't see anything that rang a bell. Like we figured, Kozak's our primary lead. He wants the disk and he's willing to go to extreme lengths to get it."

"Which means there's something on that disk he doesn't want anyone to see." Sarah took a sip of her coffee. "Kozak is linked to Andrew through Hollister Equipment. Their main office is in West Covina. I'm sure they'll let me in — I'm Andrew's widow, after all. Let's go down there and dig around, see what we can find out."

"What about your husband's personal office?"

"The office was closed after Andrew died.

It was only for show, anyway. Each of the companies he owned ran independently. Andrew liked to play, not work. He liked to keep things simple."

"Then we'll go out to West Covina, take a look at Hollister Equipment."

She nodded. "I'd better shower and get dressed." She rose from the chair, the flowered silk parting, showing a long length of her sexy legs. Jackson felt a jolt of heat that went straight to his groin.

He watched her refill her coffee cup then disappear inside the bedroom she had claimed but not slept in. He wondered where their relationship was headed — wondered if there would be any sort of relationship at all or just the memory of a heated night of sex.

Whatever happened, it was going to take patience on his part, patience and a will of steel. As he rose from the sofa, his erection hard as granite, it was all he could do not to walk through that bedroom door, join her in the shower, and make love to her until neither of them could move.

For the second time that morning, common sense prevailed, and he went in to shower and change.

ELEVEN

Sarah turned off the water and toweled herself dry. She blow-dried her hair and dressed in a beige skirt, turquoise silk blouse and sandals. When she returned to the living room, she found Jackson in a yellow short-sleeved shirt and dark chinos, drinking a cup of coffee.

God, he was handsome. She knew the iron-hard body beneath those clothes, knew the scent of him, the texture of his skin, the exact feel of the roughness along his jaw. Memories of last night did ridiculous things to her body.

"Ready?" he asked, setting the coffee cup down and striding toward her.

"I'm ready." She forced herself not to take a step backward as he approached. He was a powerful force and ignoring his sexual appeal wouldn't be easy.

They left the hotel and took the 10 Freeway out to West Covina. Hollister Equipment was in a gray stucco building on a huge open lot where a variety of heavy equipment was stored. Sarah didn't know the name of each piece, but there were heavy earth movers and gigantic dump trucks with wheels the size of a small house, big yellow Caterpillar graders, steamrollers and dozens of miscellaneous trucks of every size.

"Big operation," Jackson said.

"I've only been here once. I'd forgotten it was so impressive."

"Let's go inside, take a look around the office." His hand settled at her waist and she ignored a little spark of awareness, waited while he opened the door, then walked inside.

There were two women working, each at a beige metal desk. One of them got up and walked over.

"What can I do for you?" She was short, late thirties, blond hair teased and pulled into a twist. She stuck a pencil into her hairdo and used it to scratch her head.

"I'm Sarah Hollister." At least she was for as long as it was necessary. "The probate on my late husband's estate is moving forward and I need to take a look at some of the company files."

The blonde flicked a glance at the other

woman, older, with silver streaks in her short brown hair.

"It's all right," the older woman said. "Mr. Hollister is certainly not going to protest."

"Go ahead," the blonde said. "The records are all in the manager's office. It's right through there." She pointed toward a closed door. "Mr. Wallace is out on a job."

Good news, Sarah thought. At least she wouldn't have to concoct a story for him. Jackson followed her into the office and closed the door behind them.

"I wonder if they searched this place," he said. "If they did, they were careful not to leave any traces."

"It's one thing to tear up a cottage in Wyoming or vandalize an empty condo. Hollister is a big company that employs a number of people. They would have been worried about bringing in the police."

Sarah sat down at the desk and began to pull open the drawers while Jackson walked over to the file cabinets.

Finding nothing but the manager's personal items, she left the desk and joined him, saw him open the drawer marked J–M and begin to skim the records, searching for Martin Kozak's name.

"Here it is." He pulled out a manila file and they both read the information as he turned the pages.

"These look like mostly highway projects," Sarah said. "Kozak rented big pieces of machinery from Hollister to complete the jobs."

"Nothing here that looks suspicious."

"Let's take the file anyway," she suggested. "Just in case there's something in it we might need later on."

They made a cursory examination of the rest of the files, but saw nothing that might indicate a blackmail scheme. They left the office, the file under Jackson's arm. None of the women seemed to notice — or maybe they just didn't care.

"Where to now?" Sarah asked.

Seated behind the wheel of the Infiniti, Jackson opened the file. "Here's a project Kozak started last year. Leased a lot of equipment from Hollister. Looks like his company's still working on it."

Sarah leaned over and read the information. "They're building an overpass on Highway 91. I'll show you how to get there."

Jackson cranked the engine and they drove out of the parking lot. With the congested L.A. traffic, they didn't reach the site until almost an hour later.

Work crews were everywhere, dust flying, engine noise so loud Sarah had to shout to be heard. Jackson pulled the car off onto a dirt road that led into the construction zone and turned off the engine, staying some distance away.

"I don't want them to come over and make us leave. I think if we stay back here, we'll be all right."

A gusty afternoon breeze whipped powdery dust into the air as each piece of Hollister machinery did its job. "What do you suppose Kozak could be doing that's illegal?"

They watched the equipment moving vast loads of dirt, flatbed trucks hauling long lengths of rebar to reinforce the concrete used to support the bridge. Huge chunks of earth were being scooped out then dumped into piles that provided the height necessary to cross the road below.

"I've read about companies using inferior grade products," Jackson said, "substandard concrete or rebar they bought for a song. Ultimately the structure failed and cost lives. Could be that kind of thing."

"I remember something like that happened in a hotel in Kansas City, though I think it might have been faulty design. Walkway gave way. Killed more than a hundred people."

"Or it could be faulty compaction. It's a

lot cheaper to do a half-assed job than to spend the time necessary to compact the earth just right."

"Andrew might have stumbled across the truth. Or he might have paid someone to keep track of what was going on."

"The trick is to figure out what it was."

"And what to do with the information once we find out."

Jackson cast her a glance. "Use it to get Kozak off your back."

That sounded like a very good idea. She looked back at the massive building project. "If Kozak was doing anything that might affect the quality of the construction, wouldn't he have to deal with an inspector, someone in charge of checking to be sure the project was built to code?"

"Yeah — and that's damned good thinking. The only way Kozak could get away with substandard construction of any kind is if the highway inspector was on the take."

"How can we find out?"

"Let's go back to the hotel and make some calls, see if we can come up with a little more information." Jackson started the engine.

"Do you really think it could be that simple?"

"There's nothing simple about it. The only

reason we're following this line of thinking is that we're pretty sure something crooked is going on."

Sarah fell silent, her mind spinning with possibilities. She had known Andrew was involved in shadowy activities. She had always worried that somehow his dealings might affect her and Holly.

She shuddered, afraid to consider the price she might yet have to pay.

The suite had been cleaned and fresh sheets put on the beds. No evidence remained of their heated lovemaking last night. Still, just a glimpse through Jackson's open bedroom door sent a ripple of heat into Sarah's stomach. She quickly glanced away, then flushed to find his dark eyes watching her.

He crossed the carpet to where she stood, came up behind her, set his hands around her waist and pressed his mouth against the back of her neck. "So you just want great sex, nothing more."

"No, I . . ."

"It's been years, you said. If that's so, one night isn't going to be enough." His warm breath fanned her nape. He slid her hair aside and kissed her just below her ear, bit down lightly on the lobe.

She moistened her trembling lips, felt his

fingers working the buttons at the front of her blouse, pulling it open, sliding inside the lacy cups of her demi-bra. He grazed the tips of her breast as he pressed more kisses along her throat, kissed the shoulder he bared, unhooked the front of her bra and filled his hands with her breasts.

Sarah's knees went weak. "Jackson . . ."

"You want this, don't you? Just as much as I do?"

She swallowed, told herself to pull away, to ignore the hot little tremors that came with each tug of his skillful fingers on her nipples.

His teeth grazed her shoulder. "Tell me you want me. Say it out loud."

She whimpered.

"Say it."

She could feel his erection pressing against her bottom, remembered how good it felt to have him inside her. "I . . . want you."

She started to turn but he held her in place, leaned around and kissed her on the mouth. She sucked in a breath at the feel of her skirt sliding over her hips, exposing her bottom and the white lace thong that matched her bra. At least the expensive underwear, one of the few remnants of Andrew's money, was being put to good use.

"Very pretty," he said, running a hand over

the rounded globes, bending down to press soft nibbling kisses against her skin. "The panties, too."

He slid the thong aside, found her softness and began to stroke her. Sarah squirmed, arched into his hand. She was trembling all over, any thought of resisting a memory. She was wet. Dear God, the man could make her wet. She heard the buzz of his zipper, felt the thickness of his heavy erection. Her palms flattened on the wall as he tipped her forward, parted her legs and filled her.

Sarah gasped at the rush of pleasure, at the heat and need pouring through her.

Jackson was a fiercely demanding lover, she had learned, but as he eased himself out and filled her again, as his fingers found her cleft and stroked her to the very edge of climax, she understood that here was a man who demanded but also gave, a man who could satisfy her as no man ever had.

A man even more dangerous than Andrew.

A hot climax shook her and sweet pleasure rolled through her, filling every cell in her body. Sarah cried out Jackson's name as he surged deeply, pounded into her and brought her to fulfillment again. Then his hard body tightened, he drove into her one last time and reached a powerful release.

For long seconds they just stood there, Sarah's eyes closed, her insides still tingling, a soft smile on her lips. Jackson eased himself out of her body and disposed of his condom while she worked to straighten her clothes.

Her smile remained in place, but as she continued to spiral down and the pleasure began to fade, warning bells went off in her head and the old fear returned. Jackson was a man with the power to reach her as no man ever had — and therein lay the danger.

Silently she vowed to find the courage she would need to resist him.

Jackson sat in the living room, poring over the equipment leases and notes in the Kozak file, then he went over the probate papers again. Sarah had showered and at his insistence lay down for an afternoon nap.

She'd had little sleep last night, thanks to him. And though she had made it clear she wanted to put some distance between them, he had beaten down her defenses and taken her again.

It hadn't been difficult. All day, sparks of sexual tension had crackled between them, sparks ready to burst into a roaring blaze. Sarah was a far more sensual woman than she realized. She had been without a man for years, and it was clear the two of them were good together, that they could satisfy each other's needs.

Jackson frowned. He wanted Sarah Allen. He couldn't seem to get his fill. And yet he wasn't sure, beyond sex, what he expected of her — or what she expected of him. He wasn't sure how deeply he should get involved.

He remembered the old Sarah, driven by a fierce desire for money and social position. Maybe that hadn't changed and the attraction she felt for him came from the money and influence he now commanded.

A line from a country song popped into his head — "How do you like me now?" Now that he was wealthy and successful. Now that he was no longer just a boy from the wrong side of the tracks.

His gut was saying it wasn't so, but he didn't know her well enough to be completely sure.

And even if he decided a relationship with Sarah was what he wanted, he wasn't sure how much involvement she would allow. After ten years with an abusive husband, she might not be ready to jump back in.

He only knew he didn't want to hurt her. Whatever her thoughts and motives, Sarah and her daughter had been hurt more than enough already.

It was half an hour later when she walked into the living room in one of the hotel's fluffy white terry robes, her hair damp from the shower and curling softly around her face, looking so damned sexy he wanted to tumble her again.

"You want a Coke or something from the minibar?" he asked, careful to keep his thoughts to himself.

"Diet Coke, if there is one. That would be great."

He filled a glass with the ice he'd retrieved from the machine down the hall, walked over to the minibar and took out a Diet Coke, poured it into the glass.

Sarah was on the phone as he approached, seated on the sofa with her legs curled up beneath her, the receiver pressed against her ear. She held up the message pad and he read the words she'd written, *highway dept.*

"Yes, well, my name is Carrie Johnson," she said, making up the words as she went along. "I'm a secretary with Kozak Construction — the company that's building the overpass on Highway 91? I was wondering . . . hoping . . . you could help me."

She reached up and took the frosty glass from his hand, took a quick sip and continued her conversation.

"You see, today is only my second day on the job and I'm embarrassed to say I've managed to lose the information my boss gave me with the highway inspector's name written on it. Do you think you could look it up for me? I really hate to ask my boss for it again." She sipped her Coke. "Sure, I'll be happy to wait."

A moment later, she set the glass down and picked up the pad, plucked up the pen beside it and began to scratch out a name. Vernon Rimmer.

"He's not new, is he? He's been doing this a while?" She gave him a nod. "You're a lifesaver, Dottie. Thank you very much." She hung up the phone and looked up at him with a grin. "Here's our man."

"I didn't realize I had myself a first-class detective."

She laughed. "It's a start. Unfortunately, we need to find out if Mr. Rimmer is legitimate, and I haven't the foggiest notion how to do that."

"I'll call my brother, see if he's back from Mexico." Jackson sat down in the chair instead of sitting next to her on the sofa as he wanted to do. He had pressed her enough for now. In boxing he'd learned to bide his time, to read his opponent, then wait till the moment was right before striking. He had a lot left to learn about Sarah Allen.

Jackson picked up the receiver and called Arizona. Dev wasn't at his Scottsdale home, or in his Phoenix office, but he had been calling for messages and he was expected back soon. Jackson left word both places.

"It's getting on toward evening. We need to stop by the Blue Parrot. Afterward we'll get some supper."

"All right. I'll go get dressed. And I need to call Holly, make sure she's all right."

Jackson had already showered and changed into fresh clothes. He emptied the other half of her Coke into a glass and drank it while he waited. A few minutes later, Sarah returned to the living room wearing a slinky little black cocktail dress that made the blood in his veins rush south.

"You look gorgeous," he said. "Ought to make the boys at the Blue Parrot sit up and take notice."

She smiled, looked pleased. He was always surprised at how little it seemed to take to please her.

"Thank you."

"I'll have the valet bring the car around." He called the front desk, grabbed his light-colored sport coat off the back of a chair but didn't put it on, and they left the suite.

The car was waiting when they reached the front door. He drove out into traffic, took the 405 Freeway to the Ventura Boulevard off-ramp, then cruised the busy street until they spotted the Blue Parrot, a few miles down the road.

The place didn't look fancy, just a white stucco, flat-roofed building with a motel facing the parking lot in the rear. A blue-collar joint of the sort that might appeal to Andrew Hollister's blue-collar clientele, guys like Kozak in the construction business.

"You ready for this?" Jackson asked as he turned off the engine.

Sarah released a slow breath. "As much as I'm ever going to be. Let's go."

TWELVE

The Blue Parrot. A plastic palm tree stood at the end of a long bar lined with red vinyl bar stools. Neon beer signs on the wall, Formica tables and multicolored plastic chairs that looked as if they came straight out of the fifties. Jackson could see into a back room that had a shuffleboard and two pool tables. The place should have been smoke-filled, undoubtedly was until the city passed an ordinance against smoking indoors.

"Nice place," he said sarcastically. "I don't imagine it's the sort your husband might have frequented."

"Andrew liked the finer things in life, but he was forced to mingle with his customers on occasion. He might have come here at one time or another."

Jackson's hand went to Sarah's waist, urging her toward the bar, and she slid up on one of the stools. She tugged on the skirt of her sexy black cocktail dress, pulling it down to cover as much as she could of her shapely legs. As short as the dress was, the gesture was pretty much futile. Enjoying the view, Jackson bit back a smile.

"What'll you have?" The bartender, a blond guy slightly past his prime in a tight black T-shirt, leaned on the top of the bar. He had blue eyes and they ran over Sarah, taking in the soft swells of her cleavage exposed in the V of the dress. Jackson ignored an unexpected shot of jealousy.

"I'll have a glass of white wine," Sarah said.

"I'll have a beer," Jackson added. "Make it a Bud."

It was a beer-and-whiskey kind of place, a little shoddy, but the sparse crowd didn't look rough, just slightly worn out. Jackson sat down on the bar stool next to Sarah and casually surveyed the room, noting the aging features of the women and the disinterested expressions of the men, none of whom fit the description of the ones they were looking for.

Halfway through his beer, he returned his attention to the bartender. Earlier, he'd noticed the guy's thick biceps but figured him for a weight lifter. Then he spotted the broken nose and roughened ears.

"You look like a fighter. You box some?"

He made a slight nod of his head. "Boxed a little after high school. For a while I was the Great White Hope around here. Didn't last long." He looked Jackson over, taking in the muscles in his arms, the scar along his jaw and the one bisecting his eyebrow. "You, too?"

He nodded. "Made the Olympic team in '92. Did pretty good till some Russian kicked my ass."

The bartender hooted a laugh. "There's a gym just down the street. We get a lot of muscle-jocks in here. A few decent fighters. You want another beer? This one's on me."

Jackson shook his head. "Rather have a little information."

"Yeah?"

"I'm looking for a couple of guys — one's blond, skinny, has a tattoo on his hand that says Mother. The other one's Hispanic. Short and stout. Might be a fighter. Maybe he's one of those who come in here from the gym."

"Sounds like Billy Hinman and Jose Delgado. They hang together a lot. Billy's okay, a little slow on the uptake. Delgado thinks he's a tough guy. Competes in the local boxing competitions. I guess he's been doing okay."

Jackson pulled the napkin from beneath

his beer, wrote down his cell number, slid it and a fifty-dollar bill across the bar. "You see either one of those guys in the next day or two, give me a call."

The bartender picked up the fifty. "I see Delgado right now . . . He's just walking in the back door." He tipped his head toward the rear entrance leading in from the parking lot. Jose Delgado strode in as if he owned the place.

"Stay here," Jackson said to Sarah, sliding off the bar stool.

"Are you sure you should —"

"I won't be long." He was sure, all right. The bastard owed him for the mess he'd made of the cottage. Jackson strode the length of the bar, across the empty dance floor toward the back door. He stopped dead in front of the fighter.

"You Delgado?"

"Who wants to know?"

"I do. I believe you owe me some money."

"I don't even know you, man. Why would I owe you money?" With his dark complexion, black eyes and straight black hair slicked back from a square-jawed face, he was good-looking — or at least Jackson figured the women would think so.

"Maybe because you and your buddy broke into my property in Wyoming and tore the hell out of just about everything."

Jose scoffed, but the truth was there in his eyes. "I don't know what you're talking about, man."

"Maybe not. Tell you what . . . you give me the name of the guy who paid you to do it and we'll forget the whole thing."

"Get lost, man." He tried to walk past, but Jackson moved in front of him, used a shoulder to shove him against the wall.

"I want the name."

Delgado grinned, a look of pure anticipation twisting the contours of his face. His hand fisted, shot out with the speed and power of a cannonball, a punch that could send a man to his knees. Jackson blocked the blow, drilled him with two sharp jabs and a punch that had Delgado's head slamming hard against the wall.

The amazement on his face turned to fury. He growled low in his throat and charged. Jackson turned at the last instant, hit him with a blow that came up from the floor, and Delgado went down like a sack of oats.

Seconds passed, not quite the count of ten, Jackson figured. Delgado staggered to his feet. He shook his head and wiped the blood off his lips with the back of his hand. "You're gonna pay for that, man."

Jackson just smiled. The kid was strong as a bull, but he'd had no real training. And he let his temper get in the way of his boxing. He threw a fierce punch at Jackson straight from the shoulder. Jackson jerked sideways, missing the blow, jabbed him two more times, then went in for the kill. Two hard punches, one to the head, one to the mid-section, another blow to the head and the kid went down.

Delgado wasn't unconscious but he was smart enough not to get up. Jackson rolled him onto his back and planted a knee in the middle of his chest. "The name."

He spit out a mouthful of blood. "Screw you."

Jackson drew back his fist. "You sure that's the way you want it?"

Delgado swore a dirty word. "Kozak," he said through swollen lips.

"You went to Wyoming looking for a disk Andrew Hollister had."

"Yeah." Delgado tried to sit up but Jackson's knee forced him back down.

"The lady doesn't have it," Jackson said. "She doesn't know anything about it."

Jackson put pressure on his knee and Delgado groaned. "Mostly it was . . . a message," the kid said. "Kozak wants her . . . to find it."

Jackson came to his feet, letting Delgado go. "All right, now I'm the one sending a message. You tell Kozak if he doesn't want more trouble than he can handle, he'd better leave Sarah Hollister alone."

No one called the police. It was over too quickly and the patrons were probably used to an occasional show of bad temper. The bartender just grinned, one boxer to another, as Sarah and Jackson walked out of the Blue Parrot.

Sarah's legs were shaking. She felt Jackson's hand at her waist all the way to the parking lot. There was something about his natural sense of protectiveness she found comforting. She told herself she didn't approve of Jackson's brutal treatment of Jose Delgado, that she'd dealt with enough violence to last a lifetime.

But somehow this was different. Jackson was trying to protect her, not hurt her.

"You okay?" he asked as he waited for her to get settled in the passenger seat and snap her seat belt in place.

"I'm all right."

"At least we know for sure it was Kozak." He shut the car door, walked around to the driver's side and climbed in.

She studied his profile as he pulled the

seat belt across his muscular chest. "I remember your fight with the Russian," she said, referring to the comment he had made to the bartender. "He didn't beat you by much."

He shrugged the powerful shoulders she had just seen in action. "I lost. That was all that mattered."

"I think it mattered that you competed and gave it your best."

His dark eyes ran over her, sending a sliver of heat into her stomach. "So you watched the Barcelona Games?"

"Everyone in Wind Canyon watched. They were proud of you. So was I." Jackson seemed surprised. "I had a crush on you, Jackson. I was just afraid to let anyone know. I was afraid they would treat me the way they treated you."

He scoffed. "You had ambitions that didn't include a poor boy like me."

She glanced away, knowing it was true. "I wanted out. I admit it. I was tired of being a small-town girl. I wanted to see what life was like outside Wyoming. I wanted to travel, to visit places like Paris and Rome. Believe me, I paid for it."

Jackson made no reply, just started the engine and drove out of the parking lot. "We've got dinner reservations at a place called The Dove. It's supposed to be very good."

"I've never been there, and to tell you the truth, I'm glad. I have some pretty awful memories of dinners with Andrew."

For the first time, he smiled. "Then let's make a good memory tonight."

Sarah's heartbeat quickened. She already had too many memories of Jackson, memories of a hot, steamy night in bed with him, of outrageous sex, memories that urged her to let him make love to her again.

Not tonight, she told herself. Tonight she would say no and she would mean it.

In the meantime, she would enjoy a delicious meal in the company of a handsome man. She deserved that much, she told herself.

Tomorrow she would think of Marty Kozak and what she needed to do to make sure she and Holly were safe.

A warm, early-June sun beat down on the asphalt surrounding the Serv-U Storage facility off Sunset Boulevard west of the 405 Freeway. After Andrew's death, when his father's big Spanish-style house had been sold and finally closed escrow, the Realtor had arranged an estate sale for the furniture that remained in the house, donated miscellaneous items, then put what was left into storage.

The items in the unit weren't something Marty Kozak was likely to know about and even Sarah had no idea exactly what was in there, since none of it held the least sentimental value to her. In fact, the only memories she had of living in the house on Sunset were bitter and painful.

Including the fact that the house was the scene of the murder.

Sarah shivered though the breeze fanning the palm trees around the perimeter was warm. She had worked hard to deal with the memories of what had happened that last night in the house — the terrible fight she'd had with Andrew she had never revealed to the police.

The awful, nauseating fear.

She closed her eyes, refusing to let the unwanted memories return.

"You all right?" Jackson asked.

"I'm fine." And for the most part, she was. The images of that terrible night came mostly in nightmares, and after her move to Wyoming, they occurred less and less.

Jackson examined the padlock. "You've got the combination, right?"

She nodded. "The Realtor gave it to me before I left. I figured we'd need it once we got to California so I brought it along."

Jackson examined the lock, worked the tumblers, removed the device, then slid up the heavy rolling door.

Sarah stared at the dusty stacks of boxes and miscellaneous bits and pieces of furniture, most of which were broken or damaged, and felt a sweep of nausea. Perspiration broke out on her forehead.

Jackson caught her arm. "You look like you're going to faint. Maybe you'd better wait in the car."

She shook her head. "I'll be all right in a minute. I just . . . I wasn't quite prepared." She wasn't prepared to see a lamp Andrew had once thrown at her in a fit of temper, the expensive silk shade ripped and bent beyond repair. Or the chair he had been sitting in behind his desk that last night.

She took a deep breath and slowly released it, clamped down on the old fear she refused to let grab hold of her again.

"Not much to show for a lifetime," she said, surveying the miscellaneous items in the storage room, a carton of books meant as a donation for the library, a stack of pillows from one of the beds, the cases now yellowed and stained.

"Your life is just beginning," Jackson said.

Sarah took a deep breath, praying he was

right. "After the estate sale, Andrew's clothes and personal effects were given to the Salvation Army."

"If the disk was in any of that, it's history."

"He kept his business life completely separate, so likely it wasn't." She moved silently into the debris that had once been part of her life. "We need to go through these boxes, see what's inside."

Jackson walked past her into the storage locker, his lean body brushing against her as he moved. She told herself she wasn't disappointed that last night he had brought her back to the hotel after supper and played the perfect gentleman. She wasn't the least disappointed that he had kissed her on the forehead and told her to get some rest.

Sarah ignored a twinge of irritation at the memory. All evening, she had been constructing her defenses, preparing for the battle she would wage when they returned to the suite and Jackson began making love to her. Her biggest enemy was her own desire for him, but she was ready to say no and mean it.

Instead, Jackson had respected her wishes and ruined her plans.

She flicked him a glance. The man was

just full of surprises.

She watched him open one dusty box after another, setting anything aside he thought she might need to go through.

"These look interesting," he said about a series of boxes he found in the corner. "Looks like they may have come out of his home office."

They had, she discovered as she started on the first of three, digging out an old fax machine Andrew had never used, paper trays, a phone with the receiver missing, a broken pencil sharpener, Scotch tape dispenser, stapler and other miscellaneous objects.

But there was no notebook or disk or USB flash drive, or anything that might have concealed something like that.

Sarah dug through several more boxes, while Jackson did the same. The dust in the storage room made her eyes water and she sneezed but kept on working.

"There's more office stuff in this one," Jackson said, pulling over another dusty cardboard box. Sarah wiped her hands on her jeans, knelt and began digging again. As she lifted out a leather desk pad, she recognized the coffee cup warmer that had sat on Andrew's desk. This year's Week At A Glance calendar was among the items. She set it aside to look at later, lifted out a tray that held pencils and pens. One of the pens caught her eye. It looked different than the others, shiny black-and-gold, and she remembered seeing it in Andrew's pocket.

"What is it?" Jackson asked as she picked it up to examine it more closely.

"Andrew's pen. He carried it a lot."

"Let me see it." Jackson took it out of her hand and pulled off the top. He smiled. "Well, look what we have in here."

"Oh, my God!"

"It's a pen drive. Works like a flash drive. Information's easy to carry this way. Whether it's got the right information remains to be seen."

But she couldn't help being excited, and she could tell he was, too.

"We're about finished in here," he said. "Let's go back to the hotel and see what we've got." He made a last survey of the storage unit. "See anything we might have missed?"

She took a good long look. She was anxious to get back to Wyoming, back to Holly. She didn't want to have to return for something they had overlooked.

"We've gone through all the boxes. The rest is mostly broken furniture the Realtor couldn't sell."

"All right, then, let's go."

Sarah took the hand Jackson held out to her. It felt warm and strong and not the least bit threatening. When they reached the car, Jackson handed her the pen drive. It held the blackmail list they were looking for — she was sure of it! She would bargain with Marty Kozak and be free of the past at last.

Sarah stuffed the black-and-gold pen deep into the pocket of her dusty jeans. Sending up a silent plea, she prayed the drive held the information she needed and she could get on with her life.

THIRTEEN

Sitting behind one of the computers in the hotel business center, Sarah opened the list of files in the pen drive. "There's only three of them."

"Good, let's take a look."

Her heart was pounding. This had to be it. It had to be!

The first was labeled Calendar. Sarah opened the file to find Andrew's schedule for the month of January, the last month of his life.

"I don't see anything exciting, just his usual meetings, golf and lunches."

Jackson was kind enough not to point out the weekends Andrew had marked off to Mitzy. Sarah ignored them, as well. She closed the file and opened the next.

Disappointment struck her. "The second file has notes from a meeting with the management of Southgate Demolition. Looks like the company had a contract to demolish a building in Northridge. It was scheduled to be pulled down the end of the month."

"January."

"That's right."

"What's in the third file?"

She was afraid to open it. If the list wasn't in there, they were right back where they'd started. Sarah watched the screen, her heart thumping almost painfully. She frowned. The file opened, but she had no idea what it meant. "What is it?"

"Looks like an address."

"Yes, I see that. 1542 Rocky Mountain Road, #14A, Palm Springs. But what's that other number?"

"Twenty-eight, thirty-two, eleven. Sounds like the combination to a lock."

"Like the storage room. That was thirty-six, eighteen, three." She gazed up at him, her spirits gradually sinking. "This isn't the blackmail list we were looking for. That means it isn't the right drive."

"No, but it's not a dead end, either."

She sighed. "So we're going to Palm Springs?"

"Looks like it."

Sarah just wanted to go home. She was missing Holly and the quiet of her charming little Wyoming cottage. And as much as she enjoyed being with Jackson, the desire that simmered between them, the constant yearning, left her on edge.

"Better to go now than make another trip."

He was right. Thank God she had turned in enough articles to keep Smiley happy at the newspaper. She sighed again as she printed out the information — everything on the drive, just in case, and picked up the printed pages. "When do we leave?"

"We can make it before dark if we start now."

And the traffic in the early afternoon would be better than in the morning. "I guess I'd better go up and pack."

Returning the pen drive to her pocket, determined to hide her disappointment, Sarah started for the elevator leading up to their suite.

It was a long drive to Palm Springs from Santa Monica, but they were getting out of town just after noon so the traffic wasn't as bad as it would be later in the day. Sarah sat back in the seat, trying not to think of the pen drive and Andrew, trying not to think that somehow he was trying to destroy her even from the grave.

Determined to distract herself, she made

the mistake of looking over at Jackson. His dark gaze cut sideways, touching hers for a moment, and heat tugged low in her belly. Lord, the man could make her think of sex without saying a word.

Flustered and unwilling to let him see, Sarah dug her cell phone out of her purse. She had yet to change to a company with better service in the mountains, but this one still worked fine down here.

The first call went to the Realtor who was handling the sale of the Santa Monica condo.

"Mrs. Hollister!" Jane Perkins said. "I'm so glad you called!"

"It's Allen, now," she corrected. "Sarah Allen."

"Oh. Well, as I said, I'm extremely glad you called. You see, the thing is, yesterday I tried to show your condo to a really good buyer, a Japanese businessman who wanted something in that exact location. I was sure he would make an offer, since your place was so nice and the price is so low, but, you see, the thing is, when I opened the door — well, you just wouldn't believe it."

Oh, yes, I would, Sarah thought, relieved that now she would not be connected in any way with the break-in. The police wouldn't even have to know she was there.

"So I guess the showing didn't go all that well."

"Well, that's just it. You see, the thing is — the entire place was a shambles!" Jane went on to describe the vandalism in the condo, how the whole unit had been trashed, and Sarah pretended to be shocked.

"I've phoned the insurance company," Jane continued, "and of course, the police — but the thing is . . ."

Sarah mostly tuned out the rest. When the woman was finished, Sarah told her to contact Stan Greenberg, the probate attorney, in regard to whatever needed to be done. She hung up the phone and let her head fall back against the headrest.

"Seems like the lady had plenty to say."

Sarah sighed. "Her name is Jane Perkins. She's a friend of Stan's. I'm beginning to think she is more than a friend, otherwise, why in the world would Stan have listed the property with someone like that?"

Jackson chuckled. "You're getting cynical in your old age, Ms. Allen."

She blew out a breath. "I guess I am." She didn't tell him that being married to Andrew had irreparably destroyed whatever naive notions she'd once had about life.

"Why don't you give Holly a call," Jackson suggested. "See how she's getting along?"

She had called Wyoming that morning before they left for the storage room, but she called again now. Livvy answered then put Holly on the line.

"Mom!"

"Hi, honey, how are you doing?"

"I'm okay, but I miss you. When are you coming home?"

"Soon, baby. Maybe tomorrow." She looked over at Jackson for confirmation and saw him nodding. He was probably as eager to get back as she was. He had a ranch to run, after all, and if the address in Palm Springs turned out to be a dead end, there was nothing more they could do in L.A.

Holly chatted pleasantly, telling her about Sam and Gibby and about the pony riding lessons, about seeing her very first eagle in the sky above the pasture, making Sarah smile.

"And Livvy taught me how to make brownies."

"Good, you can make some for me when I get back."

"Do you really think you'll be coming home tomorrow?"

Sarah felt a tug at her heart. She and Holly were so very close. The little girl had

190

never really had a father. Andrew was just a shadowy part of her life, someone who was almost never there. It was the reason Holly rarely mentioned him, the reason Andrew's death hadn't hit her as hard as it might have.

"I hope so, baby. I'll call you as soon as I know for sure." Sarah hung up the phone feeling more homesick than she had before.

Jackson cast her a glance. "How's she doing?"

"She loves the boys and Livvy."

"But she misses her mother."

Sarah nodded.

"What about her dad, Sarah? How's she dealing with that? I've never heard her talk about him."

Sarah sighed, the question mirroring her earlier thoughts. "Andrew was never around. He talked about Holly as if he really cared about her, but he rarely saw her. He came home late and left early. He never had time for a child."

"We'll go home tomorrow no matter what we find. We can come back if we need to."

Relief swept through her. They were going home. She could be with her daughter, and she could get back to work. She had told her boss that she needed a few days to take care of some loose ends in L.A. Now she could get back to her job as a reporter, back to her charming little cottage and the new life she had been trying to build.

She flicked a glance at Jackson, caught the lean, hard jaw, the slight indentation in his chin. His eyes were a rich dark chocolate brown, his lashes black and thicker than she had noticed before. The hands he wrapped around the steering wheel had long, sun-browned fingers, skillful fingers that had stroked her to climax more than once.

She felt that same, sensuous tug in her belly, closed her eyes and willed herself not to remember what it was like to make love with him.

What would happen once they returned to Wyoming? Could she live in such close proximity to such an attractive man and not succumb to her desire for him?

She wasn't sure what else she felt for him. She liked him. She was grateful for his willingness to help her, valued the kindness he had shown her. Perhaps they could come to an arrangement, enjoy a friendship that included occasional sex, but went no further.

"You're awfully quiet," he said, breaking into her thoughts.

She shifted in the seat, hoped he didn't notice the flush that crept into her cheeks. "I was . . . I was just thinking about Marty

Kozak," she lied. At the moment, the man was the farthest thing from her mind.

"Delgado will deliver my message. There's a good chance Kozak will accept the fact you don't have the disk and leave you alone."

Sarah said nothing. She hoped Jackson was right, but she knew Marty Kozak.

And her cynical nature just wouldn't let her believe it.

"There it is." A small condo development in the rugged, arid mountains outside Palm Springs, a chic, expensive town in the California desert. Tile-roofed, tan and dark brown stucco, thirty-five units built around a big, kidney-shaped swimming pool. They parked the car and went in search of unit 14A, making their way along wandering pathways landscaped with rocks and cactus in a desert motif.

"There it is." Unit 14A sat on the ground floor; 14B was a second-story unit above.

"So what do you think we should do?" Sarah asked in quiet tones, her nerves kicking up.

"Let's try knocking." Jackson took her hand and started for the door. "Maybe someone's home."

It seemed obvious, but there was no way

to know what Andrew might have been doing with the condo or who might be inside. They walked the cement path, climbing an occasional wide step, then up the stairs to the covered front porch. Jackson rang the doorbell, but neither of them actually expected anyone to come to the door.

No one did.

"Let's go round back," Jackson suggested, "see if we can find a way in without being seen."

There was a walkway between each four-unit complex. They passed the single-car garage marked 14A, went round to the back and saw a door that went into the garage from the rear. Jackson tried the door but it was locked. They continued to a glass sliding door that led out onto a small patio. Jackson walked over, lifted and jerked, and an instant later, the glass door was slightly off its track and moving backward, creating an opening big enough for them to slip through.

She flicked him a glance. "A man with hidden talents."

His mouth edged up. "A trick I learned in my misguided youth."

The condo looked surprisingly clean — too clean. No dust on the countertops or the small kitchen table, and there were freshly washed dishes in the sink.

"Anybody home?" Jackson called out.

A movement in the doorway alerted them. "Don't move or I'll shoot!" A flashy blonde pointed a gun straight at Jackson. Though the woman held it arms out in front of her, her hands were shaking and it was clear she had no idea how to properly use the weapon. Which made her even more dangerous.

"Take it easy," Jackson soothed. "We didn't think anyone was home."

She was wearing very short white shorts and a black-and-white halter top — and she looked really good in them. She was perfectly tanned, had long blond hair, and she was extremely pretty.

A light went on in Sarah's head. "You must be Mitzy," she said, certain she was right. All of Andrew's women looked pretty much the same. Sarah was amazed he had ever been attracted to *her.* But then, apparently her late husband was one of those men who wanted a lady in the living room and a whore in the bedroom — literally.

Sarah forced herself to smile. "I'm Andrew's wife, Sarah."

The gun wavered. "You're . . . you're Sarah?"

"Put the gun down, Mitzy," Jackson said

with firm command. "We didn't come here to hurt you."

She tipped her head toward Jackson, but didn't lower the weapon. "Who's he?"

"His name is Jackson Raines. He's a friend. We came here to find a disk Andrew had." She caught the fear that flashed in Mitzy's blue eyes. "I think maybe Marty Kozak thought you had it. Is that the reason you're hiding out here?"

Mitzy cautiously lowered the pistol, and Jackson reached out and took it gently from her hand.

"I — I told him I didn't have the disk but he didn't believe me. I was afraid of what he might do. I had a key to the condo so I came here." So this was Andrew's little love nest, a place he came with his mistress-of-the-moment. "Andrew said no one knew about the place. He said he paid cash for it a long time ago."

Andrew actually owned something he hadn't mortgaged to the hilt? *Amazing.*

"You won't say anything, will you? You won't tell Mr. Kozak I'm here?"

"We won't say anything," Sarah promised.

Jackson held out a slip of paper with the numbers twenty-eighty, thirty-two, eight printed on it. "We just need to figure out what this means. It's probably the combination to a lock of some kind. Is there a safe or a storage room around here?"

"There's a safe in the back of Andrew's closet. I don't think he used it much. At least I never saw him. I found it when I was hanging up some of my clothes."

Some clothes turned out to be a boatload, two closets full — expensive designer dresses, slacks, shoes and purses that Andrew must have bought her.

Sarah couldn't help wondering what price, beyond the use of her incredible body, Mitzy had paid for them. One thing Sarah knew — if Andrew hadn't beat her for some imagined transgression, sooner or later he would have.

She fought to control the shudder that filtered through her body.

"Here it is." Mitzy shoved aside some of the clothes on the rod. "Behind my suit."

A lovely white Chanel. Of course, in the beginning, Andrew had bought Sarah clothes with those same expensive labels. In the past few years, she hadn't wanted them, hadn't wanted anything that came from him.

"All right, let's give it a try." Jackson moved past Mitzy. So far, he hadn't seemed to notice her gorgeous face and amazing body. Or maybe he was just more subtle than most men.

He turned the dial slowly, carefully working the tumblers into place. He must have missed a number on the first try because it didn't open. He started over, went round again, back and then forward, and *click.* The combination fell into place. Jackson turned the handle and the small safe slowly opened.

Sarah leaned forward to peer inside. "It's empty," she said, not sure if she was disappointed or relieved.

Then Jackson reached into the shadows and pulled out three narrow colored envelopes. The words *Varig Airlines* were printed on the front.

"Looks like he was planning a trip."

Sarah felt a rush of nausea. "H-he talked about it. He threatened to move us all to Rio. I told him I wouldn't go — that I wouldn't let him take Holly. We fought about it."

She looked away. They'd fought, all right. A scene that had ended with Sarah's nose bloodied and her lip split. Like most of their arguments, they happened late in the evening — downstairs in his study where he demanded her presence — long after Holly had been put to bed upstairs.

"Looks like he expected you to give in, sooner or later."

She swallowed. They had argued about it again that last night.

"I'm going," Andrew had said. *"You want to stay here, fine with me, but I'm leaving the country and I'm taking Holly with me."*

She closed her eyes to block out the rest of the ugly scene. She refused to let her mind stray past the moment when he had risen from behind his desk and started toward her, when she had felt the awful, sickening fear.

Jackson's arm went around her, steadying her. "You okay?"

"Yes, I . . . I just wish we'd found the disk."

But they hadn't, and there was no telling what Kozak might do.

"Do you think he'll give up?" Mitzy asked.

"I hope so," Sarah said.

"Sooner or later, he'll quit looking," Jackson said. "And we're still working on a couple of things that might help. Odds are he'll eventually figure the disk is lost and therefore no longer a threat."

Sarah made no reply. They were still trying to find out why Andrew had been blackmailing Kozak. If they could find the answer, they would have a bargaining chip to use against him.

She thought of Kozak and Andrew and

her mind returned to the airline tickets Jackson held in his hand. She couldn't help wondering what would have happened when she had finally convinced Andrew she wasn't going with him. Would he have forced Holly to go, changed her ticket into Mitzy's name and taken his mistress to Rio instead?

Or would he have simply taken Holly and made Sarah disappear?

FOURTEEN

They were almost home. Sarah's anticipation built as Jackson's Ford pickup rolled toward the ranch. The minute the truck pulled up in front of the sprawling two-story ranch house, Holly rushed out to great them.

"Mama! Mom!"

Her daughter was growing up. She was *Mom* now. Holly hadn't called Sarah *Mommy* since a few weeks after their arrival in Wyoming.

"Hi, baby." Sarah lifted her up and propped her against her hip. "Good heavens, I think you must have grown a bunch since I left town."

Holly giggled. "Just like Rags. He gets bigger every day." She turned. "You should see him, Jackson — I think he's gonna be really big."

"Well, maybe not too big," Jackson said, running a hand over the top of her small blond head. "Maybe just right."

Holly grinned up at him. "I'm glad you're back."

"Me, too," he said.

Sarah returned Holly to her feet and the little girl took hold of Sarah's hand. "Come on, Mom. I wanna show you Midnight. She is so cool."

"I need to take my stuff inside, then we can go down to the barn and you can show me."

"I'll take your luggage inside," Jackson offered. "You can unpack when you're finished."

He was always so thoughtful. She wished it didn't make her so nervous. She wished *he* didn't make her so nervous. Then again, maybe *nervous* wasn't the right word. She flicked him a glance, caught the heat in his dark eyes he was usually so careful to hide, and her stomach contracted. He was back in his jeans and boots and looking so damned sexy her thoughts strayed to the bedroom and she blushed.

She turned her attention to her daughter, a thread of worry filtering through her. They were home, back in Wyoming, but nothing had changed. Marty Kozak still posed a threat to her and Holly.

And Sarah still wanted Jackson Raines.

■ ■ ■ ■

"Welcome home." Livvy's robust figure stood in the kitchen when Jackson walked into the house towing his black, wheeled, carry-on bag behind him.

"It's good to be back."

"Did you get things straightened out for Sarah?"

"We're still working on it."

Livvy moved toward the sink, spatula in hand. "Your brother, Dev, called this morning. He's back in Scottsdale. I told him you'd call him when you got in."

He nodded, started toward his study, stopped and looked back. "Thanks for taking care of Holly."

Livvy smiled, stretching her double chins. "She wasn't a bit of trouble. That little girl is a treasure. She can stay with me anytime." Livvy had wanted kids when she married, he knew, but somehow it just never happened. Jackson thought Olivia Jones was also a treasure, and he was damned glad to have her there on the ranch.

"She's going to be a real heartbreaker," he said. *Just like her mother,* popped into his head. He forced the old uncertainties away and continued along the hall, went into his office, and over to his big oak desk. Picking up the telephone, he dialed his brother's home number.

"Ey, *muchacho* — how was Mexico?"

"Hot." Dev chuckled. "In more ways than one."

"Yeah, well, I hope your mind's back on business because I'm going to need a favor."

"Seems like I've heard that one before."

"True — and it probably won't be the last time."

Dev's smile reached into the phone. "This still about Sarah Allen?"

"We just got back from L.A. Went to look for the missing disk."

"I guess you didn't find it."

"Not yet."

"Why don't you bring me up to speed on this thing?"

So he did, telling his brother about the break-in at Sarah's grandmother's house before they'd left Wyoming that had put the old woman in the hospital, about the threats Sarah had received from the dark-skinned man in town, his run-in with Jose Delgado and that Delgado had a partner named Billy Hinman.

"Looks like Andrew Hollister was blackmailing Martin Kozak," he said. "We're trying to find out why."

"You're looking for leverage."

"That's about it."

"In a situation like this, leverage can be a very good thing."

"Kozak is big-time in heavy construction, builds highways and bridges, that kind of thing. Currently he's working on an overpass on Highway 91, leased the equipment from one of Hollister's companies. Could be he's cutting corners, using substandard material or something. The inspector on the project is a guy named Vernon Rimmer. I need to know if Rimmer's on the take. Any chance you can find that out?"

"Maybe. Sounds like you two have been doing your homework."

"Unfortunately, we've pretty much reached a dead end — unless you can help."

"Let me see what I can do. I'll get back to you as soon as I know something."

"Thanks, bro."

"No problem." Dev rang off, and Jackson felt a sense of relief. His brother was good. *Very good.* If they could find out what Kozak was doing, they could insure he left Sarah and Holly alone.

Jackson checked his messages, returned a couple of calls, then left the study and went out to find Jimmy Threebears. The spring branding was done, so it wasn't as busy as it had been a few weeks back, but they were moving cattle to graze different pastures and there were always fences to mend, along with just keeping track of the animals' general welfare.

He found Jimmy out in the barn, stacking some of last year's hay to make room for this summer's crop. They had weed sprayed last year and fertilized this spring so the grass was growing tall and thick, and rich in nutrients.

"Hey, boss!" Jimmy strode toward him, his long legs eating up the ground between them. "How'd it go in L.A.?"

"Not as well as I'd hoped. Dev's looking into a couple of things for me. We'll see what he comes up with. Everything okay here?"

"We could use a little rain. Weather's been pretty warm for this early in the year. Ground gets too dry, we're gonna have a problem with fires."

Jackson nodded. In the past few years, what had rarely been a problem had become a very big one. Drought and forest fires were a huge concern. And having a logging operation creating sparks with their heavy machinery could make the situation even worse.

"I guess we'd better pray for rain."

Jimmy grinned. "I'll talk to Dennis Redhorse, see what he can do."

Redhorse was the local tribal medicine man, or at least his grandfather had been. Dennis was doing his best to follow in the old man's footsteps. Unfortunately, in these modern times, a lot of the old ways were lost as they passed from one generation to the next.

Jackson just smiled. "You do that."

He looked over Jimmy's shoulder to a door leading out to the corral. Sarah sat on the fence while Sam led the little black pony, Midnight, around the ring — Holly riding in the pony saddle. A few feet away, Gibby added an occasional instruction.

"She's been doing real good," Jimmy said. "Sam's done a great job of teaching her."

Jackson watched the way Holly held the reins just like Sam told her, not too tight and not too loose, and felt the pull of a smile. She was the sweetest little girl, exactly the sort he'd want if he ever had a kid.

His gaze drifted to Sarah. The sun was gleaming on her heavy chestnut hair, highlighting fine strands of red and making her skin glow. She smiled as she watched her daughter on the pony. The soft, full lips he remembered so well curved up at the corners, and inside his jeans he went hard.

Damn. He reminded himself to stay away from her, as he had done last night and the night before that. He wanted to give her some breathing room, some time to consider what might lie ahead for them.

He wanted some time to consider those things himself.

But time wasn't going to change the hot desire he felt whenever he looked at her. Or whenever she looked at him — the way she was now.

The air seemed to heat and thicken between them. Sexual awareness crackled like invisible lightning around them. He knew she felt it, knew she fought it, just as he did, but it only made the wanting worse.

She jerked her gaze away, off toward the lane leading from the main road into the ranch. Jackson turned to see a plain brown sedan driving up the lane, pulling to a stop in front of the cottage. Two men in dark suits got out and started toward the front porch.

"I guess I better go see what they want," Sarah said, but she didn't look happy about it.

"I'll go with you."

Sarah seemed relieved. "Thanks." When they reached the cottage, she paused at the bottom of the wooden steps and looked at the men on the porch. "May I help you?"

"FBI. We need to speak to you, Mrs. Hollister — in private."

Her cheeks paled. "Could I please see your credentials?"

The men pulled out their IDs and flipped them open and Sarah climbed the steps to examine them. Jackson joined her.

"Can we go inside?" one of the agents asked, older than the other, maybe forty-five, his blond hair sparse.

"What is this in regard to?"

"As you know, your late husband was being investigated for tax evasion. We need to ask you some questions."

Sarah's head jerked up. "I — I don't know anything about an investigation. I had no idea."

Dev had mentioned it. Jackson knew the Feds had been after Hollister, but clearly Sarah didn't know.

He could see she was fighting for composure. "I'm Jackson Raines," he said to give her the time she needed. "I own Raintree Ranch."

"I'm Special Agent Lee Brooker," the blond man said. "This is Special Agent Matt Davis." Davis was tall, African-American, the shoulders of his dark brown sport coat snug over a solidly muscled frame.

"Mr. Raines is a friend," Sarah said as the men shook hands. "He'll be coming inside with me. We can speak in the kitchen."

Sarah led them into the house and they all sat down at the old oak table in front of the kitchen window. She didn't offer them refreshment, just went straight to the point. "You've come quite a distance to see me. What is it you need to know?"

Jackson didn't miss the slight tremor in her voice.

Brooker began the conversation. "As I said, your husband was under investigation for tax evasion. Since you signed on the return, so are you."

"But that . . . that isn't possible. I didn't know anything about Andrew's business. I don't even know how much he paid in taxes."

"Not enough," Matt Davis drawled, a slight Texas twang in his voice. "We figure, even if no criminal charges are filed against you, with interest and penalties, you'll owe somewhere around five million dollars."

Sarah's shoulders drooped. Her complexion had faded to the color of sand. "Andrew left me virtually penniless. I couldn't possibly pay that kind of money."

"Which you gentlemen undoubtedly know," Jackson put in. "So why are you really here?"

Brooker flicked him a look of respect, then returned his attention to Sarah. "We think your husband was blackmailing someone, maybe several someones. Whoever it was is involved in illegal activities on a very large scale. We want to know who it is and what they were doing."

Sarah swallowed. "As I said, I don't know anything about . . . about Andrew's business dealings. I'm afraid I can't help you."

"Word is your husband kept a record," Brooker continued, "probably burned onto a computer disk. It's got the names of the people he dealt with and a record of their illegal endeavors. He was trying to sell that information back to them."

"Extorting them for money," Jackson said, which they already knew.

"That's right."

"What does that have to do with me?" Sarah asked.

"From the information we've uncovered, we believe the people he was blackmailing are trying to find the disk. We think they'll contact you — if they haven't already. They won't feel safe until the information is returned to them."

"Andrew's been dead for months. Why

would they wait until now to go after the disk?"

"Probably waiting for things to cool down," Davis drawled. "Hollister was murdered. There was a police investigation. By now, enough time has passed for them to crawl out from whatever rock they were under."

"Well, I don't have it," Sarah said, "and I have no idea where to find it."

Brooker's voice softened. "We need to know who these men are, Mrs. Hollister. We want to know what they were doing and we want proof. In other words — we need the information on that disk."

"And in return," Jackson added, "you'll see that Sarah is cleared of any responsibility for Andrew Hollister's tax problems."

Brooker smiled. "That's about it."

Sarah looked sick. "I'm not a detective. I'm a mother trying to raise a child. I have no idea how to go about this kind of thing."

Brooker looked directly at Jackson. "Maybe not, but I have a feeling your friend here may be able to help you."

Sarah flicked a glance at Jackson. "But I don't know what to do. I haven't the slightest —"

"To start with," Brooker interrupted, "keep us informed. Let us know when someone contacts you. And try to figure out where your husband hid that information."

Sarah made no reply. She had wisely made no mention of their trip to L.A. or that Martin Kozak had already been pressing her for the disk.

"Sarah needs time to think this through," Jackson said, "see how she might be able to help you." They needed time, all right. Time to figure out what the hell to do.

The men rose from their chairs around the table. "You've got three days, Mrs. Hollister. We'll expect to hear from you by then."

"It's Allen," she belatedly corrected. "My name is Sarah Allen."

The men ignored her. "If you hear from someone or need our help in any way, call this number." Brooker handed her a white business card. "Be sure the line is secure. We wouldn't want Andrew's *friends* to know what you're up to. In fact, there's a very good chance that disk of his is the reason he wound up dead."

Jackson walked the men to the door, then returned to the kitchen. Sarah stood pale and shaken next to the sink.

"What . . . what am I going to do?" Her eyes slowly filled with tears. "I don't know how to catch a criminal."

She didn't resist when Jackson eased her gently into his arms, just rested her head on his shoulder. "You're going to do exactly what we were doing already. To begin with, we're going to find out why Andrew was blackmailing Marty Kozak. We just need the leverage we were after a little bit more."

"Is this ever going to end, Jackson?"

His chest tightened at the fear he heard in her voice. "We'll make it end, Sarah. I promise you, we'll find a way."

In that moment he realized he would do anything to keep Sarah safe.

And that was the moment he knew he was in trouble.

FIFTEEN

June in the mountains, wildflowers bloom-ing in fields so green it made your eyes hurt, while blinding-white snow still crowned the tops of the surrounding peaks. In the early mornings, the pasture was alive with deer.

It was tempting to stay home and simply absorb the beauty of a late Wyoming spring, watch the tiny striped chipmunks frolic on the porch.

Instead, Sarah went to work. After her visit from the FBI, Jackson convinced her that until they heard something from his brother, or Marty Kozak contacted her again, there was nothing more they could do.

"We just have to wait," he had said. "Dev will call as soon as he knows anything. Three days from now, you'll call the Feds and tell them you're willing to cooperate. That'll buy us a little more time."

"Maybe I should just tell them it's Kozak. That Marty's the guy Andrew was blackmailing."

"We still don't know why, and there may be others. You tell them about Kozak, they'll want more. We need to hold them off for as long as we can."

"All right, we wait, but in the meantime, we need to live our lives. That means I go to work and you go run your ranch."

He frowned. "If you go into town, you might be putting yourself in danger."

"I don't think Kozak is going to hurt me — not as long as he thinks there's a chance I'll get him that disk."

"Maybe. But I still don't like —"

"I need this job, Jackson. I've got a daughter to support. Besides, I enjoy what I'm doing. I've always wanted to be a writer. Someday I'd like to write a book, but for now being a reporter is enough. I'm doing what I love and I'm not going to let anyone — including Andrew's crooked *friends* — screw things up."

Jackson walked to the door, lifted his battered straw hat off the rack beside it and settled it low on his forehead. He turned to face her. "All right, if you're that determined, I guess I can't stop you. But let's get you a cell phone that works so at least we can stay in touch."

"Good idea. And I want to get internet

service. If I have to use dial-up, it's better than nothing."

He grinned. "DSL. I paid to have a line brought in from the road. It was worth it."

And so Sarah signed up with Qwest for internet and cell service. That Monday morning, she dropped Holly off at day care and went to work.

"Welcome back, stranger." That from Mike Stevens, the tall, sandy-haired reporter who worked with her at the paper. Except for the creak of the old wooden floors as she walked to her desk, the place was quiet.

"It's good to be back." She glanced around, saw that she and Mike were the only ones in the office.

"Smiley's out of town," Mike explained. "Myra isn't due in until this afternoon."

Myra Cunningham, the part-time receptionist, bookkeeper and head of the advertising section, was an older, no-nonsense, curly-haired blonde with a ready smile and an easy disposition. She and Smiley were an item, which everyone knew, though they tried to pretend it was a secret.

Sarah plunked her oversize bag down on top of her desk. "So what's been going on in town? Anything exciting?"

"Well, we had some big news day before yesterday. Bob Springer's teenage boy,

Teddy, stole his old man's car and went for a joyride with his girlfriend. Bob thought the car had really been stolen so he called the sheriff. Kid was picked up and taken to jail. Bob was so mad he left the boy there overnight."

"Might be an interesting family angle for a follow-up article."

"Yeah, if you can get the Springers to talk to you. I think it shook 'em up pretty good — their perfect, never-do-anything-wrong son arrested for stealing a car."

"Well, it was the family car, not someone else's."

"Bob and Susan didn't see it that way. Ted isn't old enough to drive. He could have killed someone."

"Or been killed himself. I'll talk to them, see if it leads anywhere."

Mike nodded. "Umm . . . by the way . . . I've been wondering . . . any chance you might let me take you out to supper sometime? Food at the Sheepherder's Inn isn't too bad. Tonight they've got prime rib."

Sarah nervously moistened her lips. The Inn was the only steakhouse around, a ten-minute drive down the road to Sheep River. It wasn't the invitation that bothered her. It was that the invitation forced her to consider her relationship with Jackson. She wondered what he would say if she accepted a date with a good-looking younger man.

"So what do you think?" Mike pressed. His tenacity was the reason he made a good reporter. She just didn't want it used on her.

"I appreciate the thought, Mike. I really do. But things are kind of up in the air right now, and I'm just not ready for that kind of thing."

"That kind of thing? Dinner, you mean? You have to eat, you know."

"Yes, but —"

"Yes, but not unless the guy asking you happens to be Jackson Raines."

Heat rushed into her cheeks. She hadn't realized her feelings were so transparent. She had no idea exactly what his feelings for her were or what hers were for him, but the truth was, he was the man she wanted to be with and if she started dating other men, he would likely start dating other women — a thought that didn't sit well.

Of course he might do that anyway. He was a man, wasn't he? Still . . .

"As I said, I appreciate the invitation . . ."

"No problem. Maybe lunch sometime — just to go over some story ideas."

She smiled. "Maybe. I could sure use the help."

Mike wandered back to his desk and Sarah went to work. She read each edition of the paper she had missed while she was away, searching for something that might develop into a human-interest story.

She found it on page three of yesterday's paper — among the foreclosure notices.

She recognized the name of the property and the borrower who had defaulted on the loan. She and Cody Ballard had gone to high school together. Cody was the son of an old-time ranching family. Apparently his father had died and Cody had inherited the Three Forks Ranch, which, like a lot of other property, seemed to have fallen on hard times.

With all the foreclosures going on in the country, there was a great deal of interest in the subject. She might be able to do a story on what happened when a lender called a loan and include information on the unfortunate lending practices that had cost a number of people their homes. She wondered if that was the kind of thing that had happened with the Three Forks Ranch.

She drove out the following morning, hoping for an interview with Cody and his wife, Marilyn. Cody was working in the hay field with their two sons, Mark and Patrick, but Marilyn was more than eager to talk.

"We had a couple bad years in a row," she said. A slender woman at least five years younger than Sarah, with long brown hair pulled back in a ponytail, the calluses on her hands said that she was a rancher's wife.

"We saw this ad on TV," she continued, "how you could consolidate your debts, you know, with an equity loan? We thought three years was plenty of time to get things straightened out. Now the loan is due and our credit's not good enough to get another one. We just don't know what we're going to do." Tears rushed into her eyes and she glanced away.

Sarah handed her a Kleenex, which she used to blot her cheeks and blow her nose.

"It's too soon to give up," Sarah said, her heart going out to the young couple. "Maybe something will come along, some way to get an extension or something."

It was so easy to get sucked into a loan that could wind up ruining you. Years ago, Andrew had gotten involved with a loan shark to pay off some of his gambling debts. He had managed to extricate himself before the leg-breaking started, though Sarah had no idea how he had done it.

Maybe he had used one of his blackmail schemes to raise the money.

"There's so much of this kind of thing

221

happening," she said. "Let me look into it, see if there are any resources for you to use."

Sarah wound up the interview, and they walked together to the door. Marilyn reached out and took hold of her hand. "Thank you, Sarah. Even if things don't work out, I appreciate your trying to help."

Sarah left feeling terrible for the Ballard family but good about a story that would give her a chance to make people aware of the dangers involved when you went into a mortgage without completely understanding the consequences. She would also talk to Jackson, see if he knew any way the Ballards might be able to hang on to the family ranch.

Returning to the office, she worked on the article the rest of the afternoon, using the computer to dig up information on mortgage companies and the problems in the subprime market. As soon as she finished, she grabbed her briefcase and was just leaving the office when the phone rang. She recognized the voice though it didn't hold the least trace of an accent — the dark-skinned, foreign-looking man who had accosted her in the parking lot.

"How was your trip?" he asked amiably, his pleasant words in contrast with the underlying tension in his voice.

"How did you —"

"We know you went to Los Angeles with your cowboy, Sarah."

"You — you followed us?"

"We didn't need to. We want that disk. We need you to get it for us and we have every confidence you will."

She swallowed, took a slow breath, determined not to let him intimidate her. "Then you'll be happy to know you're right. I'm doing everything in my power to find it. When I do, you'll be the first to know."

"I believe you, Sarah. You're trying. The problem is we need you to try a little harder."

"Who are you working for? Kozak?"

"Just get me that disk." The line went dead. For a few more seconds, Sarah held the phone against her ear. On a shuddering breath, she closed the phone and dropped it into her purse.

She told herself she wasn't frightened. She was getting used to being accosted, to people threatening her. After Andrew, she could handle it, she told herself. After Andrew, she could handle anything.

But she had Holly to think of.

She was going to speak to Jackson, see how he would feel about letting her hire Livvy to take care of Holly whenever she went to the office.

She trusted Livvy completely and Holly would be safe at the ranch. As she left the building and walked to where her car was parked in the lot, she found herself glancing over her shoulder, looking to see if someone was watching.

She wasn't as frightened this time, she told herself again.

But something warned her that might just be a mistake.

Sarah didn't tell Jackson about the phone call. She knew he would try to talk her out of going to work, and though she could do some of her work from the house, her job demanded she come into town. And so she spoke to Livvy — who refused to take money for watching Holly, until Sarah refused to leave her unless she did.

A deal was struck.

Holly stayed safe at the ranch and Sarah went to work.

The rest of the week was uneventful. On Friday, Sarah's article about the Three Forks Ranch foreclosure came out in the newspaper and several people called to congratulate her on writing a story of such importance to the community.

Jackson was one of them. "I didn't know

about the foreclosure till I saw your article in the paper. I'll call Cody, find out the amount of the loan. If Cody will sell me that triangular piece that abuts my property for a fair price, I'll see he gets a new loan on the rest of the property — at a reasonable rate, due in a reasonable period of time."

Sarah's heart warmed. "I was going to talk to you about it this weekend. I was hoping you might come up with some way to help."

"I'll call Ballard. See if we can work something out."

Sarah smiled into the phone. "I'm sure he'll be interested. I think he'd do just about anything to save his family's ranch."

Sarah rang off, thinking of Jackson and how different he seemed from Andrew, whose thoughts revolved mostly around himself.

Saturday came. Since she mostly set her own hours, she rarely worked weekends. Sarah stood at the window of the cottage watching her daughter race down the steps and off toward the corral, Rags trailing along in her wake. Holly loved it here in Wyoming. She was blossoming in the warm sun and clear mountain air. Sarah smiled, thinking what a good decision she had made in leaving the city.

If only she could find a way to solve the multitude of problems Andrew had left her.

Giving in to a sigh, she turned away from the window, meaning to finish her house-cleaning, but stopped as she spotted a compact silver car driving toward the cottage. For an instant her nerves kicked in, then the car pulled to a halt, the engine went still, and Nan Hargrove climbed out of the car, long red hair flashing in the brilliant morning sun.

Nan pulled a potted plant out of the backseat and walked toward the front porch steps as Sarah hurried to open the door.

"Nan! Come in!"

"Welcome home." Nan handed her the plant, a lovely blooming lilac. "It's a little late in coming, but as they say, better late than never. I figured you could find a place to plant it."

Sarah carried the lilac inside, set it on the coffee table, turned and gave Nan a hug. "It's wonderful. And it smells so good. You didn't have to buy it, but I love it."

"I hoped you would."

"I've been meaning to call you. Things have just been so hectic time slipped away."

"That's okay. You're just getting settled. Eventually things will calm down." She glanced around the living room, at the mismatched sofa and chairs that replaced the ones destroyed by Kozak's goons.

"Jackson ordered some new furniture. It's due in any day."

"That's nice, but the place is already starting to look like home. I like the hooked rug and the old kerosene lamps."

"Jackson found them in the top of the barn."

"You were always good at decorating. I remember your bedroom when we were kids. The whole place was done in pink and white. You had a pink-and-white-striped dust ruffle and a matching pink comforter on the bed. You even painted pink flowers on the old antique mirror above your dresser. I loved that room. It was so *girlie*."

Sarah laughed. "It was, wasn't it?" She ignored a bittersweet pang at the memory of the happy days when her parents were still alive.

Nan walked over to the window, looked out to where Jackson and Jimmy Threebears were working. They had the hood up on one of the older ranch pickups, which apparently had broken down.

"How are things going with Jackson?" Nan asked.

Something warm unfurled inside her at the mention of his name. Oh, boy, was she in trouble. "Jackson's a very nice man. He's been a good friend."

Nan's dark red eyebrows went up. "*A very nice man?* Girl, have you lost your mind? This is Jackson Raines we're talking about. Mr. Tall-Dark-and-Handsome? He's one of the sexiest men on the planet. Tell me you just think of him as a friend."

She flushed and glanced away. "All right, so maybe it's a little more than friendship." *Like spending hours in bed with him and wishing they could make love again.* "But I don't think either one of us knows where it's going." She noticed Nan hadn't turned away from the window, but seemed to be watching Jimmy, not Jackson.

"What about you? Any new men in your life?"

Nan turned and Sarah caught a flash of sadness in her eyes. "I went out with Jimmy Threebears. It was pretty much a disaster."

"A disaster? Really? Why?"

Nan blew out a breath. "Because — like half the men in Wind Canyon — Jim thinks I'm a slut."

"But that's crazy. Why on earth would he think that?"

Nan walked over and sank down on the sofa. "For a while after Ron and I got divorced, I kind of was." She smoothed a wrinkle in one of the sofa cushions. "I hung out at the Canyon Club — you know, that place out on the Sheep River highway?"

"I remember it."

"When I'd get lonely, I'd go out there. Sometimes I'd pick up a guy. I saw Jim there a couple of times. The night we went out, he pressed me for sex. When I said no, he said I put out for every other guy, why not him?"

"Lord, Nan, what did you do?"

"I slapped his face and made him take me home." She looked up and tears sprang into her eyes. "I wanted to tell him I'm not like that anymore — not for years. That I never really was that way. I didn't, of course."

"Oh, Nan."

"I've wanted to go out with him forever. I really wanted him to like me."

Sarah sat down beside her, leaned over and gave her a hug. "People make mistakes. Nobody's perfect — not even Jimmy Three-bears. Jimmy doesn't deserve you. You keep that in mind."

Nan smiled wanly. "I didn't mean to get into that. I almost didn't drive out because I was afraid I'd see him."

"Forget him. Come on in the kitchen and I'll make us a nice cup of tea."

And so she did, and they sat together

drinking Earl Grey and enjoying the pretty view outside the kitchen window, watching a fat gray squirrel foraging food from beneath a pine tree.

But long after Nan left, Sarah thought of Jimmy Threebears and the way he had treated her friend. She never would have expected Jimmy to behave so disrespectfully to a woman.

Which only went to prove how careful a woman had to be.

Sixteen

Jackson was flat-out tired. Tired of waiting for his brother to call, tired of worrying about Sarah and little Holly. Tired of waiting for Sarah to give in to her desire and invite him back into her bed.

He couldn't do much about his brother, or the problems with Marty Kozak. But he could do something about Sarah.

Saddling Galahad, a big sorrel quarter horse gelding he favored, and a paint mare named Daisy he trusted for Sarah, he led the animals toward the cottage. Holly and her puppy were playing with Sam and Giddy and their dogs out in front of the barn so he knew Sarah was home alone. Before he left the house, he'd asked Livvy to keep an eye on the little girl so Sarah wouldn't worry.

Arriving at the cottage, Jackson tied the horses to the railing in front of the flower bed, climbed the wooden steps and knocked on her door. Another quick knock and Sarah pulled it open.

"Jackson. Hi."

His gaze ran over her feminine features, pretty blue eyes and luscious curves, and the blood began to settle in his groin. Since it was far too soon for that kind of thinking, he clamped down on the heat burning through him and smiled.

"You're wearing jeans. Great, you won't have to change." He grabbed her hand. "It's too nice a day to stay in the house. Come on, we're going for a ride."

"Wait a minute —"

"Holly's with Sam and Gibby, and Livvy's keeping an eye on them."

She continued to resist, pulling against his hand, then she spotted the little paint mare. "That isn't fair. She's too pretty to resist."

"That was my plan."

"I haven't ridden in ages." But he could feel her eagerness as he led her toward the horse. "Not since I left Wyoming. I don't know if I remember how."

"It'll come back to you. It's the same as riding a bicycle — once you know how, you never forget."

She cast him a not-so-certain glance. "I hope you're right."

He led her over to the paint — brown and

white, small, well-shaped head and nice markings. "Sarah, meet Daisy. She's got a good rein and she's very sweet tempered."

Sarah scratched Daisy between the ears. "Aren't you a sweet girl?" The mare nickered softly and leaned into her hand.

"See, she likes you already."

And from the adoration on Sarah's face, the feeling was mutual. Jackson swung her up in the saddle, took a moment to check the stirrup length, saw that he'd guessed about right. She was wearing the same white sneakers she usually wore and he made a mental note to take her into the mercantile and buy her a pair of boots.

Sarah settled deeper in the saddle and took hold of the reins, placing them correctly in her left hand. She rode Daisy in a small circle, just to get the feel of the horse, and it was clear she hadn't forgotten much of anything. It was hard to live in a small, rural town in Wyoming and not know how to ride.

"Where are we going?"

"Up to the top of the ridge. I need to check on those loggers, make sure they aren't causing any trouble." And it was a beautiful ride up an easy, meandering trail. Livvy had packed a picnic lunch, and there were nice places along the way where they could stop to eat.

"Ready?"

"As I'm ever going to be."

The kids had disappeared inside the barn. Jackson led Sarah out a dirt road that followed the creek, then they branched off up the trail.

The path started up steeply.

"Jackson?" There was a hint of nervousness in Sarah's voice.

"It's only a little way to the top of the rise, then it's a gentle climb the rest of the trip. Just give Daisy her head and hang on."

Sarah handled the climb like an expert and pulled the little mare to a halt behind Galahad under a canopy of trees. She looked at him and grinned. "I forgot how much fun this is."

He smiled back at her, thinking how pretty she looked in the dappled sunlight filtering down through the branches. A rush of wanting hit him that had nothing to do with sex, then the familiar throb of desire settled deep in his loins.

The woman was in his blood, had been since he was a boy. It was a worrisome thought; one, for the moment, he chose to ignore.

The trail continued, passing grand vistas of green-grass valley below and craggy mountains in the distance where a hawk soared over the treetops. The path wound into deep, old-growth forests, and the scent of cedar and pine filled the air. Saddle leather creaked beneath him and a thick mat of needles muffled the clop of the horses' hooves.

An hour into the ride, Jackson pulled Galahad to a halt in a quiet little meadow next to a bubbling stream.

"Livvy packed us a picnic lunch." Swinging down from the saddle, he slung a rope around Galahad's neck, pulled off the bridle and tied the horse up to graze. He dragged a blanket out of his saddlebag and whipped it open on the grass then walked back to where Sarah sat on Daisy.

She was staring at the rocky, snowcapped peaks as if she had never really seen them. "Oh, Jackson, this is wonderful! Thank you so much for bringing me."

"My pleasure." He refused to let the thought linger, just slipped a rope around the little mare's neck, took off Daisy's bridle and tied her to the nearest tree. Reaching up, he lifted Sarah off the saddle, holding her so close she slid down his body as he set her on her feet.

He was hard and he let her know it. Her eyes found his and he felt the thrum of her pulse speeding into a faster gear. He kept his hands at her waist, though he wanted to move them higher, wanted to cup those sweet breasts he remembered so well.

"Livvy made us sandwiches." His voice came out gruff since his mind was not on food.

Sarah reached up and touched his face. He could read the uncertainty, knew the instant she made her decision. "Let's eat later." Twining her arms around his neck, she went up on her toes and kissed him. Her soft curves melted against him and Jackson groaned.

Damn, he wanted her.

His tongue found its way into her mouth, and she sucked on it, tangled her own tongue with his and pressed herself more fully against him. Desire slammed through him like a heavyweight punch, set off a roaring in his ears and a pounding in his blood.

Sweet Jesus. His hands found her breasts, just the way he had imagined. He palmed them, cupped them over the crisp white blouse she wore with her jeans. He told himself to go slow, but when Sarah deepened the kiss, when it turned hot and fierce, any thought of a slow, easy loving evaporated like water on a heated stone. Jackson drove his hands into her heavy hair and tilted her head back to lay claim to what was his.

Sarah couldn't think. She could barely breathe. Jackson kissed her wildly, a deep, slick kiss that fired the fever burning through her blood. She wanted this, wanted him. There was no use denying it. Jerking the snaps open on the front of his Western shirt, she ran her palms over his magnificent chest, felt the slabs of muscle tighten, felt the roughness of his curly, dark chest hair, felt his erection leap against the zipper of his jeans.

She leaned toward him, pressed her lips against a flat copper nipple, and the last of his control seemed to snap.

"I want you," he said, cupping her face between his hands. "God, I want you so damned much." Dragging her mouth back to his, he plunged his tongue inside. He walked her backward till they reached the blanket, then lowered her to the ground and came down on top of her.

Long, deep kisses followed. Wet, openmouthed kisses as he unfastened her bra then clamped his lips over a rigid nipple. He sucked until he had her moaning, stopped only long enough to tug off her sneakers, unzip her jeans and drag them down her legs. He pulled them off and his hot gaze devoured her, snagged on the little blue thong panties that barely covered the dark brown curls above her sex.

Sarah reached for him, her hands trembling as she unzipped his jeans, urging him to take them off. "I want to see you. I want to touch you, Jackson."

He clenched his jaw as if he were in pain. He was naked in an instant — boots, jeans and shirt all gone. Slabs of muscle tightened across his chest as he moved, spreading her legs, positioning himself above her.

He didn't wait, and Sarah didn't want him to, just parted her softness and found the entrance to her passage, began to ease his powerful erection inside. She was wet and slick and as the penetration deepened, the pleasure was so intense she started to come.

Sarah bit back a cry as ripples of sweetness washed over her and her body tightened around his hardened length.

Jackson hissed in a breath. "God, lady . . ."

She could see he was fighting for control, his breath coming fast, every muscle tense. His movements quickened, his hips pumping, driving him hard inside her. Pleasure swamped her, pulled deep in her stomach. He felt so good, so totally amazing. She closed her eyes and bit her lip, dug her fingers into his powerful shoulders and held on through a second searing climax.

"Damn . . ." he ground out, and finally let himself go. His skin was slick with sweat, his biceps bunching as he spent himself inside her. The muscles across his chest teased her nipples. She loved the weight of him above her, loved every inch of his rock-solid body.

She'd had sex before, but never like this, and she loved it.

I can handle this, she told herself. Sex with an incredible lover. All she had to do was keep things on an even keel — keep herself from falling in love with him.

The words stirred a trickle of unease inside her. She wasn't ready for that kind of involvement. Maybe she never would be.

I can handle it, she told herself again. She wanted this time with Jackson. After what she had suffered with Andrew, she deserved this special time with this very special man.

"All right?" he asked, slowly lifting himself from above her, lying down on the blanket beside her and easing her into his arms. Cool mountain air rushed over her bare skin, raising a fine spray of goose bumps. Sarah loved it.

"I'm fine. Wonderful, in fact."

He leaned over her, kissed her softly on

the lips. "So am I." He smiled. "Hungry? Because if we don't get dressed pretty soon, I won't give a damn about that chicken."

Sarah laughed. "I'm starving." She hadn't eaten all day. Even so, when Jackson leaned over to kiss her one last time, she slid her arms around his neck and deepened the kiss. Sparks ignited. They made love slowly this time, learning each other's body, giving each other pleasure.

After they finished, they lay there in the sunshine, Sarah on the edge of slumber till the breeze began to chill her bare skin. She leaned over for a last quick kiss, then left him there on the blanket.

While Sarah washed in the little stream and pulled on her clothes, Jackson dressed and went to retrieve their picnic lunch. As she returned to the blanket, an image stirred of him naked, all dark skin and lean bands of muscle.

She hid a small, inward smile. She hadn't realized what a brazen hussy she was until she met Jackson. Or maybe that was just the way a normal woman reacted to a man who attracted her as strongly as he did. She had so little experience with men she didn't really know.

They ate the sandwiches and drank iced tea. When they had finished, he tugged her to her feet. "I'd rather stay here and make love to you again, but it looks like it's getting ready to rain. Storms blow up fast around here. I'd rather not be stuck on the mountain."

"We're going back?"

A few drops began to fall, dappling the ground around them. "I think we'd better," he said.

"What about the loggers? I thought you wanted to check on them."

"There's a road that goes to the top. I'll take one of the ATVs and go up in the morning." Jackson hauled her into his arms and very thoroughly kissed her. "I'm glad you enjoyed the ride."

She blushed, and he laughed.

"That one, too. Come on, we'd better get going." He had readied the horses. He boosted her into the saddle, then collected his reins and swung up on Galahad. Adjusting his battered straw hat to shade his eyes, he led the way out of the meadow and they started back down the trail.

It was raining steadily by the time they reached the ranch and Sarah's gaze went in search of her daughter.

"I need to find Holly."

"I'm sure Livvy brought her into the house. Let's get you in where it's dry and

241

I'll send her home."

Sarah hesitated. She wasn't used to anyone looking after her daughter but herself.

"Come on," he gently coaxed, riding past the barn and reining up in front of the cottage. "It's getting wetter by the minute."

With a last glance back toward the ranch house, Sarah jumped down and Jackson swung down beside her.

"Sorry about the rain."

She smiled up at him. "It was worth it." She handed him Daisy's reins, went up and kissed him full on the lips. "Thanks for the lunch."

"As I said, my pleasure." The edge of his mouth curved up and the devil twinkled in those flashing dark eyes. Sarah ignored the little flutter in her stomach and the urge to invite him inside.

"Tell Holly to come straight home."

He nodded, pulled his hat farther down against the rain that was falling even more heavily, turned and led the horses toward the barn.

"Mom, I'm home!" It hadn't been ten minutes, but still Sarah was relieved to hear the sound of her daughter's voice. Everything was fine. Holly was home and safe.

"I'm in here, honey — in the bedroom."

She had finally gotten her laptop up and running and was now able to get her email. She was still subscribed to AOL so she hadn't lost any messages from her friends. Not that she had all that many.

The friends she had made in SBW, the online support group for battered women, all stayed closely in touch. One woman in particular. Patty Gorski, the founder of the small collection of women, was as tough as nails and as solid as a rock. Sarah sorted through her emails, looking for a message from Patty as Holly dashed into the bedroom.

"Hey, Mom!"

"Hi, honey." Sarah smiled down at her. "Sounds like it's stopped raining." She listened but no longer heard the soft patter on the roof.

"It's mostly stopped. Jackson says he wished it would rain all week."

Sarah shoved aside a memory of their incredible lovemaking in the meadow, knowing the danger of that line of thinking. "Your clothes are damp. You better go put on something dry."

"Jackson says the next time you two go riding, I can come with you. He says I can ride with him on Galahad — that's his horse."

"If you keep up your lessons on Midnight, someday you'll be able to ride by yourself."

Holly chattered on about her morning with Sam and Gibby — Rags had to stay outside because he was too muddy to come in the house — then dashed off to change and watch TV.

Sarah went back to her email. Among assorted spam, she found several anxious messages from Patty, who was worried about her. Patty wanted to be sure she had made it to Wyoming safely and that everything was working out all right.

Sorry to take so long getting back to you, Sarah replied. Just got my email up and running. Hope you weren't too worried. Andrew left me with some problems, but we're coping. Holly and I both love it here. Maybe someday you can come for a visit.

Sarah didn't say more. Though she and Patty had never met, in the ways that mattered the woman was the best friend she'd ever had. Patty Gorski lived in Chicago, the only daughter in a poor Polish family of six. She'd gotten pregnant her junior year in high school, had an abortion, then a year later married the guy who had fathered the baby.

For years, she had lived as a battered wife,

unable to build up the nerve to leave, but with the help of a support group, she had finally found the courage to break free.

If it weren't for Patty . . .

Sarah shook off the thought, refusing to imagine what might have happened if she hadn't become friends with such a strong, caring woman.

Sarah returned the emails in her in-box, then decided to work on the synopsis of a book she had been dabbling with for more than a year. *Trials of Passage* was the working title, a novel about a young woman from a small town trying to raise a child and make her way in a troubled world. It was loosely based on her own life, but not entirely.

There were things she would never write about, things that were too frightening or too painful — and the book *was* a novel, after all.

If she ever got the project off the ground.

"The rain's all the way stopped," Holly called out from the living room. "I'm going back out to play."

"Try to stay out of the mud!" Sarah called back to her. She glanced out the window. The ground was so dry the rain had soaked right in, but if there was a puddle, Holly was sure to find it.

The front door slammed as Holly ran out, and Sarah thought of the changes in her daughter since their move to Wyoming. Here the little girl was outside most of the time instead of inside watching TV. With the harsh winters, hot summers, bugs and wild animals, it wasn't an easy place to live, but for Sarah and Holly, the trade-off was worth it.

Sarah opened the file marked *Passage.* She hadn't worked on the novel since before Andrew died. It was something he knew she was doing, patronized her about, but didn't take seriously. Since she had been at it for what seemed ages, maybe in this instance he was right.

She was going over the opening chapter — which was as far as she had ever gotten — when she heard a faint knock at the door. Rising from the chair behind the small oak desk in her bedroom, she walked into the living room and, through the window, saw Jimmy Threebears standing on the porch.

"Hello, Jimmy."

He held his damp felt cowboy hat in his hands. "Hello, Sarah . . . I was . . . ah, wondering if you might have a minute to talk."

He was a tall man, and imposing, with all that long black hair, black eyes and dark, smoothly carved features. She opened the door, curious as to why he was there. "Come on in."

Jimmy pulled off his muddy boots and left them by the door, the way most people did in Wyoming. They walked into the living room and sat down on the sofa and chair in front of the rock fireplace.

"I saw you had a visitor yesterday." Jimmy turned the hat in his hands.

"Nan Hargrove. Yes, she was here."

"Did she . . . ah . . . tell you we went out?"

"She mentioned it. I don't know what you want me to say, Jimmy. Nan is a friend. She told me what happened, and to be honest, I was surprised you would treat her that way."

Jimmy glanced off toward the window. "That's the reason I'm here."

"I'm listening."

Jimmy released a slow breath. "I don't know exactly what happened that night. I'd been wanting to ask Nan out for a real long time. I knew Ron, her ex-husband, before the divorce. After they split up, I tried to work up the nerve to ask Nan for a date, but then I started seeing her down at the Canyon Club."

"She told me about that. It was a bad time for her, Jimmy. Her marriage had failed. Ron was gone and she was lonely."

He turned the hat in his hands. "The truth is, those times I saw her at the Club . . . I wanted to be one of the guys she went home with. I was jealous she picked one of them and not me."

"Nan's not really that kind of woman. She never was, and the way I understand it, that was several years ago."

He nodded. "I know. Like I said, I don't know what happened. I guess my feelings kind of spilled over. I took my past jealousy out on Nan."

"And you expect me to do . . . what?"

He ran a callused finger around his sweat-stained hatband. "Talk to her, I guess. See if you can convince her to give me another chance."

"I don't know if she will, Jimmy. From what Nan told me, she wanted to go out with you, too. The way you acted, those things you said . . . You hurt her, Jimmy. I don't know if she'll take the risk."

He looked her straight in the face. "I know about your husband — the way he treated you. I've never abused a woman and I never will."

When Sarah made no reply, Jimmy shoved to his feet and started toward the door.

He turned back when he got there. "Tell her I'm sorry. Will you at least do that?"

Her heart pinched. Even after Andrew, she was a sucker for an old-fashioned romance. "I'll tell her," she said softly.

Jimmy nodded, pulled open the door, picked up his boots and stepped out on the rain-soaked porch to pull them back on. He closed the door behind him, and Sarah sighed.

Everyone made mistakes. Some were smaller than others. Maybe Nan and Jimmy could get past this one. She would tell Nan what he had said and leave the decision up to her.

SEVENTEEN

Jackson sat in front of the old wood-burning stove in his study. Most of the house had been remodeled, but this room remained much as it had been when the ranch was built in the 1920s. He propped his boots up on the coffee table Jimmy had made for him one Christmas out of deer antlers. The antlers formed the legs beneath a thick slab of varnished tree trunk.

Jackson had a fire burning in the stove tonight. Though the days were growing warmer, up here in the mountains the nights were still cold — perfect weather, Jackson thought. If only the rain had lasted more than a couple of hours, the summer might be all right.

Thinking of the storm that had passed though the mountains so quickly brought memories of a grassy meadow and the beautiful woman he had made love to. The rain hadn't lasted long enough and neither had the lovemaking.

Jackson sighed, wishing Sarah were there with him, that he could pull her down on the thick bear rug in front of the iron stove, strip off her clothes, and —

The ringing of the doorbell put a stop to the train of his thoughts. It was past eight o'clock. Livvy had gone home and it was nearly dark outside. Walking out of the office, he made his way to the front door, flipped on the porch light, and opened the door.

His youngest sibling, Devlin, stood there grinning. "Hey, big brother, got an extra room for the night?"

Gabriel stood behind him. "Make that two."

"I'll be damned." Jackson shook hands with each of his brothers, pulling them into a quick bear hug, then stepping out of the way so the men could carry their duffel bags inside the house. "What in blazes brings the pair of you way up here?"

"I was in Phoenix on business," Gabe said, tossing his duffel at the bottom of the stairs. "Dev said you were having a little trouble. He had some information he figured he would rather deliver in person, so I offered to give him a ride."

"Pretty far out of the way for a side trip."

251

Gabe shrugged a set of linebacker shoulders. All of them were about the same height, Jackson being tallest, but Gabe had the most muscular build — which had proved useful since he actually *was* a linebacker on the high school varsity football team. After that, four years in the Marines, just a grunt, he'd always said, but the service had given him the confidence he'd needed to start a successful career in real estate and construction.

Jackson fixed his attention on Devlin, the pretty boy of the family, though with their startling blue eyes, both his brothers managed to charm more than their fair share of women. "So I guess you've got news."

"Big news, *hermano.* The kind that could get your lady off the hook with Martin Kozak and his bad boys."

Jackson liked the sound of that. "Why don't you two go upstairs and get yourselves settled in a couple of the spare bedrooms. I'll make us some coffee and meet you in the study."

"I take it Sarah's still living in the cottage," Dev said. He grinned. "I thought by now you'd have her moved in here."

Jackson felt an unexpected pang at the notion. "Mostly, we're just friends," he said, ignoring a memory of making love to her in the meadow.

Gabe slapped him on the back. "Yeah, right — mostly."

"She's going to want to hear this," Dev said.

"It's late and she's got her daughter to think of. We'll go over all of it again in the morning." Besides, he wanted to hear the news first, find a way to soften the blow if one was coming.

The men pounded up the staircase, and Jackson went into the kitchen and began to make coffee. He was damned glad to see his brothers, the best friends he had in the world. Only the fact they thought it was necessary to fly all the way up to deliver the information in person made him uneasy.

Dev and Gabe arrived in the study, poured themselves a mug of coffee from the pot keeping warm on the stove, then sat down on the brown leather sofa and chairs around the fire. Jackson opened the heavy iron door, tossed in a couple of logs, closed the door and joined them.

"All right, what have you found out?"

Dev didn't hesitate. "Kozak's running two or three different scams all at once. On some jobs, he's using fewer supports than the project calls for, spacing the rebar a little farther apart than is legal. In projects the

253

size of the ones he builds, it saves him millions."

"What about the inspector?"

"I'll get to him in a minute." Dev took a sip of his coffee. "Kozak's also got an interesting deal going with the labor he's hiring. The state requires the contractor to pay the prevailing wage. Kozak's bringing in Mexican illegals by the truckload, willing to work for substandard wages. I figure he's cooking the books so the state doesn't know. There may be more — I just haven't run across it yet."

"How's Kozak getting away with all this?"

"That's where his old buddy, Vernon Rimmer, comes in."

"Who's Rimmer?" Gabe asked, clearly aware of most of what Dev had been working on. Gabe owned a construction company in Dallas. Lately, he'd been doing redevelopment projects.

"Rimmer's a state highway inspector," Dev answered. "It took a little doing to find them, since they were buried pretty deep, but Rimmer's got several offshore bank accounts in the Caymans. He's on Kozak's payroll and getting paid off big-time."

"So even after paying Rimmer," Jackson said, "Kozak is still ahead of the game."

"Way ahead," Dev agreed. "And this has

been going on for years. My guess is, Andrew Hollister found out about it sometime back. Maybe he had an informant. Clearly he kept a record of what was going on."

"So what happened to make him decide it was time to cash in?" Gabe asked.

"The IRS, I'm betting," Jackson said. "Hollister must have figured he could either get enough blackmail money from Kozak to pay his back taxes, or make a deal with the Feds not to prosecute in exchange for the information on the disk."

Jackson explained about the two federal agents showing up at Sarah's door, threatening her with prosecution if she didn't help them find out who her husband was blackmailing.

"Not good," said Gabe, rubbing a hand over his square jaw.

"Maybe that's how the Feds knew Hollister had the kind of information they would want," Dev said. "He was in touch with them before he got whacked."

It made sense.

"Maybe Kozak whacked him," Gabe suggested.

"Or hired someone to do it," Dev added.

Jackson took a slug of his coffee. "The guy had enough enemies it could have been just about anyone."

"So what's the next step?" Gabe asked.

Jackson sat back in his chair. "Good question. Since the FBI is now in the game, the whole thing's a lot more complicated. In the morning we'll fill Sarah in, then put our heads together and see what we can come up with."

Dev nodded. "Sounds good to me." He yawned, rubbed the shadow of black along his jaw. "I was out pretty late last night — not that I'm complaining."

"Missy or Babs?" Gabe asked.

"Maria." He shook his hand as if he had burned it. "That lady is hot!"

Jackson inwardly sighed. Since Devlin's breakup with longtime girlfriend Amy Matlock two years ago, he was a confirmed bachelor. He went through women like a scythe through wheat. Jackson wondered whether it was really helping his brother forget the woman he had loved or if he was fooling himself.

"It's been a long day," Jackson said, rising from his deep leather chair. "I want you both to know I appreciate your help in this."

"Not a problem, bro." Dev shoved to his feet.

"I needed a vacation anyway," said Gabe, which was probably true though he would be hard-pressed to actually take one. He rose from the sofa to join his brothers. "Good night, y'all," he drawled with the slight Texas accent he had slowly been acquiring since his move to Dallas ten years ago.

"I've got a little more to do down here," Jackson said. "I'll see you both in the morning."

The men left the study and Jackson sat down in front of the stove, watching the low-burning flames through the open iron door. Propping his boots on the coffee table, he leaned back on the sofa.

Dev had found the information they needed. Now the question was, what to do with it? The things Kozak was doing weren't just illegal, they were dangerous. If one of those overpasses collapsed because of shoddy construction . . .

He didn't even want to go there.

Making any sort of deal with Kozak was no longer an option. The trick was to figure how to get the Feds off Sarah's back, stop Kozak — and keep all of them in one piece.

Sarah sat in the living room of the cottage the following morning. Across from her sat three of the best-looking men she had ever seen. Jackson, the rugged Raines brother, sat next to Gabe, who was the brawniest of the trio. Both had the same dark brown hair, though Gabe's shone with traces of red in the light coming in through the window. His square jaw led to a strong chin with the same cleft all three Raines brothers had inherited.

Dev was leaner than the other two, but with his shirtsleeves rolled up, she could see muscular forearms, hinting at a solid body that matched those of his brothers. He had nearly black hair, incredible eyes the same brilliant blue as Gabe's and thick black lashes that a cover model would kill for.

"So that's about it," Jackson said, summing up the information Devlin had discovered, drawing her mind back to the information he had been delivering, information she would rather not have known, the kind of illegal activities that made her stomach burn. "Now we need to decide our next move."

Sarah sighed. "Well, we can't let Marty Kozak continue to build bridges that might fall down. I think we should call the FBI, set up a meeting with agents Brooker and Davis."

"I think we're all in agreement on that," Dev said.

"I'll get hold of my attorney," Jackson

added. "We need someone there who knows the ropes when we talk to those guys, someone we can count on to see you get a fair deal."

Her stomach tightened. "I can't afford to hire —"

"I can," Jackson said as he had before.

Sarah came to her feet. "I can't take money from you, Jackson. I don't want to be in your debt and that's exactly where that would put me."

Gabe was staring at her with a trace of pity. "You think he'll want something in return, don't you?"

"My brother's trying to help you, Sarah," Devlin said gently. "You won't be the first person he's done that for — Gabe and I can both personally vouch for that. You won't be the last."

"And he isn't going to require any kind of repayment," Gabe finished.

She stood there feeling humiliated and embarrassed. Jackson had never asked her for anything. He had been a friend from the start, one she needed very badly. He wasn't like Andrew or any other man she had ever known.

"I'm sorry." She sank back down in her chair. "I'm not used to people helping me." She looked at Jackson and blinked to hold back tears. "Thank you," she added.

Jackson looked away from her, hiding the emotions she had read in his face — concern, relief that she had agreed, and something more she couldn't name.

"Where were we?" he said, clearly wishing to turn the conversation back to their plans.

"Thomas Carson, your attorney," Gabe reminded him. "You were going to set up a meeting with the Feds and ask Carson to be there."

"Right."

"Not in Wind Canyon," Dev warned. "We don't want Kozak or his goons getting wind of this."

"Carson's office is in Cheyenne. We'll ask for a meeting there tomorrow."

"That'll work," Dev said. "They'll be eager to know what you've got."

"I'll fly you down," offered Gabe.

Sarah took a deep breath, trying to pull her thoughts together, feeling a surge of gratitude for the help the brothers were giving her.

She looked over at Jackson, who had turned to speak to Gabe, and found herself studying his profile: the straight nose and hard jaw; the dark hair, a little too long, that brushed the collar of his Western shirt. A sweep of desire stirred deep in her stomach — which was ridiculous, considering they weren't alone and they were discussing a deadly serious situation.

Sarah returned her thinking to the problem at hand, listened as the men worked out the details. She would have to take time off work — again. But she didn't really have set hours and she could always work at home a few nights to make up the time. She was surprised when they asked her opinion and actually seemed to listen to what she had to say, including her in the planning as Andrew never would have done.

"All we need to do now is to set up that meeting," Dev said.

"I'll take care of it," said Jackson, rising from his place on the sofa, and Sarah had no doubt that he would.

As soon as the men left the cottage, Sarah grabbed her briefcase and headed into town. Holly was staying with Livvy. Earlier, the little girl had met Dev and Gabe, who both had an easy way with children and really seemed taken with the little girl.

Holly had been instantly charmed by Jackson's two handsome brothers, and disappointed she had to leave while the adults had their meeting. She did so only with the promise that the men would come down to the corral and watch her ride Midnight, which they all agreed to do.

Sarah smiled as she sat at the desk in her office reviewing the article she was currently writing. She had gotten an appointment with Susan Springer to discuss her son Teddy's arrest for joyriding in his parent's car, promising to keep Teddy's name out of the article. She explained that she wanted to write about the problems parents had today communicating with their teenage children and how important it was to keep those lines of communication open.

Susan seemed to like the idea, telling Sarah over the phone that she regretted not having talked to Teddy more about his responsibilities, as well as drugs, alcohol and sex, and that she and Bob were making much more of an effort to listen to what their son had to say.

Her interview was scheduled for two o'clock. There was still plenty of time, so Sarah called her grandmother, which she did as often as she could, wishing she could drive over to Sheep River to see her. With things the way they were, it wasn't going to happen right away.

"How are you, Gran?" Sarah asked.

"I'm doing just fine, sweetheart. Feels real good to be back home. Everything okay with you and Holly? You haven't had any more trouble like before?"

Things were far from okay, but she didn't say that to Gran. "I'm trying to get the whole thing straightened out." And maybe tomorrow, after her trip to Cheyenne, the situation would look better.

She and Gran chatted for a while, then Sarah hung up the phone on her desk, picked up her big leather purse, and started for the door, waving to Myra Cunningham as she passed the front counter.

"See ya later," Myra called out, shoving a pencil into the frizzy gray-blond curls she had pulled back into a bun.

Sarah stepped out on the boardwalk and took a couple of paces before she spotted Nan Hargrove walking toward her.

"Sarah!"

"Nan! I've been meaning to call you." *Would have if it weren't for the trouble that seems to follow me wherever I go.*

"I know it's a little late for lunch, but have you eaten yet? I thought maybe you could get away for a sandwich or something."

"I wish I had time. I have an appointment with Susan Springer to discuss an article I'm writing."

"Well, maybe next time." She started to turn away, but Sarah caught her arm.

"Listen, Nan, Jimmy Threebears came to see me. He wanted to talk about what happened the night he took you out. He asked me to speak to you about it."

Nan's fiery red eyebrows went up. "Jim asked you to talk to me?"

Sarah tugged her a little way down the boardwalk, where no one could hear. "Jimmy said he screwed up that night. He said he was jealous of the men you'd dated. He said he had been wanting to take you out for years. He said to tell you he was sorry."

"If he was sorry, why didn't he call and tell me?"

"I don't know. I guess he didn't think you'd forgive him."

Nan faintly smiled. "I might. If I thought he really meant it." She tossed her long red hair back over one shoulder. "Tell him to call me. Tell him I'll listen to what he has to say."

Sarah smiled. "I'll tell him the first chance I get."

Nan reached over and hugged her. "Thanks, Sarah. You're a good friend."

And for the first time Sarah realized that Nan was also a dear friend. The number of them had been growing since her arrival in Wind Canyon, something she hadn't really expected when she had decided to move back.

"I'll talk to you later," Sarah said with a smile as she started walking toward the parking lot.

Her smile slowly faded. She hoped Nan wouldn't rush into a relationship with Jimmy. He had hurt her once. There was no telling what kind of man he really was. He said he had never abused a woman, but verbal abuse could be just as hurtful. Still . . .

Sarah shook her head as she climbed into her blue truck. It wasn't fair to assume every man was like Andrew. Surely she should know that by now.

But deep down inside she knew that for her, trusting a man completely would never be an easy thing to do.

EIGHTEEN

Cheyenne, the state capital, was an interesting small Wyoming city. Interesting because, like Wind Canyon, the town was so completely and utterly Western. It's 1860s beginnings were apparent in the old brick buildings, the charming Victorian houses, the Wild West statues of buffalo and gunfighters that were scattered all over town — and the people themselves, men and women comfortable in worn jeans, cowboy hats and boots.

Summer visitors roamed the streets along with locals, and more would be arriving for the annual Cheyenne Frontier Days Rodeo next month. Sarah had never been to the event and she vowed to bring Holly sometime — after she got her life back in order.

Gabe's plane had landed safely. Sarah gazed out the windows of the white Buick sedan Jackson had rented at the airport and now drove toward the domed capitol building where the meeting was scheduled. As a kid, she had visited Cheyenne a couple of times with her parents, but she barely remembered.

Now that she was older, the Western atmosphere captivated her completely. It would be fun to visit the museums or check out the old steam trains that once ran on the Transcontinental Railway tracks heading through town.

Not today.

Today all she wanted to do was to finish her meeting with the FBI and get the hell out of Dodge — or in this case, Cheyenne.

Jackson walked next to Sarah along the corridor leading to the small conference room down the hall in the capitol building, an historic brick structure completed in the early 1890s.

His brothers weren't coming to the meeting. Whatever means Dev had used to gain access to Vernon Rimmer's offshore accounts was undoubtedly illegal. Dev didn't want his name connected to the case in any way. Gabe just didn't like Feds.

Jackson spotted Thomas Carson, his attorney, a tall, imposing man with dark brown hair streaked with silver though he wasn't much past forty. Jackson had filled him in on the particulars of the situation during a lengthy phone call yesterday, and earlier this morning, he and Sarah had gone to Carson's office for a discussion of the case. Jackson had no doubt Carson would be prepared.

Sarah stopped when they reached him. In the brief time she and the lawyer had spent together, she seemed to have come to trust him. "Thank you for being here, Mr. Carson."

Carson gave her a reassuring smile. "I thought we agreed you'd call me Thomas." Sarah returned his smile. "You look like you're holding up. If we're lucky, this won't take too long."

She seemed to relax a little.

"I just have a couple more questions before we go in," the attorney said.

Sarah nodded. "All right."

Thomas asked her to confirm a few more bits and pieces of information. Sarah asked him a couple of questions, then Jackson asked a few. Satisfied that they were all on the same page, Carson tipped his head toward the door.

"I think we're ready." He turned to Sarah. "Once we're inside, let me do as much of the talking as possible. Don't volunteer any information. Answer only what's asked, and look to me for a nod before you do even that."

"Okay," Sarah agreed.

"Ready?" Jackson asked her.

She took a deep breath. "I guess."

She was nervous. That much was clear, and yet when she walked into the room and caught sight of special agents Brooker and Davis seated next to an FBI higher-up — the guy with the power to make the deal — Jackson caught only the subtle squaring of her shoulders.

The men rose as she approached. "Mrs. Hollister, thank you for coming. I believe you know special agents Brooker and Davis. My name is Richard Kemp." Six feet tall, medium build, dark blond hair, power tie and a decent navy-blue, pin-striped suit.

Sarah gazed at him steadily. She was wearing a simple white cotton suit with white embroidery on the lapels, not too expensive but classy, the perfect choice for an occasion like this.

"Legally, my name is Sarah Allen. This is Jackson Raines and my attorney, Thomas Carson."

Carson was no longer the big-time Chicago lawyer he had once been, but he still had a big reputation. Business was his specialty, which meant he had worked with a number of clients in tax-related matters. And this wasn't the first time criminal charges were involved.

All of them sat down around a long mahogany table. Carson slid a manila file across the table and Richard Kemp opened it. He took his time, carefully examining the contents, then looked over at Sarah's attorney.

"According to this letter, your client wishes to trade the name of the man she believes her late husband was blackmailing, along with information about his criminal activities and proof that will lead to the man's arrest. In exchange, she wants complete exoneration from any charges resulting from the ongoing investigation of Andrew Hollister's tax records."

"As well as any other illegal matters in which he might have been involved," Carson added. "She was, after all, an unknowing participant in her husband's affairs."

Kemp flicked Sarah a glance. "We would have to know the name of the person or persons involved, the nature of the criminal activity and what you're offering as proof before we could agree. In other words we need to determine the value of what we are buying before we can make any sort of a deal."

Carson's look fixed on Kemp. "But assuming you're satisfied with what we've brought to the table — information your agents strongly indicated you needed — the government will agree."

"As I said, we'll need to hear what you have, but if the information is all you claim — and your client only culpable as an unknowing spouse, we'll accept your terms."

Jackson looked at Sarah. He could read the anxiety — and her hope that all of this would come to an end. Jackson wanted that same outcome. He cared about Sarah Allen. He wanted to explore a relationship with her and her daughter, see if there might be a future for them.

It was an idea that had started that day in the meadow. Watching her, seeing the joy on her face as she absorbed the beauty of the mountains, the way she seemed to respond to the land and to him had stirred something deep inside him. There was something about Sarah that drew him as no woman ever had, and since that day the feeling had been growing. He wanted to see where it led.

Still, there were obstacles to overcome. Three of them sat at the table across from her.

■ ■ ■ ■

For the next half hour, Sarah sat rigidly at the table listening to Thomas Carson discuss Martin Kozak's illegal activities. Carson told the FBI about the bribes a state inspector had been taking to ignore Kozak's shoddy construction practices and offered to give them the inspector's name and the account numbers that contained the bribery money he had received.

"Let me get this straight," Richard Kemp said. "Your client has somehow been able to obtain the numbers of the offshore accounts that contain the money this inspector was being paid?"

"That is correct."

"I presume this information was contained on the disk Andrew Hollister was using in his blackmail attempt."

"Ms. Allen knows nothing about the alleged disk and never has."

Kemp leaned over and said something to the blond agent, Brooker. He looked back at Carson. "If that's the case, we'll need to know how she obtained the information."

"I'm afraid that isn't possible," Carson said.

Kemp turned to Sarah. "Mrs. Hollister?"

She refused to reply to the name.

"Excuse me, I meant, Ms. Allen."

"I won't divulge my sources. That was never required when your agents came to see me demanding information."

"As I said, in order to agree to your terms, we'll need —"

"We'll give you the inspector," Jackson interrupted, "and his account information. You pressure him enough and he's going to roll over on Kozak. And you can simply follow the money. In the course of your investigation, there is every chance you'll run across other illegal activities Kozak is involved in. You'll have more than enough to prosecute."

"My client won't even need to testify," Carson added, "which means you won't need to worry about offering her protection."

The men glanced back and forth, mentally going through their options. Even their years of training couldn't mask their excitement. It was clear they were interested in Marty Kozak, maybe had already suspected his criminal activities.

"So do we have a deal?" Carson quietly demanded.

The men spoke briefly one last time.

"We have a deal," Kemp said.

"Good," said Carson with the faintest of smiles. "In reliance upon your promise here and in exchange for the information I am about to hand over, I'll expect a memo to that effect faxed to my office this afternoon."

Kemp gave a curt nod and Sarah breathed a sigh of relief. Martin Kozak would be dealt with. She would be free to get on with her life. She watched as Thomas Carson slid across the table a sheet of paper with Vernon Rimmer's name on it, along with a list of his bank account numbers in the Cayman Offshore Corporation. The knowledge of Rimmer's participation and the threat of a long jail term, Jackson had told her, would be enough to gain his cooperation and probably the return of the money.

Everyone stood up from the table.

"Thank you for your assistance, Mrs. . . . Ms. Allen."

Sarah didn't bother to smile. "Good afternoon, gentlemen." Turning, she walked out of the conference room. She had nothing more to say to the FBI.

And she hoped to God they never had anything more to say to her.

"I think we should celebrate." Jackson reached out and caught hold of Sarah's hand, gave it a gentle squeeze. "I told my brothers I'd call as soon as we had a decision." He pulled his cell phone out of the inside pocket of his navy-blue sport coat. "I know a great little restaurant we can all go to for lunch." He grinned. "I'm buying."

"I wish I could join you," Carson said, "but I had to rearrange my schedule to make time for this morning's meetings. I promise I'll make it the next time you're in town — and I'll be the one to buy."

Sarah looked up at the attorney and smiled. "Thank you, Thomas. You can't know how much this means."

"You understand, this isn't completely over — not yet. It'll take a while for the government to move on this."

"Not too long, I don't think," Jackson said. "They won't want anything to happen to their case."

"I'd say a couple of weeks. But until they have Kozak in custody and he realizes the FBI already knows about his illegal activities, you'll need to be careful, Sarah."

"I will. And thank you again." She took Carson's hand, leaned over and kissed his cheek.

Ignoring a twinge of jealousy at the smile Carson gave her, Jackson settled an arm around her waist and led her toward the white Buick parked in the lot. He dialed his brothers.

"We made the deal. We're out of the woods — mostly. I'm buying lunch at Buffalo Bill's."

"Great news!" said Dev. "We'll be there."

Jackson closed the cell and slid it into his coat pocket. "Everything's going to be okay," he said as he walked Sarah to the car.

She looked up at him. "That's what I keep telling myself."

But there was something in her face that said she wasn't completely convinced.

Two weeks passed. Sarah had seen no sign of Kozak or his thugs. She had received a single phone call from Richard Kemp, telling her an arrest had been made. That same day, Jackson got a call from his brother in Scottsdale. According to people in his L.A. office, Kozak's arrest had made the front page of the *Times*.

"Dev says it's all over the news out there." Jackson stood in the living room of the cottage, making the room feel smaller than it actually was. He had arrived with the news just moments ago. "I don't think you'll be hearing from your old buddy Kozak again." He smiled. "He's too busy trying to stay out of jail."

Sarah felt a sweep of relief so strong her legs went a little weak. Kozak had been dealt with. At last her life was her own.

Hearing a noise outside, Jackson walked over to the window to see the delivery truck pull up with the furniture Sarah had chosen to replace the pieces Kozak's goons had destroyed — a comfortable overstuffed sofa and chair in a dark green color with floral patterns in soft yellows, golds and browns, along with accent throw pillows.

"Looks like your furniture is finally here."

Excitement filled her. The cottage already felt like home, but it would be nice to have something she had picked out herself. Jackson helped the men carry the furniture inside, but she knew he wouldn't stay long. She told herself she was glad he was giving her time to get her life back in order, that he hadn't pressed her to have sex with him.

She was glad, she told herself, but as she watched him helping the men carry the old furniture out and setting the new sofa and chair in place in front of the fireplace, she noticed the way his lean muscles bunched beneath his shirt and felt a soft tug low in her belly. An hour later, when she spotted him working in front of the barn, it was all she could do not to go to him, drag him into the straw in one of the stalls, unzip his jeans and do delicious things to his magnificent body.

At the end of the day, when she saw him ride off on his beautiful horse, she wanted to follow him into the woods and demand he make love to her as he had that day in the meadow.

It was ridiculous. Embarrassing, even. She was afraid to look at him, afraid he could read the lustful thoughts she was trying so hard to hide.

Jackson didn't bother hiding his. The hot looks he gave her, the deep rusty tone of his voice when he spoke to her, told her how much he wanted her in his bed.

At least she had fulfilled her promise to Nan and spoken to Jimmy Threebears, relaying Nan's message to him.

"She said you should call her, Jimmy. She says she'll listen to what you have to say."

He just nodded, his expression solemn. "Thank you," was all he said.

Then Gran called, wanting to know how Sarah would feel about letting Holly spend a few days with her in Sheep River.

"I'm not getting any younger, you know," Gran said. "And the two of us . . . well, we've never really had a chance to get to know each other."

Sarah adjusted the phone against her ear,

the idea gaining momentum as it rolled around in her head. The threat from Kozak was past and she could certainly use a little time to herself. Raising a daughter was a full-time job. Except for the few hours she spent in town writing articles for the newspaper, she rarely had time alone.

And she could go to Jackson, accept his blatant if unspoken invitation. Sarah ignored a little tremor of heat and concentrated on her phone call.

"Are you sure you're feeling well enough, Gran? A child can be a heckuva lot of work."

"I'm not so old I don't remember what it's like to raise a child. And I feel just fine. So what do you say?"

Sarah smiled into the phone. "I know she'd love to come for a visit. I'll bring her over in the morning."

And she had been right. When she mentioned the idea to Holly, it was clear her daughter wanted very badly to go.

"Can I, Mom? Please?" Holly jumped up and down, her blond ponytail bobbing. "I never had a real grandma before."

"She's actually your great-grandmother — my mother's mother."

"Cool! I promise I won't be any trouble."

"I'm sure you'll be a good girl and do exactly what your gran tells you."

"I will, I promise."

They packed that night. Early the next morning as Holly finished dressing, Sarah summoned her courage and stepped out into the warm July morning. Jackson stood in front of the barn talking to Jimmy. The moment he saw her walking toward him, he turned and started her way. His worn jeans clung to those long sinewy legs and gently cupped the impressive bulge of his sex. The sleeves of his shirt were rolled up and she could see the powerful muscles in his forearms.

A little sliver of desire snaked through her, giving her the courage she needed to do what she had come for.

"Good morning," he said as he reached her, shoving his hat back on his head.

"Yes, it is." She smiled up at him. "It's beautiful." She flicked a glance toward the house. "I'm driving Holly over to my grandmother's place this morning. She's going to stay for a couple of days. I was wondering . . . hoping you might come over for dinner tonight. I mean . . . I owe you at least that much."

She couldn't miss the hunger that burned in those dark eyes. "I'd love to come. What time?"

"I know you start work early. How about

six o'clock?"

"Perfect," he said, his eyes still on her face.

"All right, then." For a couple of seconds neither of them moved. Sarah felt a blush creeping into her cheeks, turned and started walking briskly back to the cottage. Already her heart was pounding and all he had done was agree to her supper invitation.

The man could make her body feel hot just by looking at her.

She should have been worried. And she would be — later. For the next few days, she was simply going to enjoy being a woman. An image of Andrew flashed into her head, but Sarah firmly pushed it away. Andrew was dead. Her life was her own now.

NINETEEN

After a drive through the glorious Wyoming countryside, Sarah left Holly at her grandmother's house.

"If you need anything," she said to the slightly bent, silver-haired woman, "just call me. You've got my numbers."

"Stop worrying," Gran said. "Holly and I will be just fine. Besides, you deserve a little time to yourself."

Which she truly believed, but of course, now that it was time to actually leave Holly behind, she worried.

Still, her decision was made, and she wanted to give the two people she loved most in the world this special time together.

On the way back to town, she stopped at the market to pick up the groceries she would need for tonight's supper, along with a bottle of Chianti to go with the Parmesan chicken she planned to serve. As she climbed back into the truck, a jolt of excitement went through her. She was seeing Jackson tonight! They would make love and it would be wonderful!

From the store, she drove to her office, which was empty with Mike out on a story and Myra taking her afternoon break.

Sitting behind her desk, Sarah grinned as she opened the word file on her computer and reread the humorous article she had been working on — the mostly true story of Homer the Rebellious Squirrel, the bane of the Wind Canyon Fire Department.

Homer had been stashing pinecones in the tailpipe of a big RV near his tree. When the owner started the engine, the cones caught on fire. The exhaust spit flaming pinecones into the dry grass and set small fires all over the area.

Fortunately, the fire trucks arrived in time to put out the burning grass and keep the fire from spreading. No harm was done and Homer escaped to the safety of his tree.

Sarah leaned back, smiling, pleased with the finished article. She printed it and put it on Smiley's desk, then glanced up at the sound of the bell ringing above the door. A man walked in and her chest squeezed so hard no air could get into her lungs. For a minute she thought she might faint. The only sound she could hear was the ringing in her ears.

She knew the man with the straight brown hair, bad complexion, and nose that spread out as if it might have been broken. Still, if it weren't for his hard-as-nails, I-hate-the-world attitude, Detective Ed Mercer might have been in a strange way attractive.

Today he was dressed in khaki pants and a yellow Izod shirt. Usually he wore cheap suits and faux leather loafers. After Andrew's murder, Detective Mercer of the Los Angeles Police Department had given her nothing but trouble.

He sauntered past the counter wearing the same smug expression he had worn the last time she had seen him, walked over to her desk and propped his hip against the edge.

"Hello, Sarah."

Her mouth went paper dry. She swallowed, managed to make her voice work. "Detective Mercer. You're . . . you're a long way from home. What are you doing in Wind Canyon?"

She had never liked Mercer and suspected the feeling was mutual. During the murder investigation, one of the other detectives had told her Mercer was recently divorced and on a hate-all-women jag that seemed to have no end.

"I came here to talk to you. I think we

have some unfinished business."

She glanced around, heard Myra on her way back from lunch coming in through the back door and quickly stood up from her desk. "We can talk in the conference room." Which was about the size of a large broom closet but was a place they wouldn't be overheard.

He followed her down the hall, walked in behind her and firmly closed the door.

Summoning every ounce of her composure, Sarah turned to face him. "What can I do for you, Detective?"

"I think you know why I'm here. I told you when you left L.A. you hadn't seen the last of me."

He'd said he wouldn't be done with her until the details of the case had been tied up. She had tried not to worry about what that meant.

"So you're here because of Andrew?"

"That's right."

"I thought the investigation was over."

"It won't be over until we find the person who murdered your husband."

"But I thought . . ." She swallowed, clamped down on an urge to run out of the room and just keep going. "Lieutenant Delaney said he was sure it was someone Andrew was in business with or someone he owed money."

She didn't mention Kozak. She didn't know how much the police knew about her husband's blackmail schemes, and she didn't want to be connected in any way to Martin Kozak's arrest.

"Come on, Sarah. We both know the truth. Why don't you make it easy on all of us and admit you were the one who shot him."

Her stomach contracted so sharply she thought she was going to be sick. No longer sure her legs would hold her up, she sat down in one of the chairs around the small Formica-topped table in the middle of the room.

"What . . . what are you talking about?" But Mercer had made a similar accusation before.

"The spouse is always the most likely suspect," he had said. *"In your case, Sarah, you had more motive than most."*

He might have officially accused her, but his boss, Lieutenant Tom Delaney, had been sure Mercer was looking in the wrong direction.

"Hollister had a dozen enemies. His shady business dealings alone were enough to get him killed — to say nothing of the big boys he owed money to in Vegas. In Hollister's case,

his wife would have had to stand in line to get a shot at him."

Mercer's voice drew her out of the past. "Let's take a look at the facts," he said as he pulled out a chair, spun it around and straddled it backward. "You were there the night he was murdered. You said that when you left he was still alive, that someone came in and shot him after you were gone, but who's to say you didn't shoot him and *then* leave?"

Sarah said nothing. Her insides were shaking. She had been so sure the police were satisfied the murder had nothing to do with her.

"Then there's your motive," he went on. "You found out Andrew had a girlfriend and was buying her expensive gifts. You knew he was seeing Mitzy Bender and you didn't like it."

She stared at him in amazement. "You think I was jealous of Andrew?"

He studied her face, saw the revulsion she didn't bother to hide. "So maybe the girl wasn't the reason. Maybe it was the money."

"What money? Andrew left me buried in debt."

"True enough. And that's what our investigation discovered. But since you left, I dug up a little tidbit we missed."

She frowned. "I told you — there wasn't any money."

"No, there wasn't. But at the time, you didn't know that. Hollister had a big fat life insurance policy — two million, to be exact — and you were the beneficiary. You didn't find out he hadn't paid the premiums until he was already dead. By then it was too late."

Beneath the table, her legs shook. "You're wrong."

"Am I?"

"If . . . if you really believed I was the one who killed him, why did you wait until now?"

"I always figured you were the one who did it. I tried to tell myself I was wrong, but the more I thought about it, the more it made sense. And the idea of you getting away with murder . . . well, that just doesn't set well with me."

Sarah said nothing.

"And then just the other day, I ran across this other little loose end . . ."

She swallowed, hoped her face wasn't as pale as it felt. "What . . . what loose end?"

"Your daughter's ballet class. It wasn't over till eight o'clock that night. I guess somehow that information got overlooked. You were there to pick her up when the class finished, just like you said. But where were you between six — when you said you left the house — and eight, when you picked her up?"

"Holly's ballet class is in Westwood. I had to drive there. I — I got stuck in traffic. I told the police that at the time."

"Yes, you did. So the fact is you don't really have an alibi for the time of the shooting, which the coroner figures was somewhere between six and eight."

If she could have made her voice work, she might have said something. As it was, she didn't dare.

"There's only one thing missing," he said.

She worked up a shot of courage. "What's that, Detective?"

"The gun. I still haven't figured out how you got hold of a thirty-eight caliber revolver, or how you got rid of it."

"I don't own a gun. I never have."

"But you know how to shoot one, don't you, Sarah? A Wyoming girl? Raised out here in the Wild, Wild West?"

Sarah made no reply. She knew how to shoot. Her dad had taught her. They'd had fun target practicing and she had become a very good shot.

Mercer got up from his chair. "Don't worry, though. In time, I'll figure it out.

Once I do, you can bet you'll be seeing me again."

Sarah felt sick to her stomach. "I didn't shoot my husband."

Mercer just smiled. "I guess we'll just have to wait and see." He turned and started for the door. "In the meantime, I'm here on vacation. I've never been to Yellowstone Park. Think I'll drive on up and take a look."

Sarah didn't stand up as Mercer opened the door and stepped out into the hallway. Her legs were shaking too badly. She wasn't sure how long she stayed in the room, but she didn't make an effort to move out of her chair until Mike Stevens knocked, then opened the door.

"Sarah. I thought you'd gone home."

She summoned a little fortitude and forced herself to her feet. "I was just on my way out."

"Are you all right? You look a little pale."

She managed a shaky nod. "I'm fine." Moving past him out the door, she made her way along the hallway to her desk, picked up her purse and started to leave.

"Will you be in tomorrow?" Mike asked.

She nodded. "I — I think so. I'll see you then." Hurriedly she pulled open the door. All she could think of was reaching the safety of her home, the safety of Raintree Ranch.

She stepped out onto the boardwalk and a wave of nausea hit her. She wasn't safe at the ranch. She wasn't safe anywhere.

From the moment a bullet had pierced Andrew's heart, she had never been truly safe.

Jackson knocked on the door to Sarah's cottage at exactly 6:00 p.m. As he stood there waiting, a bottle of good red Napa Valley wine in his hand, he rubbed the toes of his boots on the back of each leg to bring up the shine and straightened the collar of his white Western shirt.

He was really looking forward to the evening, looking forward to a supper Sarah cooked especially for him, looking forward to making love to her for most of the night.

His mouth edged up. He wasn't a fool. Sarah might keep him at arm's length but she wanted him. He could see it in those clear blue eyes whenever she looked at him.

And, by damn, he wanted her.

The door swung open and Sarah's eyes widened. "Jackson! Oh, my God, is it six o'clock already? I sat down for a couple of minutes. I guess I must have fallen asleep. I — I meant to call you. Something's come up and —"

He walked into the house, over to the round oak dining table, and set down the bottle of wine. He turned to face her. "What's going on, Sarah?"

She swallowed, glanced away. "Nothing. I just . . . I fell asleep and I didn't get supper ready, that's all."

"Fine. I'll do the cooking." He turned and started into the kitchen. Sarah caught up with him and grabbed hold of his arm. She looked as though she wanted to say something but didn't quite know how.

"You . . . you can cook?"

"I didn't always have a housekeeper. In Houston, I had to take care of myself. And I like good food."

He opened the refrigerator door and looked inside, spotted the package of chicken breasts she had apparently meant to cook, took it out and set it on the counter.

"I just . . . I guess I'm not used to Holly being gone. It would be better if we made supper another night."

He opened the package. "I'm hungry. You promised to feed me. Since I sent Livvy home early and we both have to eat, we might as well eat together." He washed the chicken then started digging around, pulling out pots and pans. He knew the little kitchen, since he had furnished the place himself.

"You're staying — is that it?"

He looked at her. "Yup."

"You're not leaving me any choice?"

"Nope."

She blew out a breath and some of the tension in her shoulders seemed to ease. "Well, okay, then." Stepping up beside him, she opened the fridge and took out a head of lettuce, along with tomatoes and the rest of the fixings for a salad. "I thought Parmesan chicken breasts and a salad with balsamic vinaigrette and blue cheese crumbles."

He smiled. "Perfect." The lady was definitely gun-shy. After her no-good husband, she still had a deep distrust of men, and yet he sensed a need in her. He thought that secretly she was glad he was staying.

Not nearly as glad as he was.

Sarah held up a bottle of Chianti. "I bought this at the market. Shall I open it?"

"I brought a bottle, too. I guess we won't run out."

Sarah retrieved the bottle he had brought and set it on the counter, then opened the Chianti and poured each of them a glass. They made supper together, working jointly at the task surprisingly well. He talked about his trip up to the top of the mountain that morning to check on the loggers, and she told him about the article she had written about the squirrel. Both of them laughed at that.

Jackson ignored the little cloud that seemed to settle over her when she finished. Something was wrong but he wasn't about to press her. At least not yet.

The aroma of tomato sauce, oregano, garlic and vinegar filled the kitchen. Sarah tossed the salad and set the table, and they filled their plates and carried them into the dining area at the end of the living room.

"The place is really shaping up," he said, glancing around as he took a sip of wine. "You've got a knack for decorating, Sarah."

She smiled, seemed pleased. She pointed toward the old steamer trunk she had placed beneath the window. "I found it up in the attic. It's wonderful, isn't it? I didn't think you'd mind."

"I like to see things put to use."

She sipped her wine. "I bought that oak bookshelf down at Potter's Antiques. I gave most of my books to the library before I left L.A., but I love to read so it won't take long to fill up."

Jackson watched her, noticed that she looked a little less pale than she had when she'd first pulled open the door. They finished the meal and ate spumoni ice cream for dessert. By the time they had cleared the table, Sarah seemed completely relaxed.

"I'm glad you stayed," she said as they stood at the kitchen counter.

"So am I." He leaned toward her. He only meant to kiss her cheek, but she looked so good standing there with her dark hair loose and tomato sauce on her blouse, he couldn't resist. It was only supposed to be a thank-you-for-supper kiss, but weeks had passed and the minute his mouth touched hers, sparks seemed to leap between them.

"Jackson . . ." Sarah leaned into him and her arms went around his neck. Jackson pulled her hard against him, deepened the kiss, slid his tongue inside her mouth.

She tasted so damned good, a little like the ice cream they had been eating. He wanted to eat her up that same way. He shoved his hands into her dark hair, pulled her mouth up to his for another burning kiss.

Sarah kissed him back, pressing her full breasts into his chest, making his erection stiffen and throb against the fly of his jeans.

"God, Sarah, do you have any idea how much I want this?" He pressed himself against her, let her feel how hard he was, heard her moan. Jackson kissed her long and deep, felt her fingers move down to cup his sex, caress him through the heavy denim fabric.

"Jesus, lady . . ." He backed her up until her shoulders hit the door leading into the bedroom, unbuttoned the front of her blouse and filled his hands with her breasts. They were full and heavy, her skin soft as silk, but her nipples were stone-hard, and so was he.

He had meant to suggest a walk down by the river. He could barely walk now and he was getting harder by the minute. He cupped her face and kissed her again, long, wet and slow. Sarah squirmed against him, reached back and turned the knob on the bedroom door.

They stumbled into the room. Jackson caught her up in his arms and carried her over to the bed. He stripped away her blouse and bra, dragged off her sneakers, jeans and skimpy thong panties, then stood there for a moment admiring her. Her sweet woman's body called to him, the soft curves and lovely breasts, the thatch of dark curls that marked her sex. Her light perfume mingled with the scent of her arousal, and his mouth watered. He wanted to taste her, pleasure her the way he had the first time they made love.

He shed his boots and the rest of his clothes and joined her on the bed, came up over her and kissed her long and deep, kissed her until he had her squirming beneath him. He suckled those luscious breasts, grazed the tips with his teeth, took the fullness into his mouth.

She was ready and so was he, and yet he waited, moved between her legs and lifted her knees up onto his shoulders.

Sarah squirmed. "Jackson, please . . . I — I want to feel you inside me."

"Soon, darlin'." And then he set to work, using his hands and his mouth, tasting her, stroking her, making her come two times before he sheathed himself and entered her.

Her eyes slowly opened and catlike, she smiled. He could read the renewed desire in the way her head fell back as he began to move, her hips arching upward, taking him deeper, making him groan. She was one helluva a woman — but then he'd figured that out sometime back.

Her body quivered. Her sex pulsed around him, sending a fierce shot of pleasure roaring through him. He tried to hold on, give her as much as he could, but when she cried his name and her body convulsed around him, it drove him over the edge.

His muscles strained and tightened, jerked with the deep, intense pleasure of a mind-blowing climax. *Sweet God Almighty.*

Sarah clung to his neck and he rested his head against her shoulder as the heat spiraled down and the world slowly spun back to normal. Jackson kissed her one last time and settled himself beside her on the bed.

You're mine, he thought. *Even if you still don't know it.*

TWENTY

Sarah slept deeply. The house was quiet, just the night sounds outside the window, the crickets and the coyotes. Jackson lay beside her. Some part of her knew he was there, felt the joy of it, the rightness. And yet, even in sleep, she knew it could not last.

As she slept, her mind shifted, slipped back in time. She saw Ed Mercer standing in front of her desk at the office.

Why don't you make it easy on all of us and admit you were the one who shot him. We both know you did it.

She tossed and turned on the mattress, her legs tangling in the sheets. Perspiration soaked the dark hair at her temples. Her thoughts shifted.

Suddenly, she was back in the house on Sunset, standing in the doorway leading into Andrew's study. She'd been upstairs packing the last of her things to take to the condo in Santa Monica when he had arrived. He had called out to her, demanded she come downstairs.

"Sarah! Get down here! I want to talk to you!"

She could hear the anger in his voice, the fury.

He wasn't drunk. He didn't have to be.

As she stood in the open study doorway, she saw him rise from behind his desk.

"What . . . what is it you want, Andrew?"

"Do you think I'm a fool, Sarah?"

He was a no-good, rotten bastard, a true sonofabitch, but he was no fool. "Why would I think that?"

"Maybe because you didn't think I'd read your email, find out what you were planning to do."

He was bluffing. She had been extremely careful, deleted everything, all her messages to Patty Gorski and the other women in the support group. And she had always chosen her words with special care, sent nothing in a message that would give her away.

"I don't know what you're talking about."

He just smiled. It was the kind of smile she hated. The kind that made her stomach knot with fear, the kind that made her want to throw up.

"I told you we were going to Rio. The three of us. Did you actually think you were going to take Holly and run away?" His smile grew feral and the knot in her stomach tightened. "I went directly to the server. I saw what you wrote to those women."

She swallowed past the lump blocking her throat. "It was just conversation." She had never been specific, only hinted to Patty. But Patty had understood.

"I think it was more."

She straightened, determined not to let him know how terrified she was. "Holly and I aren't going with you, Andrew. You can leave if you want, but we're staying here."

His mouth thinned to a slash across his face. "You really believe you can defy me? You don't remember what happened the last time you tried?"

She remembered. He had beaten her so badly she'd ended up in the hospital. She'd had three broken ribs and thirty stitches in her arm. She hadn't reported him to the police, had, in fact, told the doctors he'd never touched her. She was afraid he'd take Holly and leave and she would never see her daughter again.

He stepped away from his chair, rounded the corner of his desk. Fury etched lines into his face. Anticipation glittered in his eyes. He liked this, liked to hurt her.

"Andrew, please don't do this." She forced

herself not to back away, to hold her ground and face him. It was now or never. "Stay away from me, Andrew. Don't!"

She was shouting his name and crying when a big hand wrapped tightly around her shoulder and shook her awake.

"Easy, Sarah," a deep voice said, his hold turning gentle. "It's all right, darlin'. You're only dreaming. Everything's okay."

She opened her eyes to see Jackson leaning over her, his face filled with concern. Sarah burst into tears.

Jackson eased her into his arms and held on tight. "I'm right here, honey. I've got you. No one's going to hurt you. You're safe with me."

There was a gruffness in his voice that told her how upset he was, how worried. Sarah clung to him, fighting the memories, trying to shove them back into the past, as it had taken her months to learn to do.

She hadn't had the nightmare since her arrival in Wyoming. Not until Detective Ed Mercer had shown up in her office.

He wanted to arrest her, put her in prison. He believed she was guilty of murder and he was determined to prove it. She was afraid to tell Jackson. She couldn't involve him in more of her troubles and even if she were selfish enough to do it, there was nothing Jackson could do.

Nothing anyone could do.

"Are you all right?" he asked, pressing his lips against the top of her head.

She nodded, dragged back her perspiration-damp hair. "I'm all right."

"You were dreaming about Andrew."

She swallowed. She remembered. She'd had the dream a dozen times. "It was the night he was killed. The last time I saw him."

"You want to tell me about it?"

It was the last thing she wanted. "I'd rather not talk about it."

Jackson didn't press her. "All right." Lying back down on the bed, he eased her down beside him, nestled her in the circle of his arms. "Think you can go back to sleep?"

Tears burned her eyes. She wouldn't sleep anymore tonight. After the dream, she never did. Not unless . . . She turned to Jackson, ran her fingers along his hard jaw, felt the stubble of his night's growth of beard.

"Make love to me, Jackson."

He studied her face, saw the need there. He came up over her, cupped her face in his hands and kissed her. She could feel him go hard, grow thick and pulsing against her. His kiss was enough to arouse her, the feel of his muscular body pressing her down in the mattress. He started gently, but she didn't want gentle. She wanted hard and fast, she wanted to climax and she wanted to forget.

Jackson seemed to understand. He pulled her beneath him and filled her, surged into her in a single deep thrust. Long, heavy strokes shook her. Deep, penetrating strokes made her come, then come again.

Jackson gentled his movements, kissed her softly and took her with such tenderness her eyes filled with tears.

"Jackson . . ." she whispered, wishing he had been the man she had married, the man who was Holly's father, the man she would share her life with.

It wasn't going to happen.

Andrew had seen to that.

For the next few days, Jackson spent his nights with Sarah at the cottage. He had pushed her to let him stay and Sarah was glad. She didn't dream while he was there. They made love and she slept and they made love again and it was heaven.

Then it was time to pick Holly up at Gran's, time for her brief respite to end.

"It doesn't have to be over," Jackson said as they lay in bed that night. "I can come to you after Holly goes to sleep and leave before she wakes up."

It was tempting. So incredibly tempting. But the risk was too great. Mercer was still on the prowl and sooner or later Jackson was bound to find out.

What would he think when the detective accused her of murder? What man would want a woman the police accused of killing her husband?

And there was the not-so-small matter of her heart. She was falling for Jackson Raines. She couldn't afford to let that happen. She trusted him more than any man she had ever known. Trusted him the way she had trusted her father. It wasn't enough.

Too much had happened. Too many years of abuse and misery. She couldn't take that kind of risk again.

Instead, tomorrow morning she would pick Holly up at Gran's and return to work. She had decided to let her daughter go back to the Busy Bee Day-Care Center so the little girl could play with her friends and make new ones. She prayed Ed Mercer would not return, that he would go back to L.A. and give up his search.

Surely he would, sooner or later.

Or he would convince the police he had enough evidence to charge her with Andrew's murder.

Sarah shivered.

Late in the afternoon of the next day, while Holly was outside playing with Rags and the boys, Sarah sat at the laptop computer in her bedroom. As soon as the machine geared up, she clicked on her email, watched it download, then deleted the junk mail that escaped her spam filter. There were a couple of actual messages, one of them from Patty.

Sarah smiled. Patty could be funny, and she was today, telling a story about her recent tooth surgery. According to Patty, the surgery had left a gaping hole that was meant to be filled by a porcelain tooth. While she was waiting for the false tooth to be finished, she had a minor accident, slipped and fell in her basement and hit her head on a wooden sign she was making for the shelter. Her eye turned black and blue. That, along with the missing tooth, had the women at the shelter certain that some man had beat her. They were all up in arms over it.

Sarah grinned as she read the email. She always loved hearing from Patty. She kept her reply light, but Patty was hard to fool, and apparently she was sitting at her computer when she got Sarah's email.

The reply came back:

What's the matter, kiddo? You can tell your big sister.

Why not? She knew she could trust Patty Gorski. Sarah typed in, Okay — here it is. Detective Mercer came to Wind Canyon. He is sure I killed Andrew and he is trying to prove it. He says he won't give up until he does.

Patty wrote back, Tell him to bugger off. He doesn't have anything or he would have arrested you a long time ago.

Sarah felt the pull of a smile. Patty was different from any woman she had ever met. She was intelligent. She was street-smart and she was courageous. And she had been there for Sarah when no one else gave a damn what happened to her and Holly.

Thanks, Patty. Take care of those teeth! Love you, Sarah and Holly.

She blew out a shaky breath, feeling better after talking to her friend. Whatever happened, she knew she could count on Patty.

She thought of Jackson, how protective he was, the way he had held her after her nightmare. She trusted him. She cared for him.

And she was afraid.

The Fourth of July arrived. In a small town like Wind Canyon, Independence Day was a really big deal. Sarah covered the fireworks display and picnic, which she attended with Jackson, Holly and Livvy. Jimmy invited Nan to join him and his boys, and all of them sat together to watch the colorful fireworks show.

Sarah knew Nan and Jimmy were seeing each other. She just hoped her friend took the time to really get to know the man before jumping into a relationship.

It was late by the time the fireworks were over, all the hot dogs and sodas consumed, and the folding chairs and blankets packed up for the trip back home. Jackson dropped Livvy off at her house just down the road from the ranch, then drove his big white Ford along the lane and parked in front of the cottage. Sound asleep in the backseat, Holly awakened as he began unloading the leftover picnic items they had taken with them to the park.

All of them climbed out of the truck and Jackson reached into the backseat for a bag of leftovers.

"I was wondering . . ." he said as he handed her the bag and reached for another.

"I thought maybe this weekend we might all ride up in the hills and spend the night. I think Holly would really enjoy it."

Any residual sleepiness Holly was feeling instantly faded. "Can we, Mom? Can we? Can I ride in front of you, Jackson, can I?"

He looked over at Sarah. "So what do you say?"

She should have been angry that he hadn't asked her first, considering there was no way now she could possibly say no, but instead she just thought how nice it was that he was willing to take all of them up into the beautiful mountains.

"I don't see why not," she said, and he smiled so wide her heart squeezed hard inside her.

Holly squealed and flung herself into Jackson's arms. He lifted her up on his back, locking her legs around his waist, piggyback style. "We'll ride up Saturday morning, make camp and spend the night. Maybe do some fishing up at the lake."

"Fishing! I get to go fishing!"

Sarah couldn't help laughing. "All right, you two, that's enough." Jackson set the little girl back on her feet. "Holly, it's time to go in. It's way past your bedtime."

As Sarah said the word *bed,* she made the mistake of looking at Jackson, saw his eyes go hot. Her breath caught. Just a hint of invitation and he would come in through the back door and join her in bed. Her body went liquid and warm. She wanted that so much.

Too much.

She turned to Holly, took her hand and led her up on the porch. "Good night, Jackson. Thanks for taking us tonight. It was really fun."

He just nodded, pulled his hat brim down over his eyes. "I'll see you tomorrow."

But tomorrow she would be working in town and it would be a long day. She had her story to write on the fireworks display and some shopping to do.

Ignoring a hollow feeling of regret, she opened the door and led her daughter into the house.

Jackson tossed a couple of small logs into the old iron stove in his study. Leaving the door open so he could watch the flames, he sat down on the comfortable leather sofa. All evening, his mind had been on Sarah. From the moment he had first seen her that night in the snowstorm, he'd had a feeling his life was going to change.

He sat there now, contemplating that change and his growing feelings for Sarah.

And what, exactly, he should do about them. He was deep in thought when the phone rang. Jackson came up off the sofa, walked over to his desk and picked it up.

"Hey, bro . . ." Dev's voice came over the line. "You got a minute? I'm not interrupting anything, am I?"

"I wish . . ." grumbled Jackson. "What's up?"

"To tell you the truth, I'm not sure. After I put the word out to my bloodhounds for information on Hollister, I never bothered to call them off. I figured, what the hell? You never know what might turn up."

"I take it something did."

"Maybe. I'm not sure. One of my people sent word . . . he says Andrew Hollister was getting big cash payments from a company called Ace Trucking. It's owned by a guy named Vincent Spalino."

"You think he was blackmailing Spalino?"

"I can't say for sure, but I don't think that was it. The payments had been coming in for years. Looks more like some kind of business arrangement, something they kept off the books."

"You know anything about the company?"

"Not much. I know their connection to Hollister was through Southgate Demolition, one of Hollister's companies. Apparently Ace Trucking did a lot of work for them."

"Could be kickbacks to Hollister through Southgate for getting them the work."

"Could be. I was just thinking that if Hollister was planning a trip to Rio, maybe he was stashing some of the cash he got from Spalino to set himself up when he got there."

"He'd need cash, all right. I figured that was why he made the disk — to get as much money as he could before he left the country."

"Or maybe that's one of the reasons Kozak was pressing Sarah so hard. Maybe he knew about the money. Maybe he was hoping the disk would help him find it."

"Anything's possible, I guess."

"I just thought you might want to know."

"Thanks, Dev. I appreciate it. If anything else turns up, give me a call."

"You got it."

Jackson hung up the phone. Hopefully, Sarah was out of danger, but it didn't hurt to stay informed.

He sat back down on the sofa, wondering if he should tell her about the phone call, then decided against it. She had been through enough. Hopefully, it wouldn't matter.

The fire crackled and popped against the sides of the old iron stove. Knowing warm summer nights were at hand, he enjoyed these final chilly evenings with the heat soaking into his bones.

Jackson sighed, his thoughts returning to Sarah, wishing he would be spending the night in her bed, instead of sleeping alone.

TWENTY-ONE

July in Wyoming was breathtaking; dark green pines soaring up the hillsides; the deciduous trees fully leafed out; the sky a clear, crystalline blue. A pair of eagles nested at the top of the ridge, occasionally sailing out over the mountains in search of food. Though last night had been cool, the weatherman predicted a rise in the temperature. Summer was on its way.

Sarah sat at her desk, her workday nearly over. Once she had finished her grocery shopping, she could pick up Holly and enjoy the beautiful scenery on the ride back to the ranch.

She finished her article on the Fourth of July fireworks, mentioning what a good job the Wind Canyon Fire Department had done, what a fantastic show it was and how the city's firemen had kept everyone safe.

There had only been one incident. A little after midnight, a teenage boy had accidentally set off a string of firecrackers that set the dry grass in the field behind his house on fire. The fire trucks had arrived in time to bring the flames under control and keep it from spreading into the nearby forest.

Sarah reread the article and printed it, then packed up her briefcase, said goodbye to Myra and Mike and left the office. She smiled as she made her way along the boardwalk, enjoying the lovely weather and the cloudless blue sky. At the corner, she stepped off the wooden walk into the street and an odd sense of unease struck her. The hairs on the back of her neck stood up, warning her something was wrong.

"Just keep walking," said the dark-skinned, foreign-looking man who had accosted her before.

Sarah jolted to a halt, but he grabbed her arm and dragged her forward, around the corner into the parking lot. He slammed her up against the building, the way he had before.

"You were a very naughty girl, Sarah." He was dressed in expensive tan slacks, a short-sleeved blue oxford shirt and a pair of Italian loafers that had to run at least six hundred bucks.

"I don't . . . I don't know what you're talking about." Her legs were shaking, her heart hammering away. She told herself she wasn't in any real danger. He wasn't going to do anything to her in a public parking lot.

"We know you went to the Feds. We know you had something to do with Martin Kozak's arrest."

"You're crazy."

"You met with them in Cheyenne."

The bottom dropped out of her stomach. It was clear the man had been watching her or knew someone in the FBI. "Are you one of Kozak's men?"

"This has nothing to do with Kozak."

That was some consolation, she guessed, though she had never figured Marty as the type for revenge. He was a businessman first, last and always. Money was his god — which was the reason he and Andrew had gotten along so famously.

She straightened, forced some courage into her spine. "I didn't go to the Feds. They came to me. They were investigating Andrew's tax records. They threatened to charge me with tax evasion if I didn't help them."

"Did you give them the disk? Make a deal to exchange it for dropping the charges?"

"I don't know anything about any disk. I told you that before."

His eyes drilled into her, black and fathomless. A chill swept down her spine. "Come on. We're going for a little ride."

He jerked her forward toward a row of cars across the lot, but she dug in her heels and tried to twist away from him. "I'll scream," she warned, then felt the heavy metal barrel of his pistol shoved into her ribs.

"Keep walking."

"What do you want?"

"We want you to understand what will happen to you if you open your mouth about your husband's business dealings again."

She moved a couple of feet toward the car, a nondescript white Ford sedan, probably a rental, her eyes darting right and left as she searched for an avenue of escape. She wasn't getting into a car with him. If he was going to shoot her, he'd have to do it right there in the parking lot.

Then she spotted Jackson. He was across the street, walking toward her office, more than a block away. Why his gaze happened to swing toward her she would never know, but the moment he spotted the foreign-looking man walking beside her, he started running.

The man spotted Jackson, as well. "Keep

your mouth shut, Sarah. Think of your daughter." Hurrying off toward his car, he got in and started the engine.

She was shaking by the time Jackson reached her, and the sedan was merging into the traffic in the street, then disappearing around a corner.

"Did you get the plate number?" Jackson asked, not breathing nearly as hard as she would have been if she had run that far.

She swallowed and nodded. "Wyoming plates — 23 619 N O."

"Twenty-three is the number for Sublette County. That's right here."

"I-it looked like a rental car, basic, no frills. It didn't seem to match the expensive clothes he was wearing."

Jackson glanced around, lifted his cowboy hat and repositioned it. "He's long gone by now. My truck is four blocks away or I'd take a run at finding him." He pulled her into his arms. "You okay?"

Sarah hung on to him, her tremors subsiding, thinking how good he felt and how glad she was he had come along when he did. "I'm okay."

"Tell me what happened."

Reluctantly, she moved away from him, regretting the loss of his warmth. She explained the encounter, telling him about the gun and repeating the subtle threats.

"He knew we'd met with the FBI in Cheyenne. He said he wanted me to understand what would happen if I talked about my husband's business dealings again."

Jackson rubbed his jaw. "Either someone's been keeping tabs on you or he's got an in with the FBI."

"That's what I figured." She looked up at him, felt a sudden jolt of fear. "Oh, my God — Holly!"

His glance shot down the street. He jerked out his cell phone and handed it over. "Call them. You know the number. Make sure she's okay and tell them to keep her inside until we get there."

She dialed the number with an unsteady hand.

"The day-care people won't let her leave with anyone but you, and I doubt he's willing to make a scene, but we don't want to take any chances."

One of the women at the center answered. Holly was playing Go Fish with some of the other kids. "I'll be there in just a few minutes," Sarah said, relieved. She looked up at Jackson. "She's okay."

"I figured she would be. It's you he's worried about. He thinks you know more than you do, and he wants to make sure you keep quiet. Still . . ." He urged her toward his truck, which was parked down the street. "We'll pick her up, then take that plate number over to the sheriff, see what he can find out."

Sarah stopped walking. "No way, Jackson. I'm not about to go against these people. I've got to think of Holly. I'm the only parent she's got. My daughter needs me."

"We don't know how far these guys are willing to go. Your life could be in danger no matter what you do. Have you thought of that?"

Her eyes slid closed. She swayed a little and felt his arm go around her, drawing her against his side. "I don't know how much more of this I can take." She pressed her face into his shoulder, her eyes welling with tears. "I just don't know."

"We'll get through this, darlin', I promise." He turned her into his arms and held her, smoothed back loose strands of her hair. Finally easing away, he took hold of her hand. "Come on, let's get Holly and go home."

"What about my truck?"

"Leave it here. I'll drive you into town in the morning and you can pick it up."

She didn't argue. The adrenaline rush was beginning to fade and suddenly she was exhausted. When she had awakened that morning, Detective Mercer had been her biggest problem.

Now she was right back where she'd started, trying to figure out what in God's name Andrew had done that threatened her from beyond the grave.

They drove to the day-care center and picked up Holly, fastened her securely in the backseat then headed out of town. Jackson waited until he pulled up in front of the cottage and turned off the engine before reaching beneath the seat and dragging a plastic bag out from underneath.

"I bought you each a present."

Holly sat up straighter, her eyes bright with excitement. "You bought me a present?"

"That's right." He reached into the bag, pulled out a cardboard box and handed it Holly. The other box was larger and he handed that one to Sarah. "I hope they fit."

Sarah took off the lid, saw a pair of soft brown leather cowboy boots nestled inside.

"Boots, Mama!" Tissue paper rustled as Holly pulled her pair out of the box, flashy red ones with great big eagles spread-winged on the front. "They're beautiful!"

Sarah ran a hand over the soft brown

leather, checked inside for the size. "How did you know I wore a seven and a half?"

"I looked at the shoes in your closet. I checked Holly's, too. Of course, until you try them on, you still won't know if they fit."

So they went inside and tried them. Holly's fit perfectly and Sarah's fit nicely, too.

"Thank you, Jackson."

"We're going riding, aren't we? You can't ride without a decent pair of boots."

With the boots still on her feet, Holly ran over and hugged him. "Thank you, Jackson. I love them."

"You're welcome. Just be sure to wear them around a little so you get them broken in."

"I will," Holly promised, dashing back outside to show them to Gibby and Sam. Rags rushed up beside her and started barking. Holly gave his head a quick pat and kept running.

"Until I get things straightened out," Sarah said, "I think Holly should stay here on the ranch with Livvy again."

"So do I. I'll talk to Jimmy, fill him in on what happened in town. He can talk to the hands, ask them to keep an eye peeled for strangers. They're good men. They won't let anyone on the place who doesn't belong."

Sarah nodded, her mind still spinning with worry over the man in town.

"Tomorrow I'll take you in to pick up your truck and bring it home."

"I'm going to work, Jackson. I can't hide out here like a frightened rabbit."

"The guy had a gun, Sarah. I think you should stay close to the house."

She only shook her head. "There's no way to know how long this might go on. I've got a job. I intend to keep it."

Jackson blew out a breath. "I was afraid that's what you'd say. I'll tell you what. I'll take you into town in the morning. You usually only work four or five hours, right?"

"Usually."

"Good, then I'll follow you home when you get off. While you're at work, I'm going to have that old truck of yours gone over, make sure it's in A1 condition. We don't want to chance it breaking down somewhere on the road."

She didn't like it. She treasured her independence. But for now, she knew he was right. "Okay, but after tomorrow, I'll be all right on my own."

"We'll see," was all he said.

She looked up at him as they stood at the living-room window watching Holly outside playing with the boys. Jackson was always so strong and caring. And yet she didn't want to have to depend on him. She needed to be able to take care of herself and her daughter.

Sarah's lips trembled, the situation suddenly more than she could cope with. "What am I going to do, Jackson? I can't live this way, always looking over my shoulder, never knowing if Holly will be safe."

"We're going to do exactly what we did before. We're going to find out who this guy is and who he works for. We'll figure out what it is he thinks you know and find a way to end this."

Sarah swallowed. The man who had accosted her wasn't involved with Kozak Construction. He was harder, the people he worked for clearly more dangerous. He carried a gun and though she didn't think his intention was to shoot her, she was sure he wouldn't hesitate to do it.

She looked over at Jackson, saw the determination in the set of his jaw and tried to find the courage to do whatever it was she had to do.

Jackson made arrangements to leave for California on Monday. He didn't tell Sarah. He didn't intend for her to go.

After the incident in town, he had called

in a favor and gotten an old friend at the motor vehicles department to run the plate number off the Ford. It belonged to Duff Oldman, one of the locals.

Since Duff was sixty-five years old, mostly into gardening and definitely not the criminal type, Jackson figured the guy had traded the rental plate for Duff's, used it while he was in town, then put it back on Duff's car before he left the area.

No help there.

He might be able to track down the rental car at one of the airports, but the guy had undoubtedly used a false ID.

Jackson had to go back to L.A., see where Devlin's information might lead.

In the meantime, it was the weekend and there wasn't much he could do. As promised, he would take Sarah and Holly camping. One thing he knew — once Sarah was up in the high mountains away from her troubles and fears — it would be nearly impossible for her to worry. He knew because it was what he'd done when he was a boy and his mother got drunk, or when he had to spend his hard-earned, after-school-job money to buy his family food.

What he still did sometimes when the troubled world just got too heavy to handle.

For the next two days, up in the high valleys where the air was crystal clear and the scent of pine needles and campfire smoke rode on the breeze, Sarah could forget for a while and just enjoy herself.

Or at least he hoped so.

Where this lady was concerned, nothing was ever certain.

He got up early Saturday morning, long before the sun had popped over the hill, and began to get ready for the trip — brushing the horses down; collecting the tent, sleeping bags, cooking utensils, fire grate and the rest of the overnight gear they would need.

Once he had it all together, he set the pack saddle in place on one of the mules he'd had Wheel Dillon bring in from the lower pasture, put the panniers in place and carefully distributed the weight of the gear.

They could have gone without the mule, old Salty, taken less stuff and made do, but the trip would be more fun, more like the old days when the mountain men packed into the high country to hunt and trap, and he was sure the girls would enjoy it.

Jimmy showed up about the time he was ready to saddle the horses, Galahad for himself and Daisy for Sarah. Until she was a little older, Holly would ride with him.

He found himself liking the thought of

the little girl getting old enough to have a horse of her own, then shook his head, not certain he was ready to think along those lines just yet.

"Need some help?" Jimmy walked up as he set the second saddle in place and adjusted it on Daisy's back.

"Just some company. Aside from that, I'm pretty well ready."

"Should be good weather for it," Jimmy said. "No rain in the forecast."

"I damned well wished there was. I'd be willing to put up with the wet if it helped get rid of this dry."

"I know what you mean."

Jackson tightened the cinch on Daisy's saddle, looked over at Jimmy and wondered what it was he seemed to want to say.

"You and Nan have a good time on the Fourth?" he asked, just to see if that might lead his friend in the right direction.

"Yeah, we did. We had a real good time. The boys sure like her."

He tugged on the latigo, checking to see if the cinch was tight. "What about you? You like her, too?"

"More than I should, I guess."

"Why is that? Nan seems like a nice enough gal."

"We haven't . . . well, you know, but I sure

like having her around. I've even been thinking it might be the kind of thing that could wind up permanent."

One of Jackson's eyebrows went up. Jimmy had never talked this way about a woman. "That sounds good."

"Could be. The only problem is . . ."

"The only problem is . . . ?" he prompted.

"I don't know if I can trust her."

Jackson thought back several years to the time Jimmy had mentioned his interest in dating Nan Hargrove. "You mean because of the guys she took home from the Canyon Club."

He nodded.

"She was single, Jim. She had a right to do what she wanted."

"I know. It's just . . ."

"It's just that Annie chased everything in pants and you don't want to go through that again."

Jimmy looked away. His ex-wife had been a real peach. Everyone in town knew she was wilder than a jackrabbit, but Jimmy had fallen for her anyway. Fallen for her hard. When he'd found out she was making the rounds with half the guys in Wind Canyon, it'd torn him apart.

The luckiest day of Jimmy's life had been the day Annie Baylor Threebears packed her bags and disappeared, never to be seen again. She'd signed the divorce papers, and Jimmy was free, but he'd never really gotten over Annie. Until now, it seemed.

"Give it some time, Jim. There's no rush."

Jimmy shot him a glance that traveled past him, off toward the cottage. "Back at ya, buddy. Sarah's a beautiful woman, but she's trouble. It seems to follow her around like a bad smell."

It was true. Too damned true. And yet he was in for the duration. In until whatever was going on was over.

He didn't have to think twice to know he wasn't going to be another man who had let Sarah Allen down.

Sarah hurried to catch up with Holly, who ran excitedly out of the house off toward the barn. Jackson stood waiting next to the horses, the big red gelding, Galahad, and the pretty little paint mare, Daisy. A pack mule stood at the hitching rail, his long ears twitching at the sound of Holly's small footsteps approaching.

Sarah made a last mental check of the stuff in the duffel bag she carried. Jackets, an extra pair of jeans for each of them, extra socks and sneakers in case their boots got wet. Along with a few miscellaneous personal items, she was ready — and far more excited than she had imagined she would be.

Jackson came forward before she reached him and took the canvas duffel from her hands. "This it?"

She nodded.

"Jackets in here? That high up in the hills, it still gets cold at night."

"It's all there. Once I got started, it all sort of came back. I used to go camping with my dad." She still avoided the bittersweet memory of those times. Her mother had been a true homemaker, Sarah a bit of a tomboy who loved spending time out of doors. "We really had fun."

"We're going to have fun this time." He loaded the duffel on top of the pack rack and tied it snugly in place.

"What's his name?" Holly asked, stroking the mule's soft nose.

"Salty. He can be cantankerous once in a while, but mostly, he's a good ole boy." He stroked the mule's long neck. "Aren't you, son?"

The mule brayed as if he understood, and all of them laughed.

"You ready?" he asked Holly.

"You bet!"

Jackson chuckled as he lifted her up on

the front of his saddle then swung up behind her. "You okay? Got enough room?"

The little girl grinned and nodded.

Jackson took the mule's lead rope, looped it loosely around the saddle horn, and they started off up the trail.

Holly waved goodbye to Jimmy, Sam and Gib, who came to watch them ride out, then settled in for the three-hour ride up the trail into the mountains.

"We'll camp next to the lake," Jackson said. "I've brought a couple of poles so we can fish. We get lucky, we'll have fried fish for supper."

Sarah smiled as she watched him settle himself in the saddle, Holly's back resting against his chest. She was only a little nervous watching Galahad carry Jackson and Holly up the steep section of the trail leading off the road, relaxed as they reached the top and settled into a steady pace.

Jackson rode with the same ease he did just about everything, his shoulders wide and straight, his long legs comfortable in the saddle, boots shoved into the stirrups, hat pulled low over his forehead.

Sarah felt a little pinch in her chest just watching him, thinking how good he looked, how tempting. It was the kind of pinch that wasn't good. The kind that said where this man was concerned, she could be in serious trouble.

Sitting on his horse, looking like every woman's fantasy, Jackson turned and surveyed her with a long, heated glance that ran up her jean-clad legs, settled on her breasts and told her exactly the kind of ride he would rather be making.

Sarah sucked in a breath as a shot of lust hit her so fiercely the muscles in her thighs went taut. Her jeans chafed an intimate spot between her legs and every time Daisy took a step, she felt a jolt of sexual heat.

Good Lord, three hours was going to be a lifetime! And once they got to the lake, it would only get worse. She would have to watch Jackson setting up camp, those hard muscles flexing and tightening, making her stomach twist with longing. With Holly along, there was no way they could make love, no way to find relief.

Sarah watched Jackson riding steadily up the trail, not quite sure she liked this new, sexual side of herself.

Then she smiled. It felt good to desire a man. Good to be desired. Leaning back in the saddle, she relaxed for the first time in days. She had come on this trip to enjoy herself. Whatever happened, whatever the future held in store for her, that was exactly what she intended to do.

Unfortunately in life, nothing ever went the way it was supposed to. They were just approaching the lake when Sarah heard the whine of a chain saw.

"Sonofa—" Jackson broke off in deference to Holly, snatched off his hat and resettled it on his head.

"Loggers?" Sarah pulled Daisy to a stop beside Galahad and Salty in a wide spot on the trail.

The chain saw bit in and whined, and Salty's long ears went up. He began to back away, pulling on his halter, trying to tug the lead rope out of Jackson's hand.

"Easy, son." Leading the mule a few feet away, he swung down from the saddle and tied the animal to a tree.

"They aren't supposed to be working in this section," he said as he led the sorrel back to where Sarah sat on Daisy. "This lake is surrounded by national forest, but these days that doesn't mean the trees are protected."

He lifted Holly out of the saddle and set her on the ground, and Sarah swung down off Daisy. They had stopped a number of times along the route, but still her legs were a little sore.

"You okay?"

She smiled. "I'm fine." A little saddle soreness wasn't much of a price to pay for a trip through such spectacular scenery.

Jackson reached into his saddlebags and dug out a map, spread it open on top of a rock and studied it for several moments. "I thought so." He rolled the map up. "I need to check this out. I won't be gone long." Stepping into the stirrup, he swung aboard the gelding, whirled the horse and headed up the trail.

TWENTY-TWO

"Where's Jackson going, Mama?"

The chain saw had stopped. Jackson must have reached the logging camp. The men couldn't be working that far away.

"I'm not sure, honey. Why don't we leave Daisy here with Salty, walk up the trail a ways and see?" She led the mare over and tied her to graze, then took Holly's hand and started up the trail.

She didn't like the idea of Jackson going head-to-head with a bunch of loggers by himself. If she and Holly were there — a woman and a child — maybe it would ease the situation.

She walked up the trail holding on to Holly's hand and the minute she rounded the bend, she saw them. A group of men clustered around a bunch of heavy equipment: bulldozer, flatbed trailer, some kind of crane for loading the logs onto the truck, other miscellaneous machinery. The words *Ban-*

nock Bros. Logging were stenciled on the sides of the equipment.

"Take a look at the map," Jackson was saying to what appeared to be the foreman, a big burly, barrel-chested, red-bearded man. "Pine Lake is right there." Jackson pointed down the hill. "Black Bear Summit is off to the right, and you can see Badger Pass on your left." He drew a finger along a line on the map. "You were supposed to stop about a half mile back, at the top of Buffalo Ridge."

"So what's it to you? You act like those trees are your own personal property."

"Well, they sure as hell don't belong to you. This is public land, DeSalvo. Your company managed to hornswoggle its way into a logging contract on far too big a chunk of it, but you're clearly over the boundaries that were set."

"So what? You think anyone gives a shit?"

"Wind it up, Red," Jackson warned, "and haul your crew out of here. You don't, I'm going to call the Forest Service and turn you in. I doubt the Bannock brothers will appreciate the big fat fine you cost them."

DeSalvo took a threatening step forward.

"Come on," Jackson taunted. "Throw a punch. I'd love an excuse to whip your sorry ass."

Sarah's stomach tightened. There were five of them and it was clear all of them were spoiling for a fight.

"Stay here," she whispered to Holly, then pasted on a smile, raised a hand, waved and started toward the men.

"Jackson! Jackson, there you are! I've been looking all over." She wasn't afraid the men would hurt her. They were just working men trying to do their jobs. Jackson represented a threat to their way of life and it was clearly him they wanted to stomp into the dirt.

"Take Holly and go back to the lake," Jackson warned, his gaze still fixed on the foreman he'd called Red DeSalvo.

Sarah just kept walking. She paused when she reached the circle of men. "Jackson, we need your help. We can't figure out how to pitch the tent."

He sliced her a look that could have crumbled stone, then turned back to the foreman. "Pack it up or I call the authorities. Get back to the area you're supposed to be working in."

DeSalvo looked from Jackson to Sarah, flicked a glance to where Holly stood at the edge of the clearing, then turned to his men. "Move it, boys. Let's get back up the hill."

Sarah breathed a sigh of relief. She might have smiled if she hadn't looked, just then, into Jackson's furious face.

"Let's go," he said between clenched teeth. Grabbing her arm, he whirled her around and urged her toward the trail. She knew that look, recognized the barely leashed fury in his expression.

She stumbled and nearly fell. On legs that barely held her up, she made her way along the trail, forced herself to keep walking until they rounded the bend. Her vision blurred and she realized her eyes had filled with tears. Why hadn't she seen it sooner? What had she been thinking to trust him the way she did?

She stumbled again and this time Jackson caught her. She cringed and tried to pull away, but he didn't let go. He must have seen the tears in her eyes for the color drained from his face.

"Sarah . . . my God." He stopped there in the middle of the trail and pulled her into his arms. "Honey, it's all right. Everything's okay." He held her, felt her trembling and tightened his hold around her. "Just because I get mad, doesn't mean I'd hurt you. I'd never hurt you or Holly. Never." He eased away enough to look at her. "Surely you know that by now."

The tears in her eyes rolled down her cheeks. She did know. Somewhere deep inside her, she knew he was nothing like Andrew. And she was no longer the submissive, frightened young woman she had been before. Still . . . just for a moment . . .

"Mama, are you okay?"

Jackson knelt in front of Holly. "Sometimes your mama's just too brave for her own good." He came up beside Sarah. "You weren't afraid of five big loggers, but you were afraid of me?"

She caught his incredulous expression and her lips slightly curved. Now that she thought about it, it did seem ridiculous. "I just . . . I didn't want them to hurt you."

Jackson laughed, loud and long. Then he pulled her back into his arms. "You're something, Sarah Allen. You truly are." And then he kissed her, right there on the trail in front of Holly.

"It's getting late," he said gruffly as he drew away. "We'd better get started making camp." Swinging Holly up on his shoulders, leading Galahad, he headed down the trail, walking next to Sarah. When they reached the clearing, he left the trail and walked out into the meadow next to the lake.

"I think this will do," he said, picking a spot close to the pines at the edge of the water. While Holly ran off to gather kindling for a fire — with instructions to stay in sight

— Jackson turned to Sarah.

"I'm not going to promise you I'll never get angry. You pull a stunt like that again — put yourself and your daughter in danger for any reason — I'm liable to get good and mad. I might yell. I might blow off a little steam, but I'd never hit you. I'd never do anything to hurt you. You need to believe that, Sarah, if whatever is happening between us is ever going to have a chance to work."

The words swirled around her, filled her with yearning. *If whatever is happening between us is ever going to have a chance to work.*

There was something in his eyes, something fierce and compelling, and an honesty that drew her as nothing had before. Sarah held his dark gaze for several long moments, then turned away, a new, different kind of fear settling deep inside her.

Fear of losing her independence, fear of the problems that still threatened her future.

And the fearful knowledge that she had fallen in love with Jackson Raines.

The trip was a grand success. Jackson taught Holly how to fish. They fried one of the fat lake trout they caught and ate it for supper, with camp potatoes and homemade

Dutch-oven biscuits and some of Livvy's raspberry jam.

In the morning he fixed flapjacks and bacon and they sat in the warm sun around an early-morning campfire and ate until they were too stuffed to move.

"I can't believe how good this all tastes," Sarah said, apparently impressed with his cooking. "I used to help my dad cook over an open fire. I bet I could do it again with a little practice."

"I bet you could, too," he said, thinking there wasn't much Sarah Allen couldn't do if she put her mind to it. He would never forget the way she had come to rescue him from the loggers. Or how badly it had hurt to see the fear in her pretty blue eyes when she had looked at him on the trail.

She had nothing to fear from him and never would, and he thought that maybe, little by little, she was coming to realize that.

They were tired by the time they packed up the camp that morning and left the meadow and started back down the trail. Holly fell asleep against Jackson's chest as Galahad plodded along, and seeing the trust in her sweet little face made something tighten inside him.

Though he often worked with kids during the summer, mostly with the youth boxing team, he had never realized what he was missing in not having a family of his own.

The thought intrigued him more than it should have and he forced the notion away. He wasn't ready for that kind of thinking. At least not yet.

The small band was exhausted by the time, late in the afternoon, they arrived back at the ranch. Jackson walked the girls to their cottage, then he and Jimmy unpacked the mule, unsaddled, fed and put the livestock away.

"Everything go all right?" Jimmy asked as they turned the horses and Salty out into the pasture.

Jackson glanced back up the mountain. "Aside from a little run-in with Red De-Salvo and some of his loggers. They were half a mile or so over the boundary line." His jaw flexed. "They decided to move back to where they were supposed to be."

Jimmy chuckled. "Lucky for them."

Jackson just grunted.

"I'd better go fix supper," Jimmy said. "The boys'll be getting hungry."

Jackson could see Jimmy's two black-haired sons standing out in front of the house tossing a baseball back and forth. "I guess they aren't going to summer school this year." He had noticed they were there every day, which they hadn't been last year.

"They got nearly straight A's. I figured they deserved a little time to enjoy themselves. Sam's going to start working with Wheel and a few of the hands. Gib's going to do some chores for me and Wheel. I think it'll be good for them."

"So do I." That was how Jackson had learned to love ranching, working on a ranch in the summers. He grabbed his saddlebags off the fence, turned and headed up to the house, thinking of Jimmy and Nan, wondering where the relationship was headed, trying not to think of his own uncertain relationship with Sarah.

"There's supper on the stove," Livvy said as he walked into the warm, steamy kitchen, and he was damned glad.

"Thanks."

"I made enough for the girls. I thought I'd take it over. They're bound to be tired after the trip."

"I'm sure Sarah will appreciate that. Both of them were pretty beat by the time we got home."

"Did they have a good time?"

"You'll have to ask them, but yeah, I think they did. We all did."

Livvy gave him a warm, motherly smile and went to work, serving him up a plate, then putting the rest of the roast, carrots and potatoes, and the remainder of a loaf of crusty French bread on a tray, covering the food with foil, and heading out the door.

As soon as Jackson finished eating, he started upstairs to pack for his trip to L.A. He needed to act on the information Devlin had given him on Ace Trucking, the company that had been paying big chunks of cash to Andrew Hollister. It was likely that someone at Ace was behind the assaults on Sarah. He was going to California to find out exactly what was going on.

Once he reached his bedroom, Jackson set to work. He retrieved his shaving kit and put it in the carry-on he had opened and set on his bed. He packed a couple of pairs of slacks, a clean pair of jeans and a couple of short-sleeved shirts, then added underwear and socks. He turned at the sound of a light knock on his door.

Livvy stood in the opening. "Sarah's downstairs. She says she needs to talk to you."

"Actually, I'm right here." Sarah peered at him over Livvy's plump shoulder, then frowned. "Where are you going?"

He hadn't planned to tell her. He was going to call once he got there. Didn't look like she was giving him any choice.

"Out to your old stompin' grounds. Dev called a couple of nights ago. He had information on a company called Ace Trucking. They were paying Andrew big money under the table. Ace does work for Southgate Demolition." One of Hollister's own companies. "I want to find out what they were paying Andrew for."

"And you were going to tell me about this — when?"

He shrugged his shoulders. "I didn't want you to worry."

Sarah's chin firmed as she stepped out from behind Livvy. "This is my problem, Jackson. You're not going out there unless you take me with you." She turned to his housekeeper. "Will you watch Holly while we're gone?"

"You know I will."

"There's no reason for you to go," Jackson said as Livvy slipped quietly away. "We have no idea if this has anything to do with the man who threatened you in town."

"But it might. And even if it doesn't, maybe we can find out who the guy is and why he's after me."

Jackson sighed. Half of him wanted to insist Sarah stay here on the ranch where she would be safe. The other half was already seeing her in a plush hotel room, curled up in his bed. Damn, sleeping next to her in that little three-man tent was one of the hardest things he'd ever done. He was hard again now, just thinking about it.

He definitely wanted her to go.

And he knew damn well he shouldn't let her.

"You don't have a choice, Jackson. If you don't take me along, I'll fly out there myself. I may not have a lot of money, but I've got some, enough I can afford to get there. I'll march right into Ace Trucking, tell them who I am and demand to know what's going on."

She was bluffing.

Or maybe not.

"All right, dammit, you can go."

"Fine."

He raked a hand through his hair, shoving it back from his forehead. "I'll talk to Jimmy, let him know we'll be gone a couple of days."

"What time are we leaving?"

"Plane's set to leave at 7:00 a.m."

"Then I'd better go pack." She turned and started for the door.

"So why did you want to see me?" he called after her.

Sarah turned back. "I just wanted to thank you for the wonderful trip." She smiled. "I'll see you in the morning." And then she was gone.

Sarah did her homework that night. Sitting at her desk after Holly went to bed, she opened the bottom drawer and pulled out a file that held the pages she had printed off the pen drive they had found in the storage room. One of the pages, she recalled, held notes from a meeting with the managers of Southgate Demolition. She carefully went over the notes, looking for any mention of Ace Trucking.

She found it at the bottom of the page. Ace was working on a couple of Southgate's demolition jobs, but the information was five months old, before Andrew had died, the projects probably completed by now.

Reaching over, she flipped on her laptop. When Google popped up, she typed in *Southgate Demolition.* There were several articles in various newspapers in the L.A. area, as well as the Southgate Demolition home page.

She skimmed their website, which showed color photos of buildings being torn down, then clicked on the link that read *management.* The company was currently being run by a man named Theodore Schuler. Since she had never heard the name, she figured he had probably been appointed by the probate court.

Going back to the Google list of entries, she clicked on a recent article in the *L.A. Times* naming Southgate as the company hired to demolish a six-story building in East L.A. Sarah mentally placed the location, thinking it might border a fairly rough section of town. But then much of L.A. was being revitalized. Space in a city that was growing so fast was always at a premium. Jackson's brother, Gabe, had said he was doing a lot of that kind of work in Dallas.

She jotted down the address of the project, searched a little longer but found nothing that seemed particularly useful.

Next she typed in *Ace Trucking* on Google.

The Ace home page was informative. The company was owned and operated by a man named Vincent Spalino. Though Andrew had mentioned him, Sarah had never met him. There was a photo of Spalino on the page, an older man with beefy jowls, hard black eyes and thick, iron-gray hair. He looked more like a dock worker than a businessman, which didn't seem to fit with the exotic-looking, expensively dressed man who had threatened her here in Wind Canyon.

Then again, if the man who had accosted

her was some sort of hired gun, how he dressed wouldn't matter to Spalino.

She yawned, satisfied she had learned all she could for now, turned off the computer and went to bed. They were flying out at seven and she wanted to have Holly settled with Livvy before she left the ranch.

The morning went as planned. Livvy had Holly nestled on the sofa watching cartoons in the ranch house living room by the time Sarah left. The road was clear on the way to the airport and the weather was good. The chartered, twin-engine plane departed right on schedule.

Sitting next to Jackson in one of the cream leather seats, she took a sip of hot coffee then handed him the information she had collected.

"This is the stuff we printed off the pen drive we found in the storage room and I also printed some items off the internet."

Jackson took the file. "Great minds, I guess. I went on the net last night, myself."

"Find anything?"

"I took a look at Southgate Demolition's web page and ran across the location of a couple of their current projects. I read about them in an article in *Heavy Equipment* magazine."

"I know they're tearing down a building

on Brooklyn Avenue. That's East L.A. It was mentioned in a *Times* article on city revitalization."

"They're demoing a grammar school in Monrovia, too."

"You think they'll be using Ace Trucking?"

"We're going to find out." His foam cup crackled as he took a sip of coffee. "I also made a call to my brother. I asked him if he could arrange for us to talk to his informant, the guy who told him about Ace's cash payments to your late husband."

She ignored a sudden chill. She hated any reference to Andrew as her husband. "And?"

"And he said he'd see if he could make it happen. I expect to hear from him sometime today."

Sarah leaned back in her seat. It was the logical first step. Find out what else Devlin's informant might be able to tell them — if he was willing to talk.

"You think this man will meet us?"

Jackson shrugged. "Money talks," was all he said.

Sarah opened her mouth to tell him she couldn't afford to pay the sort of money it would take, but he held up his hand and simply shook his head.

Sarah sighed. There was no point in arguing. She reminded herself what his brothers had said. Jackson was helping her. Just as he had helped people in the past and would again in the future.

She bit her lip and closed her eyes, let the drone of the engines lull her. She relaxed and grew sleepy. She was just drifting off when erotic images of Jackson began to appear in her mind. She squirmed in her seat, softly whispered his name. She wasn't sure what else she said, something provocative, it was clear, for when she opened her eyes her blouse was unbuttoned, Jackson's dark head bent to the task of suckling her breast.

"Always happy to oblige a lady," he said softly, then returned to the job at hand.

Sensation swamped her. Sarah laced her fingers in his hair to pull him closer, urging him to continue. His teeth grazed her nipple, then she felt the sweet sensation of his mouth opening to take the fullness.

Sarah moaned. Her heavy-lidded gaze slid toward the cockpit door but it was firmly closed. She glanced down to see that her slacks were unzipped as his tanned hand moved over her belly, slipped beneath the band of her thong panties into the tangle of dark hair between her legs. She was wet in an instant, plump and ready for him to take her.

"Jackson . . ." She was trembling all over,

more than eager, but there was a pilot sitting behind the cockpit door and no possible way they could make love.

"As soon as we get to the hotel," he promised, claiming her lips in a slow, ravishing kiss. "In the meantime, I'll give you something to last until we get there."

Sarah arched upward as his long dark fingers slid inside her, stroking deeply, expertly. In moments, she was hovering on the verge of climax. A glance toward the cockpit door assured her it remained tightly closed, and she gave herself over to the exquisite sensations.

"Come for me," Jackson softly urged, and the deep, sexy cadence of his voice sent her over the edge. His hard kiss swallowed a cry of passion, and he held her as she trembled, then began to spiral down.

Her tremors slowly eased, replaced by a glow of satisfaction. A last soft kiss and he let her go, settled himself back in his seat.

Sarah looked down at her open blouse and unzipped slacks and hurriedly rearranged her clothes. Embarrassment pinkened her cheeks as Jackson leaned back in his seat, a smug male smile tilting the corners of his lips.

She couldn't believe it. She had let the man pleasure her in the seat of an airplane!

She glanced toward him from beneath her lashes.

"You don't have to be embarrassed," he said, clearly reading her thoughts. "I liked it, too."

"But you didn't get to —"

"No, but I enjoyed touching you just the same."

She glanced away. He was such a virile man. He liked sex and he made no secret of it.

Sarah rose from her seat and made her way to the tiny bathroom in the rear of the plane to freshen herself. As she closed the minuscule door, she gazed into the small oval mirror on the wall. Her dark hair was mussed and a soft flush colored her cheeks. She looked, well, satisfied.

The plane hit an air pocket just then, tossing her against the wall in the narrow, confining space. She had never liked flying. She glanced back at her reflection in the mirror, saw the glow in her face, felt the sweet tingling that hadn't completely left her.

Then again, there were definitely some advantages to flying with Jackson Raines.

TWENTY-THREE

Jackson's cell phone rang as he slid behind the wheel of his rental car. They had flown into the Burbank Airport, which was close to Ace Trucking in the San Fernando Valley and not far from Southgate Demolition in Glendale. The day was California-warm, eighty-five degrees and sunny. But the weatherman had predicted light showers that night.

Jackson flipped open his phone, recognized the caller ID. "Hey, bro."

"You on the ground?" Dev asked.

"Yeah, we just landed in Burbank."

"That'll work. My guy's name is Jorge Rodriquez. He's willing to meet you — for a price."

"Not a problem. When and where?"

"Tonight. Nine o'clock. A place called the Arizona Café. It's on Valley Boulevard in Alhambra." Dev gave him directions off the eastbound 10 Freeway. "He'll be wearing an L.A. Dodgers ball cap."

"How much do you know about him?"

"Jorge worked for Hollister up until he died. Did pretty much whatever the guy wanted him to. Nothing wet, I don't think. Just errands that required tight lips and muscle when it was needed, that kind of thing. He was out of a job after Hollister got snuffed. Does a little work for a guy I know. According to him, Jorge's got a family. He needs the money. He'll tell you as much as he knows."

"Thanks, Dev."

"It may not be all that much, but you were coming out anyway, so it's definitely worth a try. I'll expect to hear from you when it's over. Take care, big brother."

Jackson leaned back in the car seat. All three brothers were protective of each other. As kids, with a mother who was mostly drunk, there was no one but the three of them, nobody else who gave a damn whether they lived or died. The feeling had stuck. Dev would be worried until he got Jackson's call.

"So what did he say?" Sarah asked from the passenger side of the rental car, a midsize, nondescript Chevy that wouldn't attract attention.

Jackson turned the key in the ignition and

the engine roared to life. "I'm meeting with his informant tonight at nine."

"*We*, Jackson. *We're* meeting him tonight."

He flicked her a glance, caught the stubborn tilt of her chin. *I'm going,* it said. *One way or another.*

He sighed, raked a hand through his hair. He put the car into gear and pulled out of the lot. "You can be a real pain in the ass sometimes, you know?"

Sarah grinned more broadly than he had ever seen her. "I'll take that as a compliment."

Jackson grumbled a word he didn't want her to hear. "Fine, but you do exactly what I tell you, okay?"

She nodded, pleased with herself for getting her way. "Okay."

He thought he understood. She was coming into her own, growing stronger every day, now that she was out from under her husband's brutal, domineering control.

"So where's the meeting?"

"Alhambra. I guess that's a town. You know it?"

She nodded. "It's south and east of here. We're staying in Burbank, right?"

"Afraid so. Nothing fancy, this time, just a little hotel I found on the internet that looked easy to get in and out of and seemed to have decent rooms."

The hotel, the Gramercy, was a little over four miles from the airport, a three-story, U-shaped building that looked clean and well cared for and had parking on all three sides. He had reserved a two-bedroom suite, small but adequate, though he hoped they would only need one of the bedrooms.

They checked in and were shown upstairs into room 318. Sarah rolled her carry-on through the door into the second bedroom.

"You sure you don't want to stay with me?" His hopes rose at the indecision he read on her face.

"I like my privacy. You don't really mind, do you?"

"Of course I mind. I want you in my bed, Sarah. I want to make love to you. I want you there when I wake up in the morning. But I know you need time and I'm willing to give it to you."

Sarah moistened her lips, making them glisten, and his blood began to heat.

"Thank you," she said softly.

He forced his thoughts in a safer direction. "We've got a little time before tonight's meeting. Let's take a drive past that demolition site I came across on the internet — the one Southgate is working on in Monrovia. I looked it up on the map and I don't think it's that far away."

"All right. Traffic shouldn't be too bad this time of day. Maybe we'll run across something useful."

They finished unpacking, then went back downstairs to the car. Fortunately, even after plowing through traffic and checking into the hotel, it was still early afternoon, not yet the rush hour, so the drive didn't take too long.

The bad news was, when they got to the demo site, it wasn't Ace but another trucking company that was busily hauling away the big chunks of cement, bent and rusted rebar, broken windows, mountains of Sheetrock and lumber, and just plain piles of trash resulting from the destruction of a cluster of buildings.

"They aren't using Ace," Sarah said, disappointed. "I wonder why."

"Maybe their bid was too high. Southgate's tearing down a school. The contract would probably be awarded by the state."

They watched the men working, the bulldozers piling up debris, skiploaders scooping it up and dropping it into dump trucks.

"Andrew owned a lot of equipment," Sarah said. "Why do you suppose Southgate needs to hire a trucking company? Why doesn't Southgate just haul the stuff away?"

"Andrew owned equipment, but not all of it was the right kind. From what we've seen, Southgate Demolition uses on-site machinery — bulldozers, pavers, skiploaders, that kind of thing. Andrew was never in the transport business."

Sarah studied the activity on the site. "Still, he owned some trucks. Maybe Ace does some kind of specialized work for Southgate. Something that requires slightly different kinds of trucks."

"Good thought. Maybe tonight good ol' Jorge will be able to tell us." And if not, maybe they would at least pick up something useful. Jackson looked at his wristwatch. The afternoon was slipping away. The traffic would be worse going back. They hadn't had anything to eat since morning, and the long plane ride was always tiring.

"Why don't we head back to the hotel? You can call and check on Holly, then we'll get something to eat and maybe catch a nap. We'll regroup and be ready for Jorge."

Sarah nodded, yawned behind her hand. "Now that you mention it, I could use a little sleep." She looked up at him and a sexy smile curved her lips. "Besides, I owe you for that little present you gave me on the plane. I wonder . . . am I officially a member of the mile-high club?"

A rush of blood went straight to his groin. "Only an associate member, but I'll be glad to remedy that on the flight back home."

Sarah laughed, but her cheeks turned red. The lady was definitely an enigma, embarrassed one minute, bold the next. She wanted a room of her own, but she wanted to have sex with him. She had a lot to figure out about herself, he guessed.

"You don't owe me for that," he said, getting back to the subject at hand, "but I'd like nothing more than to take you to bed." Leaning across the console, he kissed her long and deep.

Sarah kissed him back and he figured they had just sealed the deal.

Sarah watched the big green freeway signs for the exit off the 10 that Devlin had said to take into Alhambra. The sun was almost down, the last faint remnants of light fading along the horizon. The heat of the day was easing, as well, the temperature cooled by a layer of clouds moving over the city. A light rain had begun to fall, just enough to dampen the arid land along the highway.

Earlier, after making love, a nap in Jackson's bed, and hamburgers and French fries from the hotel's limited room service menu, they set off for tonight's meeting, leaving early enough to get there even if they ran into trouble on the road.

Another freeway sign loomed ahead of them out of the darkness. "There it is." Sarah pointed. Jackson spotted the turnoff, signaled and eased the car toward the off-ramp. A few minutes later, they were heading down Valley Boulevard in search of the Arizona Café.

It was a coffee shop, Sarah saw as they pulled into the parking lot and Jackson turned off the engine. She had no idea why it was named for another state, except maybe for the dirt and tumbleweeds around the edge of the lot, making it look like it sat in the middle of the desert.

"We wait out here until it's time to go in," Jackson said. "I doubt Jorge would want us drawing any more attention than necessary."

They waited fifteen minutes, till exactly 9:00 p.m., then got out of the car, crossed the rough pavement, and pushed through the glass doors into the small café. A mix of whites, Hispanics, African-Americans and Asians sat in booths and at the long Formica-topped counter. A good spot to meet, Sarah thought, a place where, dressed in jeans and a T-shirt, her hair pulled back in a ponytail, with Jackson in jeans and a short-sleeved shirt, they would blend in fairly well with the rest of the customers in the café.

Jackson said Jorge Rodriquez would be wearing a Dodger's baseball cap and Sarah scanned the counter in search of him. He wasn't there, or in any of the pink vinyl booths along the wall.

"He's in the back, the last booth," Jackson said softly.

Sarah spotted him, average height, muscular build, plain white T-shirt snug across his chest. Jackson's fingers entwined with hers and he led her forward.

Jorge Rodriguez pulled his cap a little lower over his straight black hair as they slid into the booth on the seat across from him. He was drinking a cup of coffee, a dark-skinned, round-faced man with black eyes and an earring in his ear.

"Why'd you bring her?" he asked Jackson sullenly. "You should have come alone."

"She's Hollister's widow. She's the one who's on the hook for his mistakes."

A waitress appeared, stringy blond hair but a friendly smile. They ordered coffee, waited till she set the heavy white china mugs down in front of them and returned to her duties.

"Tell us what you know." Jackson shoved a folded newspaper across the table. Jorge peeked inside, saw four crisp hundred-dollar bills, closed it quickly and dragged it to his side of the booth.

"Ace made a cash payment once every month. I picked up the payments directly from Spalino and delivered the envelope to Hollister personally."

"What was the money for?"

"I don't know. I overheard them talking once . . . something to do with getting rid of waste."

Sarah exchanged a look with Jackson, neither of them had a clue what that meant. Still, the information might prove useful.

"What else?" Jackson slid another hundred out on the table.

"They talked about putting it somewhere safe. They didn't say where."

"Anything else?"

"That's all I got."

Jackson dropped a five-dollar bill on the table to pay for the coffee. With a nod at Jorge, he urged Sarah up from the booth, and they walked toward the door. Clues. Like pieces of a puzzle. Separately they meant nothing, but putting them altogether might just give them the answers they so desperately needed.

Outside in the parking lot, the light rain had already stopped, leaving a pattern of scattered drops in the dirt.

"It wasn't much, was it?" Sarah said.

"Might be more than you think. We're only getting started. Let's see what tomorrow brings."

Sarah just nodded. Her mind was spinning. So much was happening. So many things seemed out of her control. She thought of the dark-skinned man in Wind Canyon who had threatened her in the parking lot. She thought of Detective Mercer, and a shudder moved down her spine.

If it weren't for Jackson . . .

A lump swelled in her throat. He was helping her now. But what would he do when he found out it wasn't just another of Andrew's crooked business partners who threatened her?

What would he do when he found out the police were after her, too?

Sarah slept poorly, even though she and Jackson had made love and he had convinced her to spend the night in his bed. Unconsciously, she snuggled closer, absorbing his warmth, his hard-muscled body enfolding her protectively even in his sleep.

Still, it wasn't enough to stop the nightmare from returning, slipping into her subconscious as it had done dozens of times before.

She was upstairs packing, getting ready to leave the house for good, when she heard Andrew's voice downstairs.

"Sarah! Sarah, come down here! I want to see you in my study!"

She could hear the anger in his voice, the fury. Fear cut through her, settled sickeningly in her stomach. Her glance strayed to the bed and uncertainty swamped her. She bit her lip, trying to decide, then stiffened her spine and moved forward. Her legs trembled as she crossed the bedroom, walked to the side of her bed and pulled the pistol out from under the mattress.

The pistol Patty Gorski had sent her.

"Use it if you have to," the brief note had said. "Don't let him hurt you again."

There were no serial numbers on the weapon. Patty was smart about those kinds of things. She'd sent it UPS, boxed like clothes ordered over the internet.

Sarah's hand shook as she stuck the gun in her purse, looped the strap over her shoulder. It took every ounce of her will to walk to the door, open it and make the trip downstairs. But the gun was there, lending her courage. She wouldn't pull it out unless she had to, but she wouldn't take another brutal beating.

She stood in the open study door, saw him rise from behind his desk.

"What . . . what do you want, Andrew?"

"Do you think I'm a fool, Sarah?"

Once she had thought he was handsome. Now his face looked pure evil. "Why would I think that?"

"Maybe because you didn't think I'd read your emails, find out what you were planning to do."

"I don't . . . I don't know what you're talking about." He couldn't know. She'd been so careful.

He just smiled. It was the kind of smile that made her stomach squeeze in fear, the kind that made her insides roll with nausea.

"I told you we were going to Rio. Did you actually think you were going to take Holly and run away?" His smile looked feral and her stomach rolled again. "I went directly to the server. I saw what you wrote to that woman."

She swallowed past the lump in her throat. "It was only conversation." She had never been specific, only hinted to Patty. But Patty knew what Sarah had suffered, understood as no one else ever could.

Sarah straightened, determined not to let him know how frightened she was. "Holly and I aren't going with you. You can leave if you want, but we're staying here."

His mouth thinned to a slash across his face. "You really believe you can defy me? You don't remember what happened the last time?"

She remembered. He had beaten her so badly she'd wound up in the hospital. She swallowed, tried to block the memory.

He stepped away from his chair, rounded the corner of his desk. Fury etched lines into his face. Anticipation glittered in his eyes. He liked this, liked to hurt her.

"Andrew, please don't do this." She forced herself not to back away, to hold her ground and face him. When he just kept coming, she drew the pistol from her purse.

Her hand shook. "Stay away from me, Andrew. I'm warning you." A noise reached her. Was someone else in the house? "I — I won't let you hurt me again."

His cruel laughter rang in her ears. The hellish sound sent a jolt of adrenaline into her blood and awakened her from the nightmare. A shot?

Or maybe it was Jackson, whose face loomed above her as he reached out and caught her shoulders.

"Sarah? Sarah, are you all right?"

She swallowed past the bile that rose in her throat. Tears welled in her eyes, began

367

to run down her cheeks. She was shaking so badly Jackson drew her into his arms.

"Take it easy, darlin'. It was only a dream."

Sarah clung to him, hung on as hard as she could.

"Easy," he soothed. "You're all right now."

She took a deep breath, exhaled slowly, fought to regain her composure. "I'll be okay. Just . . . just give me a minute."

"Take all the time you need." He stroked her hair, held her snugly against his chest. "It was him again," he said. "Andrew. You called out his name."

Her eyes slid closed. "Sometimes . . ." She swallowed. "Sometimes I remember the things he did and I get scared all over again. I wish I could forget, but at night . . . sometimes I can't."

She felt his lips against the top of her head. "It's all right, honey. Sometimes the past is hard to forget."

He talked as if he knew and she remembered his troubled childhood — the father who abandoned them, the mother who drank herself to death. Maybe he was like Patty. Maybe he understood.

They lay back on the mattress, and he curled her against his side, wrapped her in his arms as he pulled up the covers. She thought she wouldn't fall asleep, but his warmth and strength surrounded her, and she did.

The dream did not return. Jackson's presence banished it. But it would come again, she knew.

And if Mercer got his way, the nightmare she would face would be real.

Twenty-Four

Jackson was in the shower when Sarah awakened. She heard the stream of water go off in the bathroom and a few minutes later, he opened the door. A rush of steam swept into the room, hiding him for a moment from view.

"I thought I'd let you sleep," he said. "After last night, I figured you could use a little extra time in bed."

A fluffy white towel rode low on his hips, exposing a flat abdomen ridged with muscle, a broad chest and powerful biceps. She allowed her gaze to run over him and wished he had awakened her with his lovemaking instead of letting her sleep.

"Keep looking at me that way and I'll take you up on what you're thinking. I'll have you again before we leave."

She laughed, wishing she could let him. "It's too late for that. We have too much to do."

He grumbled, and then he smiled. He had the most breathtaking smile. "There's always later." He walked over to the bed and pressed a soft kiss on her lips. "You'd better get going. We're driving all the way to East L.A."

She grabbed her silk robe, rolled out of bed and headed for the shower in the other bedroom. Twenty minutes later, she walked back through the door into the living room for some of the coffee and rolls he'd had room service bring up.

She sipped the rich black brew and nibbled the sweet pastry as she talked to Holly, laughing at the story of Rags chasing a big raccoon that turned and chased him back inside the house.

She smiled as she hung up the phone. "I miss her already."

"Maybe we'll have better luck today and we can go home."

Sarah hoped so. Last night Jackson had called Devlin after their meeting with Jorge Rodriquez. Dev had asked him to phone again if they found out anything more.

Sarah grabbed her purse, anxious to get started and see what they might discover. "Ready?"

Jackson nodded, walked over and opened the door.

As they drove out of the parking lot, she studied him, thinking of the call he'd made to Devlin. "You're very close to your brothers, aren't you?"

He shrugged, but it was clear it was an important subject. "We're all we've got," he said, as if that explained everything.

Sarah settled back against the seat. "You're lucky to have them. I always wanted a sister, but Mom had to have a hysterectomy so my parents never had more children. I have a friend in Chicago who's the closest I've got to a sister. It's crazy, since we've never even met."

"How did that happen?"

"She was one of the women in the battered women's group I told you about. She was the founder, the one who got the program started. We really seemed to connect." She told him a little about Patty, how funny she could be and how strong. How she hoped someday to meet her.

"I used to call her from a pay phone whenever I got the chance. She was my rock, the reason I could get out of bed in the morning." Sarah didn't say more, didn't even tell him Patty's last name. "She's the best friend I've ever had."

Jackson cast her a sympathetic glance as he took the 60 Freeway and continued along the road. Eventually, they found their way onto Brooklyn Avenue, the location of Southgate's project.

"You got the address?" he asked.

"Right here." She pulled out a slip of paper, read him the street numbers, and both of them started searching. The location wasn't hard to find. The demolition site was marked by a wide blue sign — Future Home of Freemark Plaza — a large office complex that would be a big asset to the neighborhood.

Just like the day before, one of Southgate's Demolition teams was hard at work. But this time, an Ace company truck sat next to the six-story building being torn down.

And the difference was instantly apparent.

"Oh, my God, they're hauling asbestos," Sarah said.

" 'Something to do with waste,' Jorge said. The men must have been talking about asbestos."

Warning signs were everywhere, including on the trucks. Men completely enclosed in white protective suits, gloves, booties, and wearing sophisticated particle masks, worked in the interior of the six-story building which had been opened up on one side.

"The backs of the trucks are fully enclosed," Sarah said.

"Everything's enclosed, including the men."

The asbestos being removed were first sprayed down with water, she saw, then dropped through flexible tubing directly into the back of the trucks, or carried in tightly sealed plastic bags.

"Southgate does the demolition," Jackson said, "but they need special vehicles to haul the waste away."

They watched for more than an hour, but saw nothing but a group of men hard at work. One of the Ace trucks was finally filled and ready to leave. It had been tightly sealed to ensure none of the toxic particles escaped into the air.

"I don't know much about asbestos," Sarah said. "I know it causes cancer and lung disease."

But tonight they could find out more on the subject. Jackson had brought his laptop and the hotel provided wireless internet service.

They watched one of the trucks prepare to leave. The driver, wearing one of the white protective suits, climbed behind the wheel and drove the vehicle out through the chain-link fence surrounding the construction site.

"Come on. Let's see what happens next."

Jackson started the Chevy, waited for the truck to pass, waited a few more minutes, then pulled in with the traffic headed in the same direction.

"Where do you suppose they dump that stuff?"

"Someplace that specifically handles toxic waste. I imagine the closest location is a pretty good distance away."

It wasn't as far as they thought, a disposal site located in the City of Commerce. The driver pulled up to a guarded gate, signed something on a clipboard and drove on into the facility. Jackson waited till the truck pulled back out, then followed its return to the construction site for another load.

"I hate to say this, but everything looked perfectly legitimate to me."

From their parking spot near the site, Sarah watched the Ace truck being filled with more of the wet asbestos. "It's daylight. Nobody does anything illegal in the daytime. I think we should do this like they do on TV — go down to Ace Trucking after dark and stake the place out."

"Stake the place out?" Jackson chuckled at the term. "You really think —"

"So far Jorge's information has gotten us nowhere. Have you got a better idea?"

He rubbed his jaw. "Not at the moment.

All right, we'll give it a try. It'll be a damned long night, but I suppose it's worth a go."

They waited till eleven o'clock before leaving the hotel. Jackson helped Sarah into the car then drove toward the San Fernando Valley. The Ace Trucking compound was easy to spot. Rows of trucks sitting on an asphalt lot surrounded by a tall chain-link fence. A one-story building, flat-roofed and unimpressive, sat on one side of the compound. Inside, everything was dark.

"They look like they're locked up for the night," Jackson said, surveying the empty lot lit only by a few tall mercury lights.

"Maybe," Sarah said stubbornly. "Or maybe that's just what they want people to think."

Jackson didn't laugh. Sarah was smart. And considering the connection between Ace and Andrew Hollister — the cash payments and Jorge's comments — she just might be right.

The hours slowly passed. "You want some coffee?" he asked. They had stopped and bought a thermos at a Kmart they passed, drove through a McDonald's and had it filled with hot coffee.

"Sounds good."

Jackson poured some of the dark liquid

376

into the plastic lid and they shared it. They were parked well out of sight, in a spot behind a patch of oleanders growing next to an empty metal building.

They sipped coffee, watched and waited. It was a warm night, only a quarter moon, making it easier for them to remain hidden.

At one o'clock, Sarah gave up a weary sigh. "I guess I was wrong. We might as well go back to the hotel."

Jackson surveyed the darkness, searching right and left one last time. The hair rose at the back of his neck. "Somebody's out there."

Sarah straightened in her seat. "Near one of the asbestos trucks?"

"No, just a regular truck and trailer. The guy just opened the door of the cab. Now he's climbing inside."

For a moment the dome light went on. "Yes, I see him. Another man just got in with him."

Jackson watched as the driver started the engine and slowly pulled the vehicle toward the gate. It opened automatically, then closed behind him. The truck continued slowly down the street, its headlights turned off. They didn't go on until the vehicle was nearly a block away.

Jackson waited until the truck turned the

corner, then started the car and followed, careful to stay out of sight.

"I don't believe this," Sarah said.

"It might be nothing. Maybe just a job out of town that requires an early start."

"Or it might be what we've been looking for. Trucks don't usually drive around with their headlights turned off."

It was a little odd, he thought as the truck found its way onto the freeway. Jackson followed at a distance, taking the same on-ramp then an off-ramp several miles down the road, traveling the same streets, following a few cars behind. The truck turned into another fenced compound. The sign on the gate read, Hexel Pharmaceuticals.

The truck and trailer disappeared inside the compound, then drove through a huge roll-up door that led into an opening in one of the two-story buildings.

"Why would they need to come here in the middle of the night?" Sarah asked.

"Good question."

Fifteen minutes later the truck reappeared. When the driver drove beneath one of the lights in the yard, Jackson saw that both men were wearing hazard suits, but this time the material wasn't white, it was black.

"White stands out too much," he said.

"Which means they don't want to be seen."

They waited till the truck disappeared down the street then pulled into the traffic and followed. The vehicle made its way onto the 15 Freeway, northbound.

"This is getting very interesting," Jackson said. "Not much out here. They may not be planning to stop anytime soon."

"Looks like we may be having breakfast in Las Vegas."

Jackson chuckled, thinking it could be true.

But a couple of hours into the drive, some miles east of the small desert town of Barstow in the middle of nowhere, the truck turned onto a frontage road. To maintain his distance, Jackson pulled onto the edge of the freeway just before their car reached the off-ramp and watched the truck until it turned onto a dirt road leading farther into the desert.

Sarah swiveled in the seat to face him. "You aren't going to stop now?"

He released a slow breath, wishing he could, but knowing how important this could be. "We saw where he turned. We'll wait another couple of minutes and go after them."

They waited, Sarah on the edge of her seat

until Jackson took the off-ramp, then pulled onto the frontage road. When he reached the dirt road, he turned off the headlights.

"I hope we didn't lose them," Sarah said.

But there was no one around for miles out here. The truck was running with only its parking lights on, but Jackson could easily make it out in the distance.

"It's turning again," Sarah said anxiously.

"I see that." He followed, keeping as far back as he could. The truck pulled to a stop. The dome light went on as one of the men got out.

Jackson was a quarter of a mile away when he pulled the car over to the side of the road and turned off the engine. Reaching up, he popped the plastic cover on the dome light and removed the bulb. "You stay here. I'm going to take a closer look."

"No way. I'm going with you."

"Sarah —"

She opened the door before he could argue and started walking along the road. Both of them were dressed in black and wearing comfortable shoes. Jackson swore softly and hurried to catch up with her.

"If you're determined to go, let's get off the road so we won't be spotted."

Sarah followed his lead, staying low, weaving in and out of the sagebrush and cactus that dotted the flat desert landscape.

"What about snakes?" she whispered as they hurried along.

"Just hope we don't step on any." Up ahead, the truck was parked at the base of a barren mountain where the road came to an end. Now as they watched, the vehicle started up again, drove inside a fenced compound, then into a hole in the side of the hill.

"It looks like a mine," Sarah said softly.

Jackson nodded. "There are probably a lot of them out here."

The area was surrounded by fencing, but a lot of it was falling down. Near the gate leading into the yard, a sign hung at an angle. Dry Springs Mine. Another sign read, Axis Mining Company.

"Oh, my God."

"Yeah." Both of them recognized the names. The bankrupt mining company had been listed as one of Hollister's assets.

"I'm trying to remember . . ." Sarah said. "Andrew mentioned it a couple of times. As far as I recall, it was never productive, just an old, played-out gold mine Andrew's father bought on a whim." She looked back at the entrance where the truck had disappeared. "They must be dumping something from the pharmaceutical company in there."

"Biowaste would be my guess."

She started forward and Jackson caught her arm, stopping her. "We're pushing our luck, Sarah. We need to call the authorities."

For once she didn't argue. Whatever was going on, it appeared to be highly illegal. They needed to talk to Richard Kemp, tell the FBI what they had seen and let them find out exactly what was going on.

"Come on. Let's get out of here." Catching hold of her hand, he turned and took a step, came to an abrupt halt as he stared into the barrel of a gun.

"Too late for that," said a man's deep voice. The black hazard suit was gone. He was tall, lean and wiry, thin-faced, with hair as black as the night. Jackson might have gone for the weapon if the man hadn't swung it toward Sarah, pressed it up against the side of her head.

She made a little whimpering sound, but didn't move.

"Where's your car?" the man asked.

"Just down the road," Jackson answered.

"Let's go."

They walked along the dirt road, both of them moving in front of the man with the pistol, a big Glock 9 mm, it looked like.

He shoved Jackson toward the driver's side. "Get in and drive." He tipped his head toward Sarah. "You get up front with him."

She did as she was told while the man with the gun got into the backseat and aimed the weapon at the back of her head.

"Where are we going?" Jackson asked.

"Back to the yard. Mr. Spalino wants a word with you."

So they'd been in touch with the boss. Apparently cell phones worked even out here. Jackson started the Chevy, turned it around in the road, and headed back to L.A. He drove carefully. With Sarah the target, he couldn't afford to take chances.

It seemed to take forever to reach the trucking company back in the San Fernando Valley. The lights were on in the office when they drove through the gate, which stood open as if in welcome.

"Pull up in front."

Jackson did as directed, waited till the man climbed out of the car and yanked Sarah out, then climbed out himself. Another guy stood on the porch in front of the door, stocky, with a heavy thatch of iron-gray hair and a bulldog face.

Vincent Spalino.

"It's a little early for visitors — even

around here." Spalino tipped his head toward the man with the gun. "Bring 'em inside, Floyd."

Jackson rested a hand on Sarah's shoulder, hoping to reassure her. If Spalino wanted them dead, there was no better time or place than out there at the mine.

They walked into Spalino's office, Spartan, with a metal desk and chairs, a brown vinyl sofa that looked as if it occasionally served as a bed, and a few family photos on the wall. The door closed behind them. The tall guy, Floyd, didn't come in.

Spalino walked behind his desk but remained standing. "Take a seat."

Jackson sat down next to Sarah in cushioned metal chairs on the opposite side of the desk.

"All right," Spalino said, "who the hell are you and what the hell do you want?"

Sarah cast Jackson a glance that told him she was the one who needed to speak. "I'm Sarah Hollister — Andrew's wife. This is a friend, Jackson Raines. We came to find out why you've been making threats against me and my daughter."

"So, you're Hollister's widow."

"That's right."

Spalino sat down in his black leather chair. "Well, I've got news for you, lady. Your husband had more enemies than fingers and toes. If someone's been threatening you, it ain't me."

"The way I hear it," Jackson put in, "Andrew Hollister was blackmailing you. You figured Sarah knew you were dumping pharmaceuticals out at the mine and you wanted to make sure she kept her mouth shut."

He grunted. "First off, me and Hollister were business partners. That's all. He didn't ask for anything more than we agreed on. Hexel paid me to dump the stuff, and I paid Hollister for the use of his property. He was happy to get the money."

Jackson mulled that over. Hollister had been blackmailing Kozak, but not Spalino. "If it isn't you, it must be the pharmaceutical company."

Spalino shrugged his bulky shoulders. "Could be. The company's got real deep pockets. Hollister might have figured he could squeeze a little more out of 'em."

"Would they come after Sarah?"

"They might. It's a small company with big plans. The guys who run it haven't been around that long. They still don't know the ropes."

Meaning they were wild cards, just the sort to cause trouble.

"The dumping has to stop," Sarah said.

Spalino leaned back in his chair. "We ain't paying your husband no more. I told those guys at Hexel that sooner or later it would have to end. With Hollister dead, the mine's in probate. Better to seal it up now, before somebody starts sniffing around."

"What do you mean, *seal it up?*" Sarah asked.

He eyed her with speculation, as if weighing how much he could say. "You got the cash, right? The money your husband got paid? He was thinking of leavin' the country. I figured he was putting away a little nest egg. When he died, you got the cash so we're in this together, right?"

Sarah opened her mouth.

"She got the money," Jackson answered for her. "We're all in this together."

Spalino nodded. "The stuff's stored in fifty-gallon drums. The drums are stashed in one of the auxiliary mine shafts. A few sticks of dynamite to close the entrance to the shaft and the barrels are safely disposed of, all nice and tidy."

Jackson looked at Sarah. Now wasn't the time to argue. She made a faint nod of her head, clearly getting the message.

"What about Hexel Pharmaceuticals?" Jackson asked. "How do we get them to leave Sarah alone?"

"I'll talk to them, explain the deal." He turned to Sarah. "If they're the ones who been hassling you, they won't give you any more trouble."

Jackson caught Sarah's faint wash of relief.

"That . . . that sounds fair."

"Hey, we all came out winners, didn't we? Hexel will have to figure something out, but you know, that's their problem."

He rose from behind his chair. "Too bad about your husband. Him and me — we always got along real good."

Sarah made no reply. It was difficult to manage a nod.

"Your car's out front," Spalino said.

"Thanks." Jackson rose and so did Sarah. He set his hand at her waist and guided her toward the door.

"One more thing."

Both of them stopped and turned.

"You open your mouth to the wrong people — you won't be getting threats. You'll be dead."

TWENTY-FIVE

"I want to go home." Sarah turned as Jackson closed the door to their suite behind them. It was seven-thirty in the morning and they were just getting back to the hotel.

"All right. I'll call the airport, make arrangements to leave. We'll be back in Wyoming before dark."

Sarah paced over to the window and looked down into the courtyard. She watched a young valet pull a car up in front of the lobby, then wait for the driver to climb inside.

She turned back to Jackson. "This all seems so surreal."

"I know what you mean."

"I don't feel right about leaving that stuff in the mine. We don't even know what it is."

"Some kind of waste from whatever it is Hexel doesn't want anyone to know they're doing."

388

"I feel like I should do something, but —" She shook her head. "But I've got Holly to think of." She returned to staring out the window, watched the valet through a sudden film of tears. "How could I have married a man like that? How could I not have seen what he was like from the beginning?"

Jackson walked up behind her. Slipping his arms around her waist, he drew her back against his chest. "You were young. He was good at what he did and that included conning you."

She turned around and leaned into him, slid her arms around his neck. "I wish it had been you."

He moved a strand of dark hair off her cheek with his finger. "There's time, Sarah. You're young yet and so am I. Things can still work out."

She looked up at him and the tears in her eyes rolled down her cheeks. She stepped out of his embrace, felt a chill at the loss of his warmth. "I won't marry again, Jackson. Not ever. You might as well know that. If you're looking for a wife, you need to look somewhere else."

Jackson's gaze remained on her face. "I wasn't looking for a wife when you came along, Sarah. I'm not looking now. But unlike you, if the right person happens to come into my life — if I fall in love — I won't throw away the chance for happiness."

Sarah felt a sharp pinch in her heart. *If I fall in love . . .*

She was in love with Jackson. She didn't think he knew and she would never tell him. How could she? How could she drag a good man like Jackson into the kind of sordid life she had been living? The kind that seemed to follow her wherever she went?

"I need to pack," she said, turning away from him and heading for her bedroom.

"I'll arrange our flight home."

Sarah paused at the door and looked back at him, saw him reach for the phone. He was so handsome her heart squeezed. She had never met anyone like him. She never would again.

She was in love with him and she didn't deserve him.

She stepped into the bedroom, closed the door and leaned against it. If Spalino kept his bargain, she and Holly would be safe.

There was no reason to continue her impossible relationship with Jackson.

There was only one thing to do.

As soon as she got back to Wyoming, she was moving off Raintree Ranch.

The plane returned them safely home. Jackson drove his pickup, which he'd left at the Wind Canyon airport, back down the road to the ranch. Sarah sat in silence beside him.

"You're supposed to be feeling better," he finally said. "I've got a hunch Vincent Spalino is a man of his word, and I'm pretty sure Hexel Pharmaceuticals is behind the threats against you. Spalino will talk to them and hopefully, your problems will disappear."

She looked up at him with troubled blue eyes. "I hope you're right. I still don't like the idea of just looking the other way while Hexel dumps its garbage into the mine or somewhere else. They don't want to go to a legitimate toxic dump site because they don't want anyone to know what they're doing. God only knows what that is — or what the consequences might be."

Jackson slowed to let a deer cross the road. A small spotted fawn followed its mother. "I'll talk to Dev. Maybe we can come up with a way to handle the problem without involving you."

She nodded, sighed and settled back in the seat. She fell silent again as he turned down the private road leading into the ranch. A car sat in front of the main house, he saw as they drove up, a plain brown Ford

Taurus with bald tires that needed replacing.

Jimmy stood in front of the driver's-side door talking to the man, who had straight brown hair cut short, a bad complexion, and wore wrinkled khaki slacks. Sarah made a funny sound in her throat as Jackson pulled the pickup to a stop in front of the ranch house next to the car.

Jackson turned. "You know who that is?"

She glanced away. He could see she was upset.

"Who is he, Sarah?

She trembled. "He's . . . he's a policeman from Los Angeles . . . a detective named Mercer."

Jackson opened the door of the pickup, rounded the vehicle and helped Sarah climb down. Mercer turned away from Jimmy and started walking toward them.

"Welcome back," the man said to Jackson with a smile that looked anything but sincere. "I'm Detective Ed Mercer, homicide division, LAPD. I'd like a word with you, Mr. Raines."

"Why did you come back here?" Sarah interjected. "Why can't you leave me alone?"

"I'm just on vacation," Mercer said, "heading home after two weeks off. I told you that when I came to see you before."

Jackson looked at Sarah hard. She hadn't mentioned the detective's visit. He couldn't help wondering why.

"If you'll excuse us, Sarah," Mercer said, "I'd like to talk to your friend alone."

Jackson could see she wanted to join them, but Mercer wasn't giving her a choice.

"Holly's probably with Livvy," Jackson said. "I'll send her home."

Sarah just nodded, watching as he and Mercer walked inside the ranch house. Holly spotted him and came running in from the kitchen, bubbling with excitement.

"Jackson!" She ran to him and he lifted her into his arms.

"You keep growing," he teased, "and pretty soon you'll be too heavy for me to lift."

She giggled at that. "I'm glad you and Mama are home."

He gave her a kiss on the cheek and set her back down on her feet. "Your mama's waiting for you in the cottage."

Holly flashed a grin, then took off running, heading back into the kitchen, slamming out the screen door and racing for home.

Jackson turned to the detective. "Why don't we go into my study? We can speak privately there." He headed that way and Mercer fell in behind him. Once the door was closed, he moved toward his desk instead of the sofa, forcing Mercer to take a seat in one of the brown leather chairs on the opposite side.

"So what can I do for you, Detective?"

Mercer surveyed the study, his gaze taking in the leather-bound books on the shelves and the old potbellied stove. Though Jackson didn't even know the man, there was something about him that rubbed him the wrong way.

Mercer leaned back in his chair. "Like I said, I was just passing through. I thought I'd stop by, see if there was something you might be able to tell me about Andrew Hollister's murder."

Jackson eyed him carefully. "How could I tell you anything? I wasn't there when it happened. I didn't even know the guy."

"No, but you know the woman who shot him."

Jackson's whole body tightened. He held on to his temper, but only by a thread. "As far as I know, Sarah Allen isn't even a suspect in her husband's murder."

"Oh, she's a suspect, all right. She was there that night. It isn't clear exactly what time she left the house but she could have been there at the time the murder was committed. She had motive. It was common knowledge the woman hated her husband. Hollister had a girlfriend and Sarah found out. Oh, and there was the life insurance policy."

"What are you talking about? Sarah got almost nothing from Hollister's estate."

"True enough. Turned out the policy was expired. But then, Sarah didn't know it at the time. She didn't find that out until later."

"That's all you have? She might have been there around the time he was killed and she didn't like him?"

"Motive and opportunity, my friend. And the spouse is always the number one suspect. In this case, it all adds up."

"And how, exactly, did she kill him? Point her finger at him and pull the trigger? Sarah doesn't own a gun."

"We haven't found the murder weapon yet, but sooner or later, something's going to turn up that proves she was the one who shot him."

Jackson came out of his chair. "This conversation is over. Unless you're here with an arrest warrant, Detective, it's time for you to leave."

Mercer stood up, too. "Like I said, I was

on vacation. Two weeks this year. I just figured I'd drop by, see if you might have something you wanted to tell me."

"Yeah, well, I don't. And since this is private property, I'd suggest you get moving. I'm sure they could use your services back in L.A."

Mercer smiled the same unfriendly smile he'd flashed before. "I'll keep in touch. You never know . . . you might have a change of heart."

Jackson made no comment, just stood fuming as Mercer walked out of the study.

Change of heart? One thing he knew for sure. Where his heart was concerned, it was already too late for a change.

Sarah opened the door to let Holly and Rags out to play. She froze at the sight of Jackson standing on the porch, his fist raised to knock, as angry as she had ever seen him.

Two thoughts occurred: First, she wasn't actually afraid of him — not in a physical sense. She had finally realized Jackson would never hurt her. Second, he had come to talk about Andrew. He had spoken to Mercer. He knew the detective believed she was a murderer.

Holly and Rags rushed past him out the door, the little black-and-white dog yipping as the pair ran off to play. Sarah just stood there.

"We need to talk," Jackson said, his jaw hard as steel.

Sarah managed a nod. "Come in." She stepped back out of the way, letting him walk past her into the living room. He didn't sit down and neither did she.

"He was here before, wasn't he?"

It wasn't exactly what she expected him to say. She had expected accusations. "He was here."

"Why didn't you tell me?"

"Because I've brought you more than enough trouble already."

"That isn't good enough. What are you leaving out?"

She swallowed past the lump that rose in her throat. "I couldn't bear to see the way you would look at me once you knew the police believed I was a murderer."

Jackson released a breath. "You still haven't figured it out, have you? You still aren't sure you can trust me. I'm your friend, Sarah. Whatever you tell me, I'm not going to look at you any differently. All I've ever wanted to do is help you. I can't do that if you don't tell me what's going on."

When she didn't move, Jackson reached out, drew her into his arms, and she didn't resist. It was hard to believe he was taking her side again and yet clearly he was.

"I'll talk to Dev," he said. "Ask him to find out who this guy is and what's going on with the murder investigation."

A trickle of fear slid through her and her shoulders stiffened. "Please, Jackson." She eased out of his embrace. "I'd rather you didn't. I don't want any more trouble. Lieutenant Delaney was the detective in charge of the investigation — he's Mercer's boss. The lieutenant thinks someone Andrew owed money to killed him. I don't think the police are trying that hard to find out. I keep hoping . . . praying that in time things will settle down and this will all go away."

Jackson made no comment. Clearly he wanted to do more than ignore the matter. His jaw flexed, but he didn't argue. For now it seemed he was willing to concede to her wishes.

"Next time you tell me if someone shows up and gives you any trouble."

Sarah opened her mouth, then closed it again and simply nodded. Jackson stalked across the living room toward the door. He was still angry but not because of Mercer's accusations. He was mad at her for not asking him for help.

She watched him walk out the door and close it solidly behind him, her heart squeezing hard in her chest. He was the best man she'd ever known and she was totally in love with him.

Still, she couldn't let things continue as they were, couldn't afford to get in any deeper.

How would she ever find the courage to leave?

It was dark outside, a warm summer wind blowing through the trees, making a soft whistling sound. As Jackson walked into his study, the phone started ringing. He headed to his desk and picked it up.

"Hey, brother."

"Gabe! Been a while since I've heard from you. What's going on?"

"Just thought I'd call and see how things went in California. I spoke to Dev a couple of times, so I know a little of what's been happening to Sarah."

Jackson raked a hand through his hair. "Things have been pretty much upside down, I can tell you." He explained to Gabe about the stakeout and the waste being dumped in the mine, that it looked as if Hexel Pharmaceuticals had been behind the recent threats to Sarah, and that he hoped

Vincent Spalino would help get things worked out.

"I was just getting ready to call Dev and fill him in," Jackson said. "I meant to call earlier, but somehow time slipped away." *Somehow. Like spending the afternoon talking to a homicide detective about Sarah's possible involvement in her husband's murder.*

He didn't believe for a moment that Sarah had murdered the guy. It just wasn't something she would do. What he needed was information on Ed Mercer and he hoped Dev could help him get it.

"You're into some serious stuff, bro. If anyone can help, it's Dev. Call him tonight, Jackson. Don't screw around with this."

"I'll call him right now." Jackson hung up the phone, thinking he was lucky to have two brothers he could count on no matter how tough things got.

He phoned Dev at his Scottsdale home. After the third ring, the phone went to voice mail. "This is Dev. I'm hard at work or doing something fun. Leave your number and I'll call you."

"It's Jackson. Ring me when you get the chance."

An hour later, Dev returned the call. He sounded sleepy — or satisfied. Jackson had a feeling it was the latter. Which was an irritating reminder that he could have had Sarah this morning before he left the Gramercy Hotel, that he wanted her fiercely right now. The feeling put a grouchy note in his voice.

"I called an hour ago. I hope you were enjoying yourself."

Dev chuckled, then yawned. "The lady had to go to work early or I'd still be enjoying myself. I gather you're back in Wyoming. How did your trip go?"

Jackson exhaled deeply. "You'd better make yourself comfortable. This is going to take a while." Even over the phone, Jackson could feel his brother tense.

"Tell me," he said.

For the next half hour, Jackson relayed the events of last night, starting with the stakeout at Ace, following the truck to Hollister's abandoned mine, the trip back at gunpoint and the conversation with Vincent Spalino.

Dev whistled into the phone. "Now you know why I'm mostly retired."

"You aren't retired — which is the reason I'm calling. I need you to see if you can find out what Hexel's dumping and why. If it's nothing that will do any harm, we'll leave things the way they are. Unfortunately, considering the pressure they've been putting on Sarah, I'm thinking whatever it is, it's probably not going to be good."

"I'll see what I can do. That it?"

"There's one more thing . . . a detective named Ed Mercer. He's LAPD. Showed up at the house this afternoon. It's his second visit. He's convinced Sarah killed her husband and he's determined to prove it. It seems personal, Dev. I want to know why Mercer's made Sarah his personal target."

"I'll get started first thing in the morning." He yawned again. "Meantime, I think I'll get some sleep. I'm damned well worn out."

Jackson grumbled a curse and hung up the phone.

He sighed into the quiet of the study. He had bought himself a handful of trouble when he'd let Sarah stay in the cottage. But right now, all he could think of was climbing back into her bed.

Sarah left the real estate office on Friday afternoon, a rental flyer clutched in her hand. She had gone to the office after work, spoken to a Realtor, and the woman had shown her a small house for rent at the edge of town that she could afford. It wasn't as nice as the cottage on Raintree Ranch, but every day she spent with Jackson, the harder it was going to be to leave him.

And there was Holly to think of. Her daughter was beginning to think of Jackson as the father she'd never had. Sarah couldn't let that happen. Not when it all might come to a crashing end.

She had to move. Mercer had left her no choice. In truth she should leave Wyoming entirely. Maybe in time, she would.

But she loved her job and she loved this town. She was beginning to make friends and so was Holly. Her grandmother was here and they were becoming a family again. She would stay for as long as she could. She was making her way along the boardwalk toward the parking lot when she heard someone calling her name.

"Sarah! Sarah, wait!" Nan Hargrove waved. Strands of red hair brushed her flushed cheeks as she hurried across the street.

"Nan, it's good to see you." The two women hugged.

"You, too." Nan settled in beside her, the two of them strolling together along the walk. "I hear you've been traveling. Jimmy said you and Jackson went out to California. I hope you had fun."

Fun? Sarah inwardly shuddered at the memory of the man who'd held a gun against her head. "It wasn't exactly fun. It's a long story, Nan. Problems left by my late husband. I just can't seem to escape him, even now that he's dead."

Nan shifted her Wilkin's Mercantile bag from one hand to the other. "I guess in some ways, I was lucky. Ron and I are friends. Well, not exactly friends, but we get along. We don't try to hurt each other the way some divorced couples do."

They walked past a small shop called Mountain High, a new winter clothing store that was just getting ready to open. The town was growing, but slowly. Which suited Sarah just fine.

"So how are things going with you and Jimmy?" she asked.

Nan smiled dreamily. "I'm crazy about him, Sarah. And I think he really likes me." She stared down at her feet. "We, uh, spent the night together last weekend." She looked up and grinned. "It was fantastic. But then I always figured it would be."

Sarah couldn't help thinking of Jackson. He made her feel womanly and sexy. She had never really understood desire until she met him. And even as she had made the arrangements to move away from the ranch into the house in town, she'd wanted him. She wanted him now.

"What about you and Jackson? You guys moved in together yet?"

Sarah paused on the boardwalk. "I'm moving into town, Nan. My husband's been dead less than six months. I'm not ready to get serious with a man."

Nan's red eyebrows arched up. "You told me you and your husband had been estranged for years. It's not like you had any kind of real marriage."

"I know."

Nan's shrewd gaze searched her face. "To tell you the truth, I thought . . . well, I thought you two were in love. I mean, the way you looked at him . . . and the way he looked at you." She rolled her eyes. "You could start a fire with a look like that."

Sarah smiled, but it was tinged with regret. "What I feel for Jackson doesn't matter. I'm just not ready, that's all."

Nan gently caught her arm. "Hey. I'm your friend, no matter what happens between you and Jackson, okay?"

Her chest squeezed. She treasured what few friends she had. She was grateful to have Nan as one of them. "Thank you. You can't imagine how much that means."

Nan leaned over and hugged her. "Maybe you just need a little more time."

"Maybe." But Sarah didn't think so. Not

with a murder investigation hanging over her head.

Not with a bloodhound like Mercer digging and digging, determined to put her in jail.

TWENTY-SIX

It rained through the night, a light, soothing patter against the roof. On Saturday morning, Sarah fixed breakfast for Holly then began to sort through her belongings, what little she had left after her move from California. She had been bringing home cardboard boxes, enough to make the move into town.

Her luggage sat open on the bed, some of her clothes neatly folded inside. She carted a couple of the boxes into the living room. It was warm this July morning, a little damp from the mist that still hung in the air.

In concession to what would likely be a hot summer day, she had left her feet bare and dressed in a sleeveless white blouse and a pair of cutoff jeans. She was trying to decide whether to start in the living room or go back to the bedroom when a familiar knock sounded at the door.

She peeked out the window to see Jackson

standing on the porch, handsome as sin in his jeans, hat and boots. A memory surfaced of the last time they had made love, and a jolt of heat slid low into her stomach. She took a deep breath and opened the door, wishing the coming confrontation could be postponed for a couple more days.

Beneath the brim of his hat, his dark eyes ran over her face. "Good morning," he said.

She smiled back as he took off the hat and held it in his hand. "Good morning."

He looked past her into the living room, saw the string of open boxes and his eyebrows drew together. "What's going on?"

She thought how much she was going to miss him. How much she loved him, how hard it would be to explain.

"I'm leaving the ranch, Jackson. Holly and I are moving into town."

His frown deepened. "What are talking about?"

"I — I'll be closer to my work, and Holly . . . Holly will be closer to school when it starts. She'll have a better chance to make friends — we both will."

Jackson looked at her as if she had punched him in the stomach. He looked past her to the boxes, looked into her face again. He didn't say a word, just stepped into the living room and closed the door firmly behind him. Sailing his hat onto the table, he moved toward her, slid a hand into her hair and dragged her mouth up to his for a long, scorching kiss.

Her insides melted. Oh, God, the man could kiss. His tongue found its way into her mouth and heat and need broke loose inside her. He tasted male and sexy. His clothes carried the scent of leather and hay. Jackson deepened the kiss. Sarah felt the hardness of his erection pressing against the fly of his jeans, gripped his shoulders and just hung on.

She was way past stopping him. Instead, her tongue slid over his and everything inside her went liquid and warm.

Sarah heard him groan. Drawing her even more firmly against him, he deepened the kiss, and desire rose fierce and hot. He backed her into the bedroom, kicked the door closed with the heel of his boot, but didn't stop moving till her shoulders came up against the wall. The curtains were closed. He must have seen Holly outside playing.

"Jackson . . ."

"Maybe this will convince you to stay." He cupped her face in his hands and kissed her again then unbuttoned the front of her blouse and filled his hands with her breasts.

His tongue ringed her nipple, turned the end diamond-hard.

Her knees started shaking as he sucked in the fullness, laved and tasted, grazed her nipple with his teeth. Capturing her lips, he kissed her as he worked the zipper on her cutoff jeans, shoved them down over her hips, along with her white thong panties. They slithered down her legs and pooled on the floor and he lifted her out of them.

Sarah whimpered as he unfastened his belt buckle, unzipped his fly and freed himself, wrapped her hand around his powerful erection.

"This is how much I want you."

He was big and hard and pulsing. "Dear God . . ." He felt hot in her hand and when her fingers tightened, he hardened even more.

Jackson parted her legs and began to stroke her. One of his big hands caressed her breast, and pleasure tugged low in her belly. How could she have forgotten how good he was at this and how much she loved it?

Lifting her, propping her back against the wall, he wrapped her legs around his waist and filled her with a single deep thrust.

Sarah softly moaned.

"We're good together, Sarah — you know

how good. How can you think about leaving?"

Beneath his shirt, the muscles in his shoulders moved and tightened. Bands of muscle bunched in his chest. Sarah grabbed the front of his shirt and popped the snaps, pressed her lips against his hot, sun-darkened skin, and Jackson hissed in a breath.

Cupping her bottom in his hands, he began to move, driving himself deep inside her. Pleasure merged with the love she felt for him, heightening the sweet sensations. Her head tipped forward onto his shoulder and goose bumps feathered across her skin.

"You don't want to go, Sarah." He nipped the side of her neck and thrust deeply again. "You know you don't."

It was true. Leaving was the last thing she wanted.

Jackson drove into her, eased out and drove into her again, and a deep, sucking orgasm hit her. Moaning, she buried her face against his shoulder, but Jackson didn't stop until she came again. Then a low, growling came from his throat and he followed her to release.

Long seconds passed. Limp and sated, she held on to him as he lowered her to her feet. He zipped his jeans and fastened his buckle, bent his head and very softly kissed her.

He handed Sarah her discarded garments. "I don't want you to go."

Sarah turned away from him and began to put on her clothes, needing a moment to compose herself.

Once she was dressed. she forced herself to turn and face him. "I have to go, Jackson. It's something I just have to do."

"Even if you want to leave, you can't — at least not right now."

"Why not?"

"Vincent Spalino is dead."

"What?"

"That's what I came to tell you. Dev called this morning. Apparently one of the people in his L.A. office saw it on the news. Spalino's secretary found him this morning sitting at his desk, dead of a heart attack."

A shiver went through her. She read the worry on his face. "It wasn't a heart attack, was it?"

"Dev doesn't think so. Neither do I."

"Hexel makes pharmaceuticals. They would know what to do to kill someone and make it look like a natural death." She raised her gaze to his face. "Oh, God, Jackson, what am I going to do?"

He moved toward her, eased her into his arms. "After our trip to the mine, I'm also

412

on Hexel's radar, which means the question is the same as it always has been — what are *we* going to do?"

Sarah moved away from him, trying to think things through, trying to stay calm and failing. She saw him through a film of tears. "This is all my fault. I never should have come here."

"But you did, and I'm glad, and somehow we'll get through this."

"How?"

"I don't know yet."

She raked back her hair and glanced over at the empty cardboard boxes. "I should leave. Maybe if I did, they'd forget you're involved."

He chuckled but it wasn't with mirth. "Those guys at Hexel aren't going to forget. We have to find a way to stop them."

"Maybe it's time to call the police."

"Maybe. In that regard, it might interest you to know the reason Ed Mercer has it out for you is because you were Hollister's wife. Apparently, he got divorced about eight months ago. His wife took him to the cleaners. She got custody of his two kids and he got minimum visitation. He can't get to her, but he figures to make you and every other woman pay for what she did to him."

"Mercer may have had troubles in his marriage, but he couldn't begin to understand what it was like living with a man like Andrew. He couldn't begin to know the fear — not only for myself but for Holly."

"The good news is most of the cops think he's gone off the deep end. He hasn't got any real evidence and apparently they aren't giving much credence to his theory." He reached out and stroked her cheek. "For now, let's not worry about Mercer. Let's just figure out what to do about those guys at Hexel."

"Before they kill us, you mean. Just like Vincent Spalino."

TWENTY-SEVEN

Sarah awakened to the low roll of thunder outside the cottage. It had rained again last night, for which everyone was grateful. She glanced at the glowing red numbers of the clock on the nightstand and shot up from the bed.

It was almost nine-thirty. She hadn't been able to sleep last night so she'd taken a couple of Tylenol PM. They had worked so well she had overslept. She was surprised Holly hadn't come in to wake her hours ago. Maybe she had overslept, too.

Grabbing her fleece robe off the foot of the bed, Sarah hurriedly drew it on and walked to the bedroom door. As she stepped into the living room, the house seemed oddly quiet and a little tremor of unease went through her.

"Holly?" She opened the door to her daughter's bedroom, saw the rumpled bed, the colorful quilt that Livvy had made decorated with tiny fawns and bear cubs, but no sign of her little girl.

Certain Holly must be outside playing, she started to close the door then happened to glance at the window. She frowned as she walked toward it. Holly liked to sleep with the window partly open so she could feel the cool night air, but the window was completely closed.

She leaned in closer toward the glass panes and looked down to the ground. Big, deep footprints were stamped into the mud. Terror filled Sarah's stomach. Whirling around, the air stalled in her lungs as she caught sight of the square of paper lying on Holly's pillow. Her hand shook as she picked it up.

If you want to see your daughter alive, bring Jackson Raines and come to the old mining shack near Alpine Meadow. Take the Bear Flat Road. You've got till noon. No police or she's dead.

Biting back a cry of sheer panic, Sarah turned and ran from the room, the paper gripped in her hand. Tears threatened as she raced out of the house. Asleep on the porch, Rags's head popped up. He jumped up and barked and started running along beside her.

Through the open barn door, Sarah spotted Jackson working.

"Jackson!" She tripped and nearly fell. Tears burned her eyes. Fear made it hard to breathe. "Jackson!"

He ran toward her, caught her hard against his chest. "What is it? What's happened?"

"It . . . it's Holly." Her voice broke. "They've taken her." The tears in her eyes spilled onto her cheeks. Her hand shook as she handed him the note. Jackson scanned the words and his jaw went granite-hard.

"We'll get her back, Sarah, I promise you."

"Oh, God, Jackson —"

"It's all right. Everything's going to be okay."

"Do you know this place? Can you get there?"

Jackson caught her arm. "I know you want to go with me, but —"

She jerked away from him. "I'm going. She's my daughter. Don't you dare try to stop me."

Jackson seemed to read her determination. "All right, go get dressed. I'll get my gear and meet you at the truck."

Jackson looked up to see Jimmy Three-bears walking toward him. "What's going on? I heard you talking. What's happened to Holly?"

"It's a long story, Jim." He glanced back at Sarah and saw her dash into the cottage. "Same problem as before, different players. And these guys mean business." He handed Jimmy the note, which he read as the two of them strode toward the ranch house.

"What are you going to do?"

"They've got Holly. We've got to do whatever they say."

"These are city folks, right? How did they know that shack was even up there?"

"Must have paid someone who lives around here for information." Everyone in the area knew about the old abandoned cabin at the top of the mountain. In the winter, the local cross-country ski group took snowmobiles up there and used it as a warming hut. The rest of the year, few people bothered with it since it was difficult to reach.

"You need to call the sheriff," Jimmy said as they pushed through the back door into the kitchen. Livvy was off on Sundays so the room was cold and quiet. "You can't do this alone."

Jackson continued through the house into his study. He went directly over to the gun cabinet, unlocked it and opened the etched glass doors. Pulling out the .308 Winchester rifle he used for hunting, he set it on top of the desk, his mind running over his options — which were few and far between.

"All right, here's what we'll do," he finally said to Jimmy. "The road up to the cabin is bad in the best of weather. After two nights of rain, it's going to be a real sonofabitch. It'll take us a couple of hours to get there, even with four-wheel drive. Give me half an hour to get Holly out of there, then call Ben Weber. Tell him to get a chopper up there. He should be able to land in the meadow."

Jimmy reached past him into the gun case. He pulled out the Colt .44 revolver Jackson carried whenever he was in the mountains and laid it next to the rifle, silently telling him one was not enough.

"I've got a better idea," Jim said. "You drive the road. Make sure you get up there at exactly noon. In the meantime, Wheel and I will trailer a couple of horses and head for the trailhead. We'll ride in the back way. It's a shorter route. Should take about the same amount of time. With luck, we'll be there to cover you when you get there."

Jackson lifted his battered straw hat and tugged it into place on his forehead. "I'm not sure what we'll be facing up there, Jim. You've got your sons to think of."

"I wouldn't be much of a father if I taught them to abandon a friend when he needs my help."

Something tightened in Jackson's throat. He could always count on Jimmy. "What about Wheel? This isn't his problem."

"They took that little girl right off the ranch. Holly's been taken and that makes it his problem. Besides, I know Wheel, and I know we can count him."

"All right, we'll play it your way. Tell Sam what's going on and have him call the sheriff at exactly twelve-fifteen. That doesn't give us much room for error, but if something goes wrong, maybe Ben can get there in time to pick up the pieces."

Jimmy nodded. He shoved both guns across the top of the desk. "I've got my own rifle and Wheel's got his." He grinned. "See you at the top of the mountain, Wyatt." And then he was gone.

Thinking of the days when they were kids playing cowboys and Indians — Wyatt Earp and Cochise — Jackson collected the rifle and pistol and headed for the door, stopping only long enough to grab his jacket off the coatrack.

Sarah was waiting next to the truck, dressed in jeans and a shirt, carrying her jacket, a blanket and a canvas satchel.

"Clothes for Holly in case she needs them," she said as she climbed in, and the lump returned to his throat.

His hand tightened around the stock of the rifle. He was tired of playing games with these people. They were in his territory now, not some shadowy street in L.A. And today — one way or another — he was going to end it.

Jerking open the driver's-side door, he shoved his pistol under the seat and rested his rifle on the seat behind him. Once Sarah was buckled in, he cranked the engine, put the truck into gear and headed for the road leading up to Alpine Meadow.

Devlin Raines pulled his rental car up in front of the ranch house and turned off the engine. His brother was usually outside working, but at the moment, no one seemed to be around. Then he spotted Jimmy Threebears and the tall, lanky cowboy, Wheel Dillon, loading a couple of saddle horses into the back of a trailer.

"Hey, Jimmy!" he called as he climbed out of the car and started walking toward them.

"Dev!" Features grim, the big Sioux strode in his direction. "Am I glad to see you."

Something was wrong. Dev could hear it

in Jimmy's voice. It was the reason he had flown all the way to Wyoming. After what had happened to Vincent Spalino, he'd had a bad feeling his brother was in trouble.

"What's going on? Where's Jackson?"

"Headed for that old mine shack near Alpine Meadow. Someone took Holly. They've demanded Jackson and Sarah come up to the cabin. Wheel and I are riding in the back way."

Dev clenched his jaw. "I was afraid something like this might happen. I'll need a horse."

Jimmy nodded. "We're on a tight schedule. I'll fill you in once we're on the road."

"Let me get my boots and gear and we're out of here." He ran upstairs, slid open the closet door, and grabbed the boots and jacket he kept at the ranch for whenever he came to visit. On the way back down, he went into the study, got one of Jackson's hunting rifles, then stopped at the car to retrieve the Browning 9 mm in his shoulder holster and a pair of high-powered binoculars.

Another vehicle was pulling up just as he shut the car door. Even with the shit that was about to rain down on all of them, he couldn't stop a grin.

"Hey, Gabe! Good to see you, brother."

He and Gabe had talked last night. Neither of them had mentioned making a trip to Wyoming in case Jackson needed help, but Gabe had clearly been worried. Dev wasn't surprised to see his brother there.

"We got trouble," Dev continued. "Go get one of Jackson's rifles." He glanced down to be sure his brother was wearing his usual pair of boots. "I'll saddle you a horse."

"I brought my own firepower," Gabe said, obviously ready for whatever trouble he might find. He opened the trunk of his rental car and dragged out a jacket with something heavy in the pocket, reached back in and pulled out his big 7 mm Weatherby rifle.

The brothers strode toward the stable. Having spotted the second car, Jimmy was just tightening the cinch on a second horse. Battered hat pulled low, Wheel Dillon mumbled a greeting, then took both animals' reins and led them toward the back of the trailer. Obediently, the bay and sorrel geldings climbed in with the first saddled pair.

"Just like old times," Jimmy said, referring to their younger days when one of them always seemed to be in trouble. "I'll bring you both up to speed on the way."

Dev just nodded.

Gabe's jaw looked hard. "Let's go."

Holly huddled on an ugly brown blanket in the corner. Beneath another itchy blanket, she wore only her cotton nightgown, the one with the big-eyed owls on it. Two men sat at an old wooden table across the room playing cards. One had a scraggly blond beard and she thought she might have seen him once in town. The other man was skinny as a snake and looked just as mean.

The third man was the scariest of all, though she couldn't quite say why. Just that his nose was too long and his eyes were a shiny black. His lips were thin, too, and when he smiled at her, it made her shiver.

"I want to go home," she said, not for the first time. It took courage because they had warned her not to say it again.

"I told you to keep quiet," the man with the blond beard said, casting her a look that made her pull the blanket tighter around her.

Last night, he was the one who'd come into her bedroom. She had only seen him for a minute before he pressed something over her nose and mouth that made her go back to sleep. This morning, she woke up in the cabin with her head hurting and her mom nowhere around.

"Your mother is coming to get you," the dark-skinned man said. His hair was as black as his eyes, which always seemed to be looking at her. One of the men had called him Turk so she guessed that was his name.

"When is she coming?" Holly wasn't even sure her mom knew where she was. If she did, though, Holly knew her mom and Jackson would come for her.

The man named Turk looked at his watch. "An hour, maybe less. The road's bad. It might take a while, but your mother will be here."

"With Jackson?"

His thin lips curved. "He'll be with her." He was sure of that, she could see, and hope rose inside her. Still, she couldn't figure out why the men had brought her here. Why they had come into her room in the middle of the night and carried her out of her house.

"You two better get outside with Beckman," Turk said. "Make sure he's still covering the road. They could show up anytime now."

Holly watched the man with the scraggly beard walk out the door with the skinny man. There sure were a lot of them and they all had guns.

Fear slid through her and she shivered

beneath the scratchy wool blanket. She told herself not to cry and whenever she did, she didn't let them see.

She tried not to think what the men meant to do when her mom and Jackson came to get her. Whatever it was, she was afraid it wasn't good.

The pickup crawled along the narrow, rutted, muddy road. Thanks to the rain, it was nearly impassable in places. Mostly the truck was axle-deep in sludge, making the tires spin and the vehicle slide sickeningly on the curves.

At first, Sarah had been afraid they wouldn't be able to make it to the cabin, but Jackson knew this country and how to drive a road like this and the four-wheel truck just kept going.

"I shouldn't have taken those pills last night," she said as the vehicle rolled along in a spot that was a little less rutted. "If I hadn't been sleeping so soundly I would have heard them. I could have stopped them." Her eyes burned. She glanced out the window and hung on to her emotions, refusing to cry again. She had to be strong for Holly.

"You only took a mild sleep aid and even if you'd heard them come into the house, chances are you couldn't have stopped them. They probably would have taken you both. But they want me, too. This way, they make sure that happens."

"Why do they want us to come way out here?"

"To control the situation. As far as they know, we're the only real threat to them. They want to get rid of us before we can tell the police about the mine. And they want to take care of the matter as neatly as possible."

She clamped down on a stab of fear. "You would have gone to the police already, wouldn't you? If it weren't for my troubles with Mercer."

Jackson made no reply.

If she had known this would happen, she would have called Richard Kemp at the FBI as soon as they had talked to Vincent Spalino. But they hadn't imagined that Spalino might get killed.

"What we should have done isn't important," Jackson said. "Right now we need to focus on how we're going to get Holly and get the hell out of there."

Sarah suppressed a shudder. "What's our plan?"

"Unfortunately, until we know what we're facing, we'll have to play it by ear."

Sarah said nothing more and neither did Jackson. Both of them just watched the road, hoped and silently prayed that by some miracle — and Jimmy's and Wheel's help — somehow they would succeed.

If there was one thing Dev was good at it was digging up information. He knew people all over the country, kept in touch with old army buddies and had developed a sophisticated network of informants that had been invaluable over the years. He paid well for information and kept his mouth shut about where it came from.

Which was the reason he knew the name of the guy who was running this operation.

Or at least believed he did.

From the description Jackson had given him and the talk he'd stirred up, his name was Rene Abaz, a hired gun currently employed by Barry Helman and Frank Eldridge, the owners of Hexel Pharmaceuticals. Rene's family had been in this country since the thirties, regular upstanding citizens. His father was first-generation Turkish-American, his mother mostly French, and Rene didn't even speak his family's native language. Still, everyone called him the Turk.

Abaz was smart and he was ruthless, and

he was being well paid to cover up whatever it was Hexel was doing. And since money seemed to be no object, he had all the help he needed.

Dev swore softly as the sorrel's steady pace ate up the trail. His instincts had been warning him, but he hadn't known about Abaz until last night and he hadn't figured on how quickly the man would move.

Saddle leather creaked beneath him. He hadn't ridden in nearly two years. Under different circumstances, he would have been enjoying himself, enjoying the ride and the scenery. At the moment, he barely noticed the dark green pines and jagged peaks. He was too busy scanning the rocky slopes in search of movement, anything that might be a sign of trouble.

They were less than half an hour from the summit, had pushed hard to make up for the extra time it had taken them to get on the road.

A squirrel chirped loudly, signaling their passage along the route. The gelding's ears went up and the horse's nostrils flared. Dev's hand went to the butt of the pistol in his shoulder holster. He straightened in the saddle, felt the comforting weight of Jackson's rifle slung across his back.

Several seconds passed, time enough for

another scan of the mountains. No problem, just Mother Nature's warning system. He had learned to pay attention to it when he'd been with the Rangers.

Riding ahead of him, he saw that Gabe had also gone on alert. Seeing nothing out of the ordinary, both of them relaxed. He was glad to have his brother along. They were both ex-military, able to communicate in a language that didn't require spoken words. He didn't know much about Jimmy's friend, Wheel Dillon, but Jimmy was as solid as a stand of timber. If Jimmy trusted Wheel, then Dev figured he could trust him, too.

He checked his watch. Almost noon. They were right on schedule. Another quarter mile and they'd leave the horses, go the rest of the way on foot.

It wouldn't be long until they knew what they were up against. Dev felt the familiar adrenaline rush and prepared to do battle in a different kind of war.

Twenty-Eight

Jackson rounded the last bend. A tall, bone-thin man with an assault rifle stood on a dirt mound at the side of the road where it flattened out in front of the cabin.

"Pull up there and turn off the engine," the man instructed, pointing to a spot out in the open.

Jackson looked over at Sarah. Her face was paper-white, but her chin was set with determination. He wished he could have left her back at the ranch but there was no way. Sarah loved her daughter more than her own life. She was going after her child come hell or high water. Better to have her with him than doing something foolish on her own.

His mind strayed to the Colt revolver on the floor of the truck beneath his feet and the rifle on the seat behind him. There was no way he could take either weapon with him. He'd have to go in unarmed except for the knife he'd strapped to his calf, and they'd likely find that when they searched him.

He hoped Jimmy and Wheel had made it to the top of the trail and gotten into position. If they had, he and Sarah might have a chance.

"Both of you! Raise your hands and get out of the truck!"

Jackson looked over at Sarah. He reached out and clasped her hand, gave it a reassuring squeeze. It was a helluva time to realize how much he loved her.

He prayed he would get the chance to tell her before it was too late.

Dev crouched next to Jimmy. "Dammit, the truck just pulled up in front of the cabin. I was hoping for another five minutes."

"Gabe's in position. I saw him drop behind that rock to the left of the clearing. Wheel's moving to the right."

"You okay here?" Dev asked.

Jimmy set his rifle in a notch between two rocks and peered into the scope. "I'm just fine."

Dev used his binoculars to scan the area below. "There's a man about ten o'clock, sixty yards out. Another a little left of your three."

Jimmy used the scope to locate the threat. "I got 'em."

Dev started moving as the pickup doors opened and Jackson and Sarah slowly climbed down from inside, their hands raised into the air. Jimmy, Wheel and Gabe were all in position and so far none of them had been spotted.

Then a rifle shot roared, echoing into the hills. Rock chips flew, and Dev caught a glimpse of Wheel slamming backward, his cowboy hat spinning into the air as he hit the ground and lay unmoving.

Son of a bitch.

The crackle of a walkie-talkie split the quiet, letting the bad guys know Jackson and Sarah were not alone. It was bad news for all of them, but at least it gave Dev the shooter's position. He started moving in that direction, keeping low as he darted between the sharp-edged rocks.

In the clearing below, all hell had broken loose. A burst of rapid gunfire followed Sarah as she ran to the back of the pickup. Jackson ducked behind the door of the truck, reached beneath the seat and retrieved his revolver, dodging and weaving past a series of bullets that struck the ground as he ran to the rear of the Ford. Crouching next to Sarah, he aimed his big

Colt .44 and took out the guy firing the assault rifle, who ran for cover off the mound.

Dev moved silently, making each step count as he came up behind the first shooter. Locking an arm around his neck, he twisted, dropping the man to the ground before he knew what hit him.

It wasn't something he liked doing, but at least he hadn't forgotten how.

He crouched and used his binoculars to check on Wheel, saw that Gabe knelt beside him, working to stop the flow of blood from what appeared to be a shoulder wound. Dev headed toward the cabin in search of Holly while Gabe moved Wheel under cover and ducked back out of sight.

Dev had nearly reached the cabin when he glanced toward the rear of the truck and saw that both Sarah and Jackson were gone.

He spotted Sarah behind the thick trunk of a downed pine tree and Jackson running along the bottom of a shallow gully that bordered the road. Jackson disappeared out of sight and Dev started moving, silently praying that his brother and his lady would be all right.

Sarah's heart raced. A shot tore into the trunk of the fallen tree in front of her and she ducked out of sight. Her breath froze as she spotted Jackson to her left, moving toward a man with a thin blond beard armed with what looked like a machine gun, scanning the area with the muzzle, searching for a target.

Sarah trembled as she watched Jackson creep closer, coming up behind the man and wrapping an arm viselike around his neck. Jackson pressed his pistol against the side of the blond man's head and ordered him to drop his weapon, which fell to the ground with a noisy clatter. Then Jackson slammed his revolver down hard on the blond man's head and he collapsed into the dirt.

Sarah's heart pounded as her terrified gaze swung to the cabin. Holly had to be inside. She wondered how many more men were in there with her daughter. The shadowy outline of a figure appeared for an instant behind the window, but dropped quickly out of sight.

Jackson was heading for the cabin door. He jerked to a halt and dropped down into the rocks as the door swung wide and the tall, dark-skinned man Sarah recognized from the parking lot stepped into the opening, holding Holly up in front of him like a shield.

Sarah's stomach knotted with fear for her little girl. She stifled a terrified sob and forced herself to remain where she was instead of rushing into the clearing to beg the man not to hurt her daughter.

"Put down your weapons! Do it or the child is dead!"

Gripping his Colt in both hands, the barrel leveled at the man who held Holly, Jackson stepped out into the open. Holly's abductor held her flush against him, one arm locked around her waist, his pistol pressed against the side of her head.

"Do it, or I kill her!"

Jimmy stood up but continued to hold on to his rifle. Wheel staggered to his feet, his rifle steadied against his hip. Blood soaked his shirt and dripped onto his jeans.

"Where are you, Sarah?" the black-haired man called out as if they were old friends. Jackson recognized him as the guy who had accosted her in the parking lot.

"If you want your daughter to live, you'll come forward. Now!"

Sarah came out from behind the fallen log, her jeans and shirt covered with mud and dead leaves. Her face looked even paler than it had before, and her legs were shaking as she hurried to Jackson's side.

"Now . . . like I said, drop your weapons. Tell your men to throw down their guns,

Raines. Do it or the little girl dies."

"Do it, Jackson," Sarah begged. The terror in her voice cut into him like a blade. But if they gave up their weapons, all of them would die, including Sarah and Holly.

Jackson glanced around the clearing, stalling for time. The rest of the gunmen were all injured or dead. He knew there was at least one more man out there on his side of the fight, someone who had ridden in with Jimmy and taken out at least one of the gunmen. In the rocks to his right, a man rose up, a rifle resting against his shoulder. Jackson recognized his brother, Dev, and a fresh shot of adrenaline poured through him.

"You shoot the girl, Turk, you're a dead man," Dev said. The barrel of his rifle pointed at the gunman's head and it never wavered. "Holly's your only way out of this alive."

Sarah made a little whimpering sound.

Following Dev's lead, Jimmy and Wheel held their positions. So did Jackson, though the fear in the little girl's eyes and the terror in Sarah's face made it the hardest thing he had ever done.

"Give it up, Turk," Dev shouted. "You don't, this isn't going to end well for you."

"I've got the girl. You'd better remember that." And then he started running, holding

Holly up in front of him to keep the men from firing, moving in such a way none of them could get a clear shot without risking the little girl's life.

All of them started moving, following the pair as they raced across the clearing and disappeared behind a row of pines that stood between the cabin and Alpine Meadow.

"Holly!" Sarah cried out, stumbling as she ran after the man with her child.

Jackson raced ahead of her, moving fast, narrowing the distance between him and Holly's captor. That was when he heard it — the *whop whop whop* of a chopper. It was preparing to lift off, not landing, so it couldn't be Sheriff Weber. The chopper had brought the kidnappers up to the cabin and as soon as the man named Turk reached it, he would be gone.

Jackson ran faster, his heart pounding in rhythm with his running feet, desperate to stop the man from boarding the chopper with Holly. The blades were spinning when Jackson burst through the row of pines into the clearing, the dark-skinned man racing for the door of the helicopter.

As the chopper began to lift off, Turk dropped the child and reached for the door. A shot roared from somewhere in the rocky terrain to the right and a bullet slammed into Turk's chest. Blood gushed through the hole in his shirt as he went down, his pistol landing in the grass a few feet away.

Jackson just kept running, keeping his head low beneath the whirling blades. He grabbed Holly and cradled her protectively against his chest, then turned and raced away from the chopper. Dev and Jimmy ran forward, their rifles aimed at the glass bubble where the pilot worked the controls.

Jimmy fired a single shot through the glass just missing the pilot, who put his hands up. The helicopter began to sink back down into the deep green grass. The engine turned off, and the rotor blades began to slow.

Sarah raced toward her daughter. "Holly! Holly!"

"Mama!"

As soon as they were a safe distance from the blades, Jackson set the little girl on her feet and she rushed into her mother's open arms. Both of them started crying. Relief hit him so hard his eyes began to burn. Jackson watched the two people he had come to love so much, alive and clinging to each other, and a lump swelled in his throat.

He turned away and when he did, he saw Gabe walking toward him, his rifle slung over one wide shoulder. Relief was etched into his face. Dev was right behind him.

Both his brothers had come to help. Jackson clenched his jaw against the fresh rush of emotion that seeped into chest.

"How'd you know?" he said to Gabe, clapping a hand on his brother's shoulder.

"We didn't. Dev and I talked last night. He had a hunch trouble was about to come down. I figured a little trip to Wyoming wouldn't hurt. I guess he thought the same thing."

For the first time since that morning, Jackson smiled. "You two always did have a good sense of timing."

They walked over to where the pilot stood next to the chopper, covered by the rifle Wheel held in his hand, Gabe's makeshift bandage wrapped around his injured shoulder. A few feet away Jimmy knelt next to Turk, who lay bleeding and unconscious. Dev found some rope in the chopper, and he and Jimmy tied up the rest of the gunmen. Kneeling next to Turk, Gabe tore open the man's bloody shirt to check the wound in his chest.

"I didn't kill him," Gabe said to Jackson. "I figured the way things were going you might need him."

Gabe was a crack shot. If he'd wanted the

man dead, he would be. But his brother was right. There was still the matter of Hexel Pharmaceuticals and whatever they were dumping in the Dry Creek Mine.

The company still posed a threat that needed to be dealt with. Jackson hoped the FBI would be able to solve the problem.

Dev left them there and went to check out the cabin. His blue eyes looked hard when he returned.

"Bastards wired the place. From the way it looks, they meant for the three of you to be in there when it blew."

"You disarmed it?"

He nodded. "It's safe now."

Jackson looked at his two brothers, and gratitude for the family he had been given filled his chest. His gaze went to Sarah and little Holly, who still hung on to each other in the meadow. They were part of his family, too.

He loved them both and he wanted them with him. He just hoped he could make Sarah see.

TWENTY-NINE

Jackson believed it was over. He would never know how much Sarah wished that were true.

Though the day was warm, she sat in front of the empty hearth in her living room, feeling cold clear to her bones. Out in front of the barn, Holly laughed as she played with Rags and Sam's dog, Feather, safe once more at the ranch, accepting in the way children seemed able to do that her life was already returning to normal.

Sarah was no longer sure what normal really was.

She leaned back in the antique rocker she had retrieved from the attic just a few days before all of this started, felt the comforting back-and-forth motion.

As Jackson had hoped, Sheriff Weber and his deputies had arrived in the meadow by helicopter soon after the shooting had ended. He had taken the gunmen into custody — three wounded, one dead — and arrested the pilot. The man with the stringy blond beard had turned out to be a local, a hand who'd been fired off the Whittaker Ranch for stealing and now lived in Sheep River. He had only wanted money, he said.

Weber's pilot had flown Sarah and Holly back down the mountain along with Wheel, who'd been taken directly to the hospital. Later that afternoon, the sheriff had come to the ranch to take her and Holly's statements. He had said not to worry, that he would take care of everything.

If only that were true.

Sarah leaned back in the rocker. She was exhausted. She hadn't slept in the past three nights, not since that awful day in the meadow. Whenever she closed her eyes, all she could hear were the sound of bullets. All she could see was blood: the man on the mound with a bloody arm; the blond man moaning, pressing a hand over his bleeding head; the black-haired man, the Turk, lying in the grass, a spreading stream of crimson pumping out of his chest.

Sitting in front of the empty hearth, she thought of those men, and a memory of Andrew arose, as it had a hundred times before.

Andrew lying on the floor of the study,

scarlet soaking the front of his jacket over the perfect hole in his heart.

She squeezed her eyes shut, trying to block the memory, but it wouldn't go away.

"Do you think I'm a fool, Sarah?"

"Why . . . why would I think that?"

He just smiled, the kind of smile that made her insides roll with nausea.

"I told you we were going to Rio. Did you actually think you were going to take Holly and run away?"

She straightened, determined not to let him know how frightened she really was. "Holly and I aren't going with you. You can leave if you want, but we're staying here."

His mouth thinned to a slash across his face. "You really believe you can defy me? You don't remember what happened the last time?"

She remembered. He had beaten her so badly she'd wound up in the hospital. The fear inside her swelled, nearly overwhelmed her.

Andrew stepped away from his chair, rounded the corner of his desk. Anticipation glittered in his eyes. He liked this, liked to hurt her.

"Andrew, please don't do this." She forced herself not to back away, to hold her ground and face him. When he just kept coming, she drew the pistol from her purse.

Her hand shook. "Stay away from me, Andrew. I'm warning you." A noise reached her. Was someone in the house? She glanced around, but there was no one there. "I won't . . . won't let you hurt me again."

He laughed, the sound almost demonic. Even the gun wasn't enough to frighten him.

"You dare to threaten me? I'm going to kill you for this, Sarah. I'm going to make you disappear and then I'm taking Holly with me to Rio." He took another step closer.

"I'll shoot you. I swear it."

His lips curled. "You don't have the guts."

She tried blot out the rest, but it was fixed in her mind and it wouldn't go away — Andrew rushing forward, his features distorted in fury. She remembered closing her eyes for an instant, but she didn't remember pulling the trigger. Not the exact moment, just the roar of the bullet, and the feel of the pistol bucking in her hand.

Andrew's eyes bulged in disbelief. He took one more step, swayed and fell backward, landing on his back on the floor of the study. Fear froze her where she stood. Fear and denial.

This can't be happening! Her gaze swung toward the phone on his desk.

Call 911. Call 911.

But when she looked at Andrew, she saw that his chest wasn't moving. His eyes were staring straight up at the ceiling and she knew for certain he was dead.

Dear God, what have I done!

For several long seconds, she just stood there, listening for the wail of sirens, the gun a deadweight in her hand.

But no police cars came. No one walked through the front door. The house sat at the end of a long, private drive, and no one had heard the gunshot.

Holly's sweet face rose in her mind. If she called the police they would take her away from her daughter. Even if she could prove it was self-defense, she'd be arrested. They would put Holly in foster care. There would have to be a trial. It could take weeks, months. She didn't have money for an expensive lawyer. She might even be sent to prison.

Hysteria threatened. She thought of Holly and forced herself to stay calm.

Opening her purse, she dropped the gun back inside, her hand shaking almost uncontrollably. On legs that felt rubbery and numb, she turned and walked out of the study. She retrieved the bag she had packed, the last of her things left in the Sunset house, and headed for the car.

Stay calm, a little voice ordered.

Andrew had any number of enemies, people with a reason to want him dead. *Just keep going. Pick up Holly and drive to the condo. Pretend nothing has happened. You can do it. You have to. Holly needs a mother. Without you, she has no one.*

Sitting there now in the rocker in her cottage, Sarah brushed a tear from her cheek, fighting to bury the memories, staring into the empty hearth as if it were her empty soul.

She had tried so hard. But trouble had followed her even here. She had to leave. She couldn't face Jackson, couldn't continue the lie a moment more.

She couldn't bear to think of what he would say, of the way he would look at her if he knew she had killed her husband. The reason wouldn't matter. No man would want a woman who had done a thing like that.

And there was the future to consider, the awful certainty that in the end, Detective Mercer would come for her.

Sarah rose from the chair, feeling sick inside. She was in love with Jackson. The desperate, forever kind of love. She knew that now, had known it the moment he had run through a hail of gunfire to save her daughter. Known it by the moisture in his eyes when he realized she and Holly were safe.

He had risked his life for her and her daughter.

Sarah loved him, and now she was going to repay him for the kindness he had shown her.

She was going to leave him. She was going to give him back his life.

It would be the hardest thing she'd ever done.

Sarah didn't know how long she stood there staring into the empty hearth. At a knock on her door, she glanced up. Wearily, she crossed the living room, wondering who was there. Pausing at the window, she saw Jackson standing on the porch, looking masculine and virile without even trying. She summoned her courage and opened the door.

"I've brought news," he said as she stepped back to let him into the living room. He took off his work-stained cowboy hat and held it in one of his callused hands. He always seemed so big, larger than life. There would never be another man like him.

"Would . . . would you like something to drink? Some iced tea, or something?"

He smiled. "It's hot out there. Iced tea

sounds great."

For the past few days, he had left her mostly alone, just stopping by to check on her and Holly, but careful to give them plenty of space, time to adjust to all that had happened.

"I'll be right back." She went into the kitchen, filled two glasses with ice and poured in the sun tea she had made by setting a jar filled with tea and water out on the porch. Jackson rested his hat on the back of the sofa as she handed him one of the frosty glasses, and both of them sat down.

"You said you brought news. I hope it's good for a change."

He took a long drink of his tea, the muscles in his throat moving up and down. He set the glass down on a coaster on the coffee table in front of him. "It's kind of good news/bad news."

She braced herself. It seemed lately, everything had been that way. "Give me the good news first."

"Richard Kemp called. They've arrested Barry Helman and Frank Eldridge, the guys who owned Hexel. According to Kemp, Rene Abaz turned state's evidence, and Helman and Eldridge were charged with conspiracy to kidnap and attempted murder, and that's just for starters."

"What about the mine?"

"That's the bad news. Turns out the Dry Springs Mine didn't live up to its name."

"The springs weren't dry?"

"Not completely. There's a little town south of the mine north of Interstate 40. It's called Mineral Wells. Apparently, people there have been getting sick. The EPA tested the water and found out they had arsenic poisoning."

"Oh, my God — and it came from the mine?"

He nodded. "From an old underground spring that ran into the town's main water supply."

"Are you saying those barrels Hexel was storing were filled with arsenic?"

"Not exactly, but arsenic was in the waste that was in the barrels. Now that this is all out in the open, some of the scientists working for the lab have come forward. They say they were working on a variation of a product called arsenic trioxide. It's a powerful drug used to treat leukemia. Hexel was secretly trying to expand the applications. Helman and Eldridge believed they could make some changes to the drug and come up with a cure for cancer."

"Couldn't they do that kind of research

legally?"

"I guess their greed got in the way. Their lab wasn't approved for the use of arsenic and they didn't want to spend the time or money it would require to qualify for whatever permits were needed. They figured once they found the cure, none of it would matter."

"And Helman and Eldridge would wind up filthy rich."

"That's about it. Kemp says they'll be charged with conspiring to conceal health risks and knowing endangerment, among at least a dozen other violations. Strict liability applies in cases like this, so Hexel will be on the hook for everything that's happened in Mineral Wells. The company is out of business for good."

Sarah glanced away, guilt rising in her chest. "I wonder how much Andrew knew about this."

"Whatever he knew or didn't know had nothing to do with you. You're an innocent bystander in all of this."

She tried to convince herself, but it all came back to the question of how could she ever have married a man like that? How could she have lived with him for all of those years?

"I'd better get going," Jackson said, finishing the last of his tea and setting the glass back down on the coaster. He came up off the sofa and Sarah stood up, too. Neither of them moved. All she could think about was how much it was going to hurt to give him up.

"There's something I need to tell you," she forced herself to say.

One of his dark eyebrows lifted. "What is it?"

"I'm moving, Jackson. I've rented a place at the edge of town, just south of the road to Sheep River. I told you I was going to leave before all of this happened."

"Sarah . . ."

"I want to be closer to work. Smiley's been great or I would have already lost my job. Holly will be closer to school and I can see my grandmother more often. It'll be better for all of us."

"Not all of us, Sarah," he said softly. He reached out and rested a hand against her cheek. "It won't be better for me." His dark gaze locked with hers and she felt the pull of it deep inside her. She wanted to touch him, erase the pain in his face. "I love you, Sarah. I want you and Holly to stay here on the ranch. I want you to mar—"

"Don't say it!" She jerked away, backed up a couple of paces. Jackson wanted to marry her! It was exactly what she wanted and absolutely could not have. Dear God, she couldn't bear it.

"I — I'm not ready for a serious relationship. I don't think I ever will be."

"Sarah, listen to me . . ."

"My mind is made up, Jackson. I'm leaving." She looked at him and couldn't hold back tears. "Please let me go. Let me go and get on with your life."

Those strong, suntanned hands settled gently on her shoulders. "Tell me you don't love me and I'll walk away. I won't ever bother you again."

She bit back a sob. How could she do it? How could she lie about something that meant so very much? It took every ounce of her will, every ounce of courage she possessed.

"I don't love you, Jackson. I wish I did, but I don't."

For long moments, Jackson said nothing. Then he turned away from her, picked his hat up off the back of the sofa and headed for the door.

He stepped out onto the porch. "Whenever you're ready, I'll send a couple of the hands over to help you move the boxes." Very softly, he closed the door, the faint click as loud as a gunshot in the silence of her heart.

Sarah pressed a hand over her mouth to hold back a sob of pain. She loved him so very much.

She told herself she had done the right thing.

THIRTY

Sarah had been living in her new place in town for almost two weeks. The house was more modern than the cottage, with a newer kitchen and bath. But it didn't feel homey like the little cottage on the ranch, and it wasn't surrounded by a clear bubbling stream, beautiful vistas and towering pine trees.

The furniture inside was modern, too, and Spartan. She hadn't even brought the few antiques she had purchased for the cottage. There was no fireplace here, just a heater in the wall, and no old, worn, wooden floors. The antiques seemed to belong up there, not here.

She kept telling herself she could fix the place up a little, make it more comfortable, but so far she never seemed to find the time.

Holly didn't like the house, either. At first she had cried and begged Sarah not to move away from the ranch, but she was a sweet, loving child, and sensing her mother's unhappiness, she had resigned herself and let the matter rest.

Holly missed Jackson, though. Whenever his name came up, a wistful look crept over the little girl's face. She thought of him as the father she had never really known, and Sarah blamed herself for that, too.

That Sarah missed him didn't surprise her. She ached for the sound of his voice, the thud of his heavy boots on the wide plank floors as he walked into the cottage. She missed the warmth in his eyes whenever he looked at her, missed his lovemaking.

She swallowed past the lump in her throat. Most of the time, she was able to keep thoughts of him away. Once in a while, like today, the loneliness crept in and memories of Jackson returned, along with the terrible pain of losing him.

Sarah shook her head, forcing his beloved image away. She checked her watch, saw that it was nearly three o'clock and went in search of her car keys. Holly had spent the day with Gran, but it was time to drive out to Sheep River and pick her up.

The phone rang just as she found her key chain and picked it up off the table. Sarah walked into the kitchen and lifted the receiver.

"Ah, Sarah . . . there you are. How are you enjoying your new home?"

Her stomach instantly knotted. She knew that voice, recognized the hint of derision. She swallowed, forced a note of calm into her tone. "Detective Mercer . . . good afternoon. What can I do for you?"

"Actually, I'm just calling with a little bit of news. I thought you might be interested to know we found the murder weapon . . . the gun that killed your husband."

Nausea hit her with such force she doubled over, wrapped her arms around her waist and fought not to be sick. Drawing in a breath, she clung to her composure by a thread. "You . . . you found the gun?"

"That's right. Guess where it was?"

"Wh-where?"

"A couple of divers were doing some work under the Santa Monica pier. Imagine their surprise when they turned up a .38 caliber pistol, lying under the sand at the base of one of the pilings. I guess all sorts of things get tossed off the pier, but this was certainly one of the more interesting items they found."

Sarah said nothing. She was afraid of what her voice would sound like if she tried to speak.

"Rather an interesting coincidence

457

wouldn't you say — being as you live just a few blocks away. When did you toss it there, Sarah? Right after you shot your husband through the heart?"

She fought for control, prayed her voice would not tremble. "Any . . . anyone could have thrown it there. Unless you can prove it was me —"

"Oh, I will — sooner or later. Count on it, Sarah."

The line went dead, and for several seconds, Sarah just stood there, holding the phone in her hand. She was shaking all over, her stomach rolling, threatening to erupt.

She set the phone back in its cradle, walked over and sank down in a kitchen chair. For the past two weeks, every time she'd thought of Jackson, the notion had arisen that maybe she had made a mistake. Maybe she should call him, tell him she loved him. Tell him she wanted to marry him more than anything in the world.

But deep down, she knew she couldn't keep lying to him. That in not telling him the truth about Andrew, she was betraying his trust in the worst possible manner.

She looked back at the telephone, ominously silent now, but for exactly how long?

How long would it be until Detective Mercer came to haul her off to prison?

■ ■ ■ ■

Jackson was working in the barn when Jimmy spotted the smoke. "Hey, boss, you'd better come take a look at this."

Jackson walked out of the barn, his gaze following the direction Jimmy pointed.

"Sonofabitch." A plume of white smoke rose from the thick forest covering the west slope of the distant mountains.

"You know where that is?" Jimmy said.

"Up near Pine Lake."

"Isn't that where Red DeSalvo and his loggers were working?"

"Yeah." Jackson pulled out his cell phone. "The Forest Service is probably already on it, but we'd better call it in, just in case."

He pressed the Forest Service number that was on autodial in his cell address book, reported the fire, then went to retrieve his binoculars from the pickup and began to scan the white smoke in the distance. He glanced up at the sound of a chopper, watched it appear overhead on its way to collect buckets of water from the lake.

"Looks like they're already on it," Jimmy said.

"Looks that way."

"Maybe we'll get lucky and they'll be able

to stop it before it gets too bad." Current forest policy was to let the trees burn and just protect whatever structures might be in danger. It was probably good in some cases, clearing out the underbrush and giving the forest a chance to breathe, but it made for a long, dangerous, smoky summer, and a helluva lot of anxiety and fear.

"We'd better pull the cows out of the upper meadow," Jackson said.

Jimmy nodded, his long black ponytail shifting against the back of his neck. "I'll get the men, saddle some horses and get up there."

Wheel was out of the hospital, but not ready for such strenuous work. The men would have to go horseback. It was too dry to risk a spark from one of the ATVs, and there was a ban on the use of any machinery between noon and midnight to keep down the fire danger.

Jackson couldn't help wondering if the loggers had any part in starting the blaze, since Red and his crew weren't much good at following rules.

"Saddle Galahad," he said, "and I'll go with you."

"You got it." Jimmy waved over his shoulder as he walked away, and Jackson headed off to retrieve his gear.

At least the fire would get him away from the house. For the past two weeks, he had hardly been out of his study, just sat there staring at the walls as if they held the answer to what had happened between him and Sarah.

He was in love with her. Deeply in love, and God, it hurt. He could barely eat, couldn't sleep, thought about Sarah and Holly from morning till night. Losing her was killing him, and he didn't even know how it had happened.

From the start, he had tried to keep his distance. He had told himself not to fall for her again, not to let her hurt him the way she had before. But Sarah Allen had gotten into his blood when he was a kid of nineteen. Clearly, he had never gotten over her.

As he grabbed his saddlebags, a blanket and a jacket and headed out the door, Jackson wondered if he ever really would.

THIRTY-ONE

Sitting at the cheap pressboard desk she had purchased at the mercantile then assembled and put in her bedroom, Sarah pushed the button on her laptop, saving the article she had been writing for the newspaper, a story about Tanya Morton, last year's homecoming queen. Tanya had been chosen as a contestant on the TV show *America's Next Top Model.* Being a local girl, it was big news in Wind Canyon.

She looked out the window, saw a layer of thick smoke spreading across the mountains in the distance. She knew where the fire was — up near the lake where Jackson had taken her and Holly camping. She had seen it on the news. The air in town was smoky and miserable to breathe, and she kept worrying about Jackson, hoping the firefighters would be able to bring the blaze under control and Raintree Ranch would be safe.

She left her desk and walked over to the

window on the opposite side of the bedroom, saw Holly playing on the rope swing hanging down from the big sycamore tree out back. Rags sprawled in the grass a few feet away.

The doorbell rang as she walked out of the bedroom. Every time she heard it, a tremor of fear ran down her spine. Was it Mercer? Had he finally come to arrest her?

Relief filtered through her when she opened the door and saw Nan standing on the porch.

"Thought I'd come by and check on you," Nan said with a smile. "See how you're doing." She walked past Sarah into the house, carrying a baking pan covered with foil. "Half a chocolate cake. I couldn't eat it all and I thought Holly might like some." She glanced around. "Where is she?"

"Playing out in back. There isn't much of a yard, but it's better than nothing." Sarah took the cake and set it on the small round dining table. Nan had been to the house several times since Sarah moved in, always smiling, always cheerful. Sarah knew Nan had been worried about her moving into town from the ranch.

"So how's it going?" Nan asked. "You getting used to city life?"

Sarah laughed, thinking of the difference

between Wind Canyon and Los Angeles. "I guess so. It's certainly more convenient."

"I suppose."

For the first time, Sarah noticed her friend's puffy, red-rimmed eyes and slightly pale complexion. She frowned. "What's wrong, Nan? You look like you've been crying."

Nan sighed and sank down on the sofa. "Jimmy and I broke up."

Sarah sat down beside her. "But I thought you two were really getting along."

"I thought so, too." She pulled a Kleenex out of her purse and dabbed at her watery eyes. "He can't get past what happened when he was with Annie. She was a terrible wife and a rotten mother. She cheated on him and abandoned him and her boys. He's scared to death it'll happen again."

"You're nothing like Annie Baylor. She was no good when Jimmy married her."

"I know that and you know that. I guess Jim can't see the difference."

Sarah ignored a shot of anger. Didn't the man have enough sense to know what a good thing he had? Then again, she'd given up the best man she'd ever known. Maybe sometimes what seemed like choices weren't really choices at all.

She leaned over and hugged her friend.

"I'm sorry, Nan."

"Yeah, me, too."

Sarah blew out a breath and fell back on the sofa. "We're a real pair, aren't we?"

Nan managed a smile. "At least we have each other."

It was true. Nan had turned out to be a very dear friend, one of the best Sarah had ever had.

"I know this isn't the best time to ask," Sarah said, "but there's something I've been wanting to talk to you about."

"What is it?"

"I know how much you love children. I've seen you with Holly and I know what a wonderful mother you would make. If something happened to me . . . would you . . . would you be willing to take care of Holly?"

"What are you talking about? Nothing's going to happen to you."

"I know, but just say it did. My grandmother's too old to take on the job of raising a six-year-old. With my mom and dad gone, I don't have anyone I can turn to, and I trust you, Nan. You said you always wanted children. If something happened to me, would you be willing to raise Holly as your own?"

Nan reached over and caught Sarah's

hand. "Of course I would. I love Holly. She's the sweetest little girl in the world."

"You're a teacher. I don't think you'd have any trouble getting custody, but I could put something in writing — if you would be willing to agree."

Nan's green eyes glistened with a sheen of tears. "I'm flattered you would ask. And I would be honored to raise your little girl."

Tears welled in Sarah's eyes, too. "Thank you."

"But nothing's going to happen."

She just nodded, thinking of Ed Mercer and praying it was true.

Jackson listened to the hum of a big borate bomber flying overhead. The cattle had all been moved out of the upper pasture, down to a safer meadow to graze, and though three thousand forest acres had burned in the week since the blaze had started, the fire crews were making progress. The winds were cooperating and three choppers and two C-130s had been working to retard the flames.

There was a very good chance that this time the firefighters were going to be able to whip this thing before it got too far out of control.

Sitting behind the desk in his study, Jackson almost smiled. He'd been right about Red DeSalvo and his crew. They'd been logging during the hottest part of the day. A catalytic converter on one of the trucks had been the cause of the blaze.

It was the third infraction the Bannock Brothers had committed, and it looked like the company was going to lose its logging contract, at least in the national forest.

Couldn't happen to a bunch of more deserving guys.

Jackson leaned back in his chair, wishing he could muster the energy to do something productive. Instead, he reached over and poured himself a whiskey.

He rarely drank, but lately . . . well, it seemed like the only time the ache went away. He wouldn't let it get out of control. He wasn't the type. Still, he tipped the glass back and downed a hefty swallow. A warm numbness spread through him and the feeling of grief that seemed to haunt him faded away a little.

He was holding the glass up to the light, studying the rich amber color and contemplating a second swallow, when a familiar, sexy blonde walked into the study. Interested, dark brown eyes ran over him.

"Livvy said I'd find you in here."

Jackson set the whiskey glass down on the

desk and came to his feet. "Hello, Maddie."

He hadn't seen her since the Memorial Day celebration in the park, but in her skintight jeans and a tank that showed her impressive cleavage, Maddie Gallagher was as tall and svelte as she had always been, with miles of gleaming blond hair and legs that went on forever.

Jackson waited for the familiar stirring but it never came. "What can I do for you, Maddie?"

She crossed the room, rounded the corner of the desk and sat down right in front of him. "Jimmy called. He says you've been lonely. He thought maybe I could cheer you up."

She usually could. Leave it to Jimmy to give it a try. Maddie was sexy as hell and he was a man with a strong sexual appetite. She ran a long, manicured finger along his cheek. He hadn't shaved, he realized, thinking it must have been at least a couple of days.

"I appreciate the invitation, Maddie, I really do, but —"

She slid her arms around his neck and pulled him toward her, covered his mouth with her soft, full lips. He tried to enjoy it, should have, but all it made him feel was sad.

He eased her arms from around his neck. "Thanks for trying, Maddie. I guess I'm just not in the mood."

She shrugged her lightly suntanned shoulders. "Things change. I'm willing to wait." She slid off his desk, her breasts spilling toward him. He should take what she offered. Maybe it would help.

"Thanks for thinking of me, Maddie. Maybe next time."

"I think of you too much, Jackson." She flashed him a seductive smile as she headed toward the door of the study. "Next time I won't take no for an answer."

He didn't argue. Sooner or later, he'd have to come back to life again.

And sooner or later, he would.

Just not now, not today.

The image of another woman rose into his mind, beautiful blue eyes and thick dark hair, a body that fit perfectly with his. The memory made him hot and hard in an instant. Clearly he wasn't dead yet.

Determined not to think of Sarah, Jackson tossed back the rest of his whiskey and sat back down in his chair.

Gabriel Raines pulled the throttle back on his twin Aerostar and lined up for touchdown on the airstrip. He set down gently, heard the familiar rub of the tires on the asphalt, taxied to the hangar and turned off the engines.

Half an hour later, he was sitting behind the wheel of the brown Jeep Cherokee he had rented and was on his way down the highway. He wasn't headed for the ranch. Instead he was on the road to Sheep River.

He turned off the road at the outskirts of Wind Canyon, pulled down a narrow paved lane and stopped in front of one of three small houses in a cul-de-sac at the end.

He'd flown all the way to Wyoming to talk to Sarah Allen.

Gabe clenched his jaw. He had ignored the first call he had received. Livvy had been crying when he picked up the phone, but she was a woman and he knew from experience the female gender often went overboard on emotion. It was clear she was worried about Jackson, but Gabe assured her that in time his brother would be just fine. It was only a broken heart, after all. Nothing too serious.

When Jimmy had called, he'd begun to rethink the situation. Jackson had always been the calm one, the voice of reason among the brothers. Liv and Jim were calling Gabe, not Dev, the hothead of the three. Gabe had a temper, too, but mostly he controlled it.

"I don't know what to do," Jim had said. "Livvy and me . . . we were hoping you might be able to talk to him, help him figure things out."

And with those words, Gabe had gotten mad.

What the hell had Sarah done to his brother? Jackson was no fool. He'd been with a dozen different women. He rarely got involved, always made it clear from the start that he wasn't looking for a serious relationship, and he was always careful no one got hurt.

That he had fallen so hard for Sarah was frightening.

As Gabe turned off the motor, a fresh shot of anger slid through him. He hadn't forgotten that day in the high school cafeteria. Jackson had been stashing his money for weeks, saving a little bit here and there out of the money he earned to feed the family.

When he'd finally saved enough to go to the prom, he had worked up his courage and asked Sarah to go with him.

Sarah had ridiculed him, laughed at him in front of every kid in the cafeteria. Sarah had hurt him badly that day, but according to Livvy and Jim, not nearly as bad as she had hurt him this time.

Gabe got out of the Jeep, slamming the car door harder than he meant to. As he climbed the front porch steps, he shoved his wraparound sunglasses up on his head, took a deep breath and told himself to go easy.

He had seen the way Sarah looked at Jackson that day up in Alpine Meadow when they had gone after her little girl.

Like his brother was her storybook hero.

Like he was her man and for her there would never be anyone else.

What had gone wrong?

What could possibly have happened to change things so drastically?

Whatever it was, he meant to find out — today.

The door swung open just then and Sarah's blue eyes widened at the sight of him. Or maybe it was the way his jaw tightened when he saw her. He forced himself to relax, told himself to take things slow and easy, one step at a time.

"I need to talk to you, Sarah."

"Of course." She stepped back. "Come on in."

He started through the door and Sarah must have suddenly realized how odd it was for him to be there.

She grabbed hold of his arm. "Oh, my God — you aren't here because of Jackson!

Something hasn't happened to him! There hasn't been an accident or . . . or . . ."

Some of his anger lessened at the fear in her face. "No accident. It's nothing like that."

A breath of relief seeped out of her. She swallowed, inhaled deeply, managed to compose herself.

"It's nice to see you, Gabriel." But she looked more wary than pleased. "Would you like something to drink? A glass of iced tea or a beer, maybe?"

He didn't want a goddamn beer. His jaw tightened. "I want to know what you've done to my brother."

Her head shot up. "Wh-what do you mean?"

"I mean that since the two of you broke up, he hasn't been himself. He barely eats. He can't sleep. Livvy is terrified he's going to get sick." He took a step closer, just because he felt like a little intimidation. "My brother's in love with you, Sarah. I want to know why you led him on the way you did. Why you let him believe there was a future for the two of you. He wants to marry you. He wants to be a father to your little girl. Doesn't that mean anything to you?"

Her pretty blue eyes welled with tears he hadn't expected to see. There was a softness in Sarah he had rarely seen in a woman. He thought that must be one of the things that had drawn his brother to her.

"I didn't mean for any of this to happen," she said.

"Couldn't you tell he was falling in love with you? How could you let it go so far?"

She tried to turn away, but Gabe caught her shoulders, forcing her to face him. There was something in her expression, something so sad his chest squeezed.

"There's more going on here, isn't there? Something you're not saying, something you haven't told Jackson."

She tried to turn away, but he wouldn't let her. "Tell me what it is."

She bit her lip. He could feel her start to tremble. Gabe's hold tightened. "Tell me, dammit!"

The tears in her eyes spilled over onto her cheeks. He saw it then, saw what he had been missing, why none of this had made any sense. "My God, you're in love with him!"

Her features crumpled. A sob escaped and fresh tears flooded her eyes. "I love him so much." And then she started crying in earnest.

Every instinct urged him to pull her into his arms and comfort her, tell her everything was going to be okay.

But too much was at stake. His brother's future. Sarah's. Even little Holly's.

"I want to know, Sarah. I'm not leaving until I find out what's going on."

She looked up at him, her face as pale as glass. Her words came out so softly he almost didn't hear them. "I killed him. I killed my husband. I'm the one who shot Andrew."

Stunned silence followed. Somewhere a clock ticked. Of all the things he could have imagined her saying, this wasn't one of them.

"You killed him?"

She nodded, her whole body drawing inward as if she were in pain.

"Did you plan it? Was it murder? Did you shoot him on purpose?"

Disbelief widened her eyes. "No! Oh, God, I would never do something like that!" She swallowed, moistened her trembling lips. "H-he called me downstairs and I — I —"

"Stop right there — don't say another word. This isn't for me to hear. It's Jackson who needs to know." He glanced around. "Where's Holly?"

"She's with . . . with Nan. I had some work to do. Nan said she'd watch her for a couple of . . . of hours."

"Get your purse and let's go."

Sarah didn't argue, just woodenly picked up her bag and let him haul her out the door. He urged her around to the passenger side of the Jeep, opened the door and shoved her inside, then went around, climbed in himself and started the engine.

Sarah said nothing as he drove down the lane and turned onto the road into town, nothing as he continued on to the two-lane road headed north then turned onto the private lane leading into Raintree Ranch.

She was shaking when the big sprawling ranch house came into view. And so pale he was a little afraid.

"We're almost there," he said, driving up in front of the house, hoping that Jackson was inside as he had been all week.

Gabe turned off the engine, went around to the passenger side and helped Sarah out of the Jeep. She was silent as he took her arm and guided her through the front door into the living room.

When he walked into the study, he saw Jackson sitting in the chair behind his desk. The computer was on. He caught a glimpse of a cost analysis program but Jackson wasn't looking at the screen. He wasn't looking at much of anything until he saw Sarah.

He jerked as if he had been punched, slowly pushed to his feet. "Sarah . . ."

Jackson started to move toward her, but she held up a trembling hand. "Please . . . just stay where you are. I have something . . . something I need to tell you."

She glanced over at Gabe, who gave her a nod then took his cue and quietly closed the door, slipping off to the kitchen. He needed a strong cup of coffee. He hoped Livvy had a pot on the stove.

For several seconds, Sarah just stood there, soaking up the sight of him. It didn't matter that Jackson needed a shave or that his shirt was wrinkled. It didn't matter that he looked a little thinner than he had before. He was still the handsomest man she had ever seen.

And she was still desperately in love with him.

"Your brother brought me here," she began. "I hoped . . . hoped I would never have to tell you, but I can't go on like this any longer."

Jackson's dark eyes searched her face. "For God's sake, Sarah, what is it?"

"First, I want you to know that I lied to

you the last time I saw you. I said I didn't love you but it wasn't the truth. I love you so very, very much. I've loved you for a long time, but —"

He started to move again, but she shook her head and he stopped. "But sometimes loving someone isn't enough. I never wanted to hurt you, Jackson. I never meant for any of this to happen."

"Sarah . . ."

"I'm the one who killed Andrew, Jackson. That's the reason I can't marry you. Sooner or later the police will find out. I don't want to bring that down on you. You don't deserve it. You never have."

Jackson stood frozen.

Sarah closed her eyes, steeling herself, determined not to cry. "Now that you know, you can do whatever you feel is right. I've made arrangements for Nan to take Holly, so you don't have to worry about that."

Jackson's jaw tightened, but he still didn't move. "How did it happen? I need to know that, Sarah."

She nodded, utterly resigned and sick at heart. "He came home while I was packing. He was furious. He demanded I come down to the study. I could tell how mad he was. I could hear it in his voice."

"Come down here, Sarah."

478

"What . . . what is it you want, Andrew?"

She told him the rest, how Andrew had threatened her, how he'd told her he was going to kill her then take Holly with him to Rio. Told him everything that had happened that night.

"I had a gun," she said, her voice thick with emotion. "Patt— a friend of mine sent it to me through the mail. She said I should use it to protect myself. She said I should never . . . never let him hurt me again."

"Go on," Jackson said, his features like granite.

Her heart ached just to look at him. She had known it would be this way, known what he would think, what any man would think. She had tried so hard to protect herself from the awful look in his eyes, but it was there just the same.

She swallowed the tears in her throat and forced herself to continue. "When he started toward me, I pulled the pistol out of my purse. I told him to stay away from me. I told him I wouldn't . . . wouldn't let him hurt me again." She bit down on her lip to keep it from trembling. "Andrew just laughed. Even the gun wasn't . . . wasn't enough to frighten him."

"You dare to threaten me? I'm going to kill you for that, Sarah."

"What happened then?" Jackson pressed.

She drew in a shaky breath, forced herself to continue. "I warned him. I told him I'd shoot him if . . . if he came any closer. He said . . . he said I didn't have the guts." Her voice broke on the last. Her head was spinning, the whole room seemed off-kilter.

"Finish it," Jackson demanded.

She braced herself, shoved out the words. "Then . . . then he ran toward me. I don't remember pulling the trigger, just the roar of the gun and the feel of the pistol jerking in my hand."

She knew she was crying, could feel the wetness rolling down her cheeks. "I knew I should call 911, but Andrew . . . Andrew was already dead and I was afraid for Holly."

She dashed at the tears on her cheeks. "I kept . . . kept thinking of my little girl. What would happen to my daughter? Dear God, the trial would take months. I knew they would put her in foster care. I had no money. I couldn't afford a lawyer. If they put me in prison, what would happen . . . happen to Holly?"

She hadn't seen him move; he was simply there, pulling her against him, holding her tightly in his arms. She felt the shudder that rolled through his tall, lean body.

"Jackson . . ."

"It's all right." His hand smoothed over her hair. "You were protecting yourself and your child. You did what you had to. Andrew left you no choice."

Sarah clung to him, and she wept.

"We'll find our way through this, Sarah." He pressed his cheek against the top of her head. "Somehow, we will."

For long moments she just stood there in the circle of his arms, her heart aching with love for him, wishing she didn't have to tell him the rest. Finally, she let go of him.

"This isn't going away, Jackson." His gaze searched her face and she forced herself not to reach for him, not to step back into his arms. "Mercer called. They found the gun."

He straightened, seemed to collect himself. "What did you do with it after the shooting?"

"I — I wiped off my fingerprints. That night, after Holly went to sleep, I asked one of the neighbors to watch her while I ran a quick errand. Then I walked down to the end of the pier and tossed it in the ocean."

"How did Mercer find it?"

"He said some divers were working and they . . . they found the gun in the sand at the base of one of the pilings."

Jackson swore softly.

"Mercer won't . . . won't give up."

Jackson looked at her hard. "Neither will I."

Everything inside her seemed to cry out with regret. It was happening, exactly as she had feared. "Are you sure, Jackson? Are you sure I'm what you want?"

He moved closer. She felt his lips against her hair. "You've been what I've wanted for the past sixteen years."

THIRTY-TWO

Jackson started things rolling the following day. He and Sarah dropped Holly off at her grandmother's place in Sheep River, then headed for Sarah's newly rented house in town.

He had asked Sarah to move back to the cottage and amazingly, she had agreed.

"I never wanted to move away," she confessed. "I love it on the ranch . . . I love being with you, Jackson. I just didn't want to drag you into all of this."

But he was in the middle of it now and he was staying. They were going to see this through all the way to the end.

While Sarah went to retrieve the boxes she had saved and stored in the garage, Jackson used his cell phone to call his attorney, Thomas Carson. He finished his brief conversation and closed the phone.

"Carson's going to get back to us with a couple of names." The best criminal attorneys in the L.A. area. "Dev's on it, too."

He had known from the moment Sarah had told him the truth about the shooting what he would have to do.

What both of them would have to do.

They couldn't get on with their lives until the matter of Andrew Hollister's death was resolved. To do that, Sarah needed to come forward with the truth.

"It's funny," she said, slipping into his arms. "Now that you're with me, I'm not afraid anymore." She rested her cheek on his shoulder and God it felt so good just to hold her.

"You did what you had to."

She eased out of his embrace and he immediately felt the loss. "I keep thinking . . . maybe if I hadn't had the gun . . ."

"If you hadn't had the gun, your husband likely would have killed you. He would have taken Holly and you know what would have happened if he had." He caught her shoulders. "A man died that day up in Alpine Meadow. Things happen. Sometimes you don't have a choice."

"You weren't the one who killed him."

"No, but I would have if I'd had to. I would have done whatever it took to protect the people I love."

Sarah stared up at him. "I never thought

you'd understand. It never occurred to me that I could trust you with such a terrible secret."

"It isn't going to be a secret much longer, and once it's out in the open and all of this is settled, we can get on with our lives." He tipped her chin with his fingers. "I think we should get married. Holly would be protected. To a certain extent, so would you."

Her lovely blue eyes welled with tears. "I want that. I want to marry you more than anything in the world, but I don't want to start our lives together with this awful shadow hanging over our heads. I can't do it, Jackson. Please don't ask me."

"What about Holly?"

"I talked to Nan sometime back. She'll take Holly if it comes to that. It would be wonderful if you and Livvy would help her."

"You know we will. I'm hoping it isn't going to go that far, but if it does, Holly will have everything she needs — including people who love her."

She nodded, brushed away a tear. "Thank you." She walked into the bedroom to begin packing her clothes. He saw her there next to the bed and for the first time in weeks, allowed his mind to remember how good it had been between them. He imagined her lush body spread open on the quilt, welcoming him, taking him deep inside her. He imagined having her in every way a man could take a woman and make her completely his.

She must have read his thoughts because her gaze grew soft and warm. He could see the heat, the desire rising there, the passion that was so much a part of her.

"I feel empty, Jackson. I need you to fill me, make me believe this is all going to work."

There was nothing he wanted more. He ripped open the snaps on the front of his shirt, tugged it free of his jeans and walked toward her. He hauled her into his arms and kissed her long and deep.

He had never wanted a woman the way he wanted Sarah, never felt such satisfaction with a woman before. He meant to go slowly, to remove each of her garments and kiss the soft pale skin he exposed. He meant to spend the next few hours making slow, languid love to her. But the weeks he'd spent without her had taken their toll.

Once men were warriors and he felt that way now, his groin swelling, his erection throbbing against the fly of his jeans. He wanted to bury himself inside her, plant his seed so deeply she would never think of another man.

The sex was wild and lusty — hot, sweaty, raunchy sex that had nothing to do with love and everything to do with a man claiming his mate.

The second time was different, easy and gentle, the love he felt for her pouring out of him, the love she felt for him washing over him in a soft, sweet wave.

"I wish I could stay in this bed forever," she said with a smile as she lay contentedly beside him.

Jackson chuckled. "I don't know about forever, but I can manage a few more hours." He came up over her, kissed her and began to make love to her again.

The persistent knock at the door finally reached him. It was fierce and determined. Jackson knew in an instant who was there.

And that they had waited too long.

"Sarah Adelaide Allen, you're under arrest for the murder of Andrew Hollister." Detective Ed Mercer stood next to Ben Weber and a female deputy sheriff.

Sarah trembled, lifted her chin and stepped forward. They had dressed hurriedly, Sarah once more in her jeans, sneakers and a blue cotton blouse. Mercer spun her around and clamped a pair of plastic bands around her wrists.

"Is that really necessary?" Jackson asked, doing his best not to grab the man by the front of his coat and bust him right in the mouth. Knowing if he did, he would go straight to jail and if that happened, he wouldn't be any good to Sarah.

"Probably not," Mercer smirked, "but that's the way it's going to be."

Ben Weber looked embarrassed. "I'm sorry it turned out this way, Jackson."

"It was self-defense, Ben. And she was turning herself in. We've just been waiting for a call from her attorney."

The sheriff nodded. "I figured there was more to it. Let me know if there's anything I can do."

Jackson had known Ben Weber for years. There was a great deal of mutual respect between them. If Jackson said Sarah was innocent, Ben would give her the benefit of the doubt. Unfortunately, Ed Mercer and the LAPD weren't going to be quite that cooperative.

"I'll follow you down to the station," Jackson told Sarah. One the way, he would call Carson and Dev. One of them was sure to have a name by now. Sarah needed legal help and she needed it today.

She stopped at the bottom of the steps, turned and looked up at him. "You don't deserve this."

"Neither do you." He caught up with her, walked beside her to the door of the sheriff's car. "I'll pick Holly up at your grandmother's and take her to Nan's, explain what's happened. We'll work things out between us."

Sarah just nodded. Bright tears glistened in her eyes. "I'm so sorry."

Jackson leaned down and kissed her full on the mouth. "Just hang on, all right?"

She nodded. Mercer shoved her head beneath the roof of the patrol car and she settled inside. She didn't look at him again as the car pulled off down the road.

"So where is Sarah now?" Dev asked Jackson over the cell phone.

"Her attorney advised her to waive extradition proceedings. They're transporting her straight to L.A. I haven't left Wyoming yet. At the moment, I'm standing outside her house in town. I need to pack some clothes for Holly. She's still at her grandmother's house. I'm going to pick her up and take her over to Nan Hargrove's for the next few days, till we see what's going to happen. As soon as I get her settled, I'm heading for L.A."

"Morgan Slater is one of the best attorneys in Califoronia. He'll do a good job for Sarah."

"I checked him out. He's got one helluva reputation."

"Listen to me, bro. You need to keep your head on straight. You have to believe that Sarah's going to be all right. Hollister was a scumbag and a wife-beater. With Sarah's medical history, self-defense should be a pretty easy sell."

Jackson released a breath. "I hope you're right."

"I'll keep my ears open. I'll let you know if I come up with anything useful."

"Thanks, Dev." Jackson closed the phone and used Sarah's key to open the door to her little rental house. The place seemed forlorn without her. As he crossed the living room and went into her bedroom, he could almost hear her cries of pleasure as he had made love to her there on the bed.

He shook his head and tried to focus his thoughts on what needed to be done. Her luggage was in the closet right where she'd told him to look.

His eyebrows went up when he spotted it and he whistled. *Louis Vuitton.* He almost smiled. Sarah had kept almost nothing Andrew had given her. But what woman could resist expensive designer luggage?

He pulled down two bags made of dark brown fabric with the logo woven into the material, dark brown leather handles and brass trim, and a personal tote to match. He opened them up on the bed. Sarah's initials were imprinted in gold on each piece, which was probably the reason she hadn't tried to sell them on eBay. The bags appeared to be several years old and had seen plenty of use, but they were still in good condition.

He glanced around the bedroom, thinking the luggage was probably the most expensive thing Sarah owned. The thought occurred that if he bought luggage for Sarah, he'd buy something with a soft floral pattern, something feminine and sexy. Undoubtedly Andrew liked the prestige of his wife traveling with world-class, designer bags.

He studied the cases, a thought suddenly niggling at the back of his mind. Andrew expected Sarah to go with him to Rio. He would have insisted she use the Louis Vuitton he had bought her.

He leaned over to examine the first bag, an overnighter, about twenty-four inches. He checked all the pockets and ran his fingers along the inside lining, carefully checking every inch.

He glanced at the tote but Sarah probably

would have carried that on the plane, which meant it would have had to go through airport security. He checked it quickly, not really expecting to find anything.

He moved to the final bag, which was slightly bigger. Sliding his fingers carefully along the interior, he checked the pockets, tested each section of the lining. He was about to give up, when his fingers touched something behind one of the removable zippered pouches. Velcro buzzed as he unfastened the pouch and felt the protrusion.

His adrenaline kicked up as he pulled his pocketknife out of his jeans and cut into the lining, which had been stitched back together by hand. Reaching in, he carefully removed the item inside.

It was a USB flash drive. Small and compact, it could hold a huge amount of information. He rechecked the pocket, felt something more in the lining and pulled out a slip of paper with a row of numbers written on it.

Andrew hadn't wanted to carry the disk or the paper himself in case there was a problem, but his wife was another story. Jackson shoved the piece of paper into his pocket, walked over to Sarah's laptop and turned it on. He waited while the machine warmed up, then shoved in the flash drive.

A list of files popped up.

Good ol' Andrew, Jackson thought as he opened the first file and found exactly what he and Sarah had been searching for all along.

There was information on Martin Kozak's illegal operations, a long list detailing the man's every move.

There was information on Vernon Rimmer, the greedy highway inspector, the dates and amounts of the payoffs he had received, and the numbers identifying Rimmer's offshore Caymen Island accounts, the same ones Dev had managed to come up with.

Another file held documentation of Hexel Pharmaceuticals' activities, including the weight of the barrels of toxic waste and the dates they were delivered to the mine. There were numerous other miscellaneous infractions.

A number of other companies were mentioned, other shady deals outlined in glaring detail. None of the company names were familiar, but Jackson figured the FBI would likely know who they were.

The disk held a wealth of information.

If he was lucky, the contents would be valuable enough to exchange for dropping all the charges against Sarah. The only one who was truly interested in seeing her convicted of killing a scumbag like Andrew was Ed Mercer. Jackson had a strong suspicion, this time Mercer was going to be flat out of luck.

He grinned as he closed the files and turned off the computer, pocketed the disk and flipped open his cell phone. The first call he made was to Morgan Slater, Sarah's attorney. He filled Slater in on his find and Slater agreed to make the call to Richard Kemp at the FBI. They had to handle this very carefully, or it would be Jackson who went to jail for withholding information.

Satisfied things were progressing in the direction he wanted, he walked back to the bedroom, grabbed one of the suitcases and went in to collect some of Holly's things. As soon as he got the little girl settled, he was heading for L.A.

He wasn't coming back until he could bring Sarah home.

THIRTY-THREE

Sarah sat at a table in a room at the district attorney's office. Carolyn Gallegos, Assistant District Attorney, sat across from her, an attractive Hispanic woman in her forties. Richard Kemp of the FBI, in his dark blue suit and power tie, was also there, as well as Sarah's lawyer, Morgan Slater, late forties, salt-and-pepper hair, a man who exuded power and control.

Most importantly, Jackson sat beside her.

The deal was almost finished. The FBI was practically salivating to get their hands on Andrew's disk. Amazingly, no one really doubted her story. They knew enough about Andrew's reputation to figure it was probably true. Or maybe they figured no matter the reason she shot him, he deserved it.

At any rate, her heart was gently pulsing with hope and whenever she looked over at Jackson, she saw confidence in the hard lines of his face.

"There's just one last thing, Ms. Allen," Richard Kemp said. "We'll need to know the name of the person who sent you the gun used in the shooting."

Her stomach dropped. Her heart set up a clatter. She had no idea what to say — only what not to say — and that was Patty Gorski's name. Not even the threat of prison could pry out those words.

Jackson reached beneath the table and took hold of her hand.

Morgan Slater must have read her decision in her face because he spoke up before she could form any sort of reply.

"My client isn't certain who sent her the revolver. She belonged to several internet chat groups for battered women. Some of them knew about the beatings she had suffered at the hands of her husband. The package came anonymously, disguised as clothing purchased on the internet. There was a note but it merely said she should use the gun if necessary in order to protect herself."

"Where is that note now?" Carolyn Gallegos asked.

"I burned it months ago," Sarah answered truthfully. "I was afraid of what Andrew would do to me if he found it."

"I see," Ms. Gallegos said. And Sarah

thought that maybe she actually did. She was a woman. In her work, she must have dealt with dozens of cases of abuse. She closed the notebook sitting open in front of her. "As far as this office is concerned, the matter is resolved. Special Agent Kemp?"

He flicked a glance at Jackson, but fixed his attention on Sarah's lawyer. "If you can provide us with the disk, we'll support the district attorney's decision."

Sarah drew in a shaky breath and blinked to keep from crying.

"It's over, Sarah," Morgan Slater said gently, rising to his feet. "I'll take care of whatever paperwork is necessary. You and Mr. Raines are free to leave."

The tears rushed past her defenses and this time she could not will them away. "Thank you. Thank you so much."

Slater smiled. "It was my pleasure." And it seemed as though he meant it. His exorbitant fee aside, clearly he believed she had shot her husband in self-defense and was glad he could help. Maybe there were more people out there than she had imagined who understood what she had been through with Andrew.

She left the district attorney's office and as she descended the wide stone steps leading down to the street, held on to Jackson's hand.

He stopped when they reached the curb. "It's over, Sarah."

"I'll never be able to repay you for what you've done."

He actually grinned. "Oh, I think you will." And the look in his eyes was so hot she laughed.

"Let's get married," he said.

"Now?"

"Anytime you say."

She swallowed past the lump that rose in her throat. "As soon as we get back to the ranch, I'll marry you. I love you, Jackson Raines."

EPILOGUE

A glorious sun shone down from a sky so vibrant a blue it seemed surreal. It was amazing how quickly a wedding could be put together when the people you love all pitched in to help.

She and Jackson were repeating their vows on a grassy rise behind the ranch house. Chairs had been set up and an arbor perched at the end of a long white runner beneath the leafy branches of a pair of alder trees.

Holly was the flower girl, dropping rose petals as she walked between the rows of white rented chairs. Nan was her bridesmaid, looking radiant in a lavender tea-length gown. Her grandmother sat next to Livvy in the front row, dabbing away happy tears. Since Sarah didn't have a father, she walked down the aisle with Jimmy, while Dev and Gabe stood next to Jackson, acting as his best men.

Nan did an excellent job of ignoring her former beau, which definitely didn't please him. Sarah figured it was only a matter of time until Jimmy realized his feelings for Nan ran deep, and the two of them got back together. But, of course, she couldn't be sure.

She returned her attention to the tall man waiting for her under the white roses entwined in the arbor. In her simply cut cream silk gown trimmed with matching cream lace, she walked toward him. The dress had a narrow skirt that came to just above her knees, and she wore matching cream satin, very high heels.

Jackson looked ruggedly handsome in a black Western-cut tuxedo and black lizard-skin boots. All of the men in the bridal party wore matching suits, black boots and black cowboy hats, which seemed fitting out here on the ranch.

The service was lovely. Though Sarah barely registered the minister's words, she would never forget her husband's kiss, sweet and tender, yet fierce and utterly possessive.

All of her friends were there: her boss, Smiley Reed, and his girlfriend, Myra Cunningham; Mike Stevens; Jackson's attorney, Thomas Carson; the Whittakers from the ranch next door; Cody and Marilyn Dillon; Sheriff Webster; Fred Wilkins and his wife from the mercantile. There were at least a dozen others, longtime friends of Jackson's. It was amazing how they all managed to get there on such short notice.

Only one person was missing.

Sarah had called her, of course, and told her about the wedding. She had told her best friend everything that had happened and how it had all turned out. That the investigation was finally closed and both of them were safe. They had talked for nearly an hour.

Both of them had cried.

But Patty lived in Chicago and there was no way she could get all the way to Wyoming with only a week's notice. The airfare alone would be staggering.

Sarah felt Jackson's arm around her waist as he led her away from the big tent set up over rows of buffet tables and a dance floor.

"I've got a surprise for you."

She smiled. "A surprise?"

He just grinned and tipped his head toward the house.

Sarah's gaze swung in that direction and she froze. A robust woman with bright red hair in a short, hot pink dress ran toward her, waving and wobbling on high heels she was clearly not used to wearing. Tears sprang into Sarah's eyes.

Patty Gorski.

"My plane was late taking off," Patty said, fighting to catch her breath. "Jackson sent a car to the airport to pick me up. Thank God it was still waiting when I finally got here."

"Patty! Oh, my God, I can't believe you're really here." Sarah went into the older woman's arms and the two women hugged. "I can't believe you actually came."

"Jackson called me. He sent a ticket and made all the arrangements. He said there wasn't going to be a wedding unless I came."

"Oh, Patty." The women embraced again.

"You're prettier than your picture," Patty said, grinning up at her.

"You're shorter than I thought."

Both of them laughed.

Sarah looked over at Jackson. "This is the best wedding gift you ever could have given me. Thank you so much, Jackson."

He just smiled.

Patty eyed him from top to bottom, leaned over and whispered, "My God, he's gorgeous." She straightened and grinned. "A man like that might be enough to make me contemplate marriage again."

Sarah laughed.

Patty turned serious. "I got the check. It came special delivery yesterday. Oh, my God — half a million dollars!"

"Just remember it's supposed to be an anonymous donation."

"Well, officially it is."

The numbers Jackson had found on the paper in her luggage had turned out to be another account in the Cayman Offshore Corporation. This one belonged to Andrew. With the numbers, they were able to withdraw the money Andrew had intended to take with him to Rio, all he had left of his ill-gotten gains. It seemed only fitting that Patty Gorski's battered women's group get the benefit of the funds.

"Listen, you two," Patty said. "This is your wedding day. I can only stay a couple of hours, then I have to head back home."

"But you've come all this way!"

"I came to meet you and I came to thank you for the money. Besides, Jackson promised to bring you to Chicago. We'll have all the time we need to really get to know each other. Now go on and enjoy yourself."

Sarah looked up at her tall, ruggedly handsome husband. "I'll expect you to keep your word on that," she said with a smile.

Jackson caught her chin, bent and lightly kissed her. "Count on it, darlin'."

Sweeping Patty along with them toward the tent, Sarah made introductions, including Holly, left Patty with Livvy and went with Jackson to cut the wedding cake.

"Come on, Mom," Holly said, grabbing her hand and tugging her toward the white, four-layer cake trimmed with fresh roses. "Everybody's waiting!"

"Well, then, we'd better get it done." Sarah looked around her, at the friends and family she had come to love. "Thank you," she said to Jackson, "for everything."

He gave her a wicked smile. "You can thank me properly later."

Sarah grinned up at him, thinking how happy this man made her, imagining their wedding night.

And planning to do just that.

AUTHOR'S NOTE

I hope you enjoyed Jackson and Sarah in *Against the Wind,* the first book in my Raines Brothers Trilogy.

Gabriel's story is next. Even in the bustling city of Dallas, Gabe's Western background shines through. Gabe owns a big construction company. He's a man's man and exactly what auburn-haired Mattie Baker is looking for — even if she refuses to believe it.

But Gabe's company, Raines Construction, is being threatened by an arsonist and Gabe has to find him — before he and Mattie become the man's victims.

I hope you'll watch for *Against the Fire,* followed closely by Devlin's story, *Against the Law.*

Till then, all best wishes and happy reading,

Kat Martin

The employees of Thorndike Press hope you have enjoyed this Large Print book. All our Thorndike, Wheeler, and Kennebec Large Print titles are designed for easy reading, and all our books are made to last. Other Thorndike Press Large Print books are available at your library, through selected bookstores, or directly from us.

For information about titles, please call:
(800) 223-1244

or visit our Web site at:
http://gale.cengage.com/thorndike

To share your comments, please write:
Publisher
Thorndike Press
295 Kennedy Memorial Drive
Waterville, ME 04901